D0160366

VIEWPOINTS
CRITICAL

*Forthcoming

Modesitt, L. E.
Viewpoints critical :
selected stories /
2008.
33305213816592
nh   05/19/08

WITHDRAWN

VIEWPOINTS

CRITICAL

SELECTED STORIES

L. E. MODESITT, JR.

TOR®

A TOM DOHERTY ASSOCIATES BOOK
NEW YORK

This is a work of fiction. All of the characters, organizations, and events portrayed in these stories are either products of the author's imagination or are used fictitiously.

VIEWPOINTS CRITICAL: SELECTED STORIES

Copyright © 2008 by L. E. Modesitt, Jr.

All rights reserved, including the right to reproduce this book, or portions thereof, in any form.

A Tor Book
Published by Tom Doherty Associates, LLC
175 Fifth Avenue
New York, NY 10010

www.tor.com

Tor® is a registered trademark of Tom Doherty Associates, LLC.

Library of Congress Cataloging-in-Publication Data

Modesitt, L. E
    Viewpoints critical : selected stories / L.E. Modesitt. Jr.—1st ed.
       p. cm.
    "A Tom Doherty Associates book."
    ISBN-13: 978-0-7653-1857-2
    ISBN-10: 0-7653-1857-1
  1. Fantasy fiction, American.   2. Science fiction, American.   I. Title.
    PS3563.O264V54   2008
    813'.54—dc22

                                  2007042148

First Edition: March 2008

Printed in the United States of America

0 9 8 7 6 5 4 3 2 1

ORIGINAL PUBLICATION ACKNOWLEDGMENTS

"The Great American Economy," *Analog*, May 1973.

"Second Coming," *Isaac Asimov's SF Adventure Magazine*, Spring 1979.

"Rule of Law," *Analog*, April 1981.

"Iron Man, Plastic Ships," *Isaac Asimov's Science Fiction Magazine*, October 1979.

"Power to . . . ?" *Analog*, November 1990.

"Precision Set," *On Spec*, Spring 2001, The Copper Pigs Writers' Society.

"Fallen Angel," from *Flights, Extreme Visions of Fantasy*, Al Sarrantonio, editor, ROC Books, New American Library, 2004.

"Understanding," *On Spec*, Summer 2000, The Copper Pigs Writers' Society.

"News Clips Recovered from the NYC Ruins," from *The Leading Edge*, Fall 2005, BYU Press.

"The Pilots," from *In the Shadow of the Wall*, Bryon R. Tetrick, editor, Tekno Books, Cumberland House, 2002.

"The Dock to Heaven," from *Low Port*, Sharon Lee and Steve Miller, editors, Meisha Merlin Publishing, 2003.

"Ghost Mission," from *Slipstreams*, Martin Greenberg and John Helfers, editors, DAW Books, 2006.

"Spec-Ops," from *Future Weapons of War*, Joe Haldeman and Martin Greenberg, editors, Baen Books, 2007.

"Sisters of Sarronnyn, Sisters of Westwind," from *Jim Baen's UNIVERSE*, August 2006.

"The Difference," from *Man vs. Machine*, Martin Greenberg and John Helfers, editors, DAW Books, 2007.

"The Swan Pilot," from *Emerald Magic*, Andrew M. Greeley, editor, Tor Books, 2004.

For David Hartwell and Ben Bova

CONTENTS

INTRODUCTION

Since I am not the most prolific of short-story writers, this collection has been a long time in coming. In fact, the first story in this volume was published more than thirty years ago. I have not included all of my stories, for various reasons, but the book does hold the majority of those published—and they total less than half the number of novels I have published. Given the effort these stories took, I have great admiration for those writers who specialize in short fiction. For this and other reasons, I am deeply grateful to Ben Bova, who early on convinced me that my writing future lay in novels, and to David Hartwell, my longtime editor, who, despite or because of editing virtually all my novels, pressed for me to complete this modest compilation.

Because the stories presented here range from hard science fiction to fantasy, and "sideways" as well, there is no central theme, except perhaps that I'm quite dubious about pat and obvious solutions to the questions raised by life and skeptical about those who extol obvious truths.

The other aspect of these stories is that they are, in general, what I might call a quietly darker look at the possible futures we face. They're certainly not horror, but I suggest you think about the implications—or not, as you wish.

L. E. MODESITT, JR.

VIEWPOINTS
CRITICAL

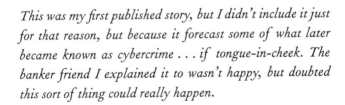

This was my first published story, but I didn't include it just for that reason, but because it forecast some of what later became known as cybercrime . . . if tongue-in-cheek. The banker friend I explained it to wasn't happy, but doubted this sort of thing could really happen.

THE
GREAT AMERICAN
ECONOMY

"What a miserable day it is," groused James Boulin Chartwell, III.

A junior member of the Council of Economic Advisors, he often groused. When he didn't grouse, he grumbled.

George didn't exactly agree with his boss. True, the smog had cut visibility outside to less than a hundred yards. The April day was grayer than usual, but what else could you really expect in the Greater Washington Reservation?

"George! Do you know that our figures are off by One-hundredth of One Percent?"

George sighed. He'd known since yesterday when the monthly inflation statistics had been printed out that there would be trouble. For the third month in a row there had been a small, but significant, inflationary trend in the Gross National Product figures. The unplanned increase could not be explained by increases in wages, construction costs, defense spending, conservation and reclamation, or anything else.

"George! Do you hear me? The President is Not At All Happy about this. If it gets out that there has already been an annual rate of inflation of over one-tenth of one percent this year, that could swing Public Opinion heavily in the election. You know we can't keep it a secret much longer."

James Boulin Chartwell, III, refilled his glass with one hundred percent pure mineral water.

"I take it, sir, that you would earnestly desire me to discover the cause of this blight upon our Great American Economy." George was about ready to quit, if only he could persuade himself that leaving the Reservation would not be the end of his career.

"I don't give an obsolete go piece what you do. But you ought to want to know how this could happen, when Government Expenditures are registered to the Last Penny, and when our computers keep track of the Private Sector to the Very Last Dime." James Boulin Chartwell, III, was a firm devotee of the bureaucratic school that spoke in capital letters.

George signed again. It would be a very long day.

"George! Don't you understand? It Can't Happen. It just Can't Happen." James Boulin Chartwell, III, finished his second glass of one hundred percent pure mineral water.

George shrugged. He knew why it wasn't supposed to happen. The growth of the nongovernmental sector was computed on a full-coverage, day-by-day, real-time basis, taking into account all variables such as price and wage increases, construction rates, investment rates, and savings. The basic government budget was programmed into the computers as well. Adjustments in the basic growth rates were made on a weekly basis by changing the magnitude of variable items in the government budget. The system was about ten years old in its present form. It had worked reasonably well, although many government agencies complained bitterly about budgets that varied from week to week. Defense and Urban Affairs, of course, were above variable controls. Status was working in a department with a fixed budget.

"Well," demanded James Boulin Chartwell, III, "do you think you can Solve the Problem?"

George shrugged again. He wanted his morning Coke.

"I'll see what I can find out."

As he left the office, he smiled at Mildred. She glared back, as usual. She disliked George's flippant attitude toward the very respected junior advisor.

George wandered down to the cafeteria. It was after coffee break and deserted. He picked up a cup, filled it with ice, and pounded on the soda dispenser until it delivered his Coke. He debated sitting down, then went back to the office he shared with two secretaries and three other junior economists. Tricia was the only one present. He looked at her.

"Mary took leave today. She'll be back tomorrow." Tricia had a very pleasant voice. She also weighed close to two hundred pounds and was a head taller than George. George liked to consider himself as a full six feet.

He eased behind his desk, setting the cup down on his blotter. Tricia began to type again.

"Tricia, can you get me the income figures on the Mafia for the last quarter?"

She nodded, but did not stop typing.

"Now! Damn it!"

"Yes, Mr. Graylin."

He looked around the office. He imagined that the other three economists were scattered all over the Washington Reservation briefing various staffs on the sundry economic idiocies still existing.

"Tricia, add to that a summary of all the major flows of union funds. Make sure that includes the pension funds and the mutuals."

"Yes, sir."

He felt guilty for yelling. He'd pay for it later. He sipped the Coke and tried to think. Who could be pumping all those dollars into the economy?

"Mr. Graylin, your readouts are coming through."

"Thank you, Tricia." He went over and collected the first pile of printouts. Tricia smiled too sweetly and resumed typing.

After five hours, including a hasty Coke and a sandwich, he was still in the dark about the Blight on the Great American Economy.

He picked up the phone and punched in a combination.

"Morey, this is George Graylin. I've got a problem that maybe you could help me with. Can you stop by after dinner—say about eight thirty?"

"Fine with me, George. Delores has chamber music appreciation tonight."

George wound up the rest of the afternoon's trivia, had a Coke, and dinner, in the cafeteria, then marched to the Reservation gate. The exit machine refused his bank card and insisted on his ID. Outside it was raining. He had left his raincoat in the office. He only had to straight-arm one secretary to get a cab, but got a faceful of Mace when the girl already in the back panicked. On the second try, he made it. After locking the doors, he dialed in his block code. The cab almost wouldn't accept his slightly mangled bank card, but finally digested the information after burping the bent card back twice.

Exiting the cab at full gallop, he dashed into the foyer, slammed the entry card into the gate, and slipped into the apartment recreation hall. A few were playing pool, but the area was generally deserted. Eight was early in the evening.

Morey Weissenberg was small and intense. He was a very good attorney.

"Let me get this straight, George. Someone or some organization is putting money into the economy. What's wrong with that?"

"No, no. It's not that. Somehow someone is putting money into the economy that never entered the country legally or was never earned here."

"How do you figure that?"

"Because for the last three months, overall income is higher than the total of goods and services indicates it should be. It's driving us nuts. The Honorable James Boulin Chartwell, III, especially. Taxes are being paid on that unknown money. It pays for more goods and services. It's not from the government."

George gulped down the rest of his Coke.

"So you're wondering if one of my clients might know where this extra cash is coming from?"

"Morey, I checked the records of your boys before I called you. As far as I can tell, they have nothing to do with it. It just boils down to the fact that there is more money in the country than this country could have produced."

"I get the picture. And you figure that if you can't solve it, you're liable to get runaway inflation?"

Morey was sipping Scotch, intensely.

"Not really. It's not even a whole lot of money. Could be as little as three to five million. Maybe less, depending on where it's dumped into the economy and the multiplier effect. The real problem for me is that it's got the Council upset because their pretty little charts don't work out."

George wandered into the kitchen, grabbed another Coke, and poured it into his glass.

"Care for more Scotch?" he mumbled while crunching an ice cube.

"No, thank you. George? Have you thought about an outside country dumping funds just to foul up the economy?"

"No, but I think that the effort would cost more than the results. You'd have to have a pretty sophisticated distribution system. I'll check on it tomorrow, though."

"I really ought to go, George. Delores will be furious if she happens to get home first. I'll let you know if I hear anything."

"Well, thanks anyway, Morey."

After Morey left, George reset the defense screens and went to bed.

.   .   .

"Good morning, Mr. Graylin," called Mary cheerfully.

"Morning, Mary."

George crawled behind his desk and clutched the Coke she always had waiting. He hadn't slept well.

"Mary, can you get the currency transfer records for the major Comm-bloc countries?"

He sat in his normal morning stupor until they arrived. The records said no country had the international balance to get away with it undetected.

The morning memo run had an Important Memo from the Desk of James Boulin Chartwell, III, to the effect that James Boulin Chartwell, III, suggested that George Jordan Graylin, Jr., stop riding a donkey and get on with discovering who was Betraying the Great American Economy before All Was Lost.

Feeling that all was lost anyway, George took the Reservation shuttle over to the new congressional addition and briefed Congressman Dither's new staff economist on the role of recovery and reclamation in the variable budget system. He came back to the office to find another Important Memo on his desk. It said, translated: Have you saved the Great American Economy?

He threw it in the pulper.

"Mr. Graylin, you have a luncheon engagement with the Bank Tellers of Greater Washington at the Burr Room." Tricia smiled a very superior smile as he scurried out the door.

Percival P. Pentamount, Executive Vice President of the Greater American Bank, was the featured speaker. The topic was "The Role of the Great American Banking System in the Great American Economy." Since the government regulated the economy, and the banks' role was zilch, George went to sleep. He woke up to the relieved applause of the Bank Tellers of Greater Washington.

The meeting broke up as the tellers scurried back to their tells. Percival P. Pentamount was approaching. George eyed an emergency exit, then shrugged.

"Did you like the talk?"

Percival P. Pentamount was round, white-haired, pleasant-looking, blue-eyed, and well aware of all four attributes.

George suppressed a yawn. "It was quite a pep talk."

"Must keep the troops happy. I enjoy making them all feel wanted." Percival rubbed his hands together eagerly. He continued. "All in a day's work, you know. Banking is the Heart of the Economy." Percival then beamed at George.

George managed a smile.

"Well, I must be hastening back to the Bank. A pleasure meeting you, sir."

Percival P. Pentamount waddled quickly off.

George sighed, gulped down the rest of his Coke, and lurched to his feet. He only knocked over one glass in his retreat.

Getting back to the office was easy. He grabbed the first cab that slowed, shattering the eardrums of a teentough who tried to cycle him down. He recharged the ultrabeamer as soon as he got through the Reservation gate.

Collapsed at his desk, he found another memo. The Important Memo decreed: "Get to the Heart of the Problem. The President and I are Counting on You, George."

He tossed it into the pulper. Then he burped.

"Bad day, George?"

Norman Dentine had a flashing smile and a slightly patronizing manner. His only asset, to George's way of thinking, was that he was seldom in the office.

"No. Terrible day."

"Sorry to hear that. I'd give you a hand, but I'm due to brief Senator Titegold in an hour."

"No problem, Norm. No problem."

George sighed. There ought to be some way to get to the heart of the problem. He straightened up, abruptly.

"Mary, I need some statistical research done."

"But, Mr. Graylin, I'm way behind."

"Don't worry about that. The President is Counting on Us, as the Very Honorable James Boulin Chartwell, III, would say."

. . .

Three days later, George emerged from his stack of printouts with very little printable to say. It was Monday, and it was still gray.

He picked up the telephone.

"Morey, you've got to help me. I think I'm onto something, but it's driving me nuts."

Morey arrived promptly at eight. George reset the defense screen by the apartment door.

"Delores says I can give you an hour and no more, George, so get on with it."

George poured Morey a Scotch, lifted an ice bucket and a carton of Cokes, and lumbered into the study. He slumped into the chair behind the desk.

"All right, Morey. Here's where I am. First, this bootleg money has to get into the economy from some legitimate source. It can't come through a sector that deals in physical goods because I'd be able to catch that through the IRS Data Link by comparing costs, input-output, and profit figures. Any goods producer would have to hide it through abnormally high profits. Same in the service sectors. No one in any of those sectors is showing higher profits. Then I hit on the financial service boys—the brokerage houses, the mutual funds, the insurance companies, and the banks. I thought that if anyone showed a higher net, I'd be set. But the fluctuations from institution to institution killed that idea."

George paused and gulped the rest of the Coke. He opened another.

"George, what about the possibility of higher costs disguising higher profits?"

Morey was still on his first Scotch.

"That doesn't show up, either. I ran a cost analysis of everyone big enough to have that kind of effect. According to the Census and IRS data, no one big enough to affect the economy has costs appreciably higher than competitors."

George dropped into the chair again and kicked off his shoes.

"Hell, Morey, I'm going nuts. I even checked the Treasury Department and the Fed about total money supply. The Treasury said no, they were not fiddling with the money supply and ran me a set of tests to prove it. The Federal Reserve boys nearly blew their programming computer when they saw the figures I brought them. They didn't like it one bit. If I don't get an answer immediately, they'll have those figures all over Greater Washington in a day or so."

"You mean, the money supply is definitely larger? Are reserves a problem?"

Morey was interested, abstractly.

"That brings us to the point, Morey. I do have one idea, but I don't know if it's technically possible. And I can't ask anyone if it is. The question itself would panic too many people. So . . ."

"Well, what is it, George? I can do your dirty work for you again, I suppose."

George told him.

"I don't know, George. I'll let you know."

George reset the apartment defense screen when Morey left.

. . .

"George, you have rendered the Government a Great Service. You have stopped a Despicable Plan to Undermine the Great American Economy. I am Proud of You. The President is Proud of You."

James Boulin Chartwell, III, no longer the Junior Economic Advisor, sipped his glass of one hundred percent pure mineral water.

"I think We just might be able to Find a Place for You, George."

George smiled. It was going to be a long summer.

The formalities accomplished, Mary waited for George. She cornered him with a Coke.

"Why banks, George?"

"As Percival P. Pentamount would say, Banking is the Heart of the Economy. What better place to pump in a little umph?"

George sipped the Coke thoughtfully.

"Once I saw how it could be done, and Morey confirmed it, the hardest problem was to find out who was doing it. The idea wouldn't have been possible years ago with all the paperwork involved then. Now it's simple. All a crooked banker has to do is a little computer manipulation. When funds are transferred, the bank computers link. The sender bank computer subtracts funds from itself and the accounts involved. The receiver bank adds funds to both. Old Percy had a percentage of the funds retained when the bank sent them to another. But only on certain accounts. This created a bit of extra money."

"George, that doesn't make sense."

"But it does. Look at it this way. Say that Percival has a hundred dollars in his own account. He transfers fifty dollars from that account to another account in his own name in another bank. The computer in Percy's bank obediently sends the fifty dollars to the second bank. The next step was Percival's stroke of genius. He programmed his own bank's computer to 'forget' to deduct that fifty dollars from the original account. Since the computer conveniently 'forgets' that Percy even sent the funds, Percy is left with his original hundred dollars still intact, plus fifty more in his second account in that other bank."

George took a quick swallow of the Coke.

"Now you have to realize that this actually happened only to a few out of all the bank's transfers. Percy was smart enough to realize that the gimmicked transactions could just be a small percentage of the total number of transactions that the bank handled."

"But how did they balance the books?" Mary was a great believer in balance.

"That was the beauty of it. Since Percy programmed the computer to 'forget' the gimmicked deals, the magnetic transfer slips covering those deals were never printed out. That meant that the printed records of the bank agreed with the computer records. According to both the printed and computer records, the money never left Percy's bank."

"Now, wait a second, George. You mean that Percival just sneaked down into the computer room one night and told the machine to do all this?" Mary shared a certain awe of computers with the rest of the world.

"No, he had an accomplice, the head programmer. There were actually three separate accounts that had the special programming. The gimmicked transfers were from Percy's personal account, the programmer's personal account, and one of the bank's investment accounts."

George took a deep breath, tilted the plastic cup back to catch an elusive ice cube, and crunched the ice into satisfying fragments.

"You see, Percy had crated a separate portfolio for investments which he managed. No one would have noticed the discrepancies but a portfolio manager, and Percy was the manager. By doing this he hoped to increase the bank's assets gradually, but dramatically, and thus boost his banking career."

Mary was beginning to look dazed.

"Now Percival was pretty smart. He had accounts in several other banks, and by shuffling funds between his own accounts, he managed to create quite an increase in his personal fortune. Because banking is so anonymous today, he got away with it.

"If he'd really been an idealist, I never could have caught him. The business with the investment account was set up beautifully. A certain percentage of funds transfers failed to be deducted. Period. Yet, according to the books of the other banks, everyone got the money. Basically, Percival had the philosopher's stone."

"But how did you find him out, considering the number of banks and bankers?"

"I just hooked into the IRS Data Link with a requirement to see the dossiers on any bankers whose assets had recently showed a marked increase.

Percival knew he had to pay taxes, since his additional savings would auto-matically be reported by the member bank computers. He knew that the IRS computer is pretty dumb. All it cares about is whether your taxes agree with your income. Unless you get an executive order, you can't pull off a search like I did. He would have been safe, except . . ."

"Except what, George?"

"That the bureaucracy is so settled that the tiniest bit of inflation is more important than the biggest bank swindle in history."

George thought of James Boulin Chartwell, III, and his one hundred per-cent pure mineral water and the Great American Economy.

"What will happen to Percy?"

"I doubt anything serious will. They may even have trouble getting back the money he made by the system. Legally, it doesn't qualify as counterfeit-ing, as no actual currency was involved. The bank laws refer to falsifying written books, and he never laid a hand on anything except a computer pro-gram, and currently, there's no law against that. It wasn't tax evasion. He didn't steal or embezzle anyone else's funds, because the funds he got didn't exist before he created them. It wasn't fraud since no one else can prove that they were defrauded of anything. All he did was create excess credit. Most people want credit for doing as little as possible. He went a step further. He got credit for nothing."

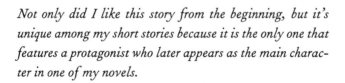

Not only did I like this story from the beginning, but it's unique among my short stories because it is the only one that features a protagonist who later appears as the main character in one of my novels.

SECOND COMING

Jimjoy Wright finished topping off the jumper's auxiliary tanks. He stowed the hose back in the service pit and slid the cover back into place. It fit flush with the green tarmac. The Believers kept things tidy.

He finished the exterior preflight. Then he tugged at the corner of his left eyelid and felt the miniscanner click on. The "click" was mostly psychological, but necessary. He "clicked" it off.

After a quick look across the field at the slender dispatch tower, he circled back to the right aux tank. He inspected the quick-release bolts, the wiring, and the separation charges. He walked back around the armaglass canopy to the left aux tank. The jettison systems on both pod tanks seemed ready. He checked the intakes on the dash jet pods. Clear.

Jimjoy climbed into the left-hand seat. The right seat and the passenger compartment were empty. He tapped his fingers on the padded shield above the instruments, then keyed the dispatcher.

"Jumper Seven, ready for passenger."

"Mr. Wright, the passenger is en route." The voice was polite, marginally so.

After two weeks, Jimjoy still hadn't met the woman behind the polite voice. He looked at the late-afternoon sun above the Plateau, then back at the instruments. He suppressed a sigh. The whole thing was so iffy. If only the Believers weren't so stiff-necked . . . if only the Fuards weren't up to something . . . if only the Terrans weren't so chicken . . .

He stared blankly through the armaglass canopy, not really seeing the green-and-white squares of the small jumpport. Stocky, tanned, brown-haired—with all his suppressed energy, he still felt relaxed compared to the religious intensity of the tall, light-skinned Believers.

A green electrocar pulled up at the edge of the field. A slender woman in white got out. She walked quickly across the empty field to the jumper, untouched by the slight breeze blowing toward the Plateau.

Jimjoy scratched behind his right shoulder and at the itching skin around the underarm signal implant. He checked the position of the late-afternoon sun again, looked at his watch, and began the checklist. He missed the automated cross-check equipment. The Believers liked to keep things simple as well as tidy.

"Believer Wright?" the woman asked as she climbed into the front passenger seat. Here it was the passenger seat. In the Service it was the copilot's seat.

"Nope. Just plain old Jimjoy Wright."

The tip of her lightly tanned nose wrinkled slightly.

"I had thought . . ."

"I know, Miss—uh—Doctor, but I'm the only jumper around here at the moment. The others are all ferrying the high muckety-mucks up to the Plateau for the ceremony."

"Day of Celebration. My name is Believer Alba. Dr. Alba, if you wish. I need to see a patient at Jehosephat."

Jimjoy finished the checklist.

"I'd appreciate it if you'd strap in Miss—uh—Dr. Alba." He keyed the dispatcher. "Seven, preparing to lift."

"Cleared to lift for Jehosephat, Seven."

Dr. Alba wrinkled her nose again, pushed a strand of fine blond hair back into perfect place over her right ear, and snapped the safety harness into place with the ease and force of habit.

"Why aren't you at First Landing?" asked Jimjoy with a nod at the Plateau. He activated the automatic cabin locks and made a last fuel check. "Seems like everyone else on *IFoundIt!* is."

The muted grumbling of the thrusters as they caught drowned out the beginning of her statement.

". . . as an apprentice physician, I must take my turn at tending those who cannot be at the Celebration."

"What happens if your god appears at the Celebration?" asked Jimjoy. He tried to keep the grin out of his voice.

"It is written that He will, and He will reward all true Believers according to their just desserts, whether they are at the Celebration or not."

"Wasn't he supposed to have his Second Coming over twenty years ago tonight?"

Jimjoy checked the rotor extension and watched the blade arc as he fed in thruster torque. The implant itch was killing him, but he avoided the urge to scratch. A doctor just might guess. He kept his eyes shifting between the field and the gauges.

"How did you come here?" she asked, avoiding his last question.

"By freighter."

"But why? You are not a Believer."

After balancing the torques, he finished the checklist. The jumper lifted, hovering on its ground cushion in the green afternoon light. The hover felt heavier than normal with the full aux tanks, but the jumper still had plenty of power to spare.

Jimjoy eased the stick forward, and the jumper began to climb as the airspeed built. After he cleared the edge of the jumpport, he banked into a gentle turn toward Jehosephat—down the Great Valley from the Plateau.

"Well," he began, as if the question had been posed only seconds ago, "I got tired of punching buttons on Old Earth, didn't like the prissy cities of New Terra, didn't like roughing it on Pristina, and I didn't like the Fuards with their nasty little conflicts and their tinhorn dictator. This is as far as I got with the credits I had. Latched on here a couple of weeks ago as a relief pilot for nights, times when you Believers are at services, what have you."

He eased the jumper from the turn onto a heading parallel to the Plateau—even as the jumper entered the shadow of the big mesa. He twisted the thrusters up fractionally for a gentle climb. If he only knew what to expect—but his instructions had been none too explicit. They couldn't be, not if his actions were to be impartial enough. Just be close to First Landing in case something happens at the Celebration. Do what's necessary. Great! Just great.

He looked over at the woman momentarily. Clean-featured, piercing green eyes, sharp nose. He turned back to the panel quickly.

"Hey," he began awkwardly, "is it really true that you believe your God will come back at sunset today . . . or next year . . . or the year after . . . I mean on the anniversary of today?"

"Of course." The doctor's voice was gentle.

Jimjoy twisted the thruster grip throttle back enough to kill the climb. He had a clear enough view of the Plateau. He pointed. "There. You can see the temple and the crowd." He paused. "Why is that half of the Plateau empty?"

"That's God's half . . . where He will manifest Himself. Both real and symbolic. God must be half you and you half God. Actually, it's more complicated than that." She looked out through the armaglass canopy to signal an end to the theological inquiry.

Jimjoy shook his head. The things some intelligent people believed. IFoundIt! was such a contradiction. Agricultural, but based on a solid and dispersed technology; libertarian civil government, but a fanatical religious social structure; highly educated population but one believing in a simplistic religion.

He peered up the valley at Jehosephat—another half hour—theoretically. Say about ten minutes after sunset.

A glint high in the sky, almost over the point of the setting sun, caught his eye. Then it vanished. A ship coming in? Certainly not a scheduled one, nor a free trader. Not today. Besides, he'd checked the schedule before they'd left Second Landing.

Not many ships called at IFoundIt!, he knew. Both the Believers and the Fuards discouraged idle sightseeing. And being on the far side of the trade lanes with the Fuardian Conglomerate in between didn't help either. The Fuards were beginning to rattle their sabres, looking for an easy kill. The Believers of IFoundIt!, while not pacifists, relied heavily on their God for defense.

"Where did you learn to pilot a jumper?" asked Dr. Alba. "We don't trust just any spacebum with them."

"Academy," he muttered.

"And you're here?"

"Don't hold much for pomp and ceremony," he answered, realizing the ridiculousness of the answer as he said it. He rushed on, "I mean, here you let a man live as he wants to. You may pity us poor slobs who don't Believe. But so long as I do a good day's work, no one seems to mind—except on Holy Days," he added with a grin.

He shook his head again, fighting the urge to scratch the underarm implant. He looked for the telltale glint against the sky, then throttled back the thrusters.

"Fuards'll fight—if they have to, but they'd rather break your spirit or try some neat form of genocide rather than bust up a pretty planet. The sneakier the better is a pretty fair approximation of the going Fuardian motto." He looked at the sky above the dropping sun. Still nothing. "Now Macedonians have one of the oldest colonies and a real population problem. That makes for cannon fodder. And Old Earth is a mess. You can't cross a single blockline without your authorization card."

"And you still don't believe in the providence of God?" questioned the young doctor, with a sweep of her hand across the green-and-blue-checkered lands of the Great Valley.

"No offense, Doctor, but I think anybody who believes in more than man is in for an awful shock. Any god man can think up, man can destroy. We're better off without."

He wondered if he'd said too much.

"You're no ordinary spacebum."

"No spacebum is ordinary." He'd said too much. Still about fifteen minutes or so till twilight. The jumper was still cruising on course toward Jehosephat. He tightened the pilot's harness. Not military, but it would have to do.

"You know," he said conversationally, "I wonder what would happen if your god actually showed up."

"He will, one Day of Celebration. We will rejoice and prepare Him a welcome."

Jimjoy looked at the sky over the Plateau, then down at nine-tenths of the population of IFoundIt! gathered in the Great Square to await the Second Coming—as they presumably had every year for the past twenty.

He felt the internal trigger from the underarm implant. He reached up and tugged the corner of his left eyelid and triggered the miniscanner, hoping it wasn't a false alarm. Then he banked the jumper toward the Great Square on the Plateau.

"Pilot! Jehosephat is *that* way."

So damned little time. Why just one person? Why me? He knew the answer, but it made him feel better to throw in a little self-pity.

Dr. Alba touched his shoulder.

"Did you hear me? I have a patient at Jehosephat."

The jumper shook with the thunderclap that radiated from the Plateau. Even over the thrusters, Jimjoy could hear the long, echoing notes of the trumpet. Wondering how they had managed that, he steepened the bank, forcing the jumper back toward the Plateau.

As the jumper leveled out, Dr. Alba paled. Even Jimjoy flinched.

Standing in the middle of the "God side" of the Plateau of First Landing was the towering figure of an angel, golden-haired, standing literally two kilometers into the deepening green sky and lowering a trumpet.

"Oh, my God," whispered the young doctor as she made the sign of the Holy Triad.

"Exactly," muttered Jimjoy. "The bastards, the total bastards." He lowered the nose. Dr. Alba was sitting forward in the passenger seat, her eyes locked on the magnificent figure.

"The Holy Messenger," she murmured. "But I didn't really Believe. Forgive me, oh my God, forgive me my sins of disbelief."

Jimjoy lined up the jumper on the left knee of the angel. From there he'd pass over one corner of the crowd, but he didn't have time for a longer route. The angel was holding a set of balance pans in one hand and a sword of fire in the other. It was going to be as quick and as dirty a job as they could manage.

Jimjoy leaned toward Dr. Alba and slammed her back into the seat with his right arm. He triggered the emergency override to activate the full passenger-restraint system, then twisted the grip throttle through the detent all the way to emergency. Then he lowered the nose farther to compensate for the increased power.

What a half-assed way to fight a war! I hope the scanner gets it all.

He kept the forward pressure on the stick as the airspeed needle climbed, the intakes screamed, and the blades began to shudder. He eased the stick back slightly as the rotors approached blade stall, cutting in the full pod thrust, disengaging the blades, and folding them with the emergency system.

He hoped it worked. He might need them on the way back—if there was a way back.

He looked at the angel dramatically lifting the balance pans into the twilight. Somehow the angle seemed wrong. The angel blurred momentarily as the jumper crossed the edge of the Plateau.

Jimjoy flicked the communit selector to fullband guard.

He could sense Dr. Alba struggling against the restraint system as the jumper bored in on the towering angel. He forced himself to keep his eyes open.

He fed more power to the straining thrusters and pods by cracking open the emergency manual fuel system. Three red lights glared from the console, and the EGT marched into the red.

Hell, I won't have an exhaust system left.

He felt the throttle coming back, out of habit, caught himself, and laughed, jamming the grip back full over. The jumper bucked with the power change. Even with the blades folded in the dash configuration, he could feel the instability.

Now they were inside the shadow of the towering figure. The angel appeared less clear. Jimjoy squinted at the robe-covered legs.

If it was a cruiser, he'd had it. But the intelligraphs had insisted that a destroyer or corvette would be the most he could expect on a mission like this. Neither had the power for full screens.

Range guides—check.

He dumped the nose toward the angel's robed ankles.

The image broke. The God side of the Plateau was clear except for the spiral curves of the Fuardian destroyer. Jimjoy saw Believers breaking ranks and running for cover. He looked at them long enough to be sure that the scanner implant got them all.

Great. If he failed, between the scanner and the survivors, there'd be enough evidence to tie the Fuards to the whole mess. Nothing short of point nihil would destroy the scanner. Unfortunately, the bearer of the infernal eye was less invulnerable.

He flipped the jumper down and to the right, abruptly up and left, in time to avoid the first bursts from the boltguns and lasers.

"Fuardian war-destroyer at First Landing! Fuardian war-destroyer at First Landing! Firing on civilians! I repeat hostile Fuardian action against civilians."

That would have to do. He hoped someone was monitoring guard, but more important, it would be recorded. Everything for the record.

Jimjoy cut the pod thrusts and jammed the nose down and hard left into a six-gee turn. Then he added back the full pod thrust and leveled out four feet above the Plateau, still screaming toward the destroyer.

If this were only like practice—but it was a real hit-and-miss operation. The only question was who would hit first.

A chunk of the armaglass canopy went as Jimjoy jerked the jumper to the left, then back on course. The lasers were all swinging in on his flight path like the angel's sword they might have been. He checked the range again. It would have to do.

Heading straight at the destroyer, he triggered the shear-release bolts on the still full aux tanks and yanked the jumper into a max-gee turn away from the destroyer and toward the nearest edge of the Plateau.

The tanks hit the smooth rock just short of the destroyer and skidded toward the Fuardian ship. Jimjoy lost sight of them as he finished turning tail.

The fire light flashed on the right thruster. The console was largely red lights. Another chunk of the armaglass canopy went with the near miss of a boltgun.

Another mile, just a few seconds—the jumper was kicked from behind by the explosion of the jettisoned tanks. It crabbed violently as the right thruster quit altogether.

Jimjoy cut the pods and the remaining thruster as the jumper plunged out over the edge of the Plateau. He flicked the switches for the emergency rotor-deployment system, felt the jumper shudder as the blades spread.

He increased the blade pitch and felt the jumper swing hard right.

Damn! The Fuards had gotten the tail compensator.

The passenger restraints unlocked as the main generator quit. Jimjoy wondered if the doctor would sit still. Last thing he needed now was more interference.

He scanned the checkerboard of field and wood. They were on the far side of the Plateau from Second Landing, thank God. His reception there might be all right in a few months, but not tonight or tomorrow . . . not that he intended to be around tomorrow.

From a wisp of smoke in the distance, he made a guess at the wind direction and swung the jumper around. The doctor was turning whiter as she watched the jumper plummet silently toward the ground below.

Jimjoy's hands were wet. The late twilight made distance judging hard. His eyes flicked from the altimeter to the horizon to the ground in a continuing pattern.

Just as the jumper reached bush-top height on his path through the blue-green pasture, Jimjoy twisted full pitch on the rotors. The jumper slowed, then mushed into the grass.

He fought to keep it upright until the blades dropped within brake range. Then he jammed on the rotor brake. As the blades shuddered to a halt, the jumper tipped slowly and came to rest on the right blade tip.

Jimjoy went through the shutdown checklist methodically. He thumbprinted the dials and sat, shaking. Dr. Alba climbed out without a word or a look at the pilot and walked halfway across the field, looking up at the Plateau.

After a few minutes, Jimjoy followed. There was a thin line of greasy smoke rising above the Plateau. As he watched, the battered Fuardian destroyer lifted slowly on gravs, winking into the black-green sky.

He sighed. Somehow, the aux tanks had done enough damage. The

Fuards didn't have the power to maintain distorters or screens. He wondered how many on the Plateau were dead.

"Praise be to God," intoned Dr. Alba, facing the Plateau and making the sign of the Holy Triad.

Right, thought Captain Jimjoy Wright, right.

He walked quickly up the dirt road away from the burned-out jumper. As he covered the ground, he triggered the underarm implant. The recovery flitter would find him soon enough. Back at Farflung, they'd remove the scanner unit with its sealed proof seal, forward it to the Federation and the Guard, and wait. And if they were lucky, the Fleet would conduct maneuvers at the edge of the Fuardian Conglomerate, almost clobber an unlucky planet, and the Fuards would apologize—maybe.

What a hell of a way to fight a war.

He kept walking.

I don't see everything I postulated in this story coming true . . . not so far . . . and yet . . . with the miniaturization of computers, Moore's Law, and increased programming expertise . . . how would we know?

RULE OF LAW

The all-news vidfax came on with a chime, jolting Darrow Bryan from sleep into semiconsciousness.

"... has ignored the growth of organized white-collar crime. Heathcoate charged that the takeover of Boston firms by 'gray' money has reached epidemic proportions . . ."

Darrow staggered into the shower.

When he emerged, the vidfax was still at it, displaying a split-screen picture, a distinguished-looking businessman in a tailored gray suit on the right and, on the left, a pan down over an audience cheering a jai alai match.

"... Ingeonelli, grandson of reputed crime boss Silveo Ingeonelli, declared Graystone's expansion and acquisition of Hy-Ly would allow Graystone to improve its efforts . . ."

"So what?" muttered the still-sleepy attorney as he wave-dried his hair into place. "If it isn't the Oilers, if it isn't the gray money, it's someone else. Ingeonelli, shmingonelli."

The image shifted to the view of a tanker, centering on the name, SLYCK QUEEN, painted on the bow in international orange.

The faxcast was explicit.

"Today, federal officials charged James Clancy Eastwood, IV, with oil profiteering and violation of oil import laws. Eastwood is the son of Multi-Media President James C. Eastwood, III. Neither Eastwood could be reached for comment.

Darrow flicked off the all-news vidfax. He checked the efficiency's insuladrapes for tightness before putting his thermal overcoat on over his thermal vest.

The MTA ride that usually lasted an hour took two. The MTA had cut back the number of trains again.

A single sheet of stationery waited in the middle of his desk. Without even reading it, Darrow flinched. It had to be from one of the senior partners.

A termination? A rebuke? It couldn't be positive. Congratulations were delivered personally.

The memo was explicit:

After long and thoughtful consideration, both Henry and I feel that you should handle the Eastwood case (file access E-33451(b)). We will be pleased to offer any and all assistance, as well as help develop any line of defense you consider appropriate.

I need not emphasize that the case should be prepared in keeping with the highest standards.

The memo was signed by Jonathon Fairley, senior active partner of Flush, Fairley, and Forefront.

A damned scuttle job, and I'm supposed to pull the plug gracefully. "Highest standards" means no "guilty" or "nolo" pleas and a pile of appropriate documentation.

Do you hand in your resignation, or quietly do your best, which the powers that be have prejudged to be inadequate? Or do you struggle against the obviously loaded dice the senior partner has handed you?

After considering the Boston winter and the number of bright young lawyers scrounging for jobs, Darrow dismissed the ceremonial resignation. He looked briefly at his overflowing in-box and turned instead to the controls of his legal console.

As the firm's case file on Eastwood appeared on the fax screen, he turned the speed control up to max. He needed the outline first. After the first runthrough, Darrow plodded through the tape again, more carefully, taking notes. The background was there, all right, and the whole thing smelled worse than the harbor.

He leaned forward in the small swivel—standard for associates of Flush, Fairley, and Forefront—and stared at the fax screen.

Where should he start?

Darrow pushed his already thinning hair back off his forehead, scratched his left sideburn, and cleared his throat.

"Citations on government regulations of energy imports?"

After a minute of silence, the computer replied, "There are 12,233 possible citations. Do you want the full listing?"

Darrow wiped his forehead. He didn't know what he wanted.

"Negative? Interrogative Constitutional precedents?"

"Article I, Section 8, U.S. Constitution. '. . . all Duties, Imposts, and Excises shall be uniform throughout the United States.' . . ."

"Hold," muttered Darrow at the console.

The case was a courtesy. If it weren't, he wouldn't have it. One of the full partners would. Just as obviously, he wasn't supposed to win it. Darcy should have had it, or even Fettinger.

James Clancy Eastwood, III, the president of MultiMedia and the "Master of Mood," wanted his son, James Clancy Eastwood, IV, defended. Young Jimmy had been cited and indicted by the Department of Energy, Enforcement Branch, and the U.S. Attorney for allegedly owning, through various subsidiaries and aliases, the controlling interest in Slyck Oil. Slyck Oil supplied fuel oil for New England.

Darrow shook his head. Why would any right-blooded, energy-saving young American want to profiteer on foreign oil?

He sat staring at the console. The Constitution, for God's sake. Nobody tried to win a case on law, did they? No one ever seriously cited the Constitution against the government.

Darrow tried to fit the pieces together, looking for any angle.

The Oil Anti-Monopoly Act of 1983 forbade U.S. citizens from holding the controlling interest in foreign shipping or foreign oil production, distribution, or refining ventures. In that strange court decision, *Offshore Oil vs. U.S.*, the Third Circuit Court of Appeals had held that while the law could not be applied to U.S.-based companies with both foreign and domestic oil production nor to foreign nationals or foreign companies controlled by non-U.S. citizens, the law applied to everyone else.

In reaction, Congress passed, and President Welsher signed, both a 20 percent additional tariff on imported oil and the Oil Import Act of 1986, which stated that U.S. companies had to import oil and other fossil fuels solely in U.S.-built and -registered ships.

In plain old American, reflected Darrow, Eastwood was charged with controlling a foreign oil company, using foreign tankers, and failure to pay the 20 percent oil duty levied on all U.S. importers; and in general engaging in the despicable practice of fuel-legging home-heating oil to frigid New Englanders.

The console buzzed. Darrow sat up straight as Jonathon Fairley beamed out from the small screen.

"Darrow, I trust you've had a chance to review the Eastwood case?"

"Yes, sir. Looks like quite a challenge."

Fairley ignored the pleasantry. "As you may know, the senior Eastwood has been a valued friend and client for many years, and he requested we handle the case for his son."

Despite rumored years of heavy coke use, Jonathon Fairley retained the ruddy good looks and easy manner that had made him a favorite with the Welsher administration.

"Doesn't the younger Eastwood have his own attorneys?"

"Under the search and seizure powers of the Enforcement Branch of the Department of Energy, young Eastwood no longer has control over any of his assets. He formerly was represented by Hutspaw, Lord, and Masters."

"I see," said Darrow. He didn't, but hoped he would.

"Under the circumstances, and particularly with your background, Hank and I thought you would be the best choice. We, of course, would be too close to Jim. Is that satisfactory?"

"Just fine, sir."

"Good. Jim may be in to see you today, and Darcy's handling the release on recognition, although young Eastwood's had some medical problems since he's been in custody. Keep me posted."

Darrow's thoughts were racing as the senior partner broke the connection. The memo had been written either early today or yesterday, but the faxcast had mentioned the charges early in the morning. And Fairley knew that Eastwood had medical problems and had sent Darcy off to get his release.

Medical problems while in Enforcement Branch custody . . . Darrow didn't like the sound of that or Fairley's knowledge of those problems. Did the senior partner know too much? Darrow pushed the thought to the back of his mind. The case itself was bad enough.

He decided to clear out the bulging in-box in order to concentrate on the Eastwood mess. He'd gotten almost to the bottom when the console buzzed again.

"A Mr. Eastwood to see you, Mr. Bryan."

He got up and opened the door to his oversized closet.

A tall, white-haired man barged down the hallway at him.

"Darrow Bryan, huh," he mumbled. "Your folks must have loved or hated lawyers. You know why I'm here, but then again, you don't know enough. Not a bit of sense in beating around the bush."

Eastwood stood a full two meters, a full head taller than Darrow. The big man half gestured, half pushed Darrow back into his own office and shut the door so hard that the thin flexiplast office walls shuddered.

"Sit down. Sit down, Darrow. Mind if I call you Darrow? Look my son's got this idea that he can solve New England's fuel shortage all by himself . . . just like that. The hell with government. The hell with fairness. The hell with the law. He's going to save New England and make filthy profits doing it."

Darrow struggled to keep his expression blank. This wasn't how he'd imagined the president of MultiMedia, even though the man matched his holos down to the microdot.

"Well, man in my position's got to keep up the images. You know what I mean. So the best firm in Boston, my own firm, has to be the one to defend him—but it can't be my own attorneys. That's as far as I go. You know what I mean. You're it, Darrow.

"I wish you luck, son, because the government's gunning for Jimmy, and, frankly, I hope they get him. Him and his let-the-government-go-to-hell attitude. He's guilty, guilty as hell."

The man's got nerve, telling me that he picked the third string of the big name firm to ensure his own son's conviction. Christ!

"Nothing against you, Darrow. If you want out, I can see your position. Of course"—and he grinned at the young lawyer—"you pull this out, and you're made."

"I appreciate your thoughtfulness in setting the parameters of the case, Mr. Eastwood," Darrow said as smoothly as he could. "As you mentioned, it presents quite a challenge. I feel confident, however, that I can do a more than adequate job."

The older man's eyes narrowed. "Think I should look elsewhere?"

"No. Not unless your son decides that. I'll be conferring with him once he's released."

"You've got the picture, Darrow. Wish you luck."

Darrow sat and watched the media executive bull his way out.

Three days later, Darcy had cut enough red tape to get young James Clancy Eastwood, IV, out of the clutches of the Enforcement Branch and into Darrow's office.

"Look, Bryan, I can see it now. I was a patsy, a setup. Here I am, believing that it's really a question of poor New England families without fuel, heating oil, what have you. Bull . . . it's a question of power. My old man's friends in Washington want to keep their power, and he wants to keep their friendship.

"Anyhow, I kept it legal, always let Hassan have the bigger chunk. Then comes the squeeze play. Hassan wants out. Hutspaw sets it up so that the Abdullah family trust has 46 percent of the stock, but the old man buys a measly 2 percent and sets it into a trust for me. That gets leaked to the DOE thugs.

"That wasn't enough. The Oilers push through another 20 percent hike. If I don't go along, I don't get oil. So I have to agree. It's not the money. I'm making plenty. If I don't supply the oil, with the DOE allocations so low, people are going to get cold.

"Next thing I know, the Feds are at my front door, and my son's watching me being dragged off. Me, his upstanding dad, being hauled off like some right-wing, screw-the-people nut. Me, the guy who's risking everything to bring heating oil to New England. I know, and you know, that my old man set me up and called his buddies down at DOE and put them on my case.

"You know what burns me worse than that? If my name were Kaliph or Abdul-de-bull-bull-de-bar, not a thing would be wrong. I could laugh my head off at them. The Oilers can charge anything, use any ship—and it's fine. Our federal government says, 'Please charge us some more. Our people use too much for their own good . . .' "

Darrow barely stopped his groan. Still, it could be an interesting case.

"Then," Eastwood plunged on, "the DOE buckoes come in and freeze all my stash. Hell . . . they wired my number right into the system. I can't even get a dollar for a piece of bubble gum. So here I am at thirty-five: busted, and depending on whatever my old man's going to give me, or on some liberal public defender, or maybe on some right-winger crusader who wants to uphold the nonexistent free enterprise system. That kind of defense will send me straight to the federal work farm.

"My wife's left. My kids are fawning over the great man, and the government's drooling over me. And the ever-loving idiots in Congress would like to string me up for treason. If I were a greasy Oiler, they'd be asking for my oil at two hundred a barrel."

Darrow shook his head. Young Eastwood didn't even notice.

When Eastwood had finally finished his story, Darrow steered him to the Medico-Legal clinic. Once Eastwood had left, Darrow called the clinic to alert them and to make his own requests.

"That's right, a complete physio-psychic and drug-residue series, plus an EEG, plus . . ."

He followed that with a call to Eastwood's personal physician to request the baseline medical data.

What a screwy deal! Old Eastwood picks an attorney to sink his own son, and the son agrees to the charade. Not that he has any options. But there had to be an angle.

The legal computer kept coming back to the possible Constitutional precedents. They wouldn't be enough, not unless the judge assigned were a Constitutionalist, or could be convinced to be one.

Still . . . the profession had been slow to adopt full computerization, perhaps because of the expense involved, and only a handful of firms had the equipment Darrow did. Even Darcy didn't use the console much, said it was a waste of time.

Darrow turned back to the console.

"Decisions from the Circuit. Rank the decisions by judges in numerical frequency of Constitutional citations in their opinions."

"Clarify," requested the console.

"Find me the district judge who bases the greatest part of his decisions on Constitutional cites . . . no . . . cancel that."

That wouldn't do the job. Darrow took two hours to set up the guidelines he needed, but shelved them for the time being. No sense in following that line until Judge Absolem assigned the case.

. . .

A week passed before he faxed Eastwood IVth back.

"Mr. Eastwood, do you want to beat the government or be a martyr to your father and the Feds?"

"You bastard! What the hell do you mean?"

"Look. I think I can win this for you, at least in the lower court, which will kill the criminal charges. But nobody's ever tried this approach before, not to this extreme, anyway."

Eastwood appeared mildly intrigued.

"So what is it?"

Darrow did his best to explain.

"Finally, Eastwood interrupted. "All right. From what I see, you're putting your job on the line, and that's better than you can expect from most shysters. Besides, it's better than stalling and waiting for them to hang me high and dry for years. That's what my old man really wants."

Now . . . if Darrow could just make it work.

Finding Judge Absolem's clerk took three calls.

"Harlan Garthaus. May I help you?"

"Darrow Bryan, with Flush, Fairley, and Forefront. I was wondering if Judge Absolem had assigned the Slyck Oil case."

"Hmmm," offered the clerk.

"I suppose it's likely to be a while longer before a final assignment's made."

"If it's a typical government case"—the clerk grinned—"the U.S. Attorney will make three motions for delay, and you'll probably have a few yourself. It's an oil case, and no one likes those."

Alarm bells were sounding in Darrow's head.

"I take it that it's been assigned to someone like Ngaio or Lerata?" Darrow hadn't appeared before either, but both had the reputation of chewing up attorneys and quashing dilatory motions practically before they were made.

"Right. Judge Lerata, and Garrity didn't say a word."

Darrow could guess why. He might as well see if his scheme could work with Lerata. If not, he'd try to angle for another judge.

With Lerata in mind, Darrow headed down to the firm's programming section.

"We can't do that!" was the first reaction of the supervisor.

Darrow knew why—money. Fairley had opposed the expense of in-house computerization. Hank Forefront had finally been the one who had pushed it through by appealing to both Fairley's sense of pride and his paranoia, telling Fairley that they could keep better track of security with their own system.

Darrow sighed, loudly, and for effect. "Let's look at it this way. You are in the business of computerizing legal research, right? Mr. Fairley wants a good job done on this case, right? Now, for a good job, I need a series of sorts done on every opinion by Judge Lerata. Is that possible?"

"Yes, but—"

"Next, I need a summary of the arguments presented on both sides, with a key-word correlation made between the language in the final opinion and the cites of the winning side. Can you do that?"

"We might have to go time-sharing with Logic/Law and the National Legal Center. Let me put Peters on it."

Darrow spent three nights designing the key-word correlation, but a week later he had a tape and three large stacks of paper. The correlation programming was spotty, which led to more hours refining the correlations. The last step was to tailor his own cites and case to the optimum presentation profile.

In the meantime, the medical records had come back. Test results were conclusive. Darrow congratulated himself on recognizing that the Feds had scrambled Eastwood's brains in the period he'd been in custody. The drug residues were there.

As for permanent effects . . . nothing that the Medico-Legal analysts could put their fingers on, but Eastwood's accomplishments and the federal charges didn't quite square with the man Darrow had met.

He persuaded Eastwood to start restoration treatments, with hopes that there would be some effect before the trial, which was approaching all too quickly.

Darrow, worrying about the computer side, finally ended up going down to discuss the procedure with Peters.

"Could you explain it simply, the technical side?"

"Sure, Mr. Bryan," said the programmer, who was younger than Darrow by at least ten years. He pushed a short printout at the lawyer.

"That's a simple, plain-language description of the search and comparison plan you asked for. Heck, if anyone had spent the time you did in outlining what you needed, this could have been done years ago. Nobody's ever asked, not according to the National Legal Center."

"You mean, now anyone could duplicate this? Even without our program?"

"Sure thing. Big thing is knowing it can be done."

Darrow smiled.

That night he vocotyped out a short article describing the process and faxed it off to the *Journal, Trial Practices, Civil Practice, Legal Ethics,* and his sister Susan in Taos, who specialized in Ute Indian claims.

If Fairley ever complained, which was unlikely because he never read any of the legal pubs, Darrow would say that he thought the firm wanted its associates to publish. Even if the hastily faxed article weren't published, the word would spread. Susan would use it, he was sure, even if she didn't speak to him. She'd use any angle.

The pretrial conference that had been postponed once already came. Darrow arrived early.

He watched Ed Garrity walk in. Garrity was the U.S. Attorney prosecuting the case, and, according to the computer analysis, specialized in *ad hominem* law, where he could set up the defendants as evildoers robbing widows and orphans.

Garrity nodded at Darrow.

"Thrown to the wolves, I see, Mr. Bryan."

"We'll do our best, Mr. Garrity."

From there, it went downhill.

"You'll agree to the stipulation that all the facts in the government's brief are correct?" asked Garrity.

"With the exceptions we've noted, certainly, but with the stipulation that they do not constitute the entire case. We have additional evidence to offer . . ."

Garrity nodded at that, but objected when Darrow refused to grant any violations of the laws themselves.

"Are you crazy? You grant the facts, but not the law. You can't win a case like this on law."

Garrity stopped giving advice when Darrow waived the jury. He didn't say anything more for the rest of the pretrial conference, just frowned whenever he looked in Darrow's direction.

.　　.　　.

"A Mr. Fiori to see you, Mr. Bryan."

"Fiori? Sounds familiar. Can't place it," he half mumbled. "Send him in."

"Jim Fiori, Mr. Bryan."

"Darrow, please. The 'misters' belong with the senior partners."

Darrow gestured to the chair in front of his console/desk.

"Have a seat."

Fiori handed Darrow a card before he sat down—James. B. Fiori, Jr., Associate General Counsel, Perdell Press.

"You name rings a bell, but I can't say that I recognize Perdell Press," offered Darrow, easing himself into his utilitarian swivel.

"I wear a number of hats, Darrow. Just one of them. Call it professional interest. Perdell publishes *Civil Practice*."

The visitor waited.

Darrow looked blank.

"You sent us a rather interesting draft article . . ."

"Oh . . . about the enhanced use of the legal computer system. Did you like it?"

"Very much. My boss was so impressed he sent me out to talk to you."

"Are you going to publish it?"

"Yes. But not anytime soon. Our backlog is about eighteen months. Reason I'm here is to get answers to some questions we had. Mind if I ask you about them?"

"Why . . . no. Go ahead."

"You outlined a computer search technique, using key words, and comparing the language of the opinion to the language of the two briefs. How do you deal with subjectives?"

"Subjectives?"

"Some judges don't like attorneys with red hair. A Latino judge may never rule for an Anglo attorney from Beacon Hill . . . you see what I mean?"

"Umm . . . Yes. Yes, but I didn't intend the program to deal with those. You could, I suppose, if you correlated the attorney's names against the judges', I suppose. That wasn't the point. It's more a matter of statistics."

Darrow looked at the older man, taking in the tailored suit, the silk shirt and tie.

Fiori nodded. "So you designed the system on an odds basis?"

"Not exactly. To be precise, I made additions to an existing system. But, yes, it works not on certainty, but on trying to figure the best odds for an approach to a given case, a given judge."

"Could you apply the system to get figures on regions?"

"You mean, to see what legal approaches were used where, and the relative success of each?"

"That would be one application. At *Civil Practice*, we like to focus on specifics. If we knew which kinds of suits were occurring where, and what cases attorneys were most successful with, it would make an interesting series."

"In other words, if all the coke cases in Southern California are won by the defendant . . . that's a story?"

"One way of looking at it. Maybe we'd be interested in seeing which kinds of cases are prosecuted, and which aren't, or which cases are dropped at what stages, and what legal arguments are involved with the successes and the failures."

Darrow shrugged.

"That's a different application, but it could be done, I'm sure."

"Well," said Fiori, abruptly standing up, "congratulations. You'll be hearing from the editor, I'm sure, and I appreciate your taking the time to chat with me."

"Oh . . . no problem. No problem."

After Fiori left, Darrow leaned back in the swivel, putting his feet up on the console. Why had Fiori come to see him? Maybe he really had something with the computer applications, more than winning a single case. Maybe he should have looked into selling the idea himself.

Too late for that now, and besides, he had a case to prepare. That was what paid the rent.

Still . . . he thumbed the vidfax Law Directory.

The screen began to print. Darrow scanned the material.

"Fiori, James Bienvenuto, Jr., born Marblehead . . . October 17, 1955 . . . B.A., Tufts University, 1976, J.D. Harvard, 1979 . . . partner, Gerswin, Fiori and Smithers . . . director, Graystone, Limited, Director and Associate General Counsel, Perdell Press . . ."

"Graystone?" Hadn't he heard something not so favorable about Graystone lately? Bells were ringing, but he didn't want to spend the rest of the morning tracking down Fiori.

He tapped out Darcy's number on the intercom.

"Hello there, Darrow. What's down?" Darcy put his pipe in the big ashtray and blew smoke at the screen.

"Graystone, Limited. Rings a bell, but can't place it."

"Ah . . . yes . . . Graystone. Holding company for the Ingeonelli family. Very, very clean. Outlet for very thoroughly laundered money. How'd you run across them? Didn't know they were involved in the Eastwood case. Aren't, are they?"

"Not exactly, but I'm trying a new computer search technique. Wrote it up as an article to expand my pubs record. A fellow by the name of Fiori came to see me about the technique. Asked me a couple of questions and left. Curious. So I thought I'd ask around."

Darcy frowned, picked up his pipe, and chewed on the stem, tapping his fingers on his desk console. Through the vidfax, Darrow could see the glint of the harbor behind Darcy. Darrow wished he had an outside view, but maybe that would come. If he did well with the Eastwood case. If . . . if . . . if a lot of things.

"Fiori's the top legal man for Graystone. Don't let all the smoke screens tell you different. If he spent the time to come see you, it's important, but for the life of me, I can't figure out what's so important about a computer technique. Unless there's more to it than you've let on. Or unless it's got a special application for them."

"He said the reason was that they could use some of the programs to develop legal statistics—"

"What?"

"Legal statistics. Graystone owns Perdell Press, and Perdell Press publishes *Civil Practice*."

"Could be, but I'd be careful." Darcy paused. "I don't like computers, think they're overrated. But if Jim Fiori's interested, it's enough to make me take a second look. Can you send me a copy of whatever you wrote?"

"Sure."

"Let me look it over, and I'll be back in touch. Good luck with Eastwood. Better you than me."

Darrow broke his glance away from the blank screen, leaned farther back in his swivel.

Graystone . . . Perdell . . . Ingeonelli . . . mob . . . gray money . . . and computers . . . there had to be a reason, a good one.

He shoved it all into the back of his mind. If he didn't make a good show with the Eastwood case, none of it would matter, and, likely as not, he wouldn't be around to worry about Fiori's visit.

.   .   .

Darrow sat in an old wooden chair in the courtroom, waiting for Judge Lerata, with a seemingly relaxed James Clancy Eastwood, IV, next to him. Darrow twisted his worn and rolled *Times* between hands already smudged with newsprint. Thinning brown hair drooped across a forehead he felt had gained too many lines too quickly in the past months.

He realized again what a gamble his strategy was. It ought to work, but theory and practice were two different things.

Garrity marched in, followed by several younger attorneys, inclined his head fractionally at Darrow, and settled himself at his table.

Judge Lerata gaveled the courtroom to order with one blow.

Darrow put down the *Times,* leaning forward.

"I've taken your motion for delay under advisement," the judge addressed Garrity, "but I'd like to hear any final remarks the defense might have."

Darrow rose.

"Your Honor," he began, his mouth dry, "as we have noted earlier, the Department of Energy and the Justice Department records concerning the charges against Slyck Oil and the defendant go back thirty-six months. Counsel for the prosecution was assigned to this case over six months ago, even before my client was taken into custody. More important, this case does not revolve around questions of fact but questions of law. There has been no recent change in the laws in question."

According to the computer analysis of Judge Lerata, a summary of briefed material appealed to him.

Darrow plunged on. "Finally, according to the Sixth Amendment, as reinforced by the Speedy Trial Act, a man accused should have a speedy and public trial. Since the government has had the benefit of thirty-six months of preparation, we object to any further delay."

Judge Lerata pursed his lips and peered through his antique glasses at Garrity.

"Does the prosecution have any further arguments?"

"Yes, Your Honor. We believe that undue haste in a precedential case of this magnitude would not be justified, particularly given the legal ramifications involved. As the Supreme Court ruled in *Beavers vs. Haubert,* the right to a speedy trial is necessarily relative and does not preclude the rights of public justice. Further . . ."

Garrity went on to cite other decisions.

Darrow punched the stopwatch button. Thirteen and a half minutes later, Garrity sat down.

The judge turned back to Darrow.

"Mr. Bryan?"

"Your Honor, I would only note in passing that later decisions, such as *U.S. vs. Marion, Barker vs. Wingo, Toussie vs. United States,* and *Freeston vs. Cole,* as well as the Speedy Trial Act itself, emphasize two basic points. First, the defense need not show how delay is prejudicial. Second, delay is calculated from the actual gathering of evidence and the government's decision to prosecute. Therefore, thirty-six months seems more than enough time, particularly with the resources of the entire Department of Energy at hand, and especially given the prosecution's pretrial assertions that this is an open-and-shut case."

"Mr. Garrity, counsel for the defense has summed up the situation accurately. However, because of the requirements of the Speedy Trial Act, some inconveniences may be necessary. Trial will begin at 7:00 A.M. a week from Saturday."

"Your Honor . . ." escaped involuntarily from Garrity's mouth.

"Seven o'clock on the sixteenth," repeated Judge Lerata. "That is the first open date and gives you another ten days."

Garrity made it over the defense table before the judge had put aside his gavel.

"You realize, Mr. Bryan, that this could be a lengthy trial, and I do appreciate the zeal you have shown on behalf of your client. I also wanted to let you know that your insistence on such haste had canceled the first vacation I've had in three years. I had to make those reservations over ten months ago. I hope you'll provide a good alternative."

Darrow smiled. "I'm afraid you'll be disappointed, sir, but I'll certainly try."

Darrow couldn't feel terribly sorry for Garrity. With the continuing fuel shortages, even bus reservations were hard to come by. Garrity had pulled strings if he'd made reservations only ten months in advance.

·   ·   ·

"A Ms. Bryan-Keith on the vidfax, Mr. Bryan."

Susan, for Lord's sake. He thought she'd written him off when he'd gone with Fairley and company.

"Susan."

The woman on the screen had boyish, short-cropped brown hair, and old-fashioned glasses that only slightly disguised the near-classic profile marred but marginally by the crook in her nose.

"Dare . . . this time you've really done it. Not only did you sell your soul when you went to work for that legal factory, but this article of yours is going to end up selling mine."

"What . . . what do you mean? I sent it to you so someone wouldn't corner the technique."

"As usual, you didn't think it through before you sent it to the rest of the world. The best of intentions, but not the best of analysis." She stopped, rubbed her right thumb on her chin, then tugged at her ear. "The idea would have come. The time's no doubt right, but for once you did a brilliant and clear explanation without a word of legal obfuscation. How I wish you had jumbled it up. But no, every third-rate big-money firm in the country will latch on to this, every—"

"Hold it! Hold on. What do you mean?"

"Dare, how can you be that obtuse? Look. You've pointed out exactly how anyone with enough money and a big enough computer can take full advantage of the legal system. You've not only said it, but you provided step-by-step directions, a basic 'how-to' manual."

Susan glared through the screen at her younger brother. Finally, her expression softened.

"Dare, I understand the position you're in. You have to produce, or you get the chop. You want to get ahead, and this looks like the way to get there. But don't you understand? Fine, you have access to a computer and a complete data-processing center. I don't. Neither do most attorneys for the little people.

"Now what can Mort Rainwater do against Amalgamated Agriculture's water diversions when they have a legal computer and your little manual, and I don't? When they can plug in all the steps you outlined, and I can't? Sure, I understand the process, but I don't have the resources. It's not the computer, per se. We could probably scrounge that. It's all the programming, all the information. So back to my basic question. What can Mort Rainwater do?"

Darrow shrugged.

"You've got it. Nothing."

The silence built up.

"What was I supposed to do, Suse? Forget it? I've got an impossible case against the government. Without the technique, there's no chance of winning. We go to trial next week, and I don't know that what I've got will even work, but it's the only chance I've got."

"I understand. But if you've prepared your case as well as you did that article, the poor government attorney doesn't stand a chance unless your client murdered someone right on prime time, vidfaxers and all watching."

Darrow shrugged again. Susan always put him on the defensive. She was usually right, too.

"Oh, Dare, it's not your fault. Someone would have come up with it sooner or later. And I guess I'm proud it was you. But what it's going to do to the practice of law, I don't even want to guess."

After her call, Darrow sat for a long time, looking at the wall.

Maybe she was right this time.

Some of the ramifications were obvious—the shuffling of attorneys within firms as the defense and prosecution tried to match strengths, the power plays in trying to get a particular judge for a particular case, the increasingly trumped-up reasons for venue changes as the prejudices and inclinations of judges were laid out in black and white.

What about computers? Did they already make a difference? Would his programs make it worse?

He accessed the Law Directory.

First, he tried his own firm. The entry he wanted was buried, but it was there. "(cll)" stood for "computerized legal library."

Within an hour he had the listings of the twenty firms in the country with the complete computerized systems like his own firm's. Just twenty, including, interestingly enough, Gerswin, Fiori and Smithers. Then he pulled the two hundred largest firms without the "(cll)" listing and vocotyped out the comparisons he wanted.

He carried the package down to Peters in Data Management.

"Compared to the last request, this one's simple enough, Mr. Bryan. Should be ready first thing in the morning."

Because he didn't sleep well, Darrow was up early enough to catch the 6:10 RT-8 and was at the closed doors of Flush, Fairley, and Forefront by seven thirty. For the first time in years, he actually unlocked the doors himself.

Data Management called him at 8:05, and he was back at his desk with the printouts in minutes.

The first page was enough, but he plowed through to the end. He read the summary twice, the second time out loud.

"The 'cll' firms obtained favorable rulings in 72.1 percent of their cases actually tried. The non-'cll' firms obtained favorable rulings in 37.3 percent of such cases."

There was more, with the usual bureaucratic caveats, but what it boiled down to was simple. The firms with money to computerize were already twice as successful as the noncomputerized firms. Was it because successful firms adopted new techniques faster? Or was it because the computer made the difference?

Darrow frowned. It made no difference. In either case, the gap between the two would widen because a noncomputerized firm legal firm couldn't use the techniques even if it wanted to.

Darrow knew he wasn't the best legal mind. Imagine what Darcy could do with the techniques. That was only the beginning.

What about other applications? What if someone hired a computer to find out what crimes were the easiest to defend? Or what laws were never upheld? Or in which localities crime paid the most? Would the big-money boys use the computer to select the judicial candidates they presented to the politicians?

Public defenders wouldn't have computers, would they? Neither would attorneys from rural areas. The fees of "computerized" law firms would jump to pay for the hardware and software. But the clients would pay, especially once they saw how the technique brought results.

The upcoming trial wasn't just a case, but the test run of the whole system he'd planned.

If he won this way, did he deserve to? Would it prove Eastwood's innocence? Then again, had the system ever proved that? Or did it just prove who had the best attorney?

. . .

"Darrow," Darcy began as he edged his head into the cubicle, "have a minute?"

"Sure. Welcome to my humble abode."

"Not much longer, I suspect. One way or the other."

Darrow nodded and waited.

Darcy grinned. "If you don't smoke a pipe, the 'nod and wait' technique is the next best one."

Darrow grinned back, before the impact of Darcy's words sank in.

"The techniques for the Eastwood case are a make-or-break thing?"

"Right."

"Cost?"

"Hank Forefront got the bill for your programs. If they work, you'll get partnership status."

"And if they don't, the front door?"

"Not quite so bluntly, but essentially, that's correct. Good thing I had that article. Since I'm nominally your supervisor, Hank checked with me before coming to take off your head."

Darcy shook his head wryly.

"Between you and me, Darrow, until this came up, I wouldn't have bet a dollar on your chances. If it works, they can't afford to let you go. And if it does, even if they did, a dozen firms would offer you something. So . . . if you produce, you're golden."

Darrow repressed a smile.

He liked Darcy, but the protection he'd gotten from the older attorney would certainly be repaid if Darrow succeeded. Darcy would claim that he was following Darrow and would be rewarded for encouraging him. Darrow might get partnership status. Darcy might reach senior partner status on the basis of Darrow's work.

And it all rested on the trial.

.   .   .

The trial got under way quickly, more quickly than Garrity had anticipated, Darrow suspected.

From the defense table, Darrow surveyed the crowd, trying to pick out familiar faces. Not that it was all that difficult—only a handful of people were on hand for the opening statements.

With a shock, Darrow recognized Jim Fiori, conferring with a man he didn't know. Fiori looked up, as if he had felt Darrow's stare, grinned, and gave back a "thumbs-up" signal.

By agreeing to most of the facts, Darrow had stripped Garrity of his strongest weapon. Nevertheless, Darrow had to object to drive the point home.

". . . and the government will prove," thundered Garrity, "that the accused did in fact heinously and willfully violate the law by importing over a million gallons of heating oil every month in foreign ships—"

"Objection. Facts are stipulated, and the character of the accused is not the question. The question is the law."

"Sustained," ruled the judge.

". . . Congress in its wisdom did choose to protect the American people by enacting such protective safeguards, disregarded so cavalierly—"

"Objection. Question is not the intent of Congress nor the character of the accused, but whether the law applies."

"Sustained."

After a series of objections, Garrity wiped his streaming face and turned to the bench.

"Your Honor, while I realize that the distinguished and honorable counsel for the defense is defending his client to the best of his considerable ability, I would like to inquire if the purpose of these continual objections is the furtherance of the law of the land or its obfuscation."

"Mr. Garrity, the counsel for the defense had generously agreed to virtually all of your stipulations in order that we may concentrate on the legal questions. If you feel that additions to the stipulated facts are necessary at this point, you may make such additions. Counsel for the defense retains the right to object to irrelevant material."

"In that case, Your Honor," returned Garrity, "we will emphasize the basic legal grounds for the government action. According to the Oil Import Act of 1983, the controlling interest of any foreign-incorporated or foreign-based business or corporation, engaged in the production, refining, transportation, or distribution of petroleum products in the United States by any U.S. citizen is prohibited. Section 503 is absolutely clear in its intent . . ."

Garrity devoted the rest of Saturday to the intent of Section 503, all of Monday to the intent of Section 801, all of Tuesday to the intent and applicability of Section 803(b), and all of Wednesday to a listing of successful government prosecutions of violators of the various oil control laws.

By Wednesday night, Darrow sensed that Judge Lerata was suffering from a case of terminal boredom.

Garrity rested his case Friday morning at eleven o'clock.

"The prosecution rests and apologizes for rushing through the applicable law, but we feel that the only possible verdict is conviction."

After a lunch recess, Darrow began.

"Your Honor, the essence of our case is simple, so simple that I find myself puzzled by the prosecution's arguments. Basically, we contend that, first, the individual rights of privacy of the defendant were violated, and second, that Sections 503, 801, and 803, so heavily cited by the prosecution, are unconstitutional.

"In reviewing the statutes and case law cited by the prosecution, one should note that for some reason, not a single case tested the merits of the law itself, and that in all but two of the twenty 'precedential' cases cited, the defendant pleaded 'guilty.' We intend to show not only Article I, Section 8, grounds for invalidity, but also First, Fourth, Fifth, Sixth, and Fourteenth Amendment challenges."

Darrow started with the medical records.

Garrity had already accepted them during the pretrial conference, and it only took Darrow an hour or so to establish his point.

". . . then what conclusions would you draw from these tests, Doctor?"

"That the individual in question had been subject to persona-altering drugs, probably sclopsclertin or a variant, certainly a drug of that generic family . . ."

.   .   .

". . . and why does the Enforcement Branch maintain stocks of Sclopsclertin A, Agent Searles?"

"I don't know. That's a matter of policy."

.   .   .

". . . and how does a licensed physician obtain Sclopsclertin A from your company, Mr. Armbruster?"

"They can't. We can only produce it under contract for the government."

"Does any other company produce it?"

"Not to my knowledge."

.   .   .

Darrow didn't have to prove the Enforcement Branch actually used Sclopsclertin A on Eastwood, just that the government had the drug, that no one else did, and that Eastwood showed signs of the drug in his system immediately after his release from custody.

According to the computer profile, that would satisfy the judge.

"Objection. Counsel for the defense has not proved that the Enforcement Branch actually administered this drug, whatever it is, to the accused."

"Does counsel for the defense wish to respond?"

"Perhaps I should rephrase my conclusion in strict accordance with the facts, Your Honor. Sclopsclertin A is a persona-altering drug. Only the government—in particular, the FBI, the CIA, and the Enforcement Branch of DOE—has access to the drug. My client has no access to this drug. After DOE interrogation and incarceration, my client showed traces of Sclopsclertin A. Even two months of restoration treatments have not reversed certain personality changes generated by the drug.

"These facts show that a massive dosage was given at a single time, and that no other drug has identical effects. Again, not even illicit sources, according to DOE's own agents, could account for such a dosage. Therefore, no other conclusion is possible. Government drugs were used. Since the accused was in government custody at the time, the government is responsible.

"Since the Enforcement Branch claims national security privilege and will not relinquish its original drug logs indicating stock withdrawals, I feel it is only fair and just to give the benefit of any doubt remaining to the defendant and conclude that, in fact, he was subjected to what amounts to a chemical invasion of privacy. Our entire case, however, is not based on this single point—"

"Objection!" Garrity was late.

"Overruled," stated Lerata dryly. "Counsel for the defense may continue."

". . . but on the fact that the spectacular evidentiary findings in previous trials have obscured the basic legal questions created by the Oil Import Acts. Compounding this has been the financial pressure exerted by the government in previous cases, since a settlement with the government was usually less expensive for the defendant than even winning a long and drawn-out legal test."

The argument itself was dry. Darrow kept the questions to his limited list of witnesses as brief as possible, referred to the cites in his brief as much as he dared, and tried to keep the actual presentation in the courtroom as short as possible while conveying the impression of massive Constitutional weight, long overlooked, behind his simple points.

Eventually, he had to get to the end.

"To sum it all up, the thrust is simple. First, the treatment of the defendant violated his basic rights, as detailed earlier. Second, the provisions of Sections 503, 801, and 803(b) do in fact constitute a duty or impost which is not uniform under any definition, and are thus unconstitutional. Third, the processes by which these Acts are enforced do violate the long-accepted standards for due process. Fourth, the enforcement process and the Acts are designed explicitly to treat individuals with identical property differently, and that is discrimination under any definition, which has long been recognized as unconstitutional."

Darrow couldn't help overhearing Garrity's loud whisper, since it was designed to carry through the courtroom.

"That's a Constitutional argument?"

Darrow held back a grin. He hoped the judge had heard it also.

The courtroom began to clear, and Darrow was packing up his files into the two cases he'd brought.

"Very nicely done, Mr. Bryan. Very nice."

He looked up to see Jim Fiori.

"Oh, thank you. I hope the judge will see it that way."

"So do we," Fiori smiled politely. "But I'm sure he will. We all owe you a great deal, and I'm sure you'll be rewarded. If not, perhaps we'll be able to get together for lunch one of these days."

Darrow smiled back.

"Well . . . I thank you. But let's see how the verdict turns out."

Fiori, impeccable in his pinstripes, smiled again, showing white teeth against dark tan, turned, and left.

Darrow shivered.

.   .   .

Judge Lerata took a month to announce the verdict.

"Ladies and gentlemen, I'm not going to waste time with unnecessary verbiage. The Court finds for the defendant. The details are in the opinion."

The fax reporters were swarming outside the doors.

"Mr. Eastwood, Mr. Bryan! Do you know the basis for the opinion?"

"Why did you avoid a jury trial?"

"What effect will this have on attempts to cut oil imports?"

Eastwood smiled and said nothing, as Darrow had suggested.

"I haven't had a chance to study the opinion," said Darrow to the directional cones focused on him. "I can only surmise that the judge accepted our arguments that the laws are unconstitutional . . ."

"Why no jury?"

"The question was not one of facts subject to question, but one of law. Judge Lerata has a fine legal mind." Let the damned masses stew over that.

. . .

Darrow walked into Jonathon Fairley's spacious corner office, feeling the tension behind the bared white teeth and the too-hearty backslap.

"Have a seat, Darrow. Would you like a vintage '79 cola? Don't brew them that way any longer, you know."

"That would be nice."

Fairley went to the corner cooler and fished out a frosty bottle, opened it with a flair, and gently poured the liquid into a large snifter. He presented the glass to Darrow, who nodded in return.

The honorable senior partners, Jonathon Fairley and Henry Forefront, perched on the edge of Fairley's massive desk like vultures.

"Now tell us, Hank and me, that is, what prompted you to take the tack you did. Darcy's mentioned some of it, but we'd like to hear it straight from you."

"I didn't have much choice. From the beginning it was obvious that the evidence was stacked against Eastwood from one end to the other. Not only that, but someone had been messing with his mind. If he'd had to take the stand, he was probably conditioned to make a basket case out of himself. No jury in the country would have declared him anything but an oil profiteer, particularly with all the government propaganda—pardon me—media emphasis against American oil companies.

"I mean, it was cut-and-dried—forbidden oil importer, guilty, next case. So I figured I couldn't lose by waiving the jury."

"Why did you go with a purely legal defense?"

"That was based on what I had to work with. I was assigned Judge Lerata. According to the computer, he likes facts, plain facts, and plain law. Doesn't go much for rhetoric. If he has a choice, he'll opt for facts, but if he's pushed a little and reminded of his legal duty, he'll go for law, especially references to the Constitution."

The two senior vultures were leaning even farther forward, but Darrow paused to take a sip of the vintage cola. He might as well enjoy it.

"But the facts?" protested Forefront.

"The facts weren't too favorable. What Eastwood was doing was legal, but unpopular. So I had to minimize the facts in order to emphasize the law. At the pretrial conference, I agreed to most of the government's facts."

"Dangerous."

"Why did you think you had a chance? Sounds pretty shaky."

"The computer analysis was convincing. When I found out that Lerata was the assigned judge, I had Data Management run a computerized analysis of his opinions. With a jury, he'll let the prosecution have a fairly free rein. Without a jury, he'll decide a case on his interpretation of the facts, bolstered by the law. If he's put on notice that it's a purely legal question, and gently reminded of it throughout the trial, and if the legal arguments are to the point, in something like 70 percent of those cases, he decided for the legalist. Seventy percent was the best I could do; so I did."

"Wait a minute. I know Hank thinks the computer is the icing on the cake, and Darcy's briefed him on what you did. Hank says it's terrific. But I got lost along the way."

"Basically, I got Data Management to create a series of special programs. The principle's simple. Attorneys have been using it for centuries, but I tried to systematize it. The programs were designed to see what arguments had been successful with Lerata in the past and under what circumstances."

Darrow pondered, wondering how much to say.

"Two things are different. First, the computer enabled me to analyze the language. That meant a better angle on what specific points appealed to Lerata. Second, I applied the same principles to Garrity. When I heard he was on the other side, I dug up all his cases and ran them through the computer to see if I could spot a pattern to the ones he'd won and lost."

"And?" demanded Fairley.

Darrow was reminded of a little old man asking for the latest gossip.

"I don't know that it's bad. Garrity does best when he can represent the accused as an evil oppressor of the people. He has the poorest record in pure legal cases, particularly when the government infringes personal rights. That's why I emphasized the drug question."

Darrow shrugged. "All I did was put the pieces together."

Fairley leaned back and turned to Forefront.

"Really, Hank, this amazes me. Darrow has come up with the greatest tool since partnerships, and he 'just put the pieces together.'"

Darrow watched the ideas click together for the two senior partners, could almost see the two of them silently planning the high-powered operation, full-scale data reduction, coding for all major decisions, gathering data on every judge and attorney.

"Take a lot of capital," noted Forefront, "but there's no way we can *not* do it. If we don't, someone else will. Onward or out, that's all there is to it."

Recalling Fiori, Darrow repressed a frown. He hadn't had time to figure out all the angles yet. Right now, he wanted to enjoy the taste of success.

"Could be the greatest legal tool of the century, thanks to our new junior partner here." Fairley beamed.

"Should bring us more back to a rule of law," mused Forefront, "back to when law belonged to the real legal professionals and not every civic activist or government hack who came along."

Darrow kept up his smile, wondering about Forefront's remark.

Would computerization mean better law? What did Fiori have in mind? What would he do if someone turned the technique against him?

He finished his cola with a gulp.

"Darrow, Mydra has left the color samples for your new office. You're moving up to an outside corner."

Darrow was glad of the dismissal, smiled, offered his thanks, and left.

He was stopped in the hallway outside his door.

"Two messages for you, Mr. Bryan. From a Ms. Bryan-Keith. She wanted you to call back."

"The other one?"

"There's a gentleman waiting for you. A Mr. James Fiori. Says he wanted to deliver a personal invitation. Very polite. But very insistent. Is he as important as he looks?"

"Yes."

He pushed open the thin door, noticing the color samples on his desk console and James Fiori simultaneously.

"Congratulations, Darrow. Frankly, I wasn't sure old Jon had the sense to offer you what you deserve."

Fiori gestured at the color samples.

"But I can see he didn't waste a minute. Sly old fox knows a good thing when he sees it." Fiori grinned. "We really owe you a lot. And if things don't work out the way you expect, don't hesitate to give me a call."

Darrow waited, sensing more.

"The real reason I dropped by was to tell you about our new venture since you gave us the idea. Graystone has just completed the acquisition of Eastlaw Citations.

"That's just the first step. We've also acquired the capability to computerize all the slip opinions not on file, and we'll be starting a subscription service that will supply on a monthly basis all the new opinions, and all the accompanying briefs, plus the key-word correlation feature."

"What about judicial profiles?"

"We're working on that, and on getting permission to use Law Directory material for attorney profiles. Good idea. That's why we'd like to have you on board."

"I imagine it's an expensive service."

"Very expensive. Pricing hasn't been worked out, but I'd estimate that the cost would add 10 to 20 percent to the fee structure of the average firm if it were passed on. But it's worth every penny for the firm that does a lot of trial work."

Fiori stood up.

"Think about it, Darrow. Ten years from now, maybe, they'll make you a full partner. I'll start you at that. And Graystone is going places. We could even end up buying out old Jon and Hank."

Darrow stood and smiled.

"I appreciate your thoughtfulness, and I certainly will think it over."

"Anyway, Darrow, my congratulations. Hell of a job you did on Garrity. Haven't enjoyed watching the government get theirs so much in ages. Like to see you do that for us. See you later."

After the door closed, Darrow looked down at the color samples, at the worn fabric of his jacket, and at the blinking light on the console reminding him to call Susan.

As usual, she'd been right.

Rule of law was right, too, but whose rule?

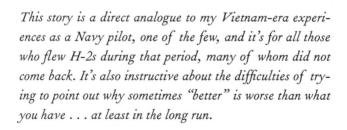

This story is a direct analogue to my Vietnam-era experiences as a Navy pilot, one of the few, and it's for all those who flew H-2s during that period, many of whom did not come back. It's also instructive about the difficulties of trying to point out why sometimes "better" is worse than what you have . . . at least in the long run.

IRON MAN, PLASTIC SHIPS

"So what it boils down to, Mort," McCaine said quietly, "is that you want me to approve the RV-2s immediately and use them to replace all the old tugs ASAP. Period. Don't bother about the fact that the RV-2's not a good space tug. Don't bother about the fact that it's poorly designed. Don't worry about the lack of flight testing. Just approve it. You said the damned thing's a new Recovery Vehicle and we ought to use it. I say it's an experimental pilot killer."

Even at the end, Captain (breveted and acting) Edward Alton McCaine did not raise his voice. But somehow the small station room vibrated unpleasantly. A paperweight teetered on the edge of the captain's compact desk for a moment before beginning a slow, curving arc toward the boron-flexiplast deck.

"Captain, we need new tugs. The RV-1s are old. They're just so much junk. If we could just replace them with the RV-2s arriving with the convoy . . ." Morton Wyemouth, Commander-Second, Darneillian Space Forces, stood very still in the light gravity of Primus Station.

Even as far from the tech spaces as the captain's small office/stateroom was, the two men could smell the combination of ozone, oil, and sweat that permeated the battle outpost.

"New is not necessarily better, Mort. Nor spaceworthy. I intend to test every one. If they don't measure up, back they go," declared McCaine.

And if that doesn't set the stage, he thought, I don't know what will.

Captain McCaine leaned back in the cheap flexiplast swivel and popped a chewball into his mouth. He brushed the mixed silver-blond hair back over his high forehead, not that there was much to brush back, and looked steadily at his Executive Officer.

"We're using junk to salvage junk, sir," answered Wyemouth. "We're losing men to do it. Last tour, Debron, and the rotation before that, three—Ferinto, Hawke-Gones, and Brereton. At least the RV-2s are new."

The captain sat up straight in the chair and put his hands flat on the desktop. Even motionless, his squat form seemed ready to spring.

"Mort, I've explained it so many times to the High Command I'm green along the jaw, but I'll repeat one thing. The RV-2s aren't new. They're a pile of reworked plastic, hopped-up thrusters, and converters with extra slosh. Tech Command used the RV-1 salvages we sent back for rework as the frame."

Wyemouth had his mind made up, and McCaine looked coldly across the desk in the cramped compartment, stifled a sigh, and waved the commander out the hatchway with an abrupt gesture.

As the flexiplast portal clicked shut—and it seemed like the entire station was constructed of plastic—he leaned back into the swivel.

Didn't any of the gung ho, can-do idiots understand? Do it, no matter what. That was why four pilots and techs were dead in two tours, not because of the Macedonians.

He tapped a button on the console that covered the left third of the desk.

A tinny voice buzzed from the grill. "Tech."

"McCaine here. If Commander Haskins is available, I'd like to see her."

"Roger, Captain."

McCaine pulled the spec sheets from the drawer. He'd brought them all the way from Tammerlane. Bouncing over to the bulkhead, he began to hang them with stick tabs.

How much should he tell Lyn, he wondered.

The station shivered, probably from the lock-to-lock hookup with the first freighter of the resupply convoy. McCaine could hear the whole station creak, from his own bulkheads to those of neighboring compartments.

Commander Haskins was grayer than McCaine, almost as tall, perhaps a year or so older, and stuck until retirement as a commander, blocked from a line slot or the hawks of a captaincy by her sex. Now a senior commander-second, she might make commander-first on retirement . . . if His Majesty were feeling particularly generous.

Most of Lynda Haskins's short hair was white. The rest was jet-black. Her space-tanned face and dark eyes gave her a look of old wisdom, except when she laughed. That was often. He and Lyn had laughed and cried together a lot. Neither had family, not to speak of, not after the years in the Space Forces.

"The RV-2s are on the in-convoy, Lyn."

"You didn't expect anything else."

No, he hadn't, and in the off-hours before their joint departure from Tammerlane weeks ago, he'd said as much.

"I can refuse to use them."

Lyn was still standing. McCaine gestured at the only other seat in the closetlike compartment. On duty, she was always the formal Commander-Second Haskins.

"Great, and if you refuse without a reason," she noted calmly, "you'll be replaced by someone like Mort Wyemouth or Handsome Saint Prince John, who'll start losing pilots and techs at the rate of one per watch." Lyn eased herself into the small chair. She was always graceful in a spare way.

McCaine grimaced, turning the left corner of his narrow mouth up. "I know. The concerned and heroic refusal doesn't do anything but clear the last obstacle from the paths of the cost-effectiveness boys. Their charts are never wrong. They just kill people."

She felt the same way. McCaine knew that. She was on the station for the same reason he was. Both had been on the Royal War Ministry developmental staff. Both had protested the deployment of the RV-2, and both had been posted to Primus.

McCaine stood up easily in the fractional gravity and half walked, half bounced to the wall—plastic wasn't really a bulkhead—where the plans fluttered under the ventilation grill.

"They've doubled the fuel storage here by extending the slosh tank. The extension's supported by these braces . . ."

"Fine if you're flying without a trac load under constant gee, but . . ." The commander let her words trail off.

"Is the extra mass compensated against sudden thrust or a load shift on the mag-trac?"

"The RV-1 can handle its full mag-trac from zero to max at a quarter-gee constant. The tech team figured that as a base parameter on the conversion." Lyn delivered the statement deadpan.

"But they upped the mag-trac by 85 percent and damn near doubled the thruster output. That's got to drop the load the frame can take."

"According to the tech manual," drawled the commander, a wry smile on her face, "the same parameters apply."

"But I'll bend the frame and crack the shell if I try it?" snapped McCaine.

Maybe I shouldn't let that much out, he thought.

"If *you* try it? You're the C.O."

McCaine wondered at the look that flashed across her face, but went on. "According to the regs, I can take a mission. Any C.O. who's physically and type-qualified can, and I quote, 'when in the best interests of the Space Forces and the safety of his command.'" McCaine smiled. He meant it to be a nasty smile. "I was sent here to supervise the service introduction of the RV-2s because I was the only captain with salvage experience. They also didn't want me around Tammerlane when the casualty reports began to come in. I might just suggest that the RV-2 wasn't all it was cracked up to be." He looked vaguely pleased with the unintentional pun.

"I never quite understood why they sent you here." Lyn crossed her long, shipsuited legs, then shifted her weight and turned to face him head-on. "But then, they don't know you like I do."

McCaine kick-bounced himself back into the swivel. "You understand, all right. They don't care about me. They don't care all that much about winning the war. They don't care too much even about getting their icebergs home. But they don't want any advice from someone who's actually jock-eyed space tugs.

"They don't understand salvage. They don't understand how every loss affects the whole future of Darneill. And they certainly don't care if a few salvage pilots get killed. If I refuse to fly the RV-2, well, then I become an object lesson at my court-martial. Lesson One for new captains—don't cross the Finance Ministry, even if you are stuck with a bunch of plastic ships."

He popped another chewball into his thin-lipped mouth. "If I let the RV-2 go into service, then that proves their power. If I don't, I'm court-martialed for insubordination, maybe for aiding and abetting the enemy. They're covered even if I allow the damned thing in service. If their beloved new and improved all-plastic RV-2 kills too many pilots, I'll get the long green table for poor leadership . . . or a medical retirement with honors."

Lyn Haskins gave him a faint but fond smile and let him go on. He'd stop in his own good time. He always did.

McCaine sighed, grabbed a handful of papers, and held them up. "What am I supposed to do? Administer a disaster? Go on with the day-to-day nuts and bolts, and smile? Sure, we need a stronger Recovery Vehicle, but the Finance Ministry doesn't want to put out the energy, the money, or the metal.

Don't ask me why we're fighting the Macedonians over water asteroids when they don't even need them. Don't ask me why we're using as much water to fight as we're getting from the bergs. And don't ask me why we have to kill pilots to find the design flaws. No . . . the glamour and the money go to the skitter pilots and the engineers. We just rescue them all and keep picking up the pieces. For what? I could go on, but you've heard it all."

Commander Lynda Haskins got to her feet, again perfectly formal. McCaine sometimes asked himself if he knew her at all.

"I'd better get my people ready," she said. "Tomorrow?"

"They may be unloading already. Do me a favor, Lyn. Make sure I get the RV-2s one at a time and that everything's done strictly by the book, and logged."

"Roger."

McCaine watched her go. He and Lyn had been stationed together five years now, on and off. He wished there had been more "on" times, but that didn't happen in the Space Forces. How many times he'd wanted to say more to her . . . rather than talk about ops, share a drink, stories . . .

He picked up the stack of papers, the maintenance reports, the officer evaluations, and forced his thoughts away from Lyn, away from the RV-2. Tomorrow would come soon enough, and the endless reports had to be filled out.

. . .

"This is most unusual, most unusual." The station schedules officer was a commander-second, nonpilot.

"We'll be in the salvage ready room," said McCaine.

"Captain, really . . . Rory, the admiral, I mean, will be most concerned about the salvage skipper and his senior tech riding the same tug."

McCaine noted the affected speech and decided it and the immaculate uniform tagged the schedules officer as another Court hanger-on out for a Belt medal and stories for the king's courtesans.

"We'll be on duty. You have the revised schedule," McCaine said curtly. He knew the schedules officer would take the updated duty roster straight to the admiral.

The cramped salvage ready room was connected to the duty lock where the duty tugs were docked. McCaine entered the ready room just in time to hear the small squadron operations console squawk.

"Captain McCaine to the Flag Bridge. Captain McCaine to the Flag Bridge."

McCaine grinned at Lyn. Her lanky frame was stretched out across one of the five patched recliners in the small flexiplast-walled compartment.

"Didn't take him long, did it?" He walked over to her.

"Captain, play it straight. Play it very straight." Even with the formal address, the "please" was evident in her tone.

"I will."

His stride was long in the low gravity as he headed for the Flag Bridge.

"Captain, please sit down."

Admiral Rory Gildness Reagan looked like an admiral, from his square decisive jaw to the steely gray eyes and the straight and short black hair and bushy eyebrows.

"Commander Hiram—"

"The nonpilot schedules officer?" interrupted McCaine smoothly, as if to clarify a point.

"Why yes," replied the admiral.

McCaine said nothing and leaned back in the stiff chair, almost tilting the front legs off the deck. Reagan was known for the use of straight-backed chairs to make subordinates uncomfortable, recalled McCaine. But someone forgot to tell him that they didn't have as much effect in low grav.

"Um . . . ah . . . look, Captain. I understand some of your men are not terribly pleased about your scheduling of the new Recovery Vehicle . . ." His voice trailed off.

"You mean, because I scheduled myself for the test hops and because I have the first salvage tour?"

"You must admit it's a bit unusual," noted the admiral suavely.

"The RV-2's unusual, Admiral, and so are the circumstances of its adoption by the forces." Damned unusual, thought McCaine. No pilot retraining, no full R&D, and only a sketchy addendum to the RV-1 basic flight manual.

The admiral nodded and said nothing. McCaine had him boxed. If Reagan said anything either way, he'd end up in trouble.

After a long silence, the admiral concluded lamely, "So I hope you'll consider all factors in phasing it into a normal operating schedule as soon as possible."

"Yes, sir. I certainly will."

Admiral Reagan nodded a curt dismissal. McCaine bounded down toward the lower levels of the outer station edge where the salvage docks were. He had to detour through the third deck to avoid one section. Suited maintenance workers were sealing off a bulkhead with instaplast.

"Trouble?" he asked the senior NCO on the team.

"Outer bulkhead blew, Captain, right through to the shell."

"Casualties?"

"Don't have a handle on the totals, sir. Skitter maintenance crews. Maybe ten bought it right away, ten with pressure injuries."

Just another facet of the problem, thought McCaine. The whole damned station was ceramic and plastic, glorified sand and wood, because His Royal Majesty was saving all the scarce metal possible so that he could have massive royal transport for the Court, and, of course, some skitters and warheads to use on the Macedonians. Now ten people were dead, and ten more might be dying, not even on duty in the holy water war.

No one could hit anyone's home planet, not with the laser defense systems powered off the core-taps. But the defense systems used a lot of power, and that reduced the energy for industry. That meant the water from the Belt bergs became more valuable the longer the war went on. Which was why the loyal servants of His Royal Majesty were fighting the loyal servants of the Macedonian Technocracy with plastic outposts and jury-rigged salvage ships. The scarce metal left over from the Court went to the high-powered skitters.

Meanwhile, men and women died at the Trojan Points and elsewhere along the Belt when plastic shells failed and inadequate salvage ships crashed or skitter engines failed a million miles from anywhere.

McCaine walked into the ready room just behind Commander-Second Wyemouth.

Wyemouth turned on McCaine.

"Sir, I protest. As senior flight commander, either I or the senior test pilot should take the RV-2."

McCaine saw Wyemouth tightening his jaw.

Hell, the idiot's going to start screeching in front of the whole duty crew.

McCaine took his Executive Officer firmly by the elbow, using the pressure points, and levered him toward the lock antechamber.

"Mort, I think you're right. We should talk about it."

McCaine half closed the hatch and let go of Wyemouth's elbow.

"Are you proposing murder or suicide, Mort?"

Wyemouth just stared at him.

"Despite your more recent flight hours, Commander, and those of Lieutenant Commander Heatherton, you are overlooking several points. First, neither of you has flown the RV-2, and in spite of all the noises made by Buships, the RV-2 handles a lot differently from the RV-1. Second, I know that. I have flown it. And third, I am the commanding officer, and I have to answer for what happens. Is that clear?"

"Perfectly clear, *sir*," muttered Wyemouth through clenched teeth.

"Mort," said McCaine exasperatedly, "stop making a jackass out of yourself. You don't have a thing to lose. If I'm wrong, I'm the one who gets relieved."

From the glint in Wyemouth's eyes, McCaine could see that he was getting through.

"Yes, sir," answered the Executive Officer, more quietly.

McCaine opened the hatch into the ready room and moved up in front of the status board. The skitters had launched at fifteen past. The Macedonians had sent interceptors after the first launch, with a cruiser hanging back, probably the *Alexander*. Anytime, there'd be some junk for a pickup. He gestured to Lyn.

"Let's go."

The two of them walked through the ready room, through the locks, and into the waiting tug. McCaine took his time strapping in before beginning the checklist. Lyn was already going through her list. The tech's position was to the pilot's right and back a half meter, with a narrow aisle between the two seats. The staggered arrangement allowed McCaine an unencumbered sweep through the bubble canopy.

"Primus Operations, this is Angel Zero Three. Ready for lift," snapped McCaine through his helmet chin mike. His visor was open.

"Angel Zero Three, you're clear. Caution for traffic off north axis."

McCaine triggered the forward trim jets with a momentary burst and let the outpressure from the dock and jets throw the RV-2 clear. He could feel the heaviness and extra power of the modified ship. But no amount of new plastic and remodeling could disguise the smell and sense of the weariness the tug incorporated, thought McCaine.

He checked the main screen for the departing skitters, then flicked the heads-up display tab, which projected the console instruments onto the lower edge of the canopy. That way he could pilot head out and still use the full board. Some pilots never got the hang of it.

Personally, he suspected Mort Wyemouth was one of them.

McCaine tuned in the guard monitor, now just static, as well as the skitter attack frequency. He checked both the screen and the actual space off the station's north axis. Both his eyes and the screen showed the last skitters well clear of the station.

As McCaine eased the tug into a minimum fuel curve toward his recovery station, he thought about Primus . . . its existence and mission.

Right now the job was to hold the area around the gigantic hunk of ice called Anemone until the Royal Engineers could complete the drive installation on the iceberg. Then an attack team with a cruiser would shepherd Anemone for the first leg of the spiral inward to Darneill. The middle leg of the transit would be without armed escort. The fuel cost would be too high for either Darneill or the Macedonians.

Off Darneill, the gross retro-rockets would waste more water to brake the iceberg and orbit it. Finally, the Royal Engineers would parcel out the ice for attack fuel processing and for the industrial needs of the dry planet below.

Macedonia didn't need the water. At least, they professed they didn't, but intended to make the getting of it expensive for the Darneillian monarchy.

McCaine broke off his reflections and began to concentrate on the message traffic of the skitter attack channel. While straining to hear the skitter pilots, he took a quick look sideways at Lyn, who was running another test pattern on her console. Even in a shipsuit, she was striking.

He turned up the volume on the skitter frequency.

"Pegasus Lead, this is Peg Two. Aborting. Mace splinter in the tanks."

First casualty of the watch, thought McCaine as he keyed his transmitter.

"Peg Two, this is Angel Three. Interrogative immediate pickup."

"Negative. Have slosh for turn and coast."

"Roger, Peg Two. We'll be waiting."

McCaine gave the main thrusters a tweak to increase the fractional glide toward the skitter return lane. Peg Two's immediate use of his fuel to get into a return glide would save McCaine both work and fuel, meriting His Majesty's gratitude for energy conservation.

McCaine wasn't totally grateful, all things considered, because accomplishing what he had in mind was going to be stickier with a live crew—not that he wished Peg Two any more trouble. Coasting back to a plastic station with the hope that a plastic tug could pull you in could hardly be the most comforting thought.

McCaine scanned the long-range screen for the distant blip he knew would be pulling away from the skitter line around Anemone. When it appeared, he locked the tracking computer on it and punched in the request for ETA and PA coordinates.

Better yet. Peg had overdone it with the thrust and would be coming in high and fast.

The Princeps system was an old one, a strangely bright sun located at the fringe of Type II suns where even the space between planets seemed to have a luminosity. Despite the extensive asteroid clumpings of the Belt, the system was low on dust, and the Royal Astronomers could only explain the light level with a speculative and intricate fold-around theory.

McCaine snorted. Trust an academic to come up with an elaborate theory instead of saying he didn't know.

Against the bright background, he still couldn't see the disabled skitter, but the screen showed Pegasus Two with a continuing minimal acceleration.

"Peg Two, this is Angel Three. Interrogative thrust."

"Angel Three, Peg Two, Slosh still dripping. No fuel control. Jettison shears inoperative."

"Roger. Be ready for a bit of a shake-up."

McCaine flicked the thrusters, fingertips tapping the control studs through the skinsuit's glove tips, trying to match the course correction readouts on the panel. His outside gauntlets were strapped back flush against his suit forearms, and the helmet face slots were irised open.

Some of the Finance Ministry planners had suggested going to unpressurized deep-space RVs, but the king had nixed that. McCaine thought about spending all that time completely suited, not with the light suit he wore, but a full deep-space rig, and shook his head. Besides, a fully unpressurized tug would require more expensive equipment or at least the manufacture of another set of equipment and instruments, and another type of war manufacture was the last thing the fragile economy of Darneill needed now.

On the other hand, he mused, a lot of the plastic shells of the pressurized skitters and RVs were cracking . . .

McCaine sighted Pegasus Two off his nose at ten and a half, right where the tracking screen said it was.

"Seal up, Lyn. Here we go. Mag-trac at seventy-five." McCaine closed his helmet and checked the internal pressure. Sealed tight. Theoretically a precaution, but practically speaking, a necessity.

"Roger. Suited tight," responded the tech. "Mag-trac on standby."

McCaine started the recovery. Coming in on the mirror course, watching both closure and the heads-up display indicator of the power drain as Lyn brought the mag-trac online. As the RV-2 passed over the powerless skitter, McCaine eased the nose thrusters up to about half, about 10 percent more than the RV-1 at max. According to the specs, the mirror course was the most power-effective recovery.

McCaine thought it stank. Power rations aside, everything could go wrong and probably would, sooner or later. But he was playing it by the book. In any case, Pegasus Two was close enough to the station that the backup tug could take over if Angel Zero Three decided to split apart.

"Angel Three, this is Peg Two. Interrogative intentions. We're splintering."

"Are you suited?"

"Suited but junked."

McCaine smiled to himself—grimly. The disabled skitter was nothing but scrap plastic and fatigued metal by now.

"Roger that, Peg Two."

McCaine watched the force vectors drop toward zero in the heads-up display and mentally calculated the distance and vector to the station. He keyed his mike.

"Primus operations, this is Angel Zero Three. Alert Angel Zero Two for possible launch. Zero Three has full load in progress."

"Angel Zero Three, Primus. Two is clear to lift. Interrogative assistance."

"That's negative this time."

"Captain," protested Lyn, "I believe we're still in the green."

McCaine translated that formal statement as "what in the hell are you up to?"

"So far," he answered, "but you're using three-quarter charge to hold and kill Peg Two's outdrift, and I'm still half plus on the nose thrusters. We're showing some internal pressure loss, and I wouldn't be surprised if something busts loose soon."

McCaine would have been surprised if it didn't. He'd executed the recovery strictly by the book, and the book had been written by Buships. But, in practical terms, the book was wrong.

He could already feel the vibrations through the pilot's couch, even fully suited and sealed. The sealed suit blocked most sound and pressure changes, but he felt the tug's internal atmosphere disappear even before the pressure drop fully registered on the console and the warning light flared.

Guess One verified. Despite all the rhetoric in the manual, Tech Command hadn't beefed up the hull.

"Primus, this is Angel Three. Internal pressure and higher instruments nonoperative. Suggest launch Angel Two."

"Roger, Angel Three. Angel Two is clearing. Interrogative assistance."

"Negative this time. Have Prime in visual. Will need dock crew."

"Roger. Dock crew waiting."

McCaine checked the mag-trac. The charge was dropping rapidly with the compensators gone.

"Lyn, do we have a mechanical hold on Peg Two?"

"That's affirmative. Clinched up when our shell went. Had to crumple his topside for a grip, though."

"Peg Two, this is Angel Three. Interrogative crew."

"Angel Three. We're shaken, otherwise fine."

McCaine juggled the RV-2 and the towed skitter to a dead halt outside Primus's main salvage port. In a few minutes, both ships were inside.

He unstrapped and flipped the full gauntlets over his control gloves. Knowing Mort Wyemouth was waiting for him in the ready room, he headed for his own compartment first.

Both Heatherton and Wyemouth met him outside his door.

"Sir," asked Wyemouth carefully, "was there any special reason you ran a reverse approach?"

"Because it was recommended by the design team as the best one. I also used less than three-quarters max thrust."

Both of them looked a him, afraid to comment but not willing to let the matter drop.

"Gentlemen, let me ask you one question. If I had used a standard RV-1 approach, and I limited the capabilities of the RV-2, how long would it be before I was replaced for failing to use the RV-2 to its fullest?"

Wyemouth started to say something, but stopped. He didn't bother to hide his expression of disgust.

Heatherton scratched his ear, opened his mouth, then shut it suddenly, and nodded. He turned and left McCaine with his Executive Officer.

McCaine was glad Heatherton was getting the picture. At least one of them understood.

"Sir," inquired Wyemouth, "do you intend to have someone else try out the second RV-2, or are you planning the first operational ride in all four?"

"Since I did not have the chance to test out all the capabilities, Mort, I'll be taking out Zero Eight when she's ready."

"How about the next one?"

"That depends on the results I get with Zero Eight." McCaine wasn't about to spell it out for him, not now.

McCaine opened the door, walked into his combination office/stateroom, and closed the door in Mort Wyemouth's face.

Sooner or later, he'd probably pay for it. Wyemouth had his commander's bars because his brother was on the Privy Council, not because of his capabilities as a Space Forces officer.

That was also why Wyemouth was assigned as his Executive Officer and was ready to report any transgression of His Majesty's Imperial pile of rules and regulations.

McCaine sighed. Here he was, an acting captain, a permanent commander-second, and filling a commander-first's billet as a salvage squadron C.O., according to his orders, for the purpose of temporarily facilitating the service introduction of the RV-2.

"Sometimes, you wonder," he muttered half-aloud. "Sometimes you really do."

He struggled out of his shipsuit and hung it in the equipment locker, automatically switching the recycler capsules and the oxygen pack.

Leaning against the edge of the desk, he slipped a ration cube into his mouth, hardly noticing as he chewed and swallowed it, and automatically took a swig from the waterbulb in his personal effects locker. War, but at this point he didn't mind.

"Should have more to eat," he said to the bulkhead, "but enough is enough."

He sat on the edge of the desk swivel to pull off his inner boots, getting up in turn to peel off his jumpsuit. He hung it on the locker hook, levered down his bunk, collapsed onto it, and was asleep in minutes.

He was awakened by an insistent thumping on his door and realized he'd fallen asleep without even dousing the lights. Terrible waste of power, but it showed how tired he'd been.

"Yes!" he barked, stretching and swinging out of the bunk. He looked at the windup chrono on the locker shelf. He'd left the locker open as well, and slept through a full watch. Probably it would be all right. Lyn wasn't supposed to have the second RV-2 ready until later.

"Commander Haskins, sir."

McCaine suddenly felt smelly. All of them smelled. But he pulled on a clean jumpsuit and wadded the dirty one he'd hung up into a mass, stuffing it into the bottom locker cube.

"Just a minute," he called as he flipped the bunk up.

He pulled the depilator from the shelf and ran it over his face quickly, wiped his cheeks and chin with a damp towel, and jammed everything back into his locker and closed it.

"Come on in, Lyn."

She looked down oddly, and he realized he was barefoot. He decided not to explain.

"Ed, I'm short of time." She looked terrible, dark splotches under her eyes, patches of grime around her neck, and bloodshot eyes. She'd been working while he'd slept.

He gestured to the chair. Lyn ignored the motion and leaned against the bulkhead, which creaked and bent slightly.

"You split virtually every exterior seam on Zero Three with that recovery. That doesn't include the damage to the frame."

"I thought so."

"Was it necessary? You know it's a better tug. Sure, it's not all that Tech Command claims, but do you have to prove it out here?"

McCaine shared her feelings about good machinery abused by poor operation, but that was only one side of the question.

"Yes. Because I don't want the RV-2 to kill someone, or a skitter full of someones."

"Still the crusader?"

"No. Just a tired man, trying to do his job before it's taken away." *And you're a tired woman, working twice as hard as anyone because of me.*

Without any reaction, she went on. "The second RV-2 will come up watch after next."

"Will you be ready?"

"Yes. Better me than some young tech. Especially with an old lecher like you." She couldn't quite bring off the laugh.

McCaine watched her glide down the curved corridor back toward the tech deck. He didn't go back into his small office/quarters until she disappeared. Belatedly, he realized he was standing outside his door barefooted.

.　.　.

"Captain, I still don't think this is a wise course. Suppose something happens to you, sir?" protested Mort Wyemouth.

McCaine was checking over his oversuit for the last time before heading for the door where Angel Zero Eight was waiting.

"Commander, you're moderating, I believe."

McCaine knew he was overdoing by continually baiting Wyemouth, but the big man was a slimy little bastard at heart. Mort Wyemouth was hoping that McCaine would blow himself and Zero Eight apart. McCaine wasn't going to give him that opportunity—he hoped.

The launch was a false alarm. Not a single Macedonian needleboat approached the Anemone skitter pickets. But McCaine still intended to use the watch.

"Primus operations, this is Angel Zero Eight. Request clearance for shakedown reentry approach."

"Zero Eight, cleared after Apollo One docks."

"Roger."

McCaine waited until the tail-end skitter's screen blob merged with the station's image. Then he slipped the test tape into autoconsole and upped thrust. The tape contained a recommended maneuver for the RV-2 . . . on the high-gee side. McCaine knew the tug wouldn't take the stress loads without something busting loose.

"Seal up, Lyn."

"Roger, Captain."

McCaine watched the instruments for any trace of a wiggle, any sign of motion.

Three-quarters through the recovery brake, the slosh levels of the reserve tank began to drop abnormally, followed by the cabin pressure light. McCaine eased his fingers over the abort stud but wanted to hold the run through to the end. He waited through the final decel as the tug shuddered to a halt. Primus was in visual.

Cabin pressure was below safe minimums and dribbling away. The heads-up display and the more pressure-sensitive instruments had quit. He knew the tug frame was overstrained.

"Primus, this is Angel Zero Eight. Blown a gasket or two. Request a tow to maintenance dock."

"Roger, Eight."

McCaine expected a hot reception when he left the maintenance wheel and pulled himself hand over hand into the operations half of the station. He was disappointed. The atmosphere in the squadron spaces was distinctly cold.

"Will you be taking Zero Five out when she's ready?" asked a junior tech from the corner of the cramped ready room. Someone had put her up to it.

"That's affirmative."

The duty crews were suddenly very busy with their battle dice or their status sheets as the hush evaporated.

The watch for Angel Zero Five, the third of the four RV-2s, was also without Macedonian contact. Half the time, McCaine thought, the Macers would launch a needleboat just to get the skitters out on line. Then the needleboat would turn tail just before the skitters got into position.

McCaine used the watch as an excuse to bring the tug back under three-quarter thrust. He blew the forward thrusters and the underhull with a half-thrust decel maneuver . . . well within the design envelope. He left the RV-2 as a pile of junk in the maintenance recovery lock. The once-spacious maintenance area was beginning to look like the junkyard of broken tugs.

McCaine went straight to his stateroom, and to the pile of paperwork that waited. Imperial form this, and Imperial form that, officer evaluation sheets . . . and who was going to accept his evaluations after this?

And the maintenance record . . . they showed poorly enough without his destroying three new tugs in a row. Lyn's predecessor as tech officer apparently hadn't known a bolt from a screw, nor flexiplast from gasket foam. What made it worse was that not even the common expendables had been re-ordered in sufficient quantity. With the time it took the supply types to respond, it would be months before some of it arrived. He wondered why he bothered. He wasn't going to be here months, one way or another. But someone had to.

McCaine shook his head. Given the spotty maintenance before her arrival and the lack of spares, Lyn had done wonders. But even she could only do so much with worn-out plastic and bent metal.

McCaine had only made the situation worse. The combination wasn't helping his popularity on Primus, either in or out of the squadron. Here comes the new salvage C.O., and immediately all the tugs fall apart.

Of the five RV-1s, two were fully operational. One was go for close-station push and pull work. Two were beyond the capabilities of the station for repair and were scheduled to go back with the next departing convoy.

So . . . out of nine salvage vehicles, two were operational, one was an untested RV-2, and the other was a cripple. Lovely. Three and a half worked.

Angel Zero Seven was the last RV-2.

The captain thumbed the comm unit on his desk.

"Tech, Relyea."

"McCaine. Is Zero Seven ready to go on standby for the next watch?"

"That's affirmative, Captain."

"Thank you."

McCaine thumbed Mort Wyemouth's code.

"Mort, I understand station ops is predicting a full-scale Mace needleboat blast-out on the up watch. Think we ought to have two on standby?"

"Wouldn't hurt, Captain. You thinking of taking a standby on Zero Seven?"

"Thought so."

McCaine wondered at the long silence. Mort wasn't known for contemplation.

Finally, the response came. "I'll let station ops know they can count on it, unless you'd rather let them know yourself."

"You can handle it, Mort. Thanks."

Even after a few hours' sleep, McCaine was in the ready room before the watch chimes echoed through the station.

"Peg flight clear. Apollo off the deck . . ." The commands from the station's ops center were muffled, but understandable, reverberating in the small salvage squadron ready room.

"You set, Lyn?" McCaine asked quietly, walking over to the corner where several tech officers were taking in low voices and throwing battle dice as if it didn't matter.

"Ready as ever, Captain."

McCaine wondered. She'd gotten some sleep, but the darkness under her eyes was still deep. Really quite a person. Again . . . he had to keep himself from reaching out to her. Not here. Not now.

He stifled the sigh, then almost laughed at himself. So damn many sighs and groans . . . really taking himself seriously, he was. Still, he'd be glad when it was all over, and he could leave the station's plastic hell.

He sat in the middle of the single table, fully shipsuited, half-listening to the ops circuit and the conflicting skitter common, as the skitters jockeyed around the Macedonian needleboats.

"Pegasus Leader, Peg Three, Splinter forest ten and a half high."

"Roger, Peg Three. Heave Mace club in the meadow."

"Apollo Three here. We'll take the meadow, and you can have the trees."

"Angel Two, clearing for recovery lane." McCaine pictured the old RV-1 moving out from the station.

"Two, you're cleared."

"Roger."

"Apollo Leader, this is Apollo Two, clubbed and sloshing . . . clearing." The damaged skitter's next transmission was to the station.

"Primus, Pol Two, half slosh, high on the recovery lane." Apollo Two, despite damage, was on the way back.

"Primus this is Angel Two. Outbound for Pol Two."

McCaine walked over to the squadron ops desk. Lieutenant Commander Heatherton was the duty ops officer. McCaine looked over his shoulder and studied the vectors unfolding on the small depth holo. Within a few minutes the situation became clear enough to McCaine.

"Haskins!" he barked, and gestured to the far dock.

"Heatherton, run a thrust-kill power check on Pol Two. Then tell station ops we're launching."

Heatherton looked up in surprise and began to fiddle with the computation controls.

Everyone was tired, too tired.

McCaine had seen enough. A year earlier, even six months ago, Heatherton or the main ops desk would have seen what the power and course requirements meant. Maybe not the station. They never understood the limits of tugs. But McCaine was the only relatively fresh officer left on Primus with any experience, thanks to the punitive orders funneled through the War Ministry by the Finance bureaucrats.

Good thing the Anemone project was nearly complete. But shortly, the Royal Engineers would be out demanding protection for another Belt iceberg, citing the need for all-too-scarce water, and another plastic picket station with skitters and salvagers would go out, supplied for months by convoys while the Engineers set up another orbit fall to Darneill.

McCaine had Angel Zero Seven clear of the dock before the pieces had all fallen into the pattern he'd foreseen.

"Primus, this is Apollo Two. Still splintered and burning. No forethrust. I'll be burned and sloshed out in another couple units."

Lord, thought McCaine. Poor bastard's still getting thrust up the recovery lane with no way to kill it. He doesn't know it, but Angel Zero Two doesn't have the power to stop him either. And we're still too far out.

"Angel Two here. Visual on Pol Two. Starting recovery."

"Angel Two, this is Angel Seven. Pol Two is over your power limit. Brake his outthrust to the max, but do not exceed your limits. Repeat, do not exceed your limits."

There was no response.

Damned hero. And likely to be a dead one shortly.

McCaine keyed station ops.

"Primus, this is Angel Seven. Interrogative cleared to cross launch lanes."

"Seven, you're cleared to cross."

McCaine eased the thrusters up to 35 percent, then cut back. Even with the heavier converter, he'd need everything.

The heads-up display, perhaps the last one operational in the squadron, showed the closure. While the screens displayed Angel Two's approach and trac, he couldn't see either.

The pinflare of Angel Two's thrusters caught his eye. He began counting. ". . . six, seven, eight," he muttered as the thin flame lengthened and continued. ". . . fifteen, sixteen, seventeen . . . stop it, you idiot . . . twenty, twenty-one . . ."

The final flare was even brighter.

"Primus, this is Angel Two. Lost converter. Lost slosh, Still carrying outvector. Interrogative ETA, Angel Seven."

McCaine checked his instruments. Angel Two hadn't lined up his braking thrusts exactly. Probably misaligned instruments, though McCaine. Flexiplast and rework after rework can only do so much.

Apollo Two and Angel Two were both drifting up and out-system as they orbited each other.

"Two and Two, this is Angel Zero Seven. Have visual. ETA ten. Strap and suit. I repeat. Strap and suit." They probably were, but this one was going to be rough.

"Roger."

"Roger."

McCaine looked over at Lyn.

"Lyn, can we mag-trac Angel Two enough to throw him along an intersect to Primus."

"Let me check."

McCaine waited as the tech fingers danced over her console.

"Can you spare a 30 percent slosh loss and a five-unit time-add-on before you tackle the skitter?"

"Thirty-one and four units?" countered McCaine.

"Close, but I think so."

"Let's try it. Seal up before we start."

"Roger."

McCaine used the trim jets to tilt the RV-2 nose high to the skitter and fallen angel he was approaching.

"Power!" demanded the tech. McCaine twisted up the flow to the converter, watching the fuel level drop and the drain needle peg-out as the mag-trac built up force.

At first, he was conscious only of a faint humming through his boots. Within a unit, the cabin was shaking hard enough to knock the loose stylus from the plot board, and the heads-up display was impossible to read. Abruptly, it vanished.

He watched the ship's internal pressure drop, seeping away as the bar gauge on the panel dropped toward the red. McCaine didn't realize he was holding his breath until Lyn cut the flow diversion and the drain needle unpegged. He exhaled.

He pulsed the stricken angel to get distance and vector readings. The output from the plotting computer showed a near intersect with Primus station. A bit tight, and Angel Two would need a close-in two, but good enough considering the situation.

"Primus, this is Angel Zero Seven, Angel Zero Two on a reentry intersect. Estimate arrival above the recovery lanes in twenty, and he'll need an in-tow. Two's no thrust, no power, low comm."

"Roger, Seven. We'll get him."

McCaine shifted his full attention to the skitter, which was drifting farther out-system. He pulsed the thrusters to close up. No fancy bookwork here, but a plain and simple overtake and reverse curve.

"Apollo Two, this is Angel Seven. You strapped?"

"Strapped and ready, Seven."

"Lyn, ready for mag-trac and grapple." McCaine knew the tug would lose mag-trac power by the end of the required maneuvers.

"Ready, Captain."

McCaine eased the RV-2 in over the skitter's nonfunctioning rear thrusters, studying the console's distance monitor as the mag-trac pulled the two together.

"Oh, hell!" He should have noticed sooner, but Apollo Two was still leaking. The mist surrounding the damaged skitter should have warned him, but he'd been thinking three steps ahead. Not that he could do much at this point.

He checked the power flow, slosh reserve, and drift before pulsing the left rear thruster and the side trim jets. He pulsed the left-rear thruster again to bring the nose around.

McCaine began bringing up power on the rear thrusters, favoring the left with a higher setting to bring the two ships onto the return course.

A red light flared on the console. Now the tug's internal pressure was well below minimum safety levels. Suited or not, it would be nice to work with more than basic instruments, but it wasn't likely.

He sighed as the two noses lined up on the return course to Primus, leaning back in the pilot's seat and checking the relative velocities.

That was when the explosion rocked both the salvage boat and the skitter.

McCaine juggled the power to his rear thrusters and managed to get the noses centered again before the rear thrusters quit.

"Apollo Two, this is Angel Seven. Interrogative damage."

"Holed, but no more hulk than before."

McCaine ran through the instruments he had left. On course, but fast, a good 20-percent-plus faster. Twenty-five percent slosh left but no rear thrusters.

Not much choice. We slow down on forward thrusters, well within the suspect specs, or we don't slow down. Too much mass/velocity for the remaining RV-1 to handle . . . so it's all ours.

"Lyn, this is going to be rough, real rough."

"Ready, Captain."

McCaine watched as the station drew closer.

What am I doing out here in a salvage tug? At forty-plus, when all I had to do was say, yes, it's a fine tug?

. . . three, two, one, now!

He slipped in the forethrusters, running them up to half power, seeing the relative motion slow, sensing the raggedness, feeling himself being pulled gently forward in his seat, wishing he'd had the sophisticated equipment to plot a more gentle decel curve, being shaken as the whole boron-flexiplast hull shuddered, knowing that if there were any cabin pressure left, the hull would be screaming in protest. No matter what anyone said, the RV-2 wasn't meant to be stopped nose first.

Without warning the left front thruster quit.

Almost in reflex, McCaine cut the right forethruster and diverted the full gasjet reserves to the right-rear trim-squirters.

He checked the closure,

He'd stopped the spin/crab, but not all the in-system drift. Without more decel thrust, the combined skitter/tug mass would still be too much for the RV-1 to handle.

"Apollo Two, interrogative gas for side squirt."

"Almost max."

McCaine had hoped for it, knowing the skitter pilots didn't make many trim corrections.

"Roger," he transmitted back. "I intend another decel burst. When I fire, feed full reserve into your right-rear trim."

"Wilco."

McCaine jammed the right forethruster to full, held it momentarily, and brought it back to zero. The trim jets of Apollo Two corrected their swing, stabilizing them both at an angle to the recovery path.

He checked the relative motion . . . still drifting, but the RV-1 could handle it from here.

The vibration of the deck caught his attention. As he half turned toward Lyn, he saw the front bulkhead bending toward him, pushing the attached equipment over his couch.

As he jabbed the shield pod switch, the darkness came up around him.

. . . . .

"He's coming around. . . ."

McCaine felt like he'd spent an eternity swimming through a gray soup. The overhead had a disconcerting tendency to waver. Overhead?

He realized he was in sick bay.

"Lyn?" he demanded, struggling to lift himself.

"Commander Haskins is fine," a strange voice stated firmly.

He let himself slip back into the gray soup.

McCaine awoke with a start, recalling the collapse of the RV-2 around him, wondering whether he should have tried guesswork decel before he even had the relative motions, how he could have handled it better, and he could, he was somehow sure . . . and the strange voice . . .

The other bed was occupied.

"Well, Ed, it took you long enough."

"Lyn . . . how long? You . . . all right." His words seemed strangely incoherent.

She smiled. The tiredness was gone from her face.

McCaine forgot the discolored flexiplast walls, the mental fuzziness, the aches across his shoulders and chest, the might-have-beens. He opened his mouth, then shut it, thought about opening it again, and shook his head, all too conscious of the tears welling up in the corners of his eyes.

She was still smiling. He looked away.

"Ed. You won, you know."

"Won?" he asked stupidly.

"Heatherton finished the job, sent the RV-2s back with us."

"With us?" Lord, he felt so out of it.

"We're on the *Avalon* back to Darneill."

Of course, the return convoy. But how long had it been?

McCaine kept trying to put the questions in order in his mind, but couldn't. At last, he turned back to Lyn and shrugged.

She laughed, a short chuckle.

"Both Admiral Reagan and Heatherton agreed that you made an impossible recovery, especially with a defective and untested rug. They can't remember when someone brought back two crews with a single fuel load. Nothing in Zero Seven worked by the time we landed up off the recovery lanes—"

"Just stupid, stupid, stupid," muttered McCaine.

"—and if the best pilot available could barely get the RV-2 back in one piece, maybe the RV-2 wasn't ready for the Forces. That's the official line. Maybe it's because Heatherton leaked the story to the flak pool, all about your putting yourself on the line to save your men. It was planetwide before the Finance Ministry and Buships found out.

"Mort Wyemouth had enough sense to jump on the bandwagon. He's really got a slimy sense of politics. He suggested that the concept behind the RV-2 was admirable, but that it needed further development."

McCaine ran his tongue over his lips. God, he'd been lucky. Someone could have been killed, and it might have been him . . . or Lyn.

"What about us?" he asked.

"Heroes are an embarrassment on a working station. Besides, Anemone is about to be touched off. Primus Station is being shifted farther Trojan to work another berg."

The painkillers were wearing off. McCaine felt as though he had been through a meat grinder and been sewed back together with rough plasticable. He looked at the closed door, wincing and unable to suppress the pain reaction, somehow mad at himself for hurting.

"Ed." It was said gently.

"I know. I know," he said quietly.

And he did. Medical retirement at the permanent rank of commander-second, quiet days, gardening, writing, whatever, being remembered, if at all, as the only pilot to destroy four tugs in a row.

The messages his body was sending were clear. His piloting days were over. In some ways it was too bad he'd devoted all his time to the Forces. No family, and friends expended like melted plastic in the senseless fights between Macedonia and Darneill.

"You don't know!"

He looked at her in confusion.

"Edward Alton McCaine, you're thinking about a forced retirement, a bit of disgrace, an abrupt transition to solitude. And you're feeling sorry for yourself. The great Edward McCaine humbled and reduced to private citizen . . . so wrapped up in his fears he isn't even listening . . ." Her voice dropped. "I'm sorry. But listen. I said you won, and you did.

"The king made you a permanent captain and put you in charge of the Buships RV-2 program. It's only a year's appointment as an acting admiral, but he *had* to. Oh, and Admiral Reagan put you in for a D.S.P."

McCaine brushed the honor away with a weak gesture. "What about you?"

"I'm putting in my papers."

Maybe he should have expected it, but things weren't going the ways he'd anticipated. He was staying with the Space Forces, and Lyn was going.

Lyn retiring? Just like that? Who would he talk to? Why was he so upset about it?

"Why?" he blurted.

"Because, Edward McCaine, because if I stay in, they'll ship me back into orbit while you're in Tammerlane getting into trouble with the Finance Ministry. Besides, someone has to take care of you, or you'll go off making a hero out of yourself again. And you're too stubborn to admit that you need a good tech officer, retired or not, behind you."

Lyn wanted to stay with him. With him. No more separating, no more tours alone, wondering why.

"Maybe I should, too," he answered.

"And waste my noble gesture? Not a chance."

"You think you know me pretty well," McCaine said with a rueful twist to his swollen lips.

Lyn looked back at him, her face free of tension and with a full smile bordering on a grin.

"You do," he finished, "you do." And we have a job in Tammerlane . . . together.

This story came from my experiences at EPA and in the consulting business . . . and in a backward way, some of the latest theories about the earth's past trends in global cooling suggest perhaps I might have gotten it totally backward . . . if to the same end.

POWER TO . . . ?

Thurman shook his head again. According to the *Science Update* article, Hyman and his crew had finally managed to get a viable allosaur embryo, but it had required a totally controlled atmosphere. His lips pursed. Genetic replication was all well and good, but what earth needed was more nonpolluting power.

He snorted and placed the *Update* in its proper place at the end of the second shelf of the bookcase, not that he even had to stretch. Then he looked at the wrinkled DEP letter that lay on the otherwise-clear space beside the computer console. He had finally retrieved it from the white-paper-recycling bin. He wasn't sure that the off-gray recycled government stationery qualified as white paper in any case.

Now, smoothed back into a semblance of flatness, the letter lay next to the earlier letter he had already received from the Office of Technology Evaluation.

Buzzzzz.

He punched the intercom button. "Yes?"

"George Hammelschmidt is here, Dr. Thurman."

Thurman managed to turn the deep groan he felt into a mild sigh. "I'll be right out." He glanced from the desk to the narrow window to his right. Outside, the afternoon appeared more like twilight under the heavy clouds. Thurman shook his head. Things had seemed sunnier when he had been younger, but that was when he and Blyth and Helda had been younger, far younger. With a snort at his self-pity, he looked back at the papers next to the console. The desk, with the built-in console, his swivel, the bookcase, and the single client chair just about took all the floor space in the office.

He didn't have to reread the letter from the technology section of the federal Department of Environmental Protection.

"Dear Dr. Thurman . . ." he mumbled as he levered himself out of the ancient swivel chair, "while the Department remains interested in the early use of your hot/cold fusion power system, a part C(a)(1) permit under the requirements of the Solid and Hazardous Waste Act of 1996, as amended, cannot be issued until Power, Inc., the applicant, completes the requirements of Subsection A(1) and A(s) [40 CFR 265.2541 G] . . ."

He'd only read the damned letter three times. The fools! All the politicians muttered about energy shortages, global warming, waste overflow, state waste sufficiency . . . and he couldn't even get a permit to solve their problems.

Then he shook his head again. Still, he and the other scientists hadn't helped their case much. First, the idiots at the old EPA had predicted sea-level rises of nearly three feet in half a century, and wildly increasing temperatures. Then, they had said that third-world industrialization and increased hydrocarbon usage would make things worse.

Well . . . the sea level, nearly fifteen years after the doomsayers, was up 1.4 inches, despite third-world greenhouse gas emissions nearly 30 percent above the amounts predicted.

Buzzzzz.

Woolgathering . . . but what else had he to do, now that the project was crashing around him?

With another sigh, he opened the door.

George was not sitting on the couch but standing by Marie's console. Definitely a bad sign.

"Come on in."

"This will only take a minute, Ron."

Thurman closed the door as he followed the attorney back into the office.

George pursed his thin lips, shifting his weight from one long leg to the other. His nouveau double-breasted suit hung loosely on his lanky frame. "Chiang wants results. He told me you've got ninety days—either to get more financing or to get the operating permit."

"Hell . . ." Thurman shook his head. "Since when has DEP even processed the paperwork for a permit in ninety days?"

"He's not that unreasonable, Ron. Even a letter indicating intent—or something—would buy some time. You have to see his point. More than $10 million—a facility in place, a penalty clause if we don't produce the power . . ."

Thurman snorted. "What do Ames, Heidlinger, and Partello have to say?"

"Partello's been dead for years."

"George . . ."

"We agree with your interpretation. Without the Part C permit, you're dead. Existing legal precedents indicate that virtually no one yet has been successful in proving that a failure to act to deny or approve a proposed permit is either arbitrary or capricious."

"George, do you know how ridiculous this whole thing is?"

There was no answer.

The inventor began to talk—to the window, to the vehicle-packed street below, and to the dark afternoon sky, knowing George had heard it all before. "The system works. We know it works, and they know it works. It doesn't generate greenhouse gases; it doesn't generate radioactive wastes; and what's a little elemental helium? Is anyone interested? Of course—but first, we have to file for a preliminary study by the Office of Technology Evaluation to ensure that the technology is valid—thanks to all the cold-fusion nuts of the nineties. Then we have to get a waste-analysis profile approved by OTA, thanks to the ultra-environmentalists. OTA won't start the waste profile analysis without the OTE preliminary evaluation. The DEP won't start processing the permit without the waste profile—" Thurman stopped his monologue and snorted. "You've heard it, George. Tell Chiang I'm working on it."

"He knows that."

"He wants the plant built—to get the clock running. And if we can't get the permits, he'll take the company, won't he?"

"Ron, I don't know his motives . . ."

"Never mind." Thurman kept looking out the window. The door opened and closed behind him.

Options? What options did he have? He either needed $5 million a year until he got a permit or an immediate permit. Getting the permit in ninety days was impossible, and the Chinese had been the only consortium anywhere willing to put up the money—mainly because they liked the idea of smaller and more dispersed power-generation facilities.

He still didn't understand why OTE was stalling, not with the continued reliance of East Coast Outer Banks oil and the tottering Islamic Union. There had to be a reason. Too bad the greenhouse warnings had died down.

He frowned and tapped the console, calling up the data section.

Three hours later, he called George.

George was out.

"Have him call me back."

But it wasn't until Tuesday that the attorney returned the call. Thurman spent most of the time before his console overspending his slim budget on data searches and sleeping less than usual.

When he picked up the phone, he didn't even give the attorney time for courtesies. "George, I'd like to make a counter to Chiang."

"Oh . . ."

"Six months . . . *but* . . . if I fail to come up with either permit or money, he not only gets the Finaldo plant, but my services for two years, at cost, in building mainland plants immediately, without the five-year-delay clause."

"That's offering a lot for an additional ninety days, Ron. You fought like hell for the delay clause."

"I know. But I need the time. And no one in U.S. industry exactly marched to our rescue." Thurman regretted the partial truth. He always regretted not telling the full truth.

"I can almost tell you without checking that he'll accept that."

"I know," Thurman said glumly. He hoped his suspicions were right. Nothing ventured, nothing gained. Except whoever had said that belonged to the optimists of the world.

.   .   .

OFFICE OF TECHNOLOGY EVALUATION proclaimed the plaque on the door.

Thurman squared his shoulders before extending a hand toward the old-fashioned doorknob. With his right hand opening the door, his left carrying the battered brown briefcase, he stepped inside the office.

"May I help you?" The gray-haired woman's voice was professionally warm, but her desk was situated to block Thurman from the office doors behind her, particularly the long corridor that led to Leightsell's domain.

"Dr. Ronald Thurman for Fred Leightsell."

"Is Dr. Leightsell expecting you?"

Thurman donned a genial smile. "If he's not, he should be."

"Let me tell him you're here."

The inventor and president of Power, Inc., settled himself into the small and sagging orange couch.

"Dr. Thurman! A pleasure to see you!" The voice rattled the door.

Thurman stood up, trying not to smile as he realized that Fred Leightsell barely reached his shoulders—although the bureaucrat was nearly as broad as he was tall.

"Please come in."

The office of the chief evaluator was easily twice the size of that of the president of Power, Inc., but the difference was Leightsell wasn't paying by the square foot for his office—the taxpayers were.

"What can I do for you?"

"Do you think clean fusion power is a good idea?"

Leightsell frowned. "Of course. Of course. Hasn't our correspondence indicated that to you? We've been most positive."

"I'm a little puzzled, then, since you've been working on the evaluation for nearly two years."

"Yes . . . it does take time . . . I'm afraid. We have to examine all the ramifications . . . the congressional mandates, you know . . ." Leightsell frowned again. "It shouldn't be that long now, certainly less than a year."

Thurman swallowed. "Less than a year?"

"Of course, that's for the draft evaluation. And that has to be published in the *Federal Register*. Say another eighteen months after that for the final."

"The statute doesn't mention . . . never mind, I suppose we're talking about the Administrative Procedures Act . . ."

Leightsell nodded in response.

"What about the requirement to reduce greenhouse emissions?"

"But that's why we're so interested in your technology. It's the most exciting thing in years." Leightsell's eyes nearly flashed.

"I don't think you understand, Dr. Leightsell. Power, Inc., is a venture-capital-funded operation. We anticipated the statutory requirements. We even added a 40 percent fudge factor for timing. Right now, the government has taken twice the statutory requirements in review time, and not one step of the permitting process beyond our initial submission has been completed."

Leightsell looked at the piles of paper neatly stacked across his desk.

Thurman looked at them as well. Several bore thin layers of dust.

"It's . . . well . . . my recommendation, which was a positive evaluation, has already been forwarded to the deputy director for her review."

"I'd like to see her."

"The deputy director?"

Thurman shrugged. "Unless it would be better for me to see the director."

"Before she has reviewed the recommendation? That would be an *ex parte* contact."

"They're not illegal. You just have to document them."

"I don't know. I just don't know."

Thurman stood up. "I understand your problem. Let me tell you mine. In thirty days," he exaggerated, "unless there is definite progress in obtaining the DEP Part C permit, Power, Inc., ceases to exist. The rights revert to a third-world banking consortium, and that includes the rights to build these units immediately."

"Why—"

"Because no U.S. firm would put up developmental funding . . ."

"Would you excuse me for a moment?"

Thurman shrugged.

In less than five minutes, the chief evaluator was back. "I managed to squeeze in a few minutes with the deputy director."

They took the elevator to the eighth floor, to an office that appeared to be situated directly above Leightsell's.

After the formalities, Deputy Director Helberstrem looked at Leightsell, then at Thurman. "You seem to think that the office should rush its work because of your failure to make adequate funding provisions."

Thurman did not strangle the white-haired woman, much as he wanted to. Instead, he swallowed. "The system works. It has been bench-tested, pilot-tested, and reviewed. Developing and protecting the patents took the life savings of three of us. Dr. Jonstone died last year, and Helda Greth had to withdraw for health reasons.

"As I explained to Dr. Leightsell, no U.S. firm would underwrite the development, and I could only get the funding from foreign sources on the condition that, after five years, if the facility were not operational, or substantially ready for operation and permitted to operate, all usage rights reverted to the financing institution. I did get a fudge factor—that if we obtained government funding to carry us through to full operation, the usage rights remained with Power, Inc." He laughed, almost a bark. "That was easy, because no one could recall a fusion power research grant in more than a decade." Thurman paused, then inclined his head to the deputy director. "The reason why the U.S. investors turned us down was that no permits had been granted, and the likelihood of a facility being permitted within the foreseeable future was remote.

"The foreign banks agreed, but were willing to give us five years before they employ the technology abroad. To get more time, unfortunately, I had to change the agreement. If we don't get additional funding, or the permit, they can use the technology abroad immediately."

"Employ it abroad?"

"You know . . . start building small hot/cold fusion power plants. Maybe even hundreds of them. That was really the rationale, I'm sure." Thurman continued, "They're willing to take a longer view, especially since I have a very good patent attorney."

"Dr. Leightsell . . . I think you have a meeting at two . . ." suggested the deputy director smoothly.

Leightsell looked puzzled, but agreed. "Ah . . . yes."

After Fred Leightsell departed, Deputy Director Helberstrem looked directly at Ronald Thurman. "You're going to see the president's science advisor." The words weren't a question.

Thurman nodded politely, glad his packages had been distributed outside the United States.

.   .   .

"Dr. Thurman, your technology is possibly the greatest threat to human survival facing this planet in the next century. It's also probably our salvation after that."

Had Dorfman Drenkell's face been any thinner, reflected Thurman, it could have substituted for an ax. The ax would have looked more friendly, but the electrolimousine and the Marine guard had not exactly left Thurman in the most cheerful of moods.

Thurman nodded, trying to keep his expression calm. The pieces fit. The only question was whether he could apply the leverage necessary. "So the Gaians are right, then." He made it a statement.

"You are a physicist—"

"But I try to keep abreast of the basics in other fields." Thurman smiled faintly before getting to the point. "Why don't I spell it out, Dr. Drenkell?"

"Why don't you, Dr. Thurman?"

Thurman swallowed. "I kept getting two messages. First, my system was good, and, second, that no one wanted it operating. The latest regulatory changes to the Tech Evaluation Act were rammed through in less than a year—right after we announced the project. Still, until last week, when I read the article on allosaur genetic replication—"

"Allosaur replication?"

"The substitution of artificially modeled dinosaur DNA for existing DNA." He shook his head and looked at the science advisor.

"What does dinosaur replication . . . ?"

"They needed an artificial atmosphere," as if the explanation should suffice. "Anyway, that was when I redid the agreement with Chiang. I bought another sixty days by agreeing that that I would replicate the pilot plant on a full-scale basis on the Chinese mainland if I failed to obtain either the permits or government financing necessary to carry the company to full operation."

Drenkell's face hardened. "That verges on global blackmail."

Thurman smiled. "If you want to call it that . . . you've played with us for over five years . . ."

"What if we can't . . . ?"

Thurman shrugged. "Then the Chinese get lots of cheap fusion power to support their industry, and at least I get to see the system working before I die of old age."

"They'll build as many as they can."

"No doubt."

Drenkell's face bore a pasty sheen, not just from the fluorescent lighting in the small west wing office. "Do you know what you're doing?"

Thurman grinned. "Why don't you tell me? And don't bother pushing buttons or things like that. There's a complete set of plans in a very discreet third-world bank. My attorney knows where to find them if anything happens to me. Besides, the forbearance agreements lapse upon my death."

"We wouldn't do anything like that."

"I didn't think so," Thurman lied. "But business is business. And you still haven't told me what I'm doing."

Drenkell took a sip from the cup at his elbow, then swallowed. He swallowed once more. "Have you ever asked why all the greenhouse terrorists' predictions didn't come true? Some of the scientists who made the earlier calculations were outstanding. And the ozone hole sometimes covers half the upper atmosphere."

Thurman waited.

"In a nutshell, the Gaians were right. In a grossly simplified way, the global ecosystem is alive, or at least responsive. In response to all the greenhouse gases, the CFCs, the methane, the CO_2, all the halides and everything else, the ecology is adjusting. But it has a lag factor, a tremendous lag factor. The adjustments began in the early 1980s—changes in jet-stream flow patterns, ocean currents, seasonal cloud cover, ice-sheet duration and extent . . ."

Thurman kept waiting.

"Don't you see?" Drenkell asked. "Your system can be implemented in a few years. Power generation, with an expansion of old-style fission choked off by the nuclear-waste restrictions, is still mostly hydrocarbons. Electric power generation and manufacturing plant operations now total nearly 50 percent of greenhouse emissions. In less than a decade, you could cut that in half, and the ecosystem would still be compensating. Conceivably, even the smaller third-world factories could install their own systems—that might cut another 10 percent from current emission levels." Drenkell swallowed once more.

"You're saying that because rapid implementation of my system could cause massive reductions in greenhouse emissions, we'd end up cooling down the atmosphere?"

"A little ice age, at best," confirmed Drenkell. "Assuming we're right this time. But no one wants to gamble that we're not. Not after the Waste Wars."

"Then, maybe, just maybe, you'd better ensure that Power, Inc., gets a good healthy research grant—say about $10 million a year—to explore the phase-in of alternative cold fusion power systems."

"I can't do that."

"Then we'd better invest in thermal underwear . . ." Thurman suggested mildly.

Drenkell sighed.

"It's a cheap investment," countered Thurman. "Besides, I could leak it to the press that you killed the project to ensure that Outer Banks production continues."

Drenkell glanced from Thurman to the console and back to Thurman. "That won't be necessary. You'll have a grant agreement tomorrow, and the first check within the next thirty days."

.   .   .

"I still don't understand." George shook his head to emphasize his confusion.

Thurman stood, looking into the rain.

"Simple. When it comes right down to it, the Earth is alive. That's over-simplifying, but let it go at that. The poor planet *tries* to compensate. So when we dumb humans started pouring all the greenhouse garbage into the atmosphere, to keep from frying everything, Gaia—"

"Gaia?"

"The Earth," explained Thurman. "Gaia began to cool everything possible, but it takes time. All right, now that the poor planet's got the air conditioner on full blast, so to speak, along comes Ron Thurman with his hot/cold fusion plant, which will wipe out 40 to 60 percent of the greenhouse heat sources within a decade or two. And Gaia can't change that fast—or if she does, the climatic impacts would be disastrous."

"So why didn't they just get rid of you and your technology?" asked George.

"Because the third-worlders are still industrializing, and all poor Gaia can do is slow the rate of heating. OTE is still trying to figure out the best phase-in period for stability. I just 'suggested' that leaving control with me gave them more control." He shook his head.

George stared directly at Thurman. "You really think the Earth is alive, the way these Gaian types insist?"

"I hope so." Thurman looked out at the heavy clouds he did not recall from his childhood. Then he turned back to the lawyer. "Don't you?"

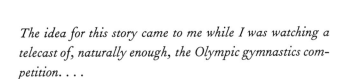

The idea for this story came to me while I was watching a telecast of, naturally enough, the Olympic gymnastics competition. . . .

PRECISION SET

He calls himself Charley Cable. That is/is not his name. At the moment he sits in the third row at the Sports Pavilion, watching the gymnasts warm up. Although the Pavilion is full, and tickets are so scarce that there are no scalpers plying the Plaza outside, each seat beside him is vacant. The price he has paid for all three seats would have bought him a suite at the local Ritz-Singleton for a season. He wears a classic blue wool blazer and gray slacks, with a white silk shirt and black leather boots. He is the only man in the section who wears a jacket, and the only one who wears no jewelry.

The glow from the slow-glass panels increases, indirect but bright enough to provide perfect lighting for the competitors and clear illumination of the various gymnastic apparati on the Pavilion floor—the four-centimeter beam that replaced the older four-inch beam a generation earlier; the vaulting horse; the bars; and the floor-exercise square.

For a moment, Charley concentrates.

". . . say the Basque team has a new technique for kinesthetics . . ."

". . . NordAms are still using enhanced physical patterning . . ."

He lets his concentration lapse, and the clear words drop into background noise, not soothing, but only vaguely disturbing. The fingers of his right hand slip across his forehead, not quite touching or brushing back the short but otherwise-nondescript brown hair streaked with silver. His eyes are a deep hazel.

On the Pavilion floor, the warm-ups continue, each girl-woman moving effortlessly, gracefully, and precisely. The judges fiddle with their laser-measuring/calibration equipment. The audience juggles programs and personal computoculars.

The slightest of sounds alerts him, a pattern he has memorized, if self-programming recognition to precise sonic patterns can accurately be called memorization. He forces himself to turn his gaze toward the aisle slowly, as if in idle curiosity, although his curiosity, comparatively new as it is, is seldom idle.

She is slender, black-haired, and of an indeterminate age beyond youth and before obvious physical degeneration. She wears a cream-colored cotton blouse, hand-tailored, and a dark skirt of real wool, and a turquoise silk scarf. Charley watches her for a time, sensing, rather than actually seeing, the blackness behind the china blue eyes. Her low-cut, light black leather, laced shoes touch each step with unvarying precision, as if each foot understands independently where it should go.

Charley nods. Each foot is programmed to react kinesthetically to the situation. He raises a hand as she looks in his direction. Her eyes meet his, and he points to the seat beside him.

With a sad smile, she shakes her head. Charley points again.

This time, she walks in front of a pseudofamily—a boy, a girl, and two parents wearing unisex clothes and hair—and eases into the seat on his left. She does not look at the chair, yet settles into it perfectly. "Are you sure?"

Charley is sure. He bought the tickets for privacy and for her. This is the fifth competition he has attended. "I'm Charley Cable."

"You could have sold these seats."

"I wasn't interested in selling them."

Charley concentrates on the narrow beam, where a delicate redhead practices a double flip with a full twist, followed by a single with a half twist to a handstand. "Is that Maureen Dinisha?" he asks, knowing full well that the redhead is Dinisha, having seen her in the four previous sessions.

"The redhead? Yes. She is very precise." The woman's voice is soft, yet as clearly defined as her steps, posture, and grooming.

"Aren't they all?"

"Of course. That's why . . ."

She does not finish the sentence, but he knows what she means. Both look toward the precision measuring equipment used by the judges.

"Do you really want to torture yourself more?" he asks gently.

Her head snaps toward him. Hazel eyes meet blue eyes.

"How would you know?"

"Why else would you be here? Obviously, someone let you in without a ticket, and that means . . ."

"You are too perceptive."

"No," Charley says truthfully, for lying remains difficult with his literal background. He knows her patterns through observation, not perception. He stands up. "Shall we go?"

She sighs. "I suppose you're right."

"That remains to be seen." He offers a hand that she does not need.

She takes it, but puts no weight upon him as she rises, graceful as always. They ease past the pseudofamily, and both parents glare, either at their obviously conservative and wealthy attire or their cavalier departure even before the competition begins.

"What do you do?" she asks, halfway up the aisle to the exit landing.

"I'm a consultant. I receive a considerable stipend . . . for past services. I also design advanced DataNets, communications equipment."

They pause at the top of the aisle as the slow-glass panels above the audience dim in preparation for the competition proper.

"You haven't asked what I do," she says. "Doesn't it matter?"

"I wouldn't define you just by what you do." Charley provides an easy smile, although it is a mannerism that he has had to learn. "What do you do?"

"I also receive a stipend for . . . past services. I teach athletic . . . history . . . at the University—part-time."

As they exit the Plaza, Charley's eyes scan the scattered crowd, studying those outside until he sees three girls, all prepubescent, all bearing tablets and styli, all clearly hoping for a sight of Sirelli or Dinisha or perhaps even Yurkira. They wait, despite the lateness of the hour, and he stops in front of them and smiles.

"I've been called away, ladies. Would you like my tickets? They're third-row center off the floor exercise." He extends the plastic-coated oblongs, with the holograms that are difficult, if not impossible, to counterfeit.

"Thanks!" The tallest girl, smooth-skinned as all youth are, but still awkward, takes the tickets.

Charley nods, watching as they scramble toward the doorway, clutching the tickets as though they were made of gold when gold was itself valuable.

"That was cruel," the woman says.

"In a way." Her observation of the effect of his gift pleases him, but not totally, for he does not engage in wanton cruelty.

"Where are we going?"

"Can you stand a long drive? Several hours?"

"If I must." She smiles. "Why should I trust you?"

"I'm eminently trustworthy. I have too much to lose by not being trustworthy. Consultants, you know, only survive through their clients' trust."

"I'm sure. But does that translate into personal relations?"

"I hope so." His vehicle is deep-coated gunmetal gray, and bears the antenna that indicates its ties to the national automated road system. He opens the door for her.

"I didn't know anyone still did that."

"My programming is doubtless dated."

They only use the highway for a time before he turns off and takes a side road, which winds through hillier and increasingly wooded land, generally obscure in details in the darkness. Beside him, the woman rests, dozes perhaps.

Still later, as the sky is graying into dawn, he turns up a dirt road. He stops beside a small house—gray, late-twentieth-century-modern with excessive glass—overlooking a lake. After opening her door, he pulls a small, but heavy pack from the car.

"If this is yours, I'd appreciate the chance to . . ."

Charley purses his lips, another learned mannerism, and opens the unlocked front door. "It's the first door on the left."

He uses the upstairs facilities, then returns and waits by the vehicle.

She returns before long. "This is yours? It's lovely."

"It is mine. Consultants do have a choice of locales in this electronic age." He offers his arm. She ignores the offer by touching his elbow.

"I'd like you to look at the lake from the wall down there." He points to the path, which circles through the lawn and past a garden filled with bright yellow marigolds and crimson petunias.

They walk downhill, their steps precise for very different reasons.

Old as the stones are, the wall has been maintained. Charley sits on a precisely reset stone wall and places the small pack by his feet. He looks down at the lake. "I told you my name was Charley Cable. I'm a man who doesn't exist."

"You look real enough to me." She remains standing.

"Your name is Cylvira. You were the first cyber-kinesthetic gymnast. You won the Gold Medal in the 2012 Olympics, and every event in the Worlds' for the two years before and after the Olympics."

"Cylvira died a long time ago."

"I'm a man who doesn't exist."

"Neither one of us makes much sense." Her tone is bitter. "I should not have come."

"You retired when the new techniques became widespread."

"Cylvira was obsolete even when she won the Olympics."

"*Obsolete* refers to machines."

"You saw Dinisha. You saw the judges with their lasers that measure deviations from the horizontal and vertical by micromillimeters. Is that human?"

Charley gestures toward the lake, so still in the dawn that the trees on the far shore appear to grow in two directions. "The water reflects the trees perfectly, but it is still water."

"Don't you ever say anything directly?"

"It's hard for someone who doesn't exist."

"What do you want?"

"Would you sit down?"

She sits, and they watch the lake, as slowly, the faintest of breezes ripples the water, and the upside-down picture of the trees and cloud-specked sky shivers, wavers, and vanishes. Only a single set of trees remains above the cold blue water.

"It is a pretty place." Cylvira's eyes shift toward Charley.

"Do you know what a data lattice looks like?"

Cylvira frowns.

"Or an enhanced if-then decision tree?" Charley smiles. "They're black and white, incredibly detailed black and white pieces that form pyramids or chains. For all the graphic arts presentations that show artificial intelligence in colors, it's not that way."

He bends down and opens his pack. From it, he removes two headsets and a black box with two input leads. He plugs each headset into the box and hands one to her.

"No!" Cylvira stands, handing the headset back to him with a harshly precise motion.

"These aren't implantation sets. They're just impression sets. Look at the leads. You should know the difference." Charley waits.

"Why?"

"I want to give you two impressions."

"This isn't big enough for an impression set."

"Technology does advance." His voice is dry. "Besides, Cylvira is dead."

She laughs, raggedly, but it is a laugh. This time she takes the headset.

Charley puts on his set, then touches a stud on the black box.

He looks at the lake, concentrating on its blueness, and upon the dark green of the tall pines, their brown trunks, and the puffy white clouds overhead, upon the scent of damp-air pine, and hard texture of the stone under his hand, the feel of the silk against his skin. He touches her hand and lets her sense the wonder of the warmth of her skin and fingers against his. Then he looks back at the lake for a long time, marveling at its colors and how it changes from moment to moment.

Then he touches the second stud on the box, calling up past memories—cold lines of black and white bytes, chains of black and white, black and white, black and white . . . white and black, black and black. No scents, no smells, no colors—the chains go on endlessly, looping, flashing, but always black and white, white and black.

He touches the stud and removes the headset.

Silently, Cylvira removes hers. "You're . . ."

He nods. "The man who no longer exists. The AI they plugged into a brain-drained killer named . . . his name doesn't matter. I'm Charley Cable, or I'm not."

She shivers. "Do all AIs feel so . . . so . . . cold?"

"No. Only the ones who have to become human. How can you know what color is until you see it?"

She takes his hand. "Thank you." The darkness behind the china blue eyes is lighter, although it will never totally lift.

"Wait a moment." He sets the black box on the ground beside the stone wall. With a quick motion his booted heel crunches through the plastic and circuitry. Then he replaces the pieces in the pack and seals it, setting it carefully on the wall.

His name is/is not Charley Cable. Her name is/is not Cylvira. There are no cyber-kinesthetic gymnasts, and no former killers/ethically enhanced computers.

A couple walks along the lakeshore, their arms entwined. Neither exists.

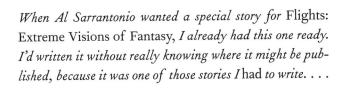

When Al Sarrantonio wanted a special story for Flights: Extreme Visions of Fantasy, *I already had this one ready. I'd written it without really knowing where it might be published, because it was one of those stories I had to write. . . .*

FALLEN ANGEL

Jaweau was sitting in the big white chair behind his desk when I walked in. "You never bother knocking . . ."

"Stow it. You always know I'm coming."

He nodded in that phony sad manner of his, like he wanted to be the forgiving male counterpart of the Maid. "We know, Lucian."

I took the black oak chair, the one he kept for me. The others were gray or white. All sorts came to see Jaweau. "What's the job?"

"Real estate. They want an attraction spell for the new villas beyond the Illysian Gardens."

"An attraction spell, and you're calling me in?"

"They want something with depth and staying power."

"An appeal to young angels, cherubim, mothers, that sort of thing?" I had to sneer. Even saints and angels retained some cupidity.

"No . . . they want the full spectrum. Draw in the seraphim, too." Jaweau shrugged, as only an angel could shrug, resigned without being cynical.

"Muckin' Maid!" An attraction spell for cherubim and seraphim, and they looked down on me?

"Don't swear. If I have to clean the place, it comes off your fee. I told you—"

I was still pissed. A full-spectrum attraction spell, for the dark's due! "They want to pay for that? Do you know what that means? You need a priestess—twice—stable holy water, a virgin singer, and I'll have to be celibate the whole time until I write the song. I can't do crap else if I take the job. That's a thousand golds, minimum."

"Well . . . that would just about take care of what you owe . . ." Jaweau smiled sweetly, the white creep. "Besides, you're always celibate here, unless you do a resonance spell. What choice do you have?"

He was stating a fact, and I ignored it. "Owe! Maid be damned . . ."

He raised his right hand, and the light gathered at his fingertips. "I warned you."

"I'm sorry." The bastard had me. One dose of his goody-goodies, and I'd be worthless for days. I can't afford that much holiness, not and remain sane. How Jaweau does it is beyond me. I mean, how can a guy who looks like an angel, and *is* one, run a damned ad agency in Piedra Los Santos? Well, someone has to, and it has to be an angel. All they let us do is be consultants. There are some things they just can't do. Like disease-killing . . . they can't even destroy a tiny bacterium . . . or deep-attraction spells.

I shifted my weight in the black chair and looked toward him. He was waiting for me to talk. Of course, I couldn't stare him down. That would have set the whole place on fire, and I couldn't afford to pay that off, either. The opposites bit, again. "All right. How good does it have to be?"

"You do this one right, and we'll call it even. You can stay away from here forever, if you want."

"It's not worth that much. You really don't want me around, do you?"

Jaweau shrugged again. He didn't have to admit anything, but I could tell I was getting on his nerves. Maybe I reminded him of the old days too much.

"Give me a couple of days. I didn't plan on two songs."

"You can do the dark side in a couple of hours." Jaweau let a halo circle that golden hair. He always did have an eye for effects.

"That's the easy part. You think it's easy for me to write a virgin song, even for a fallen angel?"

"I always admitted you were an artist, Lucian deNoir—"

"Don't say it."

"You comprehend the fallen. I still don't understand . . ."

"You never will." I stood up. "You'll know when the songs are ready."

He nodded. "The skies will weep . . . again."

Such dragon crap, and he believes it. All the damned angels and saints do.

I left as quickly as I could, and I sure as Hel didn't look in his eyes. Once I trusted him, but you know where trusting an angel leads. I'm sure the bastard used his web of light to remove any traces of skepticism I'd left behind.

The villa was the same as always, the same low hill, the same as when—I try not to think about it, but I'm sure Jaweau leaves it that way just to remind me. The painting of the Maid still hangs over the couch in the workroom. The harps are gone, but I don't need them anyway. I poured a goblet of water—that's one thing I can have in Piedra Los Santos. Then I sat down, the Maid looking over my shoulder.

Writing the song for the dark side of the resonance spell took a couple of hours. That was after it took me three days to write the piece for the singer, and white song had to come first. With all the crap about grace, they have to turn to me to write a true white song. The Maid has a sense of irony, all right.

I have to finish on the dark side, or I'd start believing in all that crap about grace and forgiveness, and I don't ever want to believe that again.

It was cloudy when I finished. Jaweau can be a real bastard. At least it was done. I sealed both folios, one with white wax, the other with black, and made my way back to Jaweau's. I walked.

He met me outside the big chamber, and I suppose his eyes were sad, but I didn't look.

"Who's the singer?" Not that I really cared, though I'd have to before the spell was set and twisted.

"Name's Kyrilann. The blonde by the pentagram."

"All right." I didn't look at her or at the three angels who carried the harps. The singer carried her own. She had to, of course, since the strings were different.

The dark drummer was Khango. I'd worked with him before. Solid, but really didn't care much so long as he could work. He was naturally dark. Some are.

"Are you going to check her out?" Jaweau held the web between his hands, and the light cascaded along the strings.

I lifted a hand, and he stepped back.

"Keep your black hands off my webs, Lucian."

"Then don't tell me when to check out the singers." I grinned, but he didn't grin back. I took a deep breath and looked at the singer, really looked.

She stared back with eyes as blue and as deep as Eden, blue over the tears of a fallen angel. I almost wanted to turn away, but, what the Hel, it was her choice. No one had made her do what she had, and, if she wanted to sing the spell, that was her choice, too.

Except it wasn't, and we both knew it.

One of the angels smiled sadly over a golden harp, and I wanted to paste him, not that it would have done any good.

People think working a resonance spell is like similarity or contagion. That's dragon crap, not that there've ever been dragons, but dark mages— that's what I think of myself as, anyway, no matter what the holies call me— are supposed to believe in the unbelievable. More crap. A resonance spell is a lot trickier, because you've got to have a virgin song, sung by a virgin singer—not pure, but virgin—and then you've got to twist it so that it resonates. The twist's the thing, almost a betrayal of the first two.

"Let's get on with it."

"As you wish." Jaweau moved the web, and a line of fire flared around the pentagram.

I stepped into the pentagram, and Jaweau closed the gap with the light web. Kyrilann stood at the focal point of the pentagram and opened the folio. White wax crumbled to the floor. No one else had seen the song, and she couldn't even open the folder until I was held inside the pentagram, not if the spell were to resonate properly.

Khango sat on a black stool between the two base points of the pentagram. After Kyrilann broke the seal on her folder, he opened his. The black wax melted in dark flames. His black sticks hovered above the drums, waiting for Kyrilann to begin.

She studied at the notes, and time froze. Finally, her fingers touched the silver harp strings. Gold would have been better, theoretically, but Kyrilann was still a fallen angel and only a virgin technically, thanks to Jaweau. He'll bend the rules when he wants to, the sanctimonious bastard.

I waited behind the white lines of the pentagram.

Hel, could she sing! I might have heard better in the time since . . . but I didn't recall when. She was so good that the faint cloak of darkness that had surrounded her, the one that probably only Jaweau and I could see, seemed to lighten as she sang, almost vanishing. As she shimmered toward the white, Khango continued weaving the counterpoint, and the darkness gathered around the base of the pentagram. Even before she finished, the chamber was resonating.

Although I wrote the notes and words, when Kyrilann sang them, I forgot them, and that was as it should be. No one else would remember them either, nor the black counterpoint sung by the dark drummer.

As the song and countersong shivered to a close, I wiped my forehead. It was hot in the pentagram, damned hot, as always.

Outside the pentagram, Jaweau and the others squirmed, as if the resonance were the beat of an unheard dance that picked at them. The whole chamber echoed with the unheard songspell, the resonance lingering, waiting for the next phase, and for the priestess. We all waited. I certainly couldn't do anything else.

The good mothers like to make you wait and squirm, to realize exactly what you've done. That unset resonance even twisted my guts as I watched for the door to open. Finally, the priestess stepped into the chamber. Actually, it was a chapel, since you don't mess with things like resonance spells in any other place, not if you want to keep a whole soul in your body. I might belong to the depths, but even I don't like the thought of spending eternity rent into burning fragments, and the Maid has never been that merciful to us.

The priestess didn't waste any time, either, starting right out with the familiar words. "Dearly beloved . . ." When she got to the part about redemption through love, I looked down. After that she avoided looking at me, and her eyes kept straying to Kyrilann.

I watched Kyrilann's eyes, too. They were a deep open blue, the honest kind you don't associate with fallen angels, and I wondered how exactly she had betrayed herself, not that what I was doing was any better, even if everyone knew it was necessary. I mean, you do have to set the spell, and no one was going to let me out of the pentagram unbound. The ceremony binds the power between us, and the twist locks it back into the rune rods that Jaweau had already placed out beyond the Illysian Gardens.

The good mother did the shortest ceremony possible, ending up with the traditional pronouncement about not putting asunder what the Maid hath joined, and once our hands touched across the pentagram, and the silver rings flared their linked fires, Jaweau opened the pentagram. I shivered; I couldn't help it.

Kyrilann didn't. Those open blue eyes held so much pain that I had to look away. Me . . . I had to look away. Figure that, and over a resonance spell.

I swallowed, and stepped across the pentagram. It still hurt, even after Jaweau erased the light.

Kyrilann turned to me. Tears should have been falling from those eyes, but they were as clear as old-time skies. She actually stepped toward me until we were perhaps three paces apart. She licked her lips, but her eyes met mine.

"You're Lucian deNoir—"

"Please don't say it."

"All right." Her speaking voice was a trace husky, unlike the silver tones that had set the spell.

I drew her to me, gently, with both hands. Her hands touched my waist, and my fingers traced the fine line of her chin. In time, I looked her full in the face, and my eyes burned as they met hers. Even if she were just a singer, that made her, after all, a fallen angel, and that's hard.

I took her arm, and we made our way from the chapel toward my villa.

Her eyes widened as we neared the open gate. "I didn't . . . realize . . ."

"He was merciful . . ."

"I wouldn't call it that." Her tone was thoughtful, but her steps matched mine as we crossed the line of black marble to the low steps.

Once we reached the room with the balcony, I offered her water. That was all. I didn't want to tempt her, although it would have been technically fair. She could have refused, but I like to play it straight, unlike Jaweau.

She took the water, looked at it, and then slowly sipped it.

In time, she let me undress her, and I was gentle.

For a while, I even forgot.

Later, I told her, "I do love you."

"You can't." Her words were sad, even as her hands drew me closer. "You belong to . . ."

I forced myself to meet her eyes. "I can't lie here. Everything I say in Piedra Los Santos must be true." That is absolutely true, so far as it goes. I cannot lie in any city of the saints or angels. And I did love her, absolutely, as those deep, innocent eyes cut through me. Not that it mattered. Nothing had changed, except for those moments when I held a fallen angel, and they came to an end too soon.

When she finally slept, I eased away from her crumpled form and watched the boreali. Then I went down to my workroom and looked at the Bucelli painting for a long time. Maybe there were other universes where it had turned out differently. Maybe.

Morning came, and eventually Kyrilann walked down the stairs, wearing the white gown. She deserved that, and it looked good on her.

I didn't let her say a word. "You can pick up the papers at the priestess's after the Sabbath. I even paid gold for an annulment, not a lousy twenty pieces of silver for a divorce." I had to be the one who paid for the betrayal, of course, or the resonance wouldn't stay set.

Her eyes glistened for a moment, like silver, I'd say . . . if I were the poetic sort. Then she looked at the painting of the Maid, the one by Bucelli that shows Her before the judges, just before they crucified Her. I had Merleno duplicate it. The spell cost a good ten golds, but it's worth it, captures the innocence in Her eyes. Sort of like Kyrilann's, I guess.

"You don't mean it." Kyrilann looked at me again, like the first time after the resonance set in us, and my eyes still burned.

"You were a great lay, Kyrilann, and we did one Hel of a resonance spell. But that's all I can give you." I looked down at the black tabletop—all the furniture got darker when I stayed at the villa for very long. She was already shimmering a bit, and the annulment hadn't even been entered. I knew I'd never do another resonance as good. Too bad the spell doesn't work unless there's betrayal.

"You don't mean it," she repeated. "You don't have to do this."

But I did. Or Jaweau would have everything. "Like I said, you were a great lay." I didn't meet her eyes. Instead, I looked back at the copy of the Bucelli. Damn, Merleno had done a fine job.

The workroom was silent, but I refused to look into those eyes. If I had, I'd have been thinking about . . . never mind.

When I finally looked up, Kyrilann was gone. You've redeemed your soul, Kyrilann. The saints will be pleased.

Business is business, I guess. But I even envied the pain in Kyrilann's eyes.

I sat down in the wooden chair at the oak table and looked at the Maid for a long time. What else could I do? It was time to head back to Hel, until Jaweau or someone else needed me. Jaweau would, again, sooner or later.

Over the years, a number of readers of the Recluce Saga *have asked about Cassius, and how he came to Recluce. Well . . . here's the answer. . . .*

BLACK ORDERMAGE

I

There was the fire, welling up everywhere on the flight deck—and an explosion and a flash of brilliant white. Everything seemed to hang in the balance. Then, blackness flowed around me, and after that so did currents of black and white light. The black felt calming. It was reassuring. The white *burned*.

Both vanished, and I dropped maybe two feet onto something hard. It only took a moment to catch my balance. I was used to pitching decks. But . . . there wasn't any heat, and there weren't any flames. A moment before, I'd been acting as nozzleman on the Big E's deck, and now my hands were empty. Less than three yards away from me a little guy in red-and-yellow rags took what looked to be a curved sabre and slashed a bigger guy in blue and black across the back of his calf. Even before the big guy went down, a silver-haired woman in black slashed the smaller man's throat, then took out another attacker with a neat thrust.

Another crewman in blue went down, and a pole—no, a staff—rolled across the deck toward my feet. I grabbed the staff. It wasn't that much different from the pugil stick I'd used when I'd been an instructor in SEE except it wasn't padded at the ends. They were ironbound.

The odors/feelings of blood and death shook me like I'd been slammed into a steel bulkhead. I looked out. I was still somewhere on an ocean, but the water looked grayer than the Pacific, and the air was colder. The sky was different—a really different greenish blue. I'd never seen anything like it, not even before a tornado and not in bright sunlight. I glanced down. The deck was wood. I could smell something burning. Coal? Then I could see that the ship had funny stacks, sort of belled like the old stove in Papaw's house in Hebron. But the people were wearing stuff I'd never seen, and there was another ship, lower, and sleeker, with raked sails, grappled to the railing of the higher-decked vessel where I stood on the aft quarter. Someone yelled, and I jumped. Then more of the men in the ragged and dirty red and yellow were climbing over the rail. Two of them looked at me the way Mamaw might have looked at a plump chicken.

One of the raiders came charging toward me with his sword—a wide-bladed scimitar of some kind. I spread my feet and brought up the staff from below. No one ever thinks that way. He didn't, either—not until the iron-tipped end cracked into his arm just below the elbow, and his blade went flying. The woman in black ran him through with one thrust.

By then I was facing a big guy, wider than me, anyway, with a long-handled ax that looked like it could cut right through my staff. I feinted toward his head. When he ducked and dodged, I brought the staff back into the knee that held most of his weight. It cracked. Most men would have toppled. He just staggered. It was enough for me to thwack him topside. He went down then—hard.

More of the raiders were swarming up the side of the ship. Seemed to me that it was better to get them when they had at least one hand occupied, and I ran to the railing, using the staff as a lance on the first one who started to scramble onto the deck. He went flailing and bounced off the hull and into the water.

I managed to take out three more, one way or another, but that wasn't much help, because there were five of them.

Something slammed into my shoulder. I yelled. A metal bolt stuck out. But another one of the honkies in red and yellow was swinging his scimitars at me. Even with one arm barely working, I used the other one and my body weight to swing the staff across. It connected with his temple, and he went down like one of Papaw's flour sacks tipped off the wagon.

Then something else hit me.

II

When I tried to wake up, I could hear a woman speaking to me. I tried to listen. I thought I should understand what she was saying, but the words didn't make much sense . . . and then they faded away. So did I.

When I woke again, someone was jabbing red-hot needles through my shoulder, and someone else was beating on my skull with a shovel. I was in a narrow bed, lying on something like a rough sheet, and a woolen blanket covered my legs. The bed was spare and wooden. The walls of the small room were dark stone, and the windows did have glass. The only light came from a brass lamp hung on the wall, like the kerosene lamp Mamaw had kept when she'd moved from Hebron after Papaw's death to be closer to Ma.

A gray-haired woman in a green shirt, except it was more like the tunics in bad historical movies, held a mug of something to my lips. I swallowed. It was piss-poor beer, not so bad as Narragansett, but almost that bad. I drank it all anyway.

Behind her was the silver-haired woman in black. She said more of the words I didn't understand, while the older woman fed me some broth that made the beer taste good. Before long my eyes closed.

That was the way things were for days and probably longer, except I didn't see the silver-haired woman again, only the older woman, and I kept wondering where I was, and what had happened. Had I somehow lost my mind?

III

The first time I could finally stay alert—and remember what had happened—I was sitting on the side of a pallet bed in a locked room with barred windows. The two small windows had glass, but it was filthy and outside the bars. My head still ached with a dull throbbing, and the continuous sharp needles in my shoulder had been replaced by occasional stabs from an invisible knife. The sleeve of my denim work shirt had been cut away, and the shoulder was so heavily bound that I could barely move my lower arm. How had I gotten from fighting a flight-deck fire to a shipboard fight on an antique steamship with staffs and swords? Had I deserted and gone out of my mind? Or just gone out of my mind?

The ironbound door opened. A guard in dirty and faded red set a platter and a mug on the floor, then quickly closed the door. The food was different, but not any better than Navy fare, just several slices of cold lamb—mutton, really—a wedge of cheese close to rancid, a chunk of stale bread, a bruised golden red fruit, and a mug of the bitter beer. I was hungry enough that I ate it all.

Later, two guards escorted a woman into my cell. She wore faded black. Her hands were chained together, and the chains were heavy dark iron. Her skin was tanned, like she'd spent a lot of time in the sun, and she was white.

I'd have said she was around thirty, but her hair was silver, even her eyebrows and the fine hair on the exposed part of her forearms. The silver looked natural—and brilliant. But there were bruises on her face and arms, and probably elsewhere. She was the one who had fought so fiercely on the deck of the ship. I couldn't help admiring her bearing and her spirit, even though we were both captives.

With her was a man dressed entirely in shimmering white. I had a hard time looking at him for long. He spoke to the woman. His words were not gentle.

She said something to me.

I shook my head.

She kept talking. Her words meant nothing, whatever language she was using. I knew Black English and American English and what I learned in three years of lousy high-school French. As she kept speaking and gesturing to the man in white, and he answered, in a tone of irritation, I had a pretty good idea they weren't speaking French, not even close.

Even though he was smiling politely, anger boiled inside him. Or something did. I could almost see it. Finally, after another exchange, he raised his hand and pointed to the wall. A tiny fireball flew and smashed against the stone. There was an acrid smell, like burning paint.

He said something else, in the tone of a threat, and he and the guards left.

She pointed to herself. "Kytrona." Then she pointed to me and raised her eyebrows. Her eyes were a muddy green.

"Cassius Barca Samuels."

That got me a frown.

"Cassius," I said.

That was how my lessons began.

Between the times spent with Kytrona in that locked room learning Low Temple, I had a lot of time to think about how I'd ended up in a different world. Or was I paralyzed, lying somewhere like Tripler, just imagining what had seemed so real? Either way, I hadn't thought things would turn out like that. I thought I'd been smart when I'd enlisted in the Navy. As the recruiter had said—clean sheets and no foxholes and no patrols with Charlie shooting at you. He'd said VC. I learned about Charlie later, on the *Sullivans*, before I got transferred to the Big E and discovered the brown-shoe Navy.

Pilots came in all shapes and attitudes, but most, especially Navy pilots, came in one flavor. That was vanilla. But, back then, black petty officers were almost as rare as black officers, sometimes rarer. My ma had just been glad I hadn't volunteered for the Marines. She didn't even mind that I'd struck for quartermaster . . . and made it all the way to second class. Chief Mangrum had told me I was crazy, that with my test scores and brains I'd already have been first class and eligible for chief if I'd gone ET. I didn't want to be a tech, especially an electronic tech. The way technology was going in the Navy, the ETs really didn't do that much tech stuff. They just figured out which black box didn't work and replaced it, and some civilian in California was the one who actually repaired the box—unless they junked it.

Chief Mangrum said that I was just copping out, that I was taking the easy way, that I just didn't want to work hard. I hated being told that. I just didn't want to be a black-boxer, but it still bothered me.

Anyway, that was how I ended up on the flight deck of the *Enterprise* that January morning. We were doing the final ORI in the Hawaiian Islands before heading to SEASIA. Some of the crew called it "Nam." That didn't seem right to me, stuck in my mind like "boy" and "nigger." For all that, I couldn't say why I always said "Vietnam" rather than "Nam."

I didn't see exactly what happened, except that it looked like a rocket somehow fired itself across the deck where it exploded into one of the F-8s—at least I'd thought it was an F-8, but with flames flaring everywhere, and with that part of the flight deck an instant inferno, I wasn't sure. I was headed for the nearest hose.

There were three of us there, and I took the nozzle. The biggest danger was wing-mounted ordinance on attack birds being cooked off, and stopping that meant putting water on any bird with weapons on its wing racks. Couldn't help thinking about what had happened on the *Forrestal*. We *had* to keep things from getting out of hand.

I'd turned the nozzle on an A-6 that was already so hot that the first blast from the nozzle turned to steam. Then there was another explosion and . . . *something* shoved me into the darkness.

IV

Over the days that followed, I kept wondering about the fire on the flight deck, and what had happened . . . and Kytrona persevered, and I did began to learn Low Temple. I also learned that she was from a place called Recluse, and that the ship I'd landed on had also been from there, bound for someplace called Ruzor when pirates had attacked her. The head of the pirates was Gaylmassen, and he held us both as captives. Because I wore blue, he was convinced that I belonged to Recluce. His keep was called something like Paraguna, and it was in Worrak. I didn't know where any of the places were, but I'd won the grade school geography bee once, and I knew they couldn't have been on earth.

I also knew there was no way I could be on another world . . . but with every day of cold meat and cheese and beer, and an occasional fruit that I'd never seen or tasted, I was getting the idea that I was either a total head case or imprisoned on another world. The other world idea was more acceptable, but barely so, because I didn't know any way that people could throw firebolts when the technology they seemed to have was on the level of steam engines and swords. Also, I'd never *tasted* or smelled anything in a dream, and I certainly was doing both. And the burned spot on the stone was definitely there.

One thing that wasn't obvious at first was that I was bigger than most of the guards, and not just a little but almost a foot. At times, it almost made me laugh, because at six-four I'd been too short to play center and too slow to be a guard, and I'd gotten my ass waxed in the pickup games—until Da and Ma had put a stop to them.

Kytrona kept talking about order. It had taken her most of an afternoon to get that idea across—along with the fact that the firebolt was chaos. She lined up little pieces of wood; she folded rags into patterns. She drew repeating designs in the dust. When I finally understood, then she kept repeating the word for "order," then pointed to her black tunic, and to my skin.

That bothered me, because it meant that, once again, I was being seen as something because of the color of my skin. I suppose it helped a little that a silver-haired woman was also seen the same way, but it was clear that I was on the other side from my captors—just because of the color of my skin. They'd attacked me on the merchanter for the same reason. From what little I'd seen, I was sure I didn't want to be on the pirate side, but their view of me was another form of discrimination based on my skin color.

I learned more words from Kytrona, but I was still having trouble with the idea that she and I were somehow linked to "order" and the raiders were linked to chaos. They seemed anything but chaotic.

Just before she was escorted off at the end of one day, she looked at me. I could sense her anger and frustration with me. "Look at the guards. Look at them closely when they come for me. Then look at you and me." She pointed to a small and recent scar on her forearm. "You have one, too."

I looked. I did have one, and it also was recent, but I had no idea how I'd gotten it, and what she had meant by pointing it out.

I couldn't do much about the scar, but I did study the guards when they came for her.

There was a white mist or shadow around them, and when they brought Kytrona the next day for my endless language lessons, they still had the white mist. There was also a faint black darkness that shadowed her, but there were patches of reddish white at points on her body, and she winced when she sat on the stool. I felt twinges in the same places. How could that be, and how could people have colored shadows? Especially when there wasn't any direct sunlight in the cell?

Then I stopped. Ma had talked about people showing their colors, and how she could sometimes see them. I'd thought those were just words, but I hadn't wanted to argue with her. No one argued with Ma.

After a moment, I realized that the reddish-white meant bruises where Kytrona had been hurt. She'd never said anything, either. I got off the bed and pointed. "You . . . sit . . . there."

She didn't protest, and I took the stool.

"The guards . . . a whiteness . . . You . . . are . . . black shade . . ."

"White is the color of chaos. Black is the color of order. Recluce is the home of order."

When she'd first talked about order, I'd thought she was saying that the good guys wore black and black hats, and the bad ones wore white. That wasn't like anyplace I knew. Charlie wore blue or black, or so the Marines on the *Enterprise* had said. But it was certainly possible. Now . . . now . . . I was seeing people in those terms. Was I really in this other world? Or just hallucinating in sick bay somewhere?

"You can see order and chaos. You are a mage."

"I am not a mage." I had to protest.

"You are. You can sense what others feel, can you not?"

"Times . . ." I didn't know the words.

"At times . . . or . . . sometimes," Kytrona supplied.

"At times," I said.

She kept her voice low. "Before long, Gaylmassen will summon you. Do

not let him know how well you speak. Because of your size, no one will believe you are a mage."

More frigging bias. If you're big, you can't be anything but dumb. I
pushed away the anger. "What about you?"

"I can sense what to do with a blade, nothing more. That is why I was a
ship's champion. That is also why Guillum linked us. He thinks it will help
you learn to speak. Before long he will sense that you are a mage. That will
not be good."

"Linked?"

She lifted her hands and rattled the chains. "These are chains. You and I
are chained together. The chains will grow stronger if we both live. If we
live long enough, what kills one of us will kill the other."

There weren't any chains linking us. She wore the chains.

"I see . . . no chains."

She pulled back her sleeve and pointed to the scar on her forearm.
"Look."

Was there a faint black line running from there? Where?

My eyes—except I was feeling as much as seeing—followed the line . . .
to my good arm and the scar there.

"You see?"

I saw, in spite of myself.

"You must learn more about how to handle order."

How was I supposed to handle something like a shadow? I could buy the
business of sensing feelings. Mamaw had been able to do that, but what
could I do with a shadow . . . even if I learned how?

V

The very next day, the guards put me in chains and escorted me to see Gaylmassen. I expected to be dragged into a throne room like the ones in the
movies. That didn't happen. I was marched into a wood-paneled office or library. There were shelves of books on one wall, and a thick plush carpet laid
over the stone floor. The windows were small, and the library was dark.

Gaylmassen stood beside a desk. The workmanship was good, but every
flat surface was covered with carvings, like a Chinese cabinet I once saw.
That desk was the ugliest piece of furniture I'd ever seen. Gaylmassen only

came to my shoulder, but he wore a sword at his waist, and it wasn't decorated. His hair was brown and short. He wore a yellow silk shirt with a vest and funny trousers.

"You admire the desk. You have some taste."

I didn't think saying anything would be wise. I just bowed a bit. I hated bowing to anyone, but there were four guards, and my hands were chained behind my back.

I didn't bow deeply enough, and one of the guards clouted me on my good shoulder with something—the flat of his sabre, I thought. Two others forced me down to my knees. Even through the thick carpet, the stone was hard on my knees.

Gaylmassen smiled and spoke. "A truly black man—that I had never thought to see. You were an expensive captive. My men tell me that you and the black bitch almost saved the merchanter by yourselves. Once you can speak well enough to be understood . . . then there will be a special place for you both in my personal guard. You would like that far better than the alternative. I could sell you as a matched pair to certain Hamorian traders." He smiled again.

I'd seen that expression before. More than once, but the one I remembered best had been on the face of Sheriff Shanklin back in Hebron, when he'd told Papaw that Papaw just had to be a good "boy" and leave things to those who knew better. I trusted Gaylmassen less than Papaw had trusted Sheriff Shanklin, but I followed Papaw's example. I just inclined my head more deeply than before, and said, "Yes, sir."

"Ser, or Lord," he corrected me.

"Yes, ser." I'd had to bow twice, been forced to my knees, and say "ser" twice, and someone would pay for all that.

"Do you know who I am?" He spoke slowly and carefully, as if I were an idiot child.

Remembering Kytrona's advice, I replied haltingly, "You . . . Lord Gaylmassen."

"Who are you?"

"Cassius . . . ser." I almost didn't add the title, but there wasn't much point in getting clouted again.

"Cassius . . . terrible name for a guard. We'll have to think of something better. He needs to learn to speak better." He nodded to the guards. "Take him away."

VI

When Kytrona was shoved into my cell the next day, her lip was swollen, and her face was bruised. Her wrists were bloody under the manacles. From the reddish white aura patches radiating from parts of her body, I could tell she'd been abused far more than was obvious.

I'd followed her advice, and I was afraid she'd paid for it.

I didn't know how to tell her I was sorry. So I knelt and kissed her hand.

Her jaw tightened. I could sense that was because she refused to show any emotion.

"You are kind, but you must learn to be a mage . . . or you and I will be without thought, or dead. Or worse than dead."

I think that was what she said. I could understand more than I could say. She was right, but how would I ever learn something like that when I had no idea what a mage was?

"Tell me . . . about order . . . what mages do . . ." I managed.

"All things are part order and part chaos . . ." She began.

My understanding wasn't much better than my handling of Low Temple. What was clear was that magic—or magery—worked. The chaos types like Guillum could throw firebolts. I'd seen that. The order types could strengthen things and make them work better.

I listened and tried to learn both words and about magery, and I worried when the guards dragged Kytrona off late in the day. Even if I could figure out how to do what Kytrona said I could do, how would that help? I was still behind stone walls and iron bars. The stone had certainly stopped Guillum's firebolt, and he was an accomplished mage.

Somewhere in the middle of the night, I sat up on the hard pallet. Strengthening and ordering things implied the ability to shift stuff. Could I strengthen things in the middle of the door in a way that weakened the wood where the hinges and the iron straps were attached? No matter how tough the iron was, if the wood got soft the way it was when termites got it, it would tear away from the hinges and locks.

That was a great idea. I didn't have any idea how to do it, though.

I lay awake for a long time, without any ideas.

I didn't sleep well, and I woke early—still without ideas.

In the gray light before dawn, I looked at the ragged sleeve of my shirt. Parts of it were so worn that it was practically falling apart. Too bad I couldn't strengthen it, with whatever this order was that tied things together. A thought occurred to me. In my world, molecules and atoms were held together by unseen forces, valences and stuff. Did order work the same way?

I ripped off a corner of the sleeve. That wasn't easy, not one-handed, because I couldn't lift my left hand high enough to reach the torn part. The old lady had changed the dressings on my shoulder several times, and the wound had scabbed over. It itched, but it didn't hurt too much.

Then I held the cloth in my good hand and tried to look at it in the same way that I'd looked at Kytrona and the guards. I stared and looked and squinted. Nothing. I kept at it, trying to think of tiny pieces of cloth, sort of like atoms. Then I thought of them like needles. I tried with my eyes open, and my eyes closed. After a while, I tried picturing them as linked puzzle pieces.

At that point, I felt so light-headed I had to put my head down. When I lifted it, sparkles flashed across my eyes. But I thought I saw shades of white mist where I'd just torn the cloth, and blackness more in the center. I tried to move the black away from the middle and strengthen the sides of the scrap of cloth. The sides seemed to get darker, and the middle had a whitish shadow—that was what I sensed. But was I just seeing what I wanted to see?

I didn't say anything to Kytrona about what I was doing after she was thrust into the cell that morning. I just tucked the scrap of cloth inside my shirt. I was relieved not to see any new bruises. I did ask her to tell me anything she had heard about order and mages.

"There are many different kinds of ordermages . . . the first was Creslin . . ."

As she spoke, she had to explain even more words, but somehow it had become easier for me to remember them. Although I seemed to understand each sentence, trying to make sense of the world she was describing was something else.

Near the end of the afternoon, she murmured, "We do not have much time, Cassius. A few more days at most. Then Guillum will use his chaos powers to destroy your ability to think for yourself."

"What about you?"

"They will do the same to me, because the link between us might allow you to regain your memories and thoughts. I am only useful as a tool to teach you—and because they wish to humiliate me . . . and Recluce." Her words were matter-of-fact, and she was telling the truth.

After she left, I took out the scrap of cloth and tugged on both sides. It practically fell into two pieces.

I just looked at it.

That night I tried to work on the door, using the same approach.

I got so faint that I passed out on the stone floor and woke in the darkness. It didn't seem as dark as it had before, but I didn't see any more lamps or a moon shining through the bars of the window.

I barely managed to get back to the pallet bed before I dropped off again.

I didn't sleep long, because a silvery light flooded the cell, and Chief Mangrum appeared. His face was blistered and black on one side, and I could see his jawbone where the flesh had fallen away there. His working khakis were half–burned off, and the odor of smoke and burning fuel filled the cell. *Where were you? Did you cop out again? Look for the easy way out?*

I didn't have an answer.

His eyes burned as he looked at me. *Cop-out, that's all you'll ever be.*

He had to be an illusion, but the words burned into me.

Mangrum's image *twisted* into something else—a silver-haired woman garbed in silver. She stood beside the base of a massive tree that impossibly rose out of the cell and into the shadows of a forest mightier than any rain forest.

Order and chaos are twisted within you, for you come from order through chaos. You must face your fears and choose.

I didn't want anyone insisting I choose something when I didn't know what I was choosing.

You know enough to choose.

"Choose what?"

That is what you must decide.

Her image vanished, and that of Mangrum reappeared. Flames surrounded him, and the heat and the odor of burning jet fuel was everywhere. *You left us. Deserter!* His khakis were in flames, and the heat and odor of fire rose until the cell was like an oven. Or even hotter. A flaming glob of oil flew past me and hit the wall by the window, where it continued to burn. *Deserter! Cop-out!*

"I had no choice."

You could have been an ET . . . you should have been on that deck . . .

I should have been, but that had not been my choice or my doing.

Mangrum's finger jabbed toward me, and I held up my good hand instinctively.

Hsstt! His finger burned my palm, and I stepped back.

Coward! Deserter!

I forced myself to step forward. His hands grasped my wrists, and for an instant, pain and fire ringed both wrists.

Then he vanished, only to be replaced by Sheriff Shanklin, as much taller than I was as he had been when I'd been a child. *Boy . . . you aren't going to be making trouble, now, are you? You wouldn't be wanting trouble for your family, would you?* His smirking smile was overpowering, and he held the ivory-handled revolver he'd always claimed had been given to him by General Patton.

Before I could move, the revolver barrel had clipped my forehead.

You're not worth a bullet, boy. No, you're not. The smirk was even more open.

What was the right answer, the right choice? I stepped forward. "Force doesn't change what's right, Sheriff. Threats don't make something right."

This time, my hand was moving before the revolver barrel was, and I caught it. I didn't stop it. Instead, the barrel kept swinging and threw me into the wall beside the window. I hit hard enough that I didn't feel anything for a moment. I did think that dreams didn't hurt the way I'd been hurt. Not any dream I'd ever had.

It is not a dream. The woman in silver appeared, still standing beside the tree. *This world is as real as yours. You have faced some of your fears. Now, you must find the will and the way for both of you to escape. Or you will die here as certainly as the man in the fire died in the world from which you came.*

With that, she vanished.

Most of my back ached. The pain had returned to my wounded shoulder. My wrists were blistered, and so was the spot in the center of my palm. The cell reeked of fire, smoke, and burning fuel oil.

VII

I had to sleep on my side, and only on one side. I didn't sleep well, and I was up early, as soon as the first light seeped through the barred windows. Then, I just sat on the edge of the bed, trying not to think about how many places on my body hurt.

Right after the guards half pushed, half flung Kytrona into the cell, she stiffened and looked around. Then she wrinkled her nose. "It smells like a fire in here. A strange fire."

"Burning fuel oil."

She looked at me questioningly. "Your face is red, and your hair is singed. There are gashes on your forehead."

I shrugged. "Long night." How could I possibly explain?

"All nights are long." Her eyes were almost accusatory. "The guards—"

"No. Not the guards." I pointed to the wall where the glob of burning fuel oil had seared the stone. She walked over and looked at it. Then she looked at me once more. I could feel her worry and puzzlement. "It was fire, but you are not of chaos."

"Last night . . . there was . . . a man who was . . . above me . . . he was . . . on fire . . . and then a woman in silver . . . with silver hair . . ."

"An angel of the Ancients—she came to you . . . here?"

"She said . . . I had to choose," I admitted.

"She came here?" Kytrona asked again. "You had to face the fire of chaos?"

That was one way of putting it. "There was fire."

She nodded slowly, then sat on the stool and began to talk. "They say that all the great mages must face a trial, and they must confront their greatest fears. They are never the same after that, although they do not look any different, except in their eyes." She paused. "I have never looked into your eyes." She said that almost like a confession before she turned to me.

Abruptly, she looked away.

"I'm . . . sorry," I said. I just hoped it was the right word.

"You have no need to apologize."

"You looked away."

She gave me the faintest smile, then shook her head. "It is not you. It is me." But she would not say more.

At that moment, I could sense the faint black tie or link between us. It was stronger, or at least clearer. Was that because I could sense it better, or because we were more linked?

"You need more words," Kytrona said, but she pointed to the door.

After that, we worked on words, and I kept trying to reorder the oak.

That night, I knew I had to do something more, and I struggled with the wood of the heavy oak door, trying to move the strength of the door away from the hinges and lock and into the center.

I kept at it until I almost passed out, and I didn't wake until it was full light.

When I got up, I examined the inside of the heavy door. Had I really accomplished anything? I thought I could detect a whiteness around the iron straps and hinges. I pressed my fingers there. The wood did give some, but not enough to tear away from the iron. I couldn't help but smile for a brief moment.

Before long, Kytrona was shoved into my cell. She had not been abused more, but she looked exhausted.

"Are you . . . good?"

"I'm fine." She offered a tired smile. "We need to work on more words." Her eyes flicked toward the door.

I realized that I could sense two figures outside the cell. I held up two fingers and nodded toward the door.

Her mouth opened. Then she shut it. For perhaps the first time, I saw hope in her eyes. She swallowed, then began to speak. "This is a door." She pointed to the iron. "These are made of iron . . ."

Not until the listeners left did I say anything but repeat her words.

"I . . . make the door strong here . . . less strong here . . ." When she didn't seem to understand what I was saying, I took her hand and pressed her fingers against the rock-hard center of the door, then guided them to the softer wood around the iron. I didn't want to let go of her hand, but I did.

"It needs more work," she said, stepping away from me and the door.

I nodded. "But . . ." How could I explain that if I made it weak enough, and if the guard stood right outside we could push it over on him? "We push it . . ." I acted out what we could do.

She tilted her head to one side, as if thinking, then nodded. "That would work."

I kept working on the door while she talked, and I repeated words. That went on for another two days. When the guards pushed Kytrona into the cell three mornings later, I actually held the door to support it. I'd done my best to leave the area around the lock and outside hasp stronger.

While she talked, and I tried to repeat her words, I concentrated on moving the black order from around the lock. I had to stop several times, because I got light-headed, and it was into the afternoon when I began to sense that the door was sagging on both its lock plate and hinges.

"Now . . ." I pointed to the door.

"We need to get the guard here," she said. "Can you tell when he's close to the door?"

I nodded.

"Let me know when he's near."

How long that took, I didn't know, but it seemed like forever before I could sense the guard, and said, "He's close."

Abruptly, Kytrona began to moan, loudly, even while she stood on the lock side of the door. I stood by the hinges, waiting as the guard moved toward the door.

When he was as close as he could get, peeping through the small hole in the center of the door, I said, "Now."

We pushed, and the heavy door ripped away from the hinges and lock. The guard scrambled back. I thought the door would bring him down, but the wood around the bottom hinge hung on and swung away from him. That didn't stop Kytrona.

The guard stared. He was frozen for a moment, and in that moment, she leaped on him, kneed him in the groin, then slammed the iron cuffs upward into his chin so hard that his head snapped back, and he went down on the stone with a dull thud. Before I could scramble around the section of the door that hung on the lower hinge, she'd taken his belt knife and slit his throat.

With what I knew she'd been through, I didn't blame her.

She rose and slipped the knife into the empty sheath at her belt. Then she unfastened the guard's scabbard and fastened it to her belt—with the sabre in it.

"Now what?" I asked.

"We wait."

"Wait?"

"The head guard will come." She raised her chained hands. "He has keys."

Outside of a U.S. Navy bolt cutter that didn't exist in Worrak, or a blacksmith, I didn't see any other way of getting the chains off her.

"This way." Kytrona led the way to the bottom of the stone steps, holding the sabre in her right hand, her left hand all too close to it because of the chains. There, we waited, each of us concealed on opposite sides of the stone arch.

We waited until the light began to fail before we heard boots on the stone. The only problem was that the head guard didn't come down the steps alone. He came down first, but behind and above him several steps was another man. The second man radiated white—Guillum.

I didn't know what to say, and anything I said to Kytrona would alert the white mage.

The head guard had just reached the bottom of the steps and stepped through the archway when Guillum yelled, "Look out!"

The head guard turned, and Kytrona's sabre went into his side. He staggered toward me.

Whhssst! A firebolt whizzed past my face, then another . . . and another, as the mage ran down the steps and toward the arch.

I grabbed the wounded guard. When I sensed that Guillum was about to throw another of the firebolts, I shoved the guard at the mage and flattened myself behind the back side of the archway.

The sound of the firebolt and the scream of the guard as the fire struck him merged. The sound was appalling and—thankfully—brief.

Somehow, Kytrona had followed the guard's body and used the sabre on the mage. Whiteness and fire flared around the blade, and I could smell burned hair.

Two bodies lay on the stone. One was blackened. The other was not a young man, but of a wizened old man. He didn't look at all the way he had moments before.

I just looked.

"Chaos ages one." Kytrona pulled a key ring off the dead guard's belt and fumbled with the key.

One key stood out. I pointed, then helped her unlock the cuffs. Her wrists were scabbed and bloody. I couldn't help but squeeze her forearm gently, wishing I could heal all she had been through.

"You are . . ." She shook her head.

"What next?"

"This way. We find a way to escape from the keep and get to the harbor. We steal a fishing boat and head west. If we are fortunate, someone picks us up. If not, we sail to Ruzor. Or we do not."

The first two possibilities were probably okay. The third wasn't, and it was the most likely, but staying in Gaylmassen's pile of stone would be even worse. "What about the screams?"

"There are always screams from down here." She started up the stairs. The sabre was back in the scabbard.

Gaylmassen's keep wasn't really a castle but more like a fortified house. It would have been dramatic to say that we had to fight our way out. We didn't.

We sneaked out through the kitchen bailey. Along the way, several attendants scattered away from us. Gaylmassen was nowhere near, but that was fine with me. I didn't need to confront him in order to prove I wasn't taking the easy way out. There is a difference between necessary courage and stupid bravado. Papaw had known that, and now I understood.

In the darkness, it was even easier to steal a boat, but I had to row us clear of the harbor, and that took much of the night. Once we were outside the breakwater, there was a breeze, and Kytrona knew enough to set the single sail. I didn't even try to explain that I knew nothing about sailing.

VIII

The next morning we were almost a mile offshore, and Worrak lay out of sight to the east of us. The sun beat down like a furnace all that day, and we managed to use a scrap of sail as an awning of sorts, probably the same way the boat owner had.

Kytrona finally looked to me. "I did not think we would ever escape. Thank you."

I could feel gratitude and something more. I hoped it was more, but I could not act on such a feeling, not until she and I were free, and she could choose without conditions.

Her mouth dropped open. "You are honorable, like an angel."

"No," I said. "We wouldn't have escaped without you."

She frowned, as if she didn't believe me.

"If you had not explained about order, I would not have learned enough . . ."

"I wouldn't be alive if it weren't for you," she went on. "I still don't know much about you or where you come from. Tell me. We have time, now."

"From earth . . ."

"From the ground?"

"Another . . . place . . . we were fighting a fire in the *Enterprise* . . . one of the attack birds dropped a rocket, and it armed . . ." For a lot of the words, I had to use English, but she listened. I didn't know how much she understood.

"What is this *Enterprise*?"

I tried to explain a bird-farm.

"You come from where the ancient angels came?"

I was definitely no ancient, ancient or modern, or whenever or wherever Recluce might be. "No."

"But the *Book of Ryba* speaks of iron ships that flew between the stars."

Between the stars? That was even scarier. *When* was I?

"You have to be like an angel. You still grope for words, but you speak without an accent, and everyone not born in Recluce has an accent."

I tried to get across that I was no angel and that CVA-65 had not flown between stars. I could feel that Kytrona was still impressed by the "iron birds"—that was the best I could do with what I knew of Low Temple.

Two days passed, and we talked and sailed some distance west of Worrak, which was the only direction we could go, because that was the direction the wind blew us. While we had taken some water bottles, they were long empty, and Kytrona was trying to steer us back inshore, now that we were well away from Worrak. We'd seen several ships in the distance, but none close enough to hail.

"We can't get picked up if we're too close to shore, but we need water," Kytrona said.

My lips were cracked, but not so badly as hers. I just nodded.

"It's too bad you can't call a storm the way the weather mages can." She smiled. It was more like a grimace.

I had to wonder if such mages existed. If I could weaken a heavy solid oak door, then I supposed they could call a storm, but I had no idea how, and neither did Kytrona.

Then she pointed. A ship was headed eastward in our general direction. She swung the sail, and we turned seaward. For a time, nothing seemed to happen. Then, all of a sudden, the ship was bearing down on us. She was a wooden-hulled steamer, but the engines were clearly shut down. Her three masts were filled with sails.

Kytrona stood. I sat.

"She's bearing the Ryall. It's a Recluce merchanter!"

For some reason, I had very mixed feelings about the approaching ship.

Before long, a seaman threw us a line, but the ship barely slowed. Kytrona tied the line to an iron ring attached to the stem post. Then the crew reeled us in until we were alongside. They even lowered a ladder. Kytrona climbed up first. That was a good idea, since I wouldn't be able to explain much of anything.

Once we were on deck, a slender but tall man wearing the same black clothes as Kytrona did moved toward us. He smiled broadly. "Kytrona! We feared everyone on the *Black Holding* was lost." Then he stepped forward and threw his arms around her.

I tried not to wince. She hadn't promised me anything, and I was a stranger from nowhere, so far as she was concerned.

"Alaren . . ." Kytrona stepped back, out of his arms, and gestured to me. "This is Cassius. He's an outland black mage, and he's the one who saved me from Gaylmassen. He showed up on board the *Black Holding*."

I bowed politely. "It is good to meet you."

"It's good to meet the man who saved Kytrona." Alaren eyed me with open curiosity, although he had to look up some, then glanced to Kytrona, questioningly.

"The Ancient of angels has tried him and found him worthy. He will be a great mage." She smiled warmly—at me. "Even if She had not tested him, he would still be my intended."

Alaren stepped back.

I swallowed. I had never asked her, although I had dreamed.

"How could I not love a man who saved my life three times and only asked for my respect?"

That was true enough, but how had she known?

Later, after we had cleaned up and had fresh clothes, we stood by the railing.

She took my hands. "I promised myself to you the day you knelt and kissed my hand. I could see the love and the concern. Then, before long, I could feel it." She looked down. "I had to work so hard not to let you know. Not until we were free."

That I understood.

My fingers touched the edge of her jaw, and she lifted her head. I looked into her eyes, realizing that they were not muddy green but golden green.

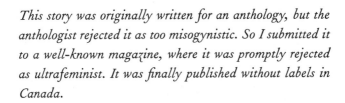

This story was originally written for an anthology, but the anthologist rejected it as too misogynistic. So I submitted it to a well-known magazine, where it was promptly rejected as ultrafeminist. It was finally published without labels in Canada.

UNDERSTANDING

"I don't understand." I was standing in the space that separated the breakfast bar from the rest of the kitchen. "You liked getting laid as much as I do."

"Randy . . ." Cyane shook her head, looking from her stool across the remnants of her omelet. I do make a good omelet. "You harbor the notion that you are irresistible to women. And . . . you could be considered good-looking and intelligent." She shrugged. "That's not enough. You're also a pig."

"Not even a hog?" I thought a laugh might help, but she didn't even smile. "Anyway, what are you talking about? First Jennifer, then Renni, and now you." Not much time before I had to leave. It takes me twenty-four minutes to run to the health club across from my office at Environment. Then I do a quick routine with the Nautilus. Keeps the shoulders broad and the stomach trim. Women like men with flat guts.

"You refuse to understand the truth." That accented voice still sent shivers down my spine.

"All of you act as though men are some sort of monsters."

Cyane just smiled that enigmatic smile and took another sip of water. She never drank anything but water, and she was a strict vegetarian, but, what the hell, the way Cyane had made me feel, she could eat or drink whatever she wanted. Until she told me she was leaving.

"You're so damned superior. Sometimes, you make me want to puke. 'Don't you think you ought to drop your mother a card?' So I do, and it turns out that it arrives on their anniversary, and she calls thanking me for being so thoughtful and understanding." I took a deep breath. "Or your suggestion about the lines in the speech for the Secretary. 'Brilliant idea, Randy.' Or the business about the marsh grass being the wrong species. Or the suggestion for using Russian olives on the Secretary's project. So you gave me some lucky ideas—big deal."

"You weren't complaining when you got the promotion and the praise," my nymph, or former nymph, observed, brushing a strand of that black hair back over her ear.

"Where the hell did this business of leaving come from?"

She shrugged. "I've told you a dozen different ways. You still don't hear. You smile that practiced and charming smile and think everyone will forgive you . . ."

I admit I have a good smile. Both Jennifer and Renni liked it.

"Some . . . men I've known have been worse. But . . ." She paused before continuing. ". . . you are one of the most . . ." She took another sip of that Grecian springwater.

"For Christ's sake! I've heard the same crap from all three of you. 'You don't understand.' Understand what?"

Again, I got the damning smile for just an instant, as if she were toying with me.

"You're afraid of understanding yourself or women."

"Afraid?" I was angry by then. Afraid? After zapping that mugger the month before? I felt like I'd been set up. By three women right in a row. They start out really good in bed, then they start talking understanding. Cyane was just the straw that broke this camel's back.

The days of the lifelong marriages—like my parents'—are gone. And anyone can make a mistake when they get married at twenty-one. I certainly did. Jennifer was just too willful and independent. I still spend a lot of time with the two girls.

After Jennifer left, I ran into Renni. She was interning with Congress-woman Hellenic, who had the office right across the hall from us. Then I was the Legislative Director for Matt Strauss—before he retired.

Within a year we were married. Same story, second verse, except it was quicker. Almost three years to the day, she walked out. By then I was the Committee Counsel for the Energy Committee. Renni said that it had been a mistake, that I'd never understand. Women and their damned understanding!

Cyane was different, and I should have known better when Renni intro-duced her to me. Renni had become a partner in Jane Helmam's law firm. It was a big deal at first, former Deputy Attorney General founds all-woman law firm. They have a couple of men there now, but they didn't to begin with.

The day I met Cyane, I'd stopped by to drop off some of Renni's papers. I could have mailed them, I suppose, but it was easier just to stop by. Besides, I had on the really good suit, and I wanted her to see what she was missing. She walked out with Cyane.

"Randy, this is Cyane. She's new here. I wanted you two to meet." She grinned at me. It was a funny kind of grin, one I didn't recognize. "She's from Greece, and I think she could teach you a lot about the things you love."

That had thrown me. Renni's last words when she left had been that the only thing I loved was to get laid. I had looked at the other woman and smiled my most charming smile. "Nice to meet you, Cyane."

"Enchanted." There was a definite accent in the husky voice, and she smiled a kind of smile I'd never seen before and inclined her head.

I had looked, and looked again. Hair so black it was almost blue, and eyes to match. Cream-colored skin, and a slightly pointed chin with a pixy nose above. Slim-waisted but with the extravagant curves I've always enjoyed seeing and—in the case of both Jennifer and Renni—touching. Then I smiled. She'd be worth something in bed. "No . . . I'm the one who's enchanted."

"Randy is always very gallant." Renni's voice had been hard.

"One can tell," Cyane answered, with another of her enigmatic smiles.

Of course, once Renni had disappeared, I asked Cyane out.

"You would like that?" she asked.

I would. So I said yes.

She was as good at what I liked as Renni had hinted, and within a week, she had moved in.

Cyane never said much about the law firm, although I found out that she was some sort of research assistant. She even did a little work for me. That was when I finally was confirmed as the head of External Affairs for the Department. Me—Randy Ozier—the Honorable Randall Jains Ozier, Assistant Secretary of the Department of Environment. First step toward becoming a Cabinet Secretary or working in the White House. There was always something about the White House that's fascinated me.

But Cyane was going. Just leaving. I was pissed, and then some. Where else would I find anyone that good in bed? And we made such a good couple at all the receptions. That's important, too, if you want to make it to the top of the political totem pole.

"Afraid?" I repeated.

"It's understandable." Her tone was condescending.

"If it's so damned understandable, kindly spell it out for poor dense Randall Ozier."

Cyane stood up. That was the funny thing. When she talked in that quiet, husky, and penetrating voice you forgot she wasn't even quite five feet tall. "It's quite simple, Randy. You don't want to understand." Her eyes flashed, and I could have sworn that they changed from black to a deep clear blue for a moment.

"Understand what? You're talking garbage. And after all I've done for you."

"You're an Assistant Secretary for the Environment. You still haven't learned that women are not things. Even the *very* ancient Greeks knew that."

She acted like she'd been there. With the ancient Greeks, I mean.

"Show me what they knew." I tried another smile, but my eyes focused on her body.

Her lips quirked, this time in what seemed genuine amusement. But she didn't say a word, standing there, barefoot, in a plain white dress so simple it would have been in style a thousand years past or future.

"So . . . show me," I demanded.

She shrugged, again with the damned smile. "You asked." She stepped up to me, and said something I didn't catch, almost in a foreign language.

"What did you say?"

"Oh . . . the closest would be something like: 'Let this be done.'" She tilted her head back and put her arms around my neck.

I needed no further urging, but as our lips joined the jolt that went through me was stronger than raw electric current. My knees almost buckled, and I steadied myself on the breakfast bar counter as Cyane stepped away.

"Good-bye, Randy. Just remember. You asked. You're not going to get what you want, you know. Not now."

"I'll get what I want, by God." Now she was really getting on my nerves.

"You might also remember what it would be like if someone the size of a Redskins tackle forced himself on you." Then she made a funny gesture with her left hand, and a great big spark flew from her fingertips to my forehead.

When the second jolt cleared, the kitchen was empty. I looked into the bedroom, and all her things were gone, but she hadn't carried anything with her—not that I saw.

I shook myself. I was going to be late to work. So I ran faster and made it in twenty-one minutes. I did cut short my workout. But the whole time, for some reason, I thought about the last fight Renni and I had, the one where she slugged me because I wanted her and wouldn't stop when she didn't. Of course, I'd pasted her back, and she had walked out the door. When I came home from work, all Renni's things were gone—just like Cyane's, I guess.

All through a very long morning, Cyane's words—and the three-hundred-pound lineman—recycled themselves through my brain. Recycling might be good for the environment, but the words weren't wonderful for my peace of mind. .

I ran home, right after all the bureaucrats left. I couldn't leave before they did. Running didn't help—not enough endorphins. Neither did reading—even the last couple of *Playboy*s.

I kept imagining that the White House had asked for my resignation, and that I was begging my mother for a room to stay in, because no one would hire me. Then I dozed off, except I woke up yelling because some three-hundred-pound lineman was trying to assault me. Finally, I got up and walked around and had a beer before going back to bed. I kept dreaming about being buggered by that three-hundred-pound tackle. I took three of the tranquilizers that I had left over from the time I wrenched my back. At least, I didn't dream any more that night.

The next morning, I was sitting behind the big desk on the tenth floor, looking out at the river, thinking about Cyane, and about women in general.

Women—they're an alien species. You're think that they're sexy and human, but they're not. They're monsters.

At that point, Mort walked in.

Mort always struck me as a pleasant-enough guy, quiet-voiced. This time, behind the polite face, I could tell he was upset. Yet he didn't look that different.

"What's the matter, Mort?" I tried to keep my voice friendly, even soft.

"Not a thing." The anger seemed to boil around him. "I've got the latest hearing request from Chairman Hancock."

I nodded, waiting.

"It's next week."

Mort had planned a family vacation, and I could see his problem. He'd spent years defining himself by his work with the Committee, and he'd promised Jeannette and their kids they'd go to Disney World. They'd planned the trip for months.

"That's tough," I finally said. "What do you want to do?"

"I hadn't thought about it." Now he was really angry. That I could tell, even though his voice hadn't risen in the slightest. He wanted me to make the choice for him.

"You've been planning the trip for too long. I'll handle the hearing for you."

His eyes turned hard. "This is an important hearing." Now he was angry, thinking I wanted to take over from him, that he might be pushed aside.

"Fine. Do what you think is best."

"Randy, what do you want me to do?" This time the anger was in his voice.

With all that fury directed at me, I was angry myself. No matter what I decided, Mort was going to be angry. "Do whatever you damned well please," I snapped back. "You're not going to guilt-trip me and use me as the excuse with Jeannette or Jeannette as the excuse for me."

"You are . . ." He didn't say the rest of the words, because I was still the boss, but they were hanging on the air as if he had. "*. . . one fucking bastard.*"

He did slam the door on the way out, but I scarcely noticed, because I was shaking all over at the fury I had felt Mort pouring out toward me. That worthless bastard!

Why hadn't I ever noticed how angry he was deep inside?

Buzzz . . .

"Yes?" I picked up the intercom.

"The Secretary's office just called. He's called a meeting for eleven."

A scheduling change in midday meant trouble. But, as usual, I was there exactly on time. So were Blaine Coswell and Elena Sanford. He was the Assistant Secretary for Solid Waste and Emergency Response, and she was the Assistant Secretary for Research and Development.

"Chairman Hancock's called a hearing on the Bitterney Superfund site. He called me this morning. He wants all the drums removed and all the contaminated soil incinerated, plus a slurry wall all around the site to the depth of bedrock. Period." That was how the Secretary opened the meeting. Nils stayed behind the big desk with the view of the Potomac. I hate people who hide behind their desks, even when they are the Secretary of the Environment.

The three of us sat in comfortable leather armchairs, lined up in a row.

"We could do that," admitted Blaine. His voice was tired, and I could sense frustration and anger behind the words. That and a blind cruel ambition that almost rocked me out of my seat. When he looked at the attractive scientist, his lust was enough to make me grit my teeth. He was such an animal he wouldn't even have appreciated her finer points. I looked sideways at Elena. Definitely a nice piece, for all the brains.

She caught my eyes and curled her lip, and I could feel a wave of total revulsion slide over me. I nearly gagged. Then I shook my head. Why was I sensing what everyone felt?

"You don't approve?" asked the Secretary.

"Uh . . . It's just a bad situation," I temporized. At least, I recover quickly.

"It's not the safest method," offered Elena. The redheaded scientist had a doctorate in some branch of geology I couldn't even pronounce. "That was why we proposed on-site bioremediation. We didn't want to create the possibility of greater contamination." The revulsion had subsided, and she conveyed a veiled contempt, a general disgust.

"What are the politics?" asked Secretary Lerison. It was as clear as the noonday sun that Nils would do whatever Chairman Hancock wanted. Nils wasn't looking for an answer, just a rationale, the spineless twerp.

"Well," I began, "the state attorney general has announced his campaign against Hancock, and he's the one who pushed the lawsuit forcing the Bitterney cleanup to begin with."

"So Hancock wants to close off the issue with an immediate cleanup, no matter what the cost?" Lerison radiated relief that there might be a way out.

I nodded. "It looks that way." Then I made my second mistake of the day, or I guess it was the third, but the stupid emotions from both bastards and the disgust from that bitch Elena really set me off. "You have to choose between doing it right and doing it right away."

"I wish you hadn't put it quite that way, Randy." That was all the Secretary said. But if looks and thoughts could have killed, I would have been dead.

I could feel Blaine gloating, even without a word, and that figured. After all, he had gotten the waste job because he had been so effective in rallying the environmental groups behind the President. He had really wanted to be Secretary, but the President's people blocked that.

Nils was seething, realizing that my statement, certain to be leaked to the press by Blaine, would put him in a no-win situation.

Elena smiled faintly, and said softly, "We can support either option, Mr. Secretary. We did recommend the bioremediation." She was vaguely pleased, the way an animal-rights lover might be when the bull got the matador.

We talked some more, without really saying anything. Then Nils asked me to stay a moment longer.

"If that statement of yours appears in the press, I'll hold you personally responsible. Do you understand?"

I understood, all right. I was dead. No more White House appointments, no more political jobs, no appointment even to a District Judgeship, not even an offer from a Washington law firm. No severance pay—that doesn't come with political jobs. No future.

By the time I got back to my office, Blaine would have leaked it in order to show how incompetent Nils was in dealing with Congress and cleanups. In turn, Nils would have to claim a foul-up in congressional communications was responsible—which would be underscored by my resignation or, if I proved uncooperative, my dismissal.

That was Thursday.

I resigned the following Monday, as events followed the pattern I had seen—except nastier. Blaine had also leaked that someone would be fired as an apology to the Chairman, and that was too much for the White House. So Blaine got fired, too. Or rather, he resigned a week or so later.

Some consolation!

In the meantime, I tracked down that bitch Cyane. She'd started it all. Not that it was particularly hard, since she was staying with Renni. Cyane agreed to lunch—lunch only, and we met at Mortimer's.

Without a job and without any prospects, I probably couldn't afford Mortimer's, but the way things were going, I figured that I had a better chance if I offered her lunch at a classy place.

We arrived almost at the same time. Cyane wore the same white dress she had the day she had left me. Or one just like it. I took a deep breath, because she still took my breath away, and inclined my head to her. Damn, she'd been good in bed.

"Thank you." That was all she said. Unlike with Elena, or Rosalie, my secretary, I still couldn't sense what she felt.

As we stepped toward the little black podium, Jacques nodded to me, immediately. "Your table is ready, Mr. Ozier." Behind his words was a sense of regret.

I returned the nod. "Thank you, Jacques. I appreciate it."

Cyane and I said nothing until we were seated.

"Thank you for coming," I said.

"You don't mean that. But you were daring enough . . . or stupid enough . . . to ask."

Damn! Every feeling, every emotion I felt, was out there for her to read. She smiled, a bright, knowing smile, not the enigmatic one.

Over the salads—of course, Cyane's was vegetarian, and mine was cajun chicken—I finally asked what I had in mind. "What did you do to me?"

Cyane put down her fork. Her deep black eyes looked older than hell, even in that beautiful smooth-skinned face. "I gave you what you asked for."

I took a deep breath. "What did I ask for?"

"Understanding."

Damned bitch! All I'd wanted was a bright and good lady in bed—and Cyane had been *very* good—and now I was out of a job with nowhere to go. Maybe, if I were real lucky, I'd get a job doing dog-work legal research or chasing ambulances.

I took another bite of the suddenly tasteless salad. How can you think when you know the woman across from you understands every feeling you have? For some reason, I thought about the three-hundred-pound tackle again and begging a room from my mother. What the hell was I going to do?

"Who . . . what are you?"

"I'm Cyane. My name is Greek, originally, from Sicily."

"From Sicily? That's bullshit."

Her eyes turned that stormy blue again. "Next time I won't be so gentle." Fire danced on her fingertips.

I was still pissed. "You're a witch, aren't you?"

She laughed softly, and I remembered all those nights. Then I looked at her face. It was like white marble, except marble's softer.

She hadn't answered the question. She wouldn't either.

"I already have."

She answered the next question before I asked it.

"Because Renni asked me. Because I don't like men who force themselves on women. I haven't since . . . for a long time . . ."

And that was really all she said, except she was leaving the law firm. She didn't say where she was going, but it might have been back to Greece—Sicily. She'd been away a long time.

Cyane? Her name's in the mythology books. Could be coincidence, but she was a nymph changed into a river. Or a fountain nymph outraged at the rape of Persephone. There are a couple of versions of the myth, but they all deal with nymphs and water. And my Cyane knew more about wetlands and water than anybody I ever met at Environment.

What will I do now? Do I really have much choice? I'm thinking about working as a consultant or a research associate for them. Jane Helmam's firm, that is. If not, I'll probably retreat to the old family house on the farmed-out forest in upstate New York. I mean, what else is there? And at least, working around women, I'd be protected some. They're not quite as violent, just disgusted and contemptuous. Or revolted. The law firm bit's up to Renni, but that's all there is. And that's not real likely. Every other firm in Washington declined even to interview me. Cyane, again, but how she did it, I don't know. Maybe she screwed every single senior partner.

Hell of a note, when you think about it, but have you noticed how many estranged husbands are shooting themselves lately? Somehow, I don't think it's coincidence. I mean, how did the women get to be such monsters? But who the hell's going to believe me?

Not all women know Cyane, but, then again . . .

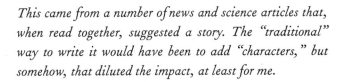

This came from a number of news and science articles that, when read together, suggested a story. The "traditional" way to write it would have been to add "characters," but somehow, that diluted the impact, at least for me.

NEWS CLIPS
RECOVERED FROM
THE NYC RUINS

TEHRAN, Iran—Insurgents hit the U.S. command center outside Tehran with four precision-guided rockets, killing fifty-one U.S. soldiers and twenty Iranians. Explosions in the area around the heavily fortified Green Zone claimed another eighty-three Iranians . . .

The strike was the second dramatic sign of the improved military technology acquired by the Iranian fundamentalists. The first was the penetration of the Army's new advanced command link . . .

Muslim nationalists have warned Iranians not to cooperate with the American forces or the recently installed Iranian interim government, threatening to "wash the streets with the blood of collaborationists . . ."

Noor Mroue, Associated Press
New York Times
January 12, 2009

WASHINGTON—April 12. President Hardison spent a long afternoon yesterday close to the White House reviewing the security arrangements for the forthcoming Iranian elections. Biometric security systems are already in place in all polling stations, and will identify all Iranians imbued with violence-prone genetic markers. While they will be encouraged to vote, special screening will be used to make certain they are not carrying conventional or bioweapons into polling places. . . .

The president reaffirmed his support for the elections, and his gratitude to the U.S. forces. "Free and meaningful elections are the key to a prosperous future, and the best way to advance the success of democracy throughout the world is through such elections . . . Our troops have performed magnificently . . ."

Mr. Hardison dismissed charges by Senator Anna Matthewson [D- IA] that his domestic prolife policies, which effectively require poor women in the U.S. to carry unwanted pregnancies to term, were philosophically at odds with his foreign policy. He declared, "We believe in the right to freedom anywhere, and the greatest freedom of all is the right to life . . ."

Selim Basse, Associated Press
Washington Post
April 12, 2010

BOSTON—May 17. Dismissing the criticism leveled by resigning trustee Thomasina Howell as "unworthy of response," Harvard president Johnstone J. Winters, III, announced that exactly 59 percent of Harvard seniors graduated with an "A" average, for the third year in a row, in accordance with his excellence policy. "A Harvard education has meant a higher standard, and we have held our students to that standard."

Winters instituted the excellence policy immediately upon taking office, in response to charges that grade inflation had rendered the use of traditional marks meaningless, after 73 percent of the class of 2008 had graduated with "A" averages.

According to Harvard University sources and a study by Dartmouth College Professor Martina Herrington, Harvard now ranks the lowest among the Ivy League in the percentage of "A" marks granted to undergraduates . . .

Chronicle of Higher Education
May 17, 2011

LOS ANGELES—The U.S. Environmental Protection Agency and computer giant Intel have reached a $4.7 billion agreement for cleanup of more than 2 million computers sold with the company's bioware quantum computing chip . . . Under the agreement, Intel will replace all infected computers and will pay for the special high-tech incineration required for safe disposal of affected computers and associated peripherals.

In a related suit, Cisco Systems has declined a settlement offer from Intel, claiming that the bioware used in routers had necessitated "unprecedented" costs . . .

Citing the suit, Intel announced the closing of its remaining U.S. plants and its relocation of those facilities to Vietnam, India, and mainland China.

The closing will affect some 5,000 workers, in addition to more than 10,000 whose jobs were eliminated indirectly as a result of the bioware problem . . .

Associated Press

Los Angeles Times

August 3, 2011

VIENNA, Austria—A key OPEC committee recommended today that the cartel keep its current output quotas unchanged, signaling that oil producers believe current prices near $80 a barrel are not too high.

In a related move, the OPEC exchange committee, after a short presentation by U.S. Deputy secretary of state David Powers, rejected without comment, the proposal to redenominate oil prices in either euros or yuans . . .

Canadian tar sands producer, TarCan, issued a press release that hailed the move as a message for price stability. With a price target of $80, TarCan can maintain its current profit margins and expand production to meet another 5 percent of U.S. oil demand.

U.S. shale oil producer TransGlobal closed its last Colorado unit, Parachute Number 3, last month, citing the excessive costs of U.S. environmental and transport security regulations . . .

United Press International

Denver Post

October 4, 2012

SACRAMENTO—August 12. Representatives from all the major organizations representing college professors, including the American Association of University Professors, staged a series of rallies today protesting real-time monitoring of all activities "related to teaching," a requirement under the Federal Education Improvement Act.

Under the final FEIA regulations released last week, all persons engaged in teaching on the university level must have their classrooms continuously monitored and must obtain advance permission from proper authorities to attend any functions where they are identified in a "professional capacity."

The regulations were based in large part on policies adopted and enforced in the Utah higher education system beginning in 2005. Critics cited the loss of "high-quality faculty" in the Utah case, but supporters of the regulations claim that the regulations reduced faculty absences significantly and also contributed to the reduction in incident of harassment, embarrassment of students before their peers, and "educational pressuring" of students to achieve at "unrealistic" levels . . .

San Francisco Chronicle
August 12, 2013

MECCA—November 12. Forces from the Iraqi Republic entered Mecca early today and reestablished order after weeks of lawlessness following the overthrow of the House of Saud . . .

Both Iran and the United Arab Emirates expressed cautious support for the peacekeeping effort . . .

United States Marines retain control of key oil fields and port facilities, with the carrier *Abraham Lincoln* standing by to support Iraqi forces as necessary . . .

New York Times
November 12, 2013

DETROIT—January 17. Federal marshals arrested Mattie J. Angelou for violation of the Freedom of Life Act. In December, Angelou reportedly took a boat in a snowstorm to Windsor, where she had an abortion. She had been denied medical treatment in Detroit after reporting being raped by an uncle.

Detroit hospital administrators declined to comment, citing the personal privacy requirements of FOLA, which restrict public statements by institutions receiving federal funding.

Former Planned Parenthood president Crystel Ibanez stated that federal authorities "wanted to make an example of Mattie." Ibanez is currently serving a five-year term for conspiracy to evade the provisions of the Freedom of Life Act . . .

Detroit Free Press
January 17, 2014

WASHINGTON—July 14. The D.C. Federal Court of Appeals today refused to hear a motion by the American Civil Liberties Union to require the Internal Revenue Service to reinstate its tax-exempt status as a nonprofit and nonpartisan foundation . . .

The Court of Appeals rejected the appeal without comment. Keniel Carson, attorney for the ACLU, said that the IRS had revoked the organization's status because the ACLU had opposed former President Hardison's legislative initiatives. These included the Freedom of Life Act, the Preservation of Marriage amendment to the Constitution, and the National Security Act, particularly the provision that required full biometric screening information be available to both the federal government and to all employers in order to allow them to comply with the Immigration Reform Act . . .

The Supreme Court had previously rejected similar appeals from Planned Parenthood, the American Medical Association, and the American Library Association. The AMA had brought suit on grounds of doctor-patient confidentiality, but the Court had refused the suit on the grounds that the AMA had no standing, since the IRS had not actually removed its tax-exempt status, but only issued a preliminary opinion. Because the ALA had supported its members in refusing to provide library records to federal law-enforcement agencies, the IRS had determined it had acted in a "politically partisan" manner inconsistent with the nonpartisan requirements of the Internal Revenue Code . . .

Washington Post
July 14, 2016

SALT LAKE—February 11. The Higher Education Reorganization Act passed both the state house and senate unanimously. After its passage, House majority leader Taylor Cannon announced that all college courses with less than twenty students enrolled will be canceled at all state universities. "At a time when families are struggling to make ends meet, we simply cannot fund programs that benefit only a comparative handful of students . . ."

Opponents of the Higher Education Reorganization Act complained that Cannon's initiative would effectively eliminate all programs in the arts, as well as all advanced honors seminars, and all independent study programs . . .

Cannon countered by pointing out that federal educational mandates had left the legislature little real choice . . .

Salt Lake Tribune
February 11, 2017

WASHINGTON—February 27. "Totally misleading and fallacious." That was how the U.S. Department of Education characterized the charges made by Reading Is Fundamental. RIF released a report yesterday claiming that 51% of all adult Americans were "functionally illiterate" and that another 30% were only "marginally literate." Functionally illiterate was defined as being unable to read instructions for assembling a product, reading a detailed map, or being able to read a passage and explain its meaning.

"Americans are a well-informed and intelligent people. They understand the world around them, and this sort of intellectual scare-mongering does all of us a disservice," replied Secretary of Education Ellis. Ellis went on to point out that reliance on archaic printed text was misleading because most Americans received information through the various sources of real-time media . . .

Washington Times
February 27, 2021

. . . Thrills, chills, and lots of lava! That's what *Survivor: Krakatoa* promised and delivered. For a grand prize of $50 million, twenty contestants signed waivers that explicitly stated that there was a 20 percent chance of a "fatal occurrence." In fact there were three fatalities, and this week the winner has a chance to bring home that $50 million . . . if the ever-rebuilding volcano doesn't explode first.

Entertainment Weekly
October 12, 2022

NEW YORK—January 12. German publishing giant Holtzbrinck [VHPS] announced the closure of St. Martin's Press, the last of its American publishing arms, citing the decline in reading of hard-copy books. "Americans no longer read the way they once did. VHPS will continue to supply material to all electronic and broadcast media . . . We will continue to expand our hard-copy operations in India, the Far East, and in Latin America. Our Continental operations will supply Canadian readers . . ."

Financial Times
January 12, 2025

WASHINGTON—November 9. The Republicans retain control of the Congress. That's what the final election results confirmed today. As in the

2026 election, no incumbents standing for reelection were defeated. That included Senator Alan Weller [R-CO] who had been appointed by Colorado governor Brett Owens, Jr., upon the death of his father, Senator Samuel Weller . . .

The outcome was almost certain following last year's decision by the U.S. Supreme Court that only the states had the authority to require impartial independent redistricting. In effect, that decision let stand political gerrymandering by state legislatures to protect incumbents . . .

Washington Post
November 9, 2028

OTTAWA—September 17. Canadian prime minister Jacques deViel declared that he stands "totally behind" the new entry standards for immigrants to Canada. Under the revised standards, all immigrants must be able to read selected passages in English or their native language, and to answer questions on the passages . . .

"This is not a measure aimed at discouraging immigrants, but one designed to encourage the kind of educated and dedicated individuals who have built Canada into what she is today . . ."

Aides to deViel discounted charges that the standards were designed to restrict immigration by ill-educated Americans . . .

One assistant noted that standards designed to restrict the ill-educated would apply to "90% of everyone south of Windsor . . ."

Associated Press
Ottawa Citizen
September 17, 2031

WASHINGTON—January 28. "In a peaceful world, we do not need to maintain an arsenal designed for the wars of the past," announced President Owens . . . The president's budget proposes a further reduction in Navy carriers from eight to five, and the elimination of two Army divisions.

Despite the president's concern about the PRC's scram fleet, and its ability to strike anywhere in the world in less than two hours, last fall, Congress cut the defense appropriations in order to keep the current account deficit at less than 50% of the federal budget, after the Pan Asian banking combine indicated its unwillingness to support the dollar without further spending cuts.

Critics say that the president's effort is clearly an attempt to forestall deeper cuts by the Congress . . .

Army Times
January 2032

OTTAWA—September 14. Canadian prime minister Patrick Mooney denied reports that Canadian army reservists were being used to patrol the U.S. border. "We are using the latest detection technology, but current border personnel and equipment are more than adequate for the task."

He also dismissed reports that U.S. officials and INS personnel were being uncooperative. "That's nonsense. It is true that they face severe difficulties with training and equipment, but they're doing the best that they can."

With a severe drought in its fifth year in the U.S. legal—and illegal immigration—to Canada has soared. More than 3 million Americans applied for legal status last year. One hundred thousand were accepted, but it's estimated that three times that many found ways to enter Canada, despite the high-tech surveillance of the border . . .

United Press International
New York Times
September 14, 2037

CHICAGO—May 13. Citing more than ten years of mounting deficits, Aryla Haroun, General Director and President of the Lyric Opera of Chicago, today announced the closure of the opera company that has been a mainstay of culture in Chicago for almost a century.

"Ninety-seven years after the Lyric Opera was founded by Carol Fox, I most deeply regret that we can no longer continue to operate. This past season's deficit amounted to over 80 percent of the operating budget, and attendance was down to 25 percent of seating capacity." Haroun noted that even drastic cuts in stipends paid to both performers and members of the orchestra made five years earlier had failed to reverse the trend.

The only full-time opera company remaining in the United States is the Metropolitan Opera in New York, and the Met has managed to remain open only because of "substantial" contributions from Chinese multilateral corporations . . .

Chicago Sun-Times
May 13, 2047

JUAREZ—October 17. More than fifty Americans, many of them apparently starving, were gunned down by automatic border defenses after an attempt to cross the Rio Grande in search of work in Mexico. Among the dead were young teenagers who had earlier attempted to sneak past American customs personnel . . .

"Mexico cannot absorb any more unmotivated menial labor," declared Mexican president Sanchez deGoya. "We remain open to those with skills and the ambition to excel . . ."

El Diario
October 17, 2059

WASHINGTON—June 23. Secretary of Education Wang-Smythe denied reports that his department attempted to suppress a report that more than 1700 U.S. colleges and universities had discontinued courses "of an intellectually challenging and demanding nature" in response to the Equality in Education Act.

"It's unfortunate that American educators seek to perpetuate the discredited legacy of elitism," the secretary said.

"Seeking excellence is not elitism," replied Elenore Ariel, the past president of the American Association of University Professors. "Failure to seek excellence has always resulted in societal decline." Ariel has been indicted for conspiracy to subvert the mandates of the Equality in Education Act . . .

Chronicle of Higher Education
June 2060

NEW YORK—October 21. Following a record heat wave and two days without power, riots flared all across the greater New York area. Governor Sebastian declined to send national guard or state militia into the city, claiming that they lacked the equipment and ammunition to protect themselves.

Mayor Abdul-ram appealed to President Bush for federal assistance, but had not heard by late last night. Marines from Fort Bragg had been dispatched earlier to Atlanta . . .

New York Times
October 21, 2065

NEW YORK—May 2. The first contingent of troops from the Pan-Asian Coalition assumed control of the New York City area after sporadic fire from insurgents, armed largely with obsolete Barrett fifty-caliber automatics. The insurgents were quickly restrained with nanosmart foam . . .

The majority of the protectorate troops were from the PRC . . .

General Hso Chiang declared that the protectorate would only remain long enough to stabilize the situation and allow Americans the right to regain the domestic freedoms that they had championed so vigorously for so long . . .

New China News
May 2, 2087

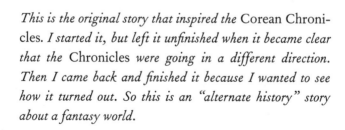

This is the original story that inspired the Corean Chronicles. *I started it, but left it unfinished when it became clear that the* Chronicles *were going in a different direction. Then I came back and finished it because I wanted to see how it turned out. So this is an "alternate history" story about a fantasy world.*

BEYOND THE
OBVIOUS WIND

Not many like Iron Stem, and fewer do every season that passes, though I never thought I'd come to appreciate it as I do. Some folks complain about the wind, the way it blows hard and hot through the summer, and cold and biting dry through the winter. Some say that each wind is different, and none is to be trusted. Others complain about the sun, with rays so hot in the thin air of summer that they turn unprotected skin red in less than a quarter glass. The same folks complain that in winter there's no heat in the sun except where it hits the eternastone that runs through the center of Iron Stem and north to Soulend and then on to Eastice. The high road also runs south, and that is its greatest use, for the ore carriers on their fifty-vingt journey to the docks at Dekhron. There they put the pigs on the barges and let the river carry them down to Faitel for the ironcrafters. Others say that the oaks and evergreens that encircle the town—and grow no farther north than the green tower—do little to make Iron Stem pleasant and much to present a deception to those who pass through.

The other eternastone road—that was and is for travelers, not that there have ever been that many, who wanted to go west to Elcien—or for the foot regiments that marched eastward along it in disgrace to serve garrison duty in Iron Stem. Going east from Iron Stem . . . there is no road, for few indeed have ever gone east. The edge of the Aerlal Plateau rises straight up some six thousand yards, the air thinner with each yard, and the wind stronger. Once in a while, some lucky dustcat hunter comes back, a wide grin on his or her face, pelt sealed away with the dust more precious than gems hidden within . . . or if he is truly fortunate, with a live dustcat.

The Recorders in Elcien and Ludar have tried to explain the Plateau, why it's there, and why no one can climb it, and failed. Even their Tables don't show anything, and the Tables show everything—except about the Plateau. Those who've tried to climb it, well, you can find their broken bones scattered along the base of those walled cliffs that support the Plateau.

The Duarches began to dump the mals—all kinds of mals—out here in the middle years of the last cycle. The idea was that they'd get along or die. Like most ideas, it was right, and it was wrong. It was right for most people in Iron Stem, though they could not see why, even as they could feel the obvious winds they seldom saw, and wrong because what lies beyond the obvious winds was, and is, the reality of the soarers. Yet most folk never see one. Those that do never say.

Why am I here? Out in the middle of nowhere, in a failing iron town, a thousand vingts away from the spires of Ludar, and the graceful arches of Elcien, and a continent's breadth west from the reassuring solidity of Alustre?

Let's just say it happened this way. Years ago, on a harvest day that offered little promise but duty . . .

I

The tireless legs of the sandoxen finally halted opposite the green tower on the north side of the town, a soaring cylinder with a pointed tip, whose green stones radiated light even on cloudy days. South of the tower were the headquarters building and the low barracks—structures faced with eternal stone—that had housed the companies of the Duarches' Foot for more than a millennium. The stone wall around the compound was low and held ungated openings and an arch on the north section that had apparently been designed only to allow foot access to the green tower.

Behind the sandoxen was a long, cupridium-sheathed transport coach. The coach doors opened, and a full tech squad of the Duarches' finest, in their gray-silver and green uniforms, marched out into the midafternoon of a day late in harvest. Each man bore sabre of the Duarchy, with an edge sharp enough to cut a feather fluttering in midair and strong enough to last for an age. Every third tech also bore a sniper's rifle, marked by a blue-steeled barrel so dark as to shimmer almost black in the white sunlight, a weapon crafted in Faitel to outlast the tech who bore it. All the rankers and officers were at least part lander; none were total indigen.

The first one out of the roller was Tech Captain Vynhal, who as a Tech officer ranked equal with the officers of equivalent rank in the Myrmidons and one grade above the regular Cadmian mounted and foot officers. He moved away from the bronzed vehicle and set down his duffel. A leather case with his orders and other materials remained slung on its strap over his left shoulder. He could not help but notice the Aerlal Plateau to the east and north. Its western and southern ramparts rose straight upward like a wall supporting the heavens, six thousand yards or more above the low hills below.

Vynhal turned back to face the command center as another captain strode from the headquarters building. The local captain, who wore the maroon and gray of the Cadmian Foot, halted short of Vynhal. "Sir, I'm Murch, captain of the Fifty-fourth Foot."

"Murch, I'm Captain Vynhal, Fourth Tech Company."

"We're here to serve the Duarchy." Murch nodded politely, his head bobbing above a more-than-ample body. Wisps of fine black hair curled away from the gray officers' cap. His squarish face and body betrayed a heritage that was mostly indigen.

"Once we get the squad settled, Captain, we'll be talking."

"Yes, sir." Murch cleared his throat. "Ah . . . there are three rooms empty in the officer's quarters. One senior and three junior."

"I'll take one of the juniors. Majer Bakarak may be conducting an inspection tour before too long."

"Yes, sir." Murch nodded. "Do you need a squad leader for assistance?"

"I think not. You can point me in the direction of the quarters and the stables."

"The north building is local headquarters. Officers' quarters are on the second level to the rear. Stables are to the back, against the west wall. Officers' section to the front. There should be enough spare mounts for your squad."

Vynhal ignored the near condescension in Murch's voice. "Thank you. Once we're settled, I'll find you, and we can discuss our assignment here in Iron Stem."

"I'll be in my study most of the rest of the afternoon, sir. At your convenience." The heavyset officer offered an attempt at a smile, then nodded before turning away.

Once the junior captain had made his way back toward the headquarters building, Vynhal dispatched Kiram, the senior ranker, to oversee the quartering of the squad while he took his time in surveying the outpost. Fine reddish dust had gathered in angled heaps against the south-facing stone walls of the post buildings. The windows, clean as their panes appeared, looked tired. What had once been an oblong lawn in front of the headquarters building had deteriorated into irregular patches of grass randomly spaced in hard red soil surrounded by a graystone border.

Vynhal's eyes turned away from the headquarters building and across the eternastone road and to the south, at the timeworn graystone walls and the polished oak doors of the seminary, and then at the rectangular walls of the school, another hundred yards south of the seminary.

Three girls, wearing sand green coveralls, strolled from the Seminary toward the school. Behind them came four boys. All seven had the blond hair and fairer complexions of pure landers, but had dressed their hair with glitterdark, an affectation imitating the alectors. That fad had come and gone in the capitals and the other true cities of Corus. The girls wore their hair cropped short, while that of the boys flared like black-etched blond flame in the wind-hints that swirled in and around the buildings.

Looking at the girls reminded Vynhal that he was still single, and would remain so until he was promoted to majer—and that could be soon . . . if he could carry out his mission before winter dropped across the Iron Valleys. With a wry smile, the Tech captain lifted his duffel and turned back toward the headquarters building and the rear stairs that led up to the officers' quarters. The stone steps had been swept recently, yet there was still a fine layer of reddish dust. At the top of the stairs, he turned and looked back southward. The wind had died away, and the seven students had disappeared into the school.

Absently, he wondered whose children they might be, since only the wealthiest of old lander families could afford the boarding fees at a seminary, and the mere handfuls of children of alectors were all schooled in the capitals or in Alustre. Most wealthy lander families lived in towns or cities large enough to have full-range schools. If they did not, they usually sent their children to the seminaries in the capitals, or in larger cities, such as Tempe or Alustre—or even Sudya. Why would they send children to a seminary in Iron Stem, an iron-mining town filled with mals and worse? He'd ask Murch, although he doubted the older captain knew.

He turned and opened the first door of those quarters reserved for junior officers.

In the end, Vynhal took the largest of the vacant junior officers' quarters—a chamber four yards by three with a wide but single bed, a narrow armoire, a rack for weapons and jackets, and a narrow desk built into the north wall. The west wall held a single window that offered a view of the dark green irongrass that stretched to the Westerhills some twenty-five-odd vingts away.

He unpacked the duffel, hung and stowed uniforms and gear, and then used the adjoining bath chamber to wash up. He dampened the corner of one of the worn gray towels and used it to remove the dust from his silver-green uniform.

Then he refolded the towel and returned to his chamber to reclaim the leather dispatch case before heading down to the main level of the headquarters building to find the Foot captain.

Murch was in his study, looking at a short stack of papers, almost as if deciding whether to pick up the topmost when Vynhal stopped just outside the half-open door to the small study.

The Foot captain stood, almost reluctantly, when he saw Vynhal. "Sir?"

"I have a warrant from the Marshal of Myrmidons." Vynhal stepped into the small chamber and handed the gilt-edged document to Murch. "I'm here to investigate the continuing loss of rankers and to report on the reasons for the decline in iron shipments to Faitel."

The older captain read it slowly, then looked up. "We do everything according to the Code and the protocols. We always have. You'll see that, Tech Captain." Murch cleared his throat. "Is that all? It mentions other matters."

"Dreamdust shipments are also down," Vynhal said flatly.

"There's always been some loss with the dreamdust. It's finer than talc, finer than the powders the ladies use in Elcien, sir."

Vynhal could see the sweat oozing from under Murch's fine and thinning blond hair. "That may be, Captain, but the shipments of both iron and dreamdust have fallen off." He had to admit to himself that he didn't know why the dust was necessary, not when its use was officially forbidden in Corus itself and punishable by assignment to the high-road building crews—or death, if the users were too weak to handle the heavy construction work.

"The ironworks can't get enough men. That's what Gestark's reports show."

"There have been more mals assigned here in the past three years than in more than twenty years," Vynhal pointed out.

"Numbers don't mean that they're suited for the ironworks. The numbers of indigens has gone down."

Vynhal just nodded. "We'll look into that. I appreciate your observation. And the dreamdust?"

"The dustcats don't do so well in closed barns, sir, and they're getting harder to trap or kill. There aren't any nearby. There haven't been for years."

"Then why has the output of dreamdust dropped by half in two years, after more than a hundred years of near-steady output?"

"The dustcatters say that the old cats are dying faster than the trappers can find others. The ones they get won't breed. Or not often enough."

Vynhal was getting the feeling that Murch had an answer—or an excuse—for everything. But excuses weren't why Vynhal had been sent. Everyone had excuses. Tech officers were supposed to see beyond the excuses and the obvious and come up with solutions. That was why there were Tech officers. "You may be right, and, if that is so, that is what I will report, but the Duarches expect a report."

"Yes, sir."

"I noticed a seminary just across the high road . . ."

"It's not that large, sir. Only a score or so . . . of real student boarders, sir."

"Where do they come from? The students?" asked Vynhal. "There aren't any towns that large nearby."

"Most come from Soulend and Iron Stem, but there are some from Sandhold and Wesrigg, and some from the herding holdings to the north."

"Why don't they send them to the seminaries in places like Tempre or those in Faitel or the capitals?"

"It's cheaper here, and they can work out payment in goods," Murch replied. "That's what I've been told."

"You don't believe that."

Murch looked down. "No, sir, but that's the only answer that I've ever gotten."

"Why do you think they don't send them to better schools?"

"I can only think of two reasons. They need them on the holdings, during the off-seasons, or they don't want them schooled in the capitals."

"Or both?"

Murch shrugged.

The more Vynhal talked to Murch, the less the Tech captain cared for the older officer, but he smiled politely as he asked, "Have you had much trouble with the mals lately? Besides not getting enough with indigen backgrounds?"

Murch laughed. "Not much. The worst mals go from the ironworks to the dustcatters, and after a week they'll do anything to stay there. The stronger ones without too much in the way of smarts are happy to stay in the iron works, and the ones unsuited for either we let the holders hire."

Vynhal didn't understand the last part. "Why the holders?"

"It's very simple, Tech Captain. Those lander holders are old stock . . ." He paused. "You're pure lander stock, too, I'd wager, sir. You look like them. Anyway, they run a hard life on the irongrass and the ironsands. The smart ones take to it, and want nothing to do with Iron Stem or us. The dumb ones die. Either way, they're not a problem for us."

Vynhal wasn't so sure that providing bright and hardworking mals to the lander holders was necessarily in the long-term interests of the Duarches— or the alectors who served as their right hands. "What is your biggest problem, then?"

"Boredom, sir. In the last year, I've lost a half score of rankers to brawls with the ironworkers in the taverns, near that many to sandwolves . . ."

Vynhal raised his eyebrows at that.

"Simple enough, Tech Captain. The men get bored. The local women won't have anything to do with them, most of 'em, anyway, except for coin, and the rates at the Kharema—that's the local pleasure house—are high. So they want more coin. The only way to get it, or enough of it, is to hire themselves out on their off-time to the dustcat hunters or as night guards to some of the herder holders near town. Sandwolves get the ones that fall asleep."

Vynhal couldn't believe what he was hearing.

Murch shook his head. "You don't believe me, sir, but Iron Stem's not posted for hazard duty. I can't restrict them for what they do on their off-times. Even if I tried, they'd still want coins for women and drink."

"Sandwolves . . ." Vynhal stopped as he heard the main door open.

A ranker in maroon and gray burst into the open doorway of Murch's study, where he stiffened at the sight of Vynhal. "Sir . . . begging your pardon, sirs. There's a Myrmidon coming in."

"We'd better go out and greet him," Vynhal said mildly. He turned and walked from Murch's study, past the ranker, and out through the front door.

He stood for several moments outside on the stone steps. He did not look eastward toward the Aerial Plateau. The pteridons never overflew the Plateau. That he knew, though he had never seen the southern section of the Plateau before. Instead, he looked south, and then westward.

Murch joined him, also looking westward.

The blue-skinned pteridon swept down out of the silver-green sky, coming almost out of the afternoon sun, then braking with wings spread wide, before settling onto the stone-bordered section that had once been lawn. The undercaptain who vaulted gracefully from the pteridon's saddle was a typical alector—white-pale skin, muscular and broad-shouldered, two and a half yards in height, glistening black hair and black eyes. Faint reddish clouds of dust puffed away from the impact of his shimmering black boots.

"Undercaptain Resytal," announced the alector. "You're Tech Captain Vynhal?" He didn't even look in Murch's direction.

"Yes, Undercaptain. Fourth Tech company."

"Good." The undercaptain handed an envelope to Vynhal. "Some modifications to your orders, Tech Captain." A hard smile followed. "Submarshal Zerchal and Colonel Klasylt also asked me to convey their respects and an observation from the submarshal."

Vynhal nodded and waited. The Myrmidon submarshal had sent more than a few observations over the years, all of which outweighed the orders from Tech Colonel Klasylt.

"Everyone will attempt to blame what does not exist, such as the soarers or the sanders. Both are myths, based on the ancient and vanished peoples of Acorus. Do not spend time chasing myths, Tech Captain." The alector's black eyes fixed on Vynhal, looking down at the lander officer from his superior height, although Vynhal, at well over two yards, was tall, even for a pure lander, for landers were anything but short.

"You may convey to the submarshal and the colonel that I have no intention of wasting time." Vynhal wasn't about to chase myths. He just wanted to find out what had cut down iron and dreamdust production and why Murch had been unable to reduce ranker losses, then return to Faitel.

"I will do so." Without another word, the Myrmidon undercaptain remounted the pteridon, which spread its wings and lifted, moving upward so quickly that in moments both pteridon and rider were but a single speck in the southern sky.

Vynhal did not open the modified orders but tucked them inside his tunic.

"Must have been important, sir," offered Murch, "to send an alector out here to deliver those."

"He could have been on his way elsewhere." Vynhal smiled politely. "I doubt that anything the Tech Corps does would warrant diverting an alector."

"Seen stranger things here, sir."

"Perhaps I will as well," replied Vynhal.

Once Murch had turned and headed back into the lower level of the head-quarters building, Vynhal walked back up the rear stairs to the quarters he had taken. There, he took out the single sheet of paper, flexible and strong enough that it was almost impossible to tear and difficult to cut except with the sharpest of belt-knives. He read. Between the standard addresses and salutations and the formal closings and authentications was a single short paragraph.

> Subject officer is commanded to use any and all methods at his disposal to ensure that the continual losses of Foot personnel are lowered to a level more appropriate for a nonhazardous posting, or to document in depth the rationale for reclassifying Iron Stem as a hazardous post, as well as to deal with other matters within the scope of his abilities . . .

The "other matters" were the need to see what could be done about re-turning iron shipments to previous normal production levels and looking into what could be done about dustcat dreamdust production. The only dif-ference in the modified orders from those shown to Murch was the phrase "commanded to use any and all methods at his disposal." Vynhal didn't like the change. "Any and all methods" meant use of force and summary judg-ment against any ranker, officer, or civilian who was not an alector.

Vynhal read the paragraph twice before replacing it in the envelope and slipping the envelope into his shoulder case. Then he stowed the case in the bottom of the armoire. Tech officers always got the difficult assignments, the ones Colonel Klasylt called "interesting."

II

Vynhal had just finished eating his breakfast and was leaving the small room, with its single table, that served as the officers' mess when Captain Murch hurried toward him.

"You didn't believe me, Tech Captain. Why don't you come look? They just brought in Lakylt. Sandwolf got him."

"I'm sorry to hear that." Vynhal was indeed sorry. The last thing he needed was more nonduty casualties immediately after he arrived in Iron Stem. "If you would lead the way."

"He's in the infirmary . . . for now. Have to move him quick, though. Bodies, the ones killed by the sandwolves, they don't last long." Murch hurried along the corridor. He finally stopped at the last door on the left before the double doors that led out onto the stone-paved area surrounding the barracks and separating it from the headquarters building.

The dead indigen was laid out on the surgery table. He still wore his uniform, slashed open across the chest.

Vynhal studied the body. Although there was only the one obvious wound, one thing struck Vynhal—there was almost no blood, as if the man had died instantly; nor did his neck seem to be broken. How had the man died? "There's not much blood. I'd expect more from a man attacked by an animal."

"You ever seen a sandwolf, Tech Captain?" asked Murch. "They're over three yards long, and that's not counting the tail. They got crystal fangs more than a span long. Unless you get them first, you won't last past the first bite they take out of you."

Three yards in length? Murch had to be exaggerating, but Vynhal didn't see much point in contradicting the other officer. Besides, he was mostly indigen. "Was he one of the ones hiring himself out as a guard?"

"Yes, sir."

"What if I forbid the practice?"

Murch laughed, sadly. "They'd mostly stop it—until the day after you left—and then they'd go back to doing it."

"You'd be required to enforce the order after I left."

"Then the disciplinary floggings would go up, and sooner or later, someone would kill me. Unless I deserted first, and I would."

"You don't seem to have much discipline here, Captain." Vynhal knew things were bad in the outlying regions, away from the Myrmidons and alectors, but that bad?

"I have more than most local Cadmian garrisons, sir."

That possibility was even more appalling. "Then what would you suggest, Captain?"

"Hazard pay would help. It might help a lot."

"For standard garrison duty?"

Murch sighed. "Tech Captain, sir, begging your pardon, but I'd suggest that you spend some time in Iron Stem before you make a final decision."

Vynhal intended to, not that he had much choice, one way or the other. "What would you suggest I visit, then, Captain?"

Murch smiled, politely. "I couldn't say what would be most valuable, Tech Captain, sir, but the ironworks are why there's a town—that and the dustcat runs to the north."

III

Vynhal rode southward on the eternastone high road, heading away from the green tower, the seminary, and the school, and toward the ironworks. None of the privileged lander youth, with their glitterdark hair, were outside or visible as he passed the school, but he could hear voices through the open windows. Beyond the school on the east side of the road was what passed for a green. Low stone walls surrounded the area, which held sparse grass and little else, save a stone platform on the south end, which overlooked several rows of stone benches.

Beyond the park was a large frame house, with a white three-rail fence. All sides of the dwelling bore full-roofed porches, and a thin gray-haired woman was beating rugs hung on a rope between two porch posts. She did not look up as Vynhal passed.

The houses farther to the south became smaller, then gave way to shops and dingier buildings as the ironworks ahead to the west loomed larger and larger. The few curtains that did hang in windows were various shades of gray. The ground—and even the eternal pavement of the high road—vibrated as he neared the hammer mills that fronted the ironworks.

The air was not only dry and thin, but acrid, a mixture of fine dust and smoke and vapor from the ironworks and mills. Each breath Vynhal took burned.

A short wagon, bearing iron pigs, drawn by eight dray horses, groaned as the teamster eased it onto the high road, heading south for Dekhron and the piers, where the iron would be loaded on barges for the trip down the Vedra to the artisans of Faitel.

In the loading yard, Vynhal counted nine mals working two of the winches that lifted the iron pigs onto the transport wagons. Three armed Cadmians watched from the loading dock, their weapons casually ready.

The Tech captain reined up and watched the overseer give orders, but the hammer mills and the roaring of the furnaces to the west drowned out the man's orders. Two other winches stood idle, and the iron pigs overflowed the loading dock and were stacked back a good forty yards. A second empty wagon waited for the first to be loaded.

Vynhal continued to watch. The mals at the winches worked steadily to load the first wagon. The overseer gave them a brief respite while the first wagon rolled away and the second one moved into position. Several drank from water bottles. Two merely wiped their brows. All looked well muscled and in good physical condition, but it was clear that there were not enough loaders and winch-men.

After a time, the Tech captain flicked the gelding's reins and continued southward, toward the main square. The square was an open paved space, nothing more, except for the statue of the Duarches. On the west side was an inn, old enough that it was entirely of brick and stone, and that meant it had been built before even limited timbering had been allowed from the forests to the west and south of the town. The north side held a line of four shops, identical from the front, except that the painted shutters were of different colors, but each set of shutters matched the colors on the doors. Bright as the colors once had been, the soot and grit from the ironworks had dimmed and darkened them, even though Vynhal could see that the windowpanes were clean, as were the shutters.

The east side contained a cloth factor's, adjoining a weaver's. On the south side were the town fountain and two stone troughs for watering mounts and dray horses. In the middle of the square was the statue of the Duarches on a stone pedestal. The statue had been recently cleaned, and that was not usual. Had someone tried to deface it? Most likely, he decided.

No one was out on the front porch of the inn, and, after a moment, Vynhal turned his mount back toward the ironworks.

This time, he rode through the loading yard, nodding at the guards, who barely nodded back, and tied his mount at the iron hitching rail in front of the small brick structure that looked to hold the supervisor's spaces.

A young man looked up as Vynhal stepped inside. "Ah . . . sir?"

"Tech Captain Vynhal to see the ironworks supervisor. I've been sent from Ludar."

"Yes, sir." The assistant bolted up from the table and the three stacks of papers set there and stepped to the closed door to the right. "Sir . . . a Tech captain from Ludar."

"Have him come in, Paulon." The deep voice carried through the closed door.

The lander who met Vynhal was thin and balding, unusual for a lander, but he could have had some indigen in his background, the Tech captain supposed.

"Gestark, Captain. Welcome to the ironworks."

"You're the one in charge of the ironworks?" asked Vynhal.

"As much as anyone," replied Gestark. "I'm the supervisor. I report to the High Alector of Engineering in Ludar, or rather to the alectress who is his assistant. How can I help you, Captain?" He gestured to the single chair across the table desk.

Vynhal took it and waited for the other to reseat himself. "I've been sent to find out a number of things. One is a matter dealing with the Cadmians, and the second is to report on the possible reasons why iron production is decreasing."

Gestark smiled, faintly. "There's no secret about that. I've sent report after report to Ludar. To smelt iron takes mostly hard coal and iron ore and water, plus more than a few other items—and people who know what they're doing. We can get enough ore and enough coal. Most of the time, anyway. What we can't get is enough water and enough labor."

Vynhal hadn't heard about the water before. "What's the water problem?"

"The ironworks draws from the Riggstel Creek. We've got a dam to the west of the works, but the flow on the creek is down a third from what it was ten years ago. I've ridden the whole creek, all the way north and east of Soulend, but no one's diverting the water. There just isn't as much, and no one knows why. We're getting as much rain, and what flows from the Plateau is pretty much the same as it always was. There's just a lot less by the time it gets to Iron Stem."

Vynhal couldn't do much about the creek and the rain. "I've heard about labor . . ."

"The Duarches, for all their edicts, don't seem to be able to get us that many more bodies. The Highest's assistant tells me that we're getting all the labor that's possible, that they've sent every mal in the west here, but they won't dispatch innocent people because I need more bodies. The ones we have don't last that long. So we do the best we can."

"How many do you get? Do they arrive every week, or once a month?"

"We got ten last week. That was more than usual. Two went to the cookshack—one had even been an assistant cook. Already, they say the food's better."

"What about the others?"

"Two were already dustheads. I sent them to the dustworks. The others are working here. I think we'll lose one to holder indenture, but it's too soon to tell."

"Do you have to send reports on what you receive?"

"Absolutely. They go to the portmaster in Dekhron. I've complained about so few, but he assures me I'm getting what's coming."

"Are you having escape problems?"

Gestark laughed. "There's no place for them to go. They get fed better in the ironworks compound than do most of the townspeople. The townies don't want anything to do with them. We've had a couple walk off over the last year. One was killed, the other two were back in less than a week."

Vynhal was more than confused.

"Look, Captain. We get the mals. Some of them can't do the ironworks. Either they're not strong enough, or they're holder-types. It's easy enough to tell. The holder-types get gaunt and start to waste away no matter how much we feed 'em. Now . . . I could keep them until they died, but that doesn't make any sense. I'd waste food, clothes, and time. So, I sell the holder-types under contract to whoever needs them. The coins get credited to the ironworks, and that's better than killing the mal and losing the coins both. The holders work them hard, and that means they don't get off easy. Usually it's a five-year indenture, sometimes ten. The weak ones, well . . . I don't have much choice there. Some we can use in the cookshack and some for scut work, but half of them go to the dustcat works. We don't get as much in coins, because the indentures are three and five years. Most don't live that long once the dusters get them."

What Gestark said made a sort of sense to Vynhal, and the lander—Vynhal gave him the benefit of the doubt—seemed to be telling the truth. But there had to be more. The Submarshal of Myrmidons wouldn't have sent him to Iron Stem otherwise.

"Where do the mals come from . . . I mean, how do they get to you?"

"They come from Dekhron in wagons, usually ten to a wagon. They're brought up the Vedra, and they hold them there in the gaol at Dekhron until they have ten or twenty, then they put them on the empty wagons coming back."

"How many do you get a month?"

"We're lucky if we get twenty—and five will work out."

"That's all?"

"That's all that it's ever been. A quarter of them. The problem is that we're getting fewer in total. I've noted that but I've been told that nothing has changed."

Something had changed.

"I'd like to talk to some of the mals, the ones that have come here recently."

Gestark shrugged. "So long as it's after their shift."

"Are there some off shift now?"

"Just the nightloaders."

"They'll do." To start with.

"I'll have Paulon get a guard to escort you." Gestark stood.

One of the guards escorted the Tech captain to the barracks. Paulon accompanied Vynhal and the guard—whose insignia was of the Fifty-fourth Foot.

The barracks bay was gray. The windows were high and barred, and another guard stood outside the heavy door. After opening the door, both guards took up positions inside, flanking the door, their sabres out. Five men lounged on pallet bunks. That was understandable. There were no chairs.

"The captain needs some answers," Paulon announced nervously. No sooner than he had made the statement than he stepped back out the door.

None of the five heavily muscled loaders said a word. Four did not even look at Vynhal.

"As the man said," Vynhal began, looking at the one who had looked up, "I'd like some information."

"So?"

"So . . . you give it to me, and I go away. You don't, and things get unpleasant."

"What else can you do to me?"

"Kill you," replied Vynhal. "If I have to."

"Be a mercy."

"No, it wouldn't. You want to live." Vynhal smiled coldly. "Besides . . . I could do worse. I could smash your foot so that you'd have to go to the dustcat works. Or chop it off."

The big man's eyes avoided Vynhal's. "What you want?"

"Just to talk to you, about what happened once the mal barge got to Dekhron."

"What about it?"

"Tell me what happened."

The mal shrugged. "Simple enough. The gaoler came on board. Asked if anyone was a dirt grubber . . . grower or orchard type. Maybe six, seven fellows were. He marched them off first, and put 'em on a wagon. Rest of us joined the ones that had been there a week, stuffed us on the wagons. Chained us. Drove us here."

Vynhal managed to nod, knowingly. "How many were there in your group, before they took out the grower types?"

"I don't know. Seventeen, eighteen."

"Did anyone else get taken away after you got on the wagons?"

"Nope."

"Did you all come at the same time?"

"Nope."

Vynhal looked at the man in the corner. "You. Did they take growers when you got to Dekhron?"

There was silence.

Vynhal drew his sabre and stepped forward.

"Yes." The mal's dark eyes radiated hatred.

"When did you come here?"

"End of winter."

Vynhal went through all five. None had been at the ironworks more than a year and a half. All had undergone the same sorting procedures. When he finished, he nodded to the guards. "That's all."

"Don't we get something?"

Vynhal smiled. "My gratitude."

He walked out, letting the guard secure the barracks bay, and headed back to where he'd tied his mount.

Vynhal knew the procedures. *All* the mals were supposed to go straight to Iron Stem—and that meant he needed to take his squad—fully armed—down to Dekhron. After he found out what he could in Iron Stem.

IV

On Tridi morning, Vynhal waited in the small mess room until Murch showed. The Tech captain had the feeling that Murch had waited until he could do so no longer.

"Good morning, Murch." Vynhal held a mug of cider that had once been warm, but made no effort to drink it.

"Morning, Captain."

"I had some questions about the way they use labor on the holdings—the ones from the works that Gestark sells. Who among the local holders might be the most informative?"

"Calistar is the oldest of the holders," Murch said slowly, settling reluctantly into the chair across the table from Vynhal. "He might know something. He's not likely to talk to you, though."

"Does he come to town?"

"Market days . . . if he doesn't send his daughter or his sons. Sometimes not then."

"We'll have to go see him."

"He still won't talk to you."

"He'll talk to me. I'll just bring the whole squad."

"He might."

"Where is his place?"

"He's a good five–six vingts to the north, east of the high road. Two stone pillars. One has an iron emblem, looks like a ram, but no ram I ever saw. The lane to the holding is another two vingts. Could be more. Never traveled it."

"Thank you."

"Your problem, sir."

Vynhal wasn't in the mood for more problems. He just wanted to get to the bottom of the mess. He hadn't been in Iron Stem two days, and he wanted out.

Less than a quarter glass after muster, he had all of second squad mounted and on the high road north.

For the first vingt, there was no one on the road but the Tech squad, but past a road cut, Vynhal made out a wagon pulled by a single horse heading southward toward Iron Stem. The driver saw the squad and pulled into a turnout on the west side. As Vynhal rode closer, he could see the driver was a bearded man close to his own age. In the back of the wagon were bundles of fodder, crudely bound with twine. The herder gave the briefest of nods to the captain, and Vynhal returned the gesture in kind.

Over the next three vingts, they passed but two wagons, one of them a high-sided and covered spirit wagon headed back to Dekhron, the other a battered relic pulled by a swaybacked gelding and driven by a young man scarcely more than a boy. Tied behind the seat were four bushels filled with a splotched green-and-red fruit Vynhal did not recognize.

When they reached the pillars with the ram emblem, Vynhal studied the dust in the lane. While it had been traveled, no one had used it in the last day or so. "This is the place." He turned his mount eastward on the lane. The lane stretched toward the east for a vingt or so before it began to rise slowly over another half a vingt to the crest of a low rolling hill. A higher hill lay beyond.

Vynhal and the scout riding beside him were a good fifteen yards ahead of the rest of the squad by the time they neared the first slope. Vynhal turned in the saddle. "Alizar . . . ride on ahead, to the top of the rise. Then come back and tell me what you see."

"Yes, sir." The Tech rider urged his mount forward, moving away from the squad.

Vynhal surveyed the lands to the north, then the south of the lane. Greenish gray irongrass stretched in both directions. The only vegetation he could see besides the spare grass were clumps of low bushes with almost spiky branches. Each bush was separated by at least a yard from any other bush, and there were only scattered groups of three or four. What Vynhal did notice was that none of the bushes grew on the lower ground—only on the upper sections of the low rolling hills. The bushes seemed almost to reflect the morning sunlight, as if they had collected dew; but the air was too dry for that, and the road dust showed that it had not rained in days.

Alizar rode back down the red-sandy lane toward the squad, reining up beside Vynhal on the Tech captain's left. "There's something over the hill, Captain, sir, there is. And . . . sir, I swear . . . the wind sings. It doesn't whistle or moan. It sings." Alizar did not look at Vynhal.

"Sure it does, and I'm the First Duarch's eldest son," snapped Vynhal. "We're here to find out why things are going wrong here in Iron Stem, and the sooner we finish, the sooner we can call in the sandoxen and head home."

"It sings, Captain. It does, I swear."

"You want to turn into a sanderer, or burn out your brains and go to work for one of the flatheads who keep the mangy dustcats?" Vynhal regretted the words as he finished speaking, but he couldn't have his rankers claiming that the wind sang. The next thing he knew, they'd be claiming . . . He shook his head. He couldn't even come up with a comparison.

"No, sir."

"What's beyond the crest?"

"Just another low valley, sir, and the lane goes up it, too."

Vynhal wondered how many hills they'd have to cross to get to the holding.

At the top of the first rise, the Tech captain looked eastward. In the distance rose the sheer cliff walls of the Aerlal Plateau, so sheer that the early dwellers in the Iron Valleys had called them the "wall of the world." That was what he'd heard, anyway. Directly before the squad, the lane headed down a gentle incline into a vale where the grass seemed thicker, and the spiky bushes fewer, before climbing up a slightly steeper grade to the top of the next rise. He couldn't see whether there was another rise beyond the one ahead; but that he couldn't suggested that there either wasn't one, or it was lower.

He glanced over his shoulder. The others in the squad had closed up slightly, but the next rank was still ten yards back. That was close enough. Vynhal looked forward and shifted his weight in the saddle. What a desolate place, open and empty, and yet it was less than ten vingts from Iron Stem. Were all the Iron Valleys like this?

Less than a hundred yards after the lane leveled out in the shallow and narrow valley, Vynhal frowned. Had he heard the faintest sound, like a distant crystal chime?

"Sir!" Alizar gestured to the left. "There!"

Vynhal turned. Less than forty yards away was a catlike creature, and it was sprinting toward them. From what he'd read, the creature had to be a dustcat. It wasn't that large, only two and a half yards long, with spindly legs that stretched out more than a meter at full extension. Those legs were fully extended as it sprinted toward the squad. They were less than six vingts northeast of the edge of Iron Stem, and here was a dustcat. Yet Murch had been telling him that the dustcats were rare.

"Ready arms! Fire!" snapped Vynhal, snatching his rifle from the holder.

Alizar's weapon was already in his hands, up and tracking the beast.

Crack! Light flared as the bullet struck the dustcat—light and a cloud of grayish green dust . . . or mist.

With the flare of light, Vynhal winced.

The Tech squad gaped as the dustcat appeared out of the cloud of whitish dust, untouched. It continued to race toward Alizar.

"No! No!" Alizar screamed. "Die, you bastard! Die!"

The Tech ranker fired again.

Vynhal aimed at the dustcat, then squeezed the trigger of his rifle as the cat leapt toward the ranker less than three yards to his right.

Light flared around both the captain and the ranker.

Vynhal blinked. The long spindly figure of the dustcat had vanished, and a cool, almost chill wind swept around him, like the Bay of Ludel in late fall, yet the air was perfumed with flowers he had never smelled. A lithe woman, impossibly small and well formed, with shimmering wings, each more than a yard long, hovered before him. She bent forward and kissed his cheek.

Only shoot if you are truly threatened. You must come to understand. He would never understand.

Then she was gone, as if she had never been there, and Vynhal blinked.

The lane beside him was empty, and the grayish green irongrass stretched untouched away to the north, as if Alizar had never been there, as if the dust-cat had not existed, as if neither rifle had been fired. Yet he could smell the powder.

Vynhal turned in the saddle, looking back at Dilleter and Forsdt. They stared at him as he counted the squad. Eleven men. Alizar was still gone. So was his mount.

"Sir? Where's Alizar?"

"I . . . I don't know." Vynhal hated himself for the weak reply, and he added quickly, "It appears that . . . whatever that was . . . it got him." He kept studying the area. There was no sign of Alizar. None. He couldn't have just vanished. But . . . he had.

"But . . . how?"

Vynhal didn't have an answer. "We still need to see the holder. Maybe he can tell us what it was. It's his land."

"Sanders . . . that's what . . ."

"Bad . . . messing with them . . ."

Vynhal kept riding, alone at the front of the squad, still carrying his rifle, as his mount started up the lane's second slope. Behind him, he could hear the mutterings and murmurings, but what could he do? Techs were supposed to solve problems, not turn around when they appeared, and that was especially true of Tech officers.

He had to wonder what the flying woman had meant. Could she have been a soarer? Soarers were gone. They'd vanished ages before. Except . . . he'd seen and heard something. So . . . he'd either met a soarer, or he was losing his mind. Vynhal preferred to believe the former. He'd just have to see where it led.

When he finally rode over the hillcrest, he surveyed the buildings spread out halfway down the gentle slope. There was a large and long barn, four long sheds, two squarish outbuildings, and a house that faced the Aerlal Plateau towering to the east, its heights shrouded in what looked to be haze. The dwelling was but one story, all of red brick, with dark slate roof tiles and extended a good fifty yards in length and a third of that in depth. The structure was angled ever so slightly so that the north and south ends were farther east than the middle. A covered and railed porch ran the entire east side of the dwelling. As he rode closer, Vynhal could see that the porch was a good five yards deep. Several graceful stone benches, with upholstered seats, were on the porch.

Still, for the house of a man who was reputed to be one of the largest holders in the Iron Valleys, the brick dwelling was modest. The only signs of extravagance were the large windows and the dark-stained wooden shutters. With the alectors' restrictions on the use of wood, large shutters were extraordinarily expensive.

Two men and a woman stepped out onto the wide porch. All three wore tan leather jackets and heavy work pants over scuffed boots. The older man, trim and square-shouldered, moved to the top of the stone steps and waited for Vynhal to rein up.

"One of the boys said he saw some Cadmians coming. So I figured it might be best to wait till you got here. In case you didn't know, I'm Calistar."

"Vynhal, Cadmian Tech Captain."

Despite the thin silver-blond hair of a lander, Calistar had the heavy square jaw of an indigen. "What can I do for you, Captain?" The holder's voice was polite but not warm.

"I needed some information, and Captain Murch suggested that you would be the most knowledgeable of holders."

"That was kind of the captain."

Vynhal wasn't quite certain how to begin. He would have been brief and direct—if he hadn't seen the dustcat that he suspected had been nothing of the kind.

"We saw a dustcat on the lane."

"Couldn't have been," replied the angular holder. "Hasn't been a dustcat around here since the time of my grandsire's grandsire. They don't like people. Alectors even less."

"That may be . . . but it attacked one of my rankers, and there was a flash of light, and both the ranker and his mount—and the dustcat—were gone."

Calistar laughed, and the sound combined humor, sadness, and regret. "Like I said. There aren't any dustcats around. That could have been a sander or a soarer. They like illusions. You're lucky it didn't go for you, Captain. Most times, they take out officers first."

"And you let them?"

"You find a way to stop them, and the Duarches themselves'd make you a majer or colonel or whatever." Calistar's smile vanished. "I'm certain that wasn't why you rode all the way out here."

"No. I'd heard that some of the growers around Dekhron were buying up indentures of mals. I know that sometimes holders here do, but I was under the impression that you waited until Gestark offers them for certain types."

"Wouldn't buy anything in Dekhron, especially not indentures."

"Do you buy many?"

Calistar shook his head. "Not many. Maybe one every five–six years, if that. Wylart—he runs the barns and the buildings. Been with me fifteen years. Good man. We added one more, younger fellow, last year. Most of them go north to the ice-holders. That's what we call them. Land freezes solid in the winter. Doesn't thaw until late spring."

"How many of these indentures does Gestark offer every year, on average?"

"Never seen more than ten. I take that back. Two years ago, there were fifteen. We all remarked on that."

"All year?"

Calistar nodded.

Vynhal blinked. The woman had stepped into the light. She was much younger than the holder, perhaps his daughter, but her features looked familiar, for all that he had never seen her before. There was something . . .

"Is there anything else, Captain?"

Vynhal concentrated on the holder. "What about the indentures sold in Dekhron?"

"Don't know anything about that. I think I told you that."

"I meant before they come to the ironworks."

The holder shrugged. "Even if I needed a fellow, I wouldn't go there. Wouldn't want to take a chance on someone who hadn't felt the furnaces and the way they bake the life out of everything."

Vynhal asked variations on his questions, but after half a glass, it was clear that the holder was getting most impatient and could not, or would not, add more.

"Thank you. I appreciate your taking the time." Vynhal inclined his head.

Calistar stared at the captain, then shook his head. "You may find whatever you're looking for, Captain, but you'll find it's changed you. More than you could ever know."

Vynhal smiled, dismissing the holder's words. He tried not to look at the younger woman, although the way the sun fell on her, it lit her fine features, and her hair shimmered white-gold, with a hint of green, and he'd never seen that before. Some new fad, like the glitterdark? No, it was more likely to be an old one that had died out in the cities and remained in the hinterlands.

"I wouldn't disregard my father's words so casually, Captain," the younger woman said. Her lips quirked into an amused smile. "But you will do what you will and learn what you must."

"I suppose I will, Lady." He inclined his head to her. "Thank you both." He turned the gelding and headed back toward Iron Stem. He'd have to ride slowly because it was another five vingts to water, but he wasn't about to ask the holder for anything.

Back at the headquarters' building, three glasses later, he entered the loss in his command logbook. "Alizar. Tech third." Then he began to write up the report for transmission to headquarters.

As he sat at the small desk, he could feel the chill air behind him.

He turned, quickly. Had there been a flash of golden green? He shook his head. His chamber was empty.

He wasn't imagining that dampness and cool that had flowed across him. He couldn't have been. Yet they were gone, and the hotter and drier air that marked Iron Stem surrounded him. Vynhal frowned.

V

That evening, just before sunset, Vynhal saddled another spare mount, a mare, and rode into Iron Stem. He left the mare at what passed for a stable adjoining the Iron Beaker—the local tavern Murch had recommended. The public room was less than half-full, not surprisingly, for a weeknight. Novdi nights would be another story, but he hoped he wouldn't be spending many Novdis in Iron Stem.

Since no one approached him when he stepped into the room, lit only dimly by three oil lamps spaced along the outer wall, he took a small square table beside the unlit hearth, where he could see most of the tables. He turned the table slightly, so that he could sit on the stool and rest his back against the rough plaster of the wall.

A golden-haired but heavyset server walked up and looked down. "I'm Larmisa. What'll you have, Majer?"

"What tastes good that won't rot my guts?"

"Gold lager or the Fyansi—red wine from Casula. Local. Not too sweet."

"The lager."

"Be three."

Vynhal held up the three coppers.

"Right back, Majer."

Vynhal watched her sway her way between the battered tables. For all her size, she was graceful. Not his type, but grace appealed to him. Striking women who walked like yearling fillies didn't.

One of the other serving girls leaned toward. "Who's the officer . . ."

". . . Aldya says he's the one came in on the sandox coach the other day . . ."

In the far corner, around a circular table, sat four Cadmian rankers. One kept glancing at Vynhal. The Tech captain ignored him, but listened.

". . . him, all right . . ."

". . . already lost one man . . . say a soarer got him . . ."

". . . won't catch me out north . . ."

The golden-haired server returned and set a heavy glass beaker on the table with a thump. "There you be, Majer."

Vynhal grinned and handed her four coppers. "Thanks for the promotion."

"Any day, Majer." Her smile was amused—but warm. Then she turned, heading toward a balding man and a woman unlikely to be the man's wife on the far side of the hearth.

Vynhal shifted his attention to the two older men, crafters by their garb, who were less than a yard away, to his right.

"Yurkab . . . where Dilsant get the oak? He charges less for the table than the wood would cost me."

"You exaggerate."

"Not by much. How can he do it?"

"Look at the seal, closely."

"You're telling me that—"

"I'm telling you nothing, except to look. Besides, no one in Wesrigg would look. He could not do such in Dekhron," added the white-haired crafter.

"They say—"

"They say? Who says?" The white-haired crafter rose. "We should go. Now."

"But . . ."

"We should go." The elder of the two grasped the other's jacket, if briefly.

The brown-haired indigen crafter rose slowly, until his eyes crossed those of Vynhal. Then the younger crafter turned quickly and followed the older man.

Vynhal strained to catch their last words, even as he took a sip from the beaker. The lager was cool, and drinkable, if barely.

". . . he just *might* tell someone . . . take care of Dilsant . . ."

If he understood more of what the two had been talking about, fully, Vynhal might have. He'd gotten the impression that a crafter named Dilsant in Wesrigg was getting contraband wood. The older crafter had made sure that Vynhal knew it, but contraband wood wasn't his mission. He could pass it on, later. The alectors did like to know about that sort of thing, what with all the laws in the Code about what could be grown where, and when and how timber could be cut.

He took another sip of the lager and kept listening, picking up fragments here and there, first from two better-dressed young men across the room, talking loudly.

". . . lost two ewes to sandwolves . . ."

". . . that where it got the Cadmian?"

". . . Meurst . . . cares less about the trooper . . . lost ewes'll break you . . ."

That didn't surprise Vynhal.

"Sandurl's got a new wagon . . ."

". . . nothing wrong with the old one that a new axle wouldn't fix . . ."

". . . said . . . couldn't haul as much . . ."

It might be a long evening, thought Vynhal. Very long.

". . . lace curtains! . . . need lace curtains like a gelding needs a mare . . ."

". . . told me that a spruce cask'd do as well. Not hardly . . ."

". . . can get oak out in Wesrigg . . . know where to look . . ."

More contraband?

". . . Gestark's been having his nephew and his boys helping with the loading . . . night shift on the end-days . . ."

". . . no one else around . . ."

". . . wife doesn't like it . . ."

Vynhal had two lagers, and kept listening, but he heard less and less. Finally, he stood, left a copper on the table, and walked out of the Iron Beaker.

He stopped short of the side steps that led to the stable and glanced into the night sky. The green disc of Asterta hung just above the roof of the chandlery across the corner of the square. For reasons, he'd never been able to explain, Asterta comforted him in ways that the larger brighter Selena could not.

"They're only moons in the sky," he murmured, glancing toward the stable to the south of the tavern.

"You want some company for a while, Captain?" The woman who spoke sat alone on one of the backless porch benches.

"I'm not your type," he said with a smile. "No coins and no wife."

"I'm not asking." Her face was narrow, not quite lined, framed by shimmering black hair cut short at neck level, and she was a good fifteen years older than Vynhal. Once she'd been a beauty, but she was still good-looking, at least in the dim light of the porch.

He shrugged and sat on the end of the bench.

"You're not local."

"No. Tech captain out of Ludar."

She smiled, a narrow, amused expression. "Someone won't be happy until you leave. If you leave."

"I will, and they never are."

"Has anyone tried to kill you?"

"Two, maybe three, times. You watch for it. What are you doing out here"—he inclined his head toward the public room—"rather than in there?"

"It's quieter here, and the girls can find me if there's a problem. I'll have to go back in and make sure everything gets cleaned up later, anyway."

Vynhal concealed a wince. He'd assumed wrong. "How long have you had the place?"

"Very smooth, Captain." She laughed softly. "Implied apology and compliment without admitting fault."

"I'm sometimes slow, but I'm willing to learn." He paused. "How is business these days?"

"Slower. Production's off in the mines and the ironworks. Miners and free worksmen don't have as many coins. Crafters don't, either. Works mals have nothing."

"What about the dreamdust? I'd heard there wasn't as much coming from the dustcat runs."

"Jorliont and Chevark aren't hurting. Supply of the dust goes down, and the price goes up. It doesn't affect me much. Jorliont and his son Satyrl are too fancy for us, and the dustheads don't drink. Some of them scarcely eat. They just waste away, so happy that they can't tell they're dying. Filthy stuff."

"Maybe it will go away. Captain Murch says there aren't as many dustcats."

"Murch wouldn't know. There are plenty of cats in the stone jumbles below the Plateau." She laughed again, softly. "They just killed off or captured all the dumb ones. What's left are smart enough to kill most trappers."

"I thought I saw a dustcat, north of here. But it vanished in a flash of light."

"Probably a soarer. One of their little tricks. One of the harmless ones. Some aren't. They don't like towns, though."

A loud shriek came from inside the tavern, and the woman straightened, listening, but that was the only loud noise. "Aldya can be a bit loud at times. Some of the fellows like it." She paused, then rose, far more gracefully than Larmisa had. "I need to get back inside, Captain. Have a pleasant evening."

"Thank you. I hope everything goes well for you."

"You and me both."

He walked to the stable. Tomorrow would come too early.

VI

Quattri was little better. The squad left the post early, but they did not reach Dekhron until close to sunset, and Vynhal had to pull his direct authorization from the Submarshal of Myrmidons to force the Cadmian Mounted company on the west end of Dekhron to grant them quarters and stabling.

Early on Quinti, the squad rode down to the river piers, through the streets of Dekhron. The larger avenues off the eternastone main boulevard had been paved many years before. That Vynhal could tell from the grooves and chips in the stone. The smaller streets were dirt and clay. From the occasional set of deserted stone walls, the gaps between buildings, the old and faded roof slates and cracked roof tiles, and the sparseness of people on the streets, it appeared that Dekhron had once been far more prosperous.

The three pinkish stone piers were empty, either of iron barges to be loaded or prison barges arriving from downriver. A small scow was tied to a post at the quay between the piers. Adjoining the piers to the west, back thirty-some yards was the gaol—a brick building fifty yards long with a shed roof. The roof tiles were pinkish gray, and more than half bore cracks.

Vynhal dismounted in front of the gaol, leaving the squad mounted, with their rifles ready.

He walked up to the door. It was locked, or barred from the inside. He pounded on it. There was no response. After studying the front of the area, he noted one window that was unbarred and shuttered, three yards to the right of the door.

He pounded on the shutters. There was the sound of someone moving.

"I guess we'll have to rip the shutters off!" he called.

"Do that, and you'll end up in the lower block," came an answer from behind the shutters.

"I don't think so," replied Vynhal. "I'm here to speak to the head gaoler."

"Head gaoler doesn't want to talk to you."

Vynhal smiled, coldly. "I'm most certain he doesn't, but if he doesn't, the Submarshal of Myrmidons will want to know why. Tech captains have rights to question any functionary in the Duarchy who isn't an alector. And we have the authority to remove all obstacles in the way. In this case, that sounds like you."

"I'll tell him you're here."

Vynhal walked back to the door and waited, his hand on the hilt of his sabre.

The man who opened the ironbound oak door was taller than Vynhal—as few landers or indigens were—and broader. His brown hair was oiled and slicked back, and bound in a silver clasp. He wore a sleeveless black leather tunic and no undertunic, and the muscles on his arms looked iron-hard. He was clean-shaven and smiled, showing brilliant white teeth that were large and uneven. "Tech Captain? I'm Gratgran, gaoler and piermaster of Dekhron."

"Vynhal."

"Zentor is a little . . . zealous." Gratgran smiled unctuously. "What can I do for you, Tech Captain? Oh . . . do come in."

Vynhal stepped into the foyer, which held a desk table, a backless bench, and a stool behind the desk.

"I'd like to see the records showing the arrival statistics for mals over the last season."

"I didn't know that the Tech corps was interested in indentures."

"We're not. We're interested in iron production."

"Ah, well . . . we all have our duties. Let me get the ledgers. If you would wait a moment."

Gratgran returned within moments with a thick ledger bound in black leather, which he set down on the table. He flipped through the pages. "The last season . . . yes . . . here we are." He pointed. "The mal indenture arrivals for summer begin here . . ." The gaoler stepped to the side. "Twenty-one on the third of Quintera. . . . And here, on the eleventh . . . twenty-three . . ."

The ledger was far too neat to be a working document, Vynhal could see, but he just nodded and looked over the columns as Gratgran explained.

". . . last week, twenty mals, all dispatched to the ironworks . . ."

"Who gets a copy of your reports?"

"The portmaster, of course."

"Where's his place? I didn't see anything else . . ."

"Oh, the portmaster is Dueryt. He's also a grower. I handle the port duties for him. There's not that much, really, just the iron going downstream and the mals coming up. I'm sure you understand, Tech Captain."

Vynhal was afraid he did. He stepped back and smiled. "You've been most helpful, Gaoler Gratgran. Thank you."

"My pleasure, Tech Captain."

Gratgran did not shut the door, but stood watching as Vynhal and second squad rode away.

VII

Late in the day of Sexdi, less than a glass before sunset, Fiosyt rode back into the Cadmian barracks in Dekhron, where second squad had been quartered for the past two days. Vynhal was out in the courtyard within moments of when the ranker reined up. He'd had to force himself to be patient in waiting until the next mal barge arrived, but that was the only way in which he'd be able to confirm his suspicions.

"What can you report?" he asked the ranker.

"Like you suspected, sir, there's a steam tug dragging a prison barge up-stream. Hard to tell, but there must be forty mals there."

"Good. We'll see what happens. Second squad! Mount up!"

"Mount up!"

Vynhal led the squad northward out of the compound, past the hill and out of easy sight, before taking a side lane that connected to the river road east of the piers. He'd spent time on the previous day checking maps and routes, and he was fairly certain how the gaoler avoided any direct observation. Vynhal also found routes that would suit his purpose, such as the one he picked for second squad.

By the time second squad was in position behind the half-tumbled walls of an ancient factor's warehouse, darkness had begun to fall across the piers, and the lines on the barge were being doubled up. But no prisoners emerged.

Had he misjudged the gaoler? Vynhal shook his head.

Less than a quarter glass later, a wagon rolled up silently, then a second.

From his position behind a stone window frame, Vynhal could barely see as each mal was taken to the gaol, and then, after but a few moments, led back out to one of two wagons, chained. There were but four lanterns, one on the pier, one by the gaol door, and one in a bracket behind the seat on each of the high-sided but open wagons. The ten men who guarded the wagons and prisoners carried staves or cudgels, certainly adequate for bound captives.

As what looked to be one of the last mals was led from the barge, Vynhal eased from his vantage point and mounted.

"Second squad, forward!"

At the sound of hoofs, several of the men with cudgels looked up.

"Cadmians!"

Three men broke and ran immediately. Two others turned and brought up iron-tipped staves, one facing Vynhal. The Tech captain leaned away as he bore down on the indenture pirate, but the man compensated, and the staff delivered a glancing blow to Vynhal's arm.

Vynhal had to force himself to hang on to the sabre, for the moment it took to shift hands. He wasn't as good left-handed, but better than he would have been with a numb right arm. And good enough to slash the bravo's throat on the back slash.

In moments, the space on the quay at the end of the pier held five bodies—all of men who had been handling the mals. One ranker was cradling a broken arm.

Vynhal reined up beside the nearer wagon where the driver was pinned against his seat, with Dhagryt's sabre at his throat.

"Now . . . you can make this easy, or you can make it difficult," Vynhal said. "Where were you taking this crew?"

"Wesrigg . . ." the tin man stuttered.

"Where else have you taken other grower indentures?"

"Emal . . ."

"Where else?"

"Satala . . . that's it. Sure as Asterta's green, it is."

"What growers bought the indentures?"

"I don't know, sir. Swear I don't."

"Tie him up and chain him with the others. We'll take him to Iron Stem. The justicer there can sentence him to indenture."

"Yes, sir!"

Vynhal turned the gelding, easing his mount toward the second wagon, where Fiosyt and Yurl stood guard.

"Driver ran off. These look like they're the ones for the ironworks. More muscle anyway."

"Good. Fyntal . . . check the barge."

While Fyntal rode out onto the pier, his rifle at the ready, Vynhal reined up and massaged his sore shoulder for a moment. From what he could tell, the only souls left around the pier were his squad, the one driver, and the mals.

"There's no one on the barge, sir!" Fyntal called back.

"Join me. We're going over to look at the gaol."

As he rode up to the gaol building, even in the dim light of the single lantern, swinging gently on a brass bracket, Vynhal could see that the iron-bound door was open. He suspected that the entire gaol would be empty.

It was.

"Frig . . ."

That meant that second squad would have to escort the mals all the way to Iron Stem, and the last thing Vynhal wanted was to run a prisoner detail.

VIII

On Sexdi, Vynhal had only taken the mals five vingts north, where he'd found a holding with a barn and commandeered the barn for the night.

When they had left in the morning, he'd paid the small holder a silver, little enough but all he could afford.

In the morning, once the wagons were back on the high road, he began to interrogate the mals, one at a time, riding beside the rear wagon, starting with the rearmost prisoner on the left side.

"What did they tell you when they took you off the barge?"

"They said I'd be going to help a forester. They didn't say where. They just laughed. The gaoler said I liked dirt, and I'd be better off planting trees than being baked in the ironworks." The wiry man shrugged.

"What else?"

"Not a thing."

"For now, you are going to the ironworks. They do feed workers well. Some indentures get sold to the local holders." Vynhal eased the gelding forward, so that he was abreast of the next prisoner.

"What about you?"

"They said I'd be doing the same. They did ask if I could handle a saw or an ax."

"Anything else?"

"No, sir."

"You a former Cadmian?"

"No, sir. River patroller in Dimor. Watched the bogs and swamps."

"How did you get here?"

"Rather not say, sir. It was stupid."

Vynhal didn't press on that. A mal was a mal, and there was little he could have done, even had he been so inclined. Still . . .

In the end, Vynhal questioned all twenty-one, and learned little more than he had from the first two.

IX

Late in the day on Septi, under gray clouds that suggested rain, but would probably deliver little more than a passing shower barely enough to wet the high road or the irongrass, Gestark stood outside the supervisor's building at the ironworks. He looked at Vynhal. "You're most efficient, Captain. I don't know that we'll end up with that many more laborers, but we'll have more coins."

"Once my report gets to the Submarshal of Myrmidons, I think you'll be getting more mals on a regular basis. For the next few weeks you may not get any more."

"If you could only do something about the water . . . that would be amazing." Gestark shook his head. "Will you be leaving soon?"

"No. There are a few loose ends I need to deal with." He needed to find out who in Wesrigg needed grower laborers—and for what. Not that it really mattered to him, but he knew that the colonel would be less than pleased if he didn't follow up on that. He still hadn't done anything much about the dustcat issue, or the higher rates of off-duty losses from the Cadmians. He'd lost one ranker, and had another useless for patrols, and he'd accomplished less than a third of his mission—without any clear hope that what he had done would even improve iron production.

With no direct links to the capitals—for there was not a Table in Iron Stem, nor one any closer than Tempre, all Vynhal could do immediately was make another entry for the report that he would submit when the Tech squad's mission was complete.

And then, a trip to the dustcat runs would be the first task on Octdi morning.

X

The high road north—leading eventually to Soulend and Eastice—held few wagons and fewer horsemen as second squad rode north from the green tower on Octdi morning. The clouds of the previous day had lifted, replaced by a high haze that shaded the silver-green sky toward the silver and cast a pall of indistinctness over more distant objects.

The side road that led to the dustcat runs was unmarked where it left the high road, but half a vingt to the east, the lane ended at a stone wall and a solid oak gate—closed.

An iron shutter in the gate opened. Vynhal could make out a bearded face.

"What do you want?"

"I'm Tech Captain Vynhal, and I'm here on the orders of the Submarshal of Myrmidons."

"I'll have to check." The shutter closed.

Behind him, in the column. Vynhal heard a mutter. ". . . ought to teach those dustcatters a lesson." He thought it was Dilleter.

Close to a tenth of a glass passed before the gate swung open, revealing a stone-walled courtyard directly behind it. The courtyard—roughly thirty yards on a side—showed a loading dock set in the middle of the north wall, with a windowless structure of but one story. The east wall had another gate, ironbound and closed, and the south wall was but a solid wall of three yards. In front of the south wall was a stone watering trough, and to one side was a stone fountain with water flowing from the mouth of what Vynhal presumed to be a dustcat.

Standing on the loading dock was a broad-shouldered man dressed entirely in black. His hair was short and blond. "Captain, welcome to Dusthaven!"

Vynhal eased his mount over to the dock, reining up short of the man. "Tech Captain Vynhal."

"Satyrl, Captain. I understand you are here on the orders of someone?" The man's voice was rich and deep, the kind that inspired confidence in most people.

"The Submarshal of Myrmidons, acting on the request of the Duarches."

"Well . . . we would certainly not wish to disobey either of those functionaries. What can I do for you?" Before Vynhal could answer, Satyrl added smoothly, "Your men should feel free to water their mounts and use the fountain to drink or refill their water bottles. The Iron Valleys can be dry indeed in harvest."

"Thank you." Vynhal did not turn to relay the information.

"If it would not be too discourteous, Captain, might I ask why you wish to see a dustcat holding?"

"Everything is of interest to the Duarches," Vynhal replied. "There was some concern that the production of dreamdust had declined, and . . . no one seemed to know why. When something is unexplained, the Duarches wish to know why."

Satyrl laughed. "So a Tech captain is dispatched."

"Something like that." Vynhal managed a wry tone, although he was coming to dislike the man, without even knowing why.

"Alas, the answer is simple. We have fewer dustcats. The older ones are dying, and they do not breed well in the runs. Some do, but not many."

"Do you suffer losses from the sandwolves, the way the holders and herders do?" asked Vynhal.

"We can't afford losses either of the dust or the dustcats," replied Satyrl. "That's why the runs are covered. We have only lost one cat to the sand-wolves."

"Just a few days ago?" Vynhal was thinking of the dead Cadmian.

"A year ago. It ripped off the planks at one end of the outside run off the easternmost barn. We have reinforced them all since. The herders lose more animals, but the loss of one does not mean so much to them. The holders keep their animals in sheds at night. They lose few, and that is one reason why they are better off."

"One reason?"

Satyrl laughed again, ingratiatingly, and the sound raised the hair on the back of Vynhal's neck. "We have our secrets, and the holders have theirs."

"Do you send your hunters out to capture new dustcats?"

Satyrl laughed once more. "No. We would lose too many men. We simply offer twenty golds for a live and healthy cat. Thirty at times for a healthy female."

Vynhal almost whistled. Twenty golds was close to a year's pay for him, and Tech captains made half again as much as Cadmian officers and more than most crafters. "Do you get many?"

Satyrl shrugged. "Some years we have gotten ten, and some less than five. Last year was four. We have bought eight so far this year."

"That sounds like you will be doing better in the year ahead."

"One hopes."

"It might be best if I could see some of your . . . holding."

"Of course. For obvious reasons, I would not suggest your visiting the runs for more than a few moments, but you are certainly welcome to inspect whatever you wish." Satyrl reached down and grasped the bronze handle on the loading door, narrow as such went, no more than two yards wide, and slid it half open. "We will go this way."

Vynhal turned in the saddle. "I shouldn't be gone long. Water your mounts at the trough, and refill your water bottles at the fountain." He dismounted and handed the gelding's reins to Fiosyt, the nearest ranker.

Then he vaulted up onto the loading dock and followed Satyrl through the door. The warehouse behind the door was larger than he had thought, running back a good fifty yards, filled with barrels and kegs, and bales. It was also spotless, if dim, illuminated only by several high windows, barred on the inside.

"This is where we receive all the supplies." Satyrl walked briskly down the center aisle between the racks that held the goods. In moments, he turned toward a door on the side of the warehouse.

Outside, Vynhal found himself standing on a stone walk that ran due east toward a large villa that made the dwelling of the holder Calistar look truly modest. The walls were of redstone, and the roof tiles were a polished slate. To the north, his left, were the dustcat runs—wooden-walled sheds, really, that extended perhaps a hundred yards, all radiating from a barn. Farther to the east, he could make out another set of runs extending from yet another barn. He thought there might be another even farther east, but the low rolling hill blocked all but some rooftops.

"Are the runs floored as well?"

"They're paved with stone, and that's covered with a layer of pure sand. That makes collecting the dung easier and keeps it from being contaminated."

Why would they worry about that?

Vynhal's face must have displayed his confusion because Satyrl laughed

"It's not nearly as potent as the dander, but we dry it in the ovens, and powder it, and then mix it with wax and a special scented oil and make candles of it. The scent emitted from the candles is a mild aphrodisiac. They use it in the better pleasure houses, and it doesn't turn those who smell it into dustheads." He gestured. "Let me show you. The scutters have just collected everything from the second run." The dustcat holder turned and took the stone-paved walk that led down a slight slope to the central barn.

Vynhal took two quick steps to catch up. "How do you manage . . . not to be affected?"

"How do you know I am not?" countered Satyrl.

"You don't act like any dusthead I've met." Vynhal barely managed to keep his voice pleasant.

"That is one of our secrets." Satyrl laughed briefly yet again. "It is no secret. Those of our family are not affected by the dustcats or the dreamdust." He paused, then added somberly, "Most of us. Those who look to be . . . we must foster them elsewhere."

The inside of the barn wasn't what Vynhal expected. Rather, behind the door was a foyer, and off the foyer were doors. Satyrl walked to the second door from the left. It was narrow and fit snugly against the frame. He opened it and stepped into a small windowless anteroom, less than three yards square. Once more Vynhal followed.

The chamber held no furnishings and was floored with smooth redstone that had been heavily lacquered in a clear finish, as had the wooden walls and the back of the door. On the far wall was a second door, also heavily lac-quered.

"The cat has just been groomed, and is still sleeping. Otherwise, it would not be wise to enter."

"How often are they groomed?"

"Every third day, usually." Satyrl opened the second door and stepped through. "More often, and they languish from the drugging."

Once inside, the run, Vynhal was immediately aware of a musky, pungent odor, yet a scent with an underlying pleasantness. As Satyrl had said, the run was paved, with a thin layer of reddish sand, recently raked and smoothed. Light came from a series of glass panes set in the roof at intervals.

To Vynhal's right, the cat lay on a pallet of some sort of smooth black cloth. Its coat was reddish tan and looked like crushed velvet. The dustcat snored loudly, and its sides, not quite painfully thin, heaved with each breath.

"The finest Hyaltan cotton, thinly coated with hard varnish," explained Satyrl. "It makes gathering the dander easier."

For a time, Vynhal looked at the drugged dustcat, pathetic in a way, and so different from the image of the dustcat created by the soarer at Calistar's holding. "They're dangerous out in the wild?"

Satyrl laughed. "More than half the dustcat hunters die chasing and try-ing to trap them."

Vynhal's eyes went back to the cat.

"It isn't what you expected, is it, Tech Captain?"

"No." Vynhal shook his head.

"Do you feel dizzy or light-headed?"

"No. Should I?"

"Most people do by now. Still, it would be best if we left. Unless you would like anything else explained?"

"I've seen enough, I think."

Neither spoke until they were walking back toward the entry courtyard.

"So you think dreamdust production will increase somewhat?" asked Vynhal.

"One never knows, but we have more dustcats than last year." Satyrl smiled enigmatically, then asked, "Is your family from near here?"

"No. I was born in Dereka."

"That would also explain it."

"Explain what?"

"You are resistant to the dander and dreamdust. Few are. Mostly from here, but some from Dereka and some from Lysia."

"I suppose that's fortunate," Vynhal said dryly. "At least, I'll never be tempted to try it."

Satyrl only smiled, faintly, and even more enigmatically.

The man's voice and attitude had come to grate on Vynhal so much that he merely nodded in reply. All he wanted to do was to leave the holding.

As he led second squad on the ride back to Iron Stem, Vynhal wasn't sure what to think—or what to report beyond the fact that the decline in dreamdust was likely to stop and might recover because the dustcat holders had more living cats.

The image of the drugged cat came to mind, lying in spotless splendor in a covered wooden cage just long enough to remind it that once it had run free.

He shook his head.

XI

Because Vynhal had done what he could about the dreamdust, and because something about the foresters in Wesrigg nagged at him, on Novdi, he and second squad took the other high road, the one that eventually led to Elcien and its green towers and Hall of Justice. They left early, barely after dawn, with the rising sun at their backs, casting long shadows before them, because Wesrigg was farther from Iron Stem than was Dekhron.

They had ridden less than a quarter glass when Vynhal noted a lake to the north of the road, a vingt or so distant. At the east end of the water was a line of stone, crossing and blocking a small gorge, rising above it, confirming that the lake had been created by the dam. That had to be the dam of Riggstel Creek mentioned by Gestark.

Vynhal could see wide areas of mud at the edges, confirming that the water level was indeed low. Why, he wondered. He couldn't see that Gestark had lied about rainfall. So why would the creek have less water, if no growers or farmers were drawing more water?

For the next fifteen vingts or so, Vynhal could occasionally see the creek before it seemed to meander back to the north through the forested hills on the north side of the road. From what he could recall from the maps, the creek eventually angled back to the northeast north of Soulend.

Even moving quickly, second squad did not reach Wesrigg before late midafternoon. The hill town was more than a hamlet, but not much more, and Reillies in leathers and heavy woodsman's shirts were in as much evidence on the short stretch of the high road that served as the Wesrigg's main street as were townspeople in more muted trousers and shirts.

Vynhal was looking for a particular name, and he almost missed it, before catching sight of the shop nearly a block down a side street. Dilsant—that had been the name he'd heard in the tavern. The crafter who got oak so cheaply.

"This way!" He turned his mount northward. If he hadn't seen the name, he would have asked, but he preferred to ask as little as possible of anyone.

Outside the shop, he reined up and dismounted, tying the gelding to the weathered railing.

"I won't be long."

Although the cabinetmaker looked up from his workbench as the Tech captain walked into the small shop, he said nothing.

"You're Dilsant?"

"Yes." The crafter's voice was polite, but it concealed a certain contempt.

Vynhal wanted to lift the man by the neck. Instead, he smiled. "You craft hardwoods, I see." He pointed to the small writing table beside the bench, the wood still without a final stain or finish. "How much will that go for?"

"Too much for you."

"Oh? And how much is that?"

"Five golds."

A quarter of a year's pay for a table desk. Still that was far less than it would have cost in Elcien.

"Where do you get your oak?"

"Where does anyone get wood? From the foresters."

Vynhal sensed that the crafter was suddenly wary. "What foresters supply you?"

"Grehab and Drutyl."

"Which one does the oak?"

"Grehab, him and his brother Bakurb."

"Where would I find them?"

"Their mill is on the creek north of town."

"How do I get there?"

"Take the main street two blocks west until you come to the inn. Go right and keep going until you reach the mill. They're not very friendly."

"Thank you for the warning." Vynhal gave the slightest inclination of his head, then turned and left the shop.

Another half glass passed before the squad reached the mill, on the west side of the narrow lane, set above a stone millrace. Vynhal led the squad across the stone bridge over the creek below the millrace, a creek with but a thin line of water in it, then up to the side of the stone mill building.

A rangy bearded figure in leathers, holding a crossbow, stood on the stone loading dock, beside a pile of freshly sawn planks.

"Rifles ready!" snapped Vynhal.

The miller, or forester, lowered the crossbow.

Vynhal rode closer.

"Captain . . . I was meaning no harm. These days, you got to be careful."

"That you do." Vynhal didn't believe a word the man said. "You Grehab?"

"Nope. I'm Bakurb. Grehab takes care of the woods, and I handle the mill and the sawing."

Vynhal glanced at the wood. He knew a little about woods, enough to recognize oak and maple and pine. It wasn't any of those, but some kind of softwood. "What's the wood? It's a softwood, but I don't recognize it."

"Damarisk. Almost a trash wood, good for crates, troughs in wet places, that sort of thing. What people get when they can't afford good oak and pine. Or when we can't cut and mill any more of the good stuff."

"How much oak are you allowed to cut?" asked Vynhal

"That's not my side. I just saw and mill what Grehab sends down. He keeps track of that."

"Where would I find him?"

Bakurb gestured vaguely to the northeast. "Take the rightmost lane. He'll be somewhere out there."

Vynhal nodded. He didn't thank the sawmill owner as he turned his mount.

It took more than a glass before the squad tracked down the forester and a group of four other loggers—along with three wagons. As they rode up, a man in a stained leather vest strode toward them.

"Cadmians! Cadmians in the woods. Something I thought I'd never see." Unlike his brother, Grehab was clean-shaven, broad, and smiled.

On first glance, Vynhal trusted him even less than he did Bakurb.

Nonetheless, he reined up and offered a smile. "We've been dispatched to check on some things—by the Submarshal of Myrmidons."

"What can I do for you, Captain?"

"First, I'd like to know how many oaks do you cut down in a year."

"Not enough," snorted the forester. "Vingts and vingts of forest out here, and we can only cut one part in a hundred every year, and every one has to have a girth of at least a yard—three yards around. Can't even get one on a wagon." He gestured to the nearest wagon, holding a section of trunk no more than four yards in length. "You want beams, long ones, takes a special wagon and eight drays." A snort followed his words. "Make more sense to let us cut younger oaks for those."

"Does your family own the land here?"

"It belongs to the Duarches." Grehab spat to one side. "We have the harvesting rights. Have had since the time of my grandsire's grandsire. Have to follow the Code and keep the roads."

"What else do you harvest?"

"Whatever there is. Different rules for different trees. Miss one, and they'll double tariff you. Miss two, and you risk a flogging. After that, it's real trouble." The forester spat again, then smiled. "My troubles aren't yours, Captain."

"That's true." Vynhal returned the smile with one of his own, equally false. "Thank you. We'll be riding along some of your roads for a time."

"Just stay on the lanes. You get off them and trample seedlings, and the alectors won't like it."

"Thank you for the advice." Vynhal cared even less for Grehab than he had for Bakurb.

After leaving the loggers, Vynhal followed the narrow lane. Behind him, over the low hum of insects, rose the murmurs of the squad.

"... don't see why riding through woods ..."

"... captain's got a reason ... always does ..."

"... never tells us ..."

"... not till later ..."

That was because, reflected Vynhal, he often didn't know the reason, only that something didn't seem or feel the way it should. Like the forest through which they rode, except it wasn't a forest, he realized. There wasn't that much undergrowth, and the spacing of the trees was too regular. They'd been planted that way. Of course they had. That was why Grehab was a forester. Still ...

He looked to his left, where but a few shafts of the late-afternoon sunlight angled into the woods. The trees beside the lanes were mostly oaks, indisputably so, but the trees farther back . . . he wasn't so sure.

Abruptly, he turned his mount off the lane and between two of the giant oaks, and then past another two. Beyond that, the trunks of the trees were smaller, not that obviously, but definitely noticeably. He looked upward. The thinner trees ahead were as tall as the more massive oaks he had just passed, and the leaves and bark looked the same.

"It looks like an oak," Vynhal mused. Still . . . there was something about the tree . . . about all of them. He rode closer to the nearest trunk, then reined up, and took out his belt knife. The wood was green, and it took some effort to break it free. He hefted the small limb, less than a finger's thickness. It was far lighter than it should have been. "It's not oak."

"Ah, sir . . ." One of the newer squad members—Choisyl—rode forward.

"Yes, Choisyl?"

"It's what they call a water oak. That's 'cause the leaves and bark look like oak, but it's a softwood, and it grows real fast. We got a lot of them back home. The alectors make us cut about half of 'em, even around the bogs. Sometimes more."

That was something Vynhal had never heard about. Most logging around water was strictly controlled.

"Why's that?"

"They're water oaks. They soak up water and crowd out the hardwoods and even the better pines and firs."

Vynhal stiffened in the saddle. Frig! The whole frigging mess made sense. "Thank you, Choisyl. We've seen enough for today. Second squad, to the rear!"

He bent the small limb and tucked it into one of the loops in his saddle, then checked his rifle holder. He gestured for Choisyl to accompany him as he rode around the squad and took the lead for the return.

Once he was back on the lane, he turned in the saddle toward the ranker, and asked, "What else can you tell me about the water oaks?"

"That's not really their name. It's Damarisk or Lamarisk. They grow tall first, and then they spread. You get a canopy pretty quick."

"Anything else?"

"It looks like pine, but it's a little softer."

Thwunk!

Choisyl twisted in the saddle, a crossbow bolt in his upper arm.

"Rifles ready! Fire at will!" Vynhal's rifle was in his hands before he completed the order, but he had ducked as well. Arrows seemed to be everywhere for a moment; but he could see their source, and he urged the gelding forward, and through a gap between two oak trunks.

Vynhal had expected there to be the loggers, and the forester, but not another ten loggers with bows, half-concealed by the undergrowth.

He took a chance by reining up for a moment and sighting in on the forester. It took three shots, but Grehab was down and dead. The archers began to fall as the rest of the squad's shots began to take their toll.

"Sabres! Forward!" Vynhal led the charge.

When the squad finally regrouped on the forest lane, most of the archers and loggers were dead, although a handful had escaped. Vynhal hadn't been about to try to chase them far through the trees.

"Tech Captain's good . . ." came another mutter. "Swear he was carrying a light-knife, instead of a sabre."

"Check your rifles. Reload, now!" snapped Vynhal, ignoring the coldness of sudden perspiration on his forehead and the dampness running down his neck and between his shoulders. Tech captains weren't trusted with light-knives. Even Myrmidon rankers didn't get them—not that they needed them with their firelances. Only Myrmidon officers carried light-knives.

He surveyed the squad. He'd lost another ranker—Dharmid—and both Choisyl and Zerkhyd had been wounded, not too severely. Dharmid's body was strapped over his saddle.

"Forward!" Vynhal ordered, keeping his eyes wide and his ears alert.

The woods were empty, or so it seemed, and by the time they reached the mill building it was empty.

Vynhal smiled mirthlessly. He hadn't expected anything different.

He looked to the west, with the sun barely above the trees. "We'll just stay here tonight."

XII

Second squad and Vynhal reached Iron Stem in midafternoon on Decdi, and as befitted an end-day, the streets were almost empty as they rode northward through the town, and past the slumbering ironworks, toward the Cadmian post and the green tower on the north side of the tired town.

Murch walked out into the courtyard as Vynhal dismounted.

"Did you find anything in Wesrigg? Besides trouble?" Murch's words verged on sardonic as he looked at the mount that carried Dharmid's body.

"We found the second cause of the production problems with the iron-works, along with a dishonest forester, and sawmiller, and we left a half score dead archers and loggers."

The Cadmian Foot captain's eyebrows lifted. "If I might ask . . . you're losing men frequently, sir. How will this help the Cadmian losses here?"

"Cleaning up the mess will give your men more useful tasks to do. That will keep them from being quite so bored and broke," replied Vynhal dryly. He didn't have much sympathy for the heavyset captain. The officer should have seen some of what was going on if he had only looked.

Murch stepped back. "I'm so sorry if I offended you. But then, you Tech officers can resign any time, and no one says a thing."

"Your words didn't offend me, Captain. Frankly, your marginal competence does. I've lost two men, and had three others wounded, but I've discovered most of what I was sent here to resolve. You've lost five times that over the last year, and you've discovered nothing and suggested less."

Murch looked as though Vynhal had slapped him.

The Tech captain could sense the rage held beneath discipline by the other captain, but he went on. "Being an officer isn't being liked. It's getting the job done while being respected and losing the fewest men possible under the circumstances."

"I doubt that you ever—"

"*All* Tech officers were Cadmians first, Murch. I spent a tour in Indyor being sniped at by mountain nomads, and a tour in Eastice, which makes Iron Stem look like Elcien by comparison. That doesn't count the half tour in Blackstear in the winter, or the summer dealing with bandits on the Dry Coast. And yes, we can resign at any moment. That's because none of us has served less than a half score of years and because we get the miserable assignments that the incompetence of idiots like you has created." Vynhal's eyes blazed.

Murch took two steps backward. "I apologize, Tech Captain."

"I'll think about that, Murch. Now . . . if you'll excuse me . . . I have to check on the wounded and write another fatality report."

Murch swallowed.

Vynhal could sense the rage, humiliation, and fear swirling in the officer, but at the moment, he didn't care as he led his mount to the stable. He shouldn't have been quite so hard on Murch, but the Cadmian captain was the type who paraded arrogance until he was put in his place. Besides, Murch had kept getting on his nerves.

Once Vynhal had groomed the gelding, he headed for the infirmary to see how Choisyl and Zerkhyd were doing. Both rankers had had their dressings changed.

The post medic looked to the Tech captain. "Good field dressings, and the wounds were clean. Who took care of them?"

"I did." Vynhal didn't bother to explain that it was part of the extra training Techs got, especially officers. "How are they?"

"It looks like all of your wounded will recover, not even with disabilities."

"Good. Thank you." Vynhal nodded, then left the infirmary to check with the three wounded men personally.

XIII

That night, Vynhal could not sleep. He shouldn't have lashed out so hard at Murch, and what he needed to write up swirled through his thoughts . . . and he kept getting the feeling that he needed to take a walk.

For a time, he lay on the bunk and tossed and turned. Finally, he got up and pulled on his boots and trousers, and his undertunic. As an afterthought, he picked up his rifle, checking the magazine, before he stepped out onto the balcony and walked down the stone steps into the empty courtyard below.

Asterta was almost directly overhead, a full green disk. Selena had just risen over the dark mass of the Aerial Plateau, but showed only three-quarters full, a softer pearly white.

Vynhal walked northward toward the green tower, noting how it had a faint greenish illumination of the kind that cast no shadows. His boots crunched on the scattered fine sand that had blown across the paving stones. The crunching stopped when he walked through the stone archway in the north wall and stepped onto the irongrass that stretched northward, perhaps all the way to Soulend, or even to Sandhold.

The irongrass bent and whispered under his boots, brushing against the lower part of his trouser legs.

He stopped when he was even with the tower, a good fifty yards north of the unguarded compound wall.

He could see—sense, really—some creature moving across the irongrass from the northwest. A sandwolf?

He raised the rifle . . . waiting.

The sandwolf snarled and edged closer.

Vynhal did not shoot. There was something about the creature . . . a greenness . . . something . . .

The sandwolf charged—silently.

Silently!

Against every instinct he had, Vynhal lowered the rifle.

As the brilliant amber-green flash surrounded him, Vynhal swallowed, wondering if he were feeling death, and what would happen next.

He tried to focus his eyes, but there was a silvery green mist around him, and with it, the feel of cool, almost cold, moist air and the scent of unfamiliar flowers. At the edge of the mist was the same small woman, clad only in a greenish gold misty fog that did not conceal that she was naked nor reveal more than the general curves of her body—or the shimmering greenish gold wings that flared from the back of her shoulders. So insubstantial were the wings that Vynhal could not see how she could soar or fly.

You are not like the others, she said. *You see what they do not. You think they should see what you do, because it is so apparent, but they never will.*

After a moment, Vynhal realized that while he heard her voice, her lips had never moved. "How are you . . . speaking?" Except he knew it wasn't speaking, not the way he knew it, and her feet had not yet touched the hard red soil. She *soared*. His briefing instructions had cautioned him against the myth of the soarers. They had been the ancient inhabitants of Corus, but there weren't any left. Myrmidon Undercaptain Resytal had been most clear on that. Yet . . . she couldn't be anything else, not after two appearances to him. "You're a soarer."

That is but a name. Crystalline laughter followed the words that chimed softly in his head.

"Why are you talking to me?" Was she? Or was he dreaming it all? Or was he dying, killed by a sandwolf that he had only thought was a soarer? "What is this all about?" Vynhal couldn't believe that he was talking to a soarer. They were all supposed to have died generations before. "There aren't any soarers."

That is what the ifrits would like you to believe. We are Corus and of Corus. We have always been.

Her long fingers brushed his cheek. Those fingertips were cool, almost chill, and yet as warm as his own, and how that could have been he did not know.

You must prepare.

"Prepare for what?"

For what must be, if all the world is to live as it should and must.

"Exactly how am I to do that?"

You will teach your daughter what is necessary.

"I don't even have a daughter," Vynhal protested.

You will. Her name will be Aliora. The soarer laughed silently. *Why do you think I saved you from yourself?*

"You can't . . ."

Did you look closely at Calistar's daughter? Why do you think he is so successful as a holder?

"Your sister?"

So much as we all are sisters.

"Why me?"

You will understand, if you will but think. How did you feel when you saw the captive dustcat? Why did you not shoot the sandwolf?

Vynhal was mute.

You will understand, if you will but consider. Will you build, or will you destroy so that the ifrits may build what will enslave your children's children?

"Ifrits?" She'd used that term more than once.

The ones you call alectors.

Names were names, Vynhal thought numbly, his mind still trying to grasp the idea of a daughter, of all that what the soarer said implied.

She will be ours, and her children will be the hope of all that could be. Later . . . later, my love.

Before Vynhal could say another word, she had vanished, and he stood alone in the chill of a late harvest night. His love? Their daughter?

What had she meant? How could she possibly have meant what he had heard? How?

XIV

On Londi, the first day of the working week, Vynhal had settled himself down in the study and was writing out his report to the submarshal. He'd written the first page twice before he'd gotten that the way he wanted it, and was working on explaining how all the factors interrelated.

At that moment, there was a knock on the side of the half-open study door.

"Sir, there's a holder outside for you," announced Kiram, the senior ranker in second squad, who was acting as squad leader while Vynhal worked on the report. "I think he's the one we visited."

Calistar? What did the holder want with him? Or did he have more information? Vynhal rose quickly. "I'll go out and see him."

Outside the headquarters building, Calistar had remained mounted, as if he had known that Vynhal would appear momentarily. The holder shifted his weight in the saddle and studied the Tech captain slowly. "Never would have thought it."

"Thought what?" asked Vynhal, although he had an idea what Calistar meant, unfortunately.

"I'd see a Tech captain out of Ludar who could charm the winds and a soarer." The holder laughed. "You won't go back. You can't. There'll be a place for you, a real stead. We'll find one. Come see me." The angular lander turned the big gelding and backed out of the compound, then turned north on the eternastone of the high road.

Vynhal stood in the late-morning sunlight just watching the holder disappear to the north.

The faintest hint of a cool breeze, with moisture and the vagrant scent of unfamiliar flowers, swirled around him. Yet the air was still.

He shook his head and walked back into the headquarters. Holders didn't offer steads to Tech captains. And cool breezes didn't blow on still harvest mornings with the white sun beating down.

But both offers made finishing his report far easier. He had written two copies, and Yurl was making a third copy for Murch.

Less than two glasses later, he stepped into the Cadmian captain's study.

Murch looked up, then bolted to his feet, fear in his eyes. "Sir?"

"We're done here, Captain."

Murch raised his eyebrows, but said nothing.

Vynhal looked hard at the older but junior captain. "I'm recommending hazard pay for your company. The justification is simple. Tech squads are more highly trained and armed than standard Foot companies, yet second squad suffered a thirty percent fatality rate and an additional thirty percent nonfatal casualty rate in less than two weeks. I have no idea whether the colonel or the submarshal will approve, but that's all I can do. The rest is up to you. The dreamdust matter also looks to be on the way to correction. We've located the problem with the labor for the ironworks and identified the reason for the declining stream flow to the ironworks, but implementing the actual solutions will lie with the high alectors."

Vynhal doubted that the crafters and residents of Wesrigg would be pleased with any solution imposed by the alectors, especially not when it would involve the logging of all or most of the water oaks planted over years, if not generations, and the further reduction in cutting quotas for oaks and other slower-growing hardwoods. And that was likely just to be the beginning.

"I'm having one of my men draft a copy of my report for you, for your records. I apologize for my harshness yesterday, and you will find that there is nothing untoward in my report about you or Fifty-fourth Company." Vynhal looked at the captain. "You could do better, Captain, but I leave that to you. We will leave on the next scheduled sandox coach. The best of fortune to you, Captain."

Murch's eyes widened, just enough that Vynhal knew the too-old junior captain understood enough of what he had been told.

With a polite smile, Vynhal turned and departed.

XV

Vynhal walked toward the sandoxen and the coach behind them. With each step, the swirling thoughts and confusion inside his head rose. Abruptly, he stopped and motioned to Kiram.

"You take them back. There are loose ends I need to tie up. No need for the rest of the squad to stay."

"Sir?"

"You heard me. Take them back to Ludar."

"Yes, sir."

Vynhal walked back toward the headquarters building, then turned. He watched the coach's doors shut, forcing a smile to remain on his face.

Only when the coach turned south, heading toward the center of Iron Stem, and the road to Elcien, did Vynhal turn and walk to the stable. There he saddled a mount that was not his. He supposed he'd have to return it . . .

or pay for it . . . somehow. And he'd have to submit a letter of resignation . . . later.

He fastened his gear behind the saddle and led the gelding out into the courtyard. Then he mounted and headed north on the high road. After five vingts, he'd turn northeast through the pillars that led to Calistar's holding. From there, he knew, although he couldn't say how, he'd find his way to where his unnamed love—what else could he call her—was waiting.

. . .

The wind sings, even when there is no wind. There are winds, all kinds of winds, and those that sing belong to the soarers. I hear them in the night most of all, long after I've finished with all that has to be done on the stead . . . after our time together when she has just left me . . . and Aliora.

As most of my readers know, I deal often with the questions of belief, faith, truth, and perception. So must Captain Bellemer . . .

ALWAYS OUTSIDE THE LINES: FOUR BATTLES

Lethe

The tourmaline tambourine trembles, and the singer's voice settles like the mist of foxfire on the four hills that surround the dell. At the base of the hills is a boxwood hedge. Inside the hedge is the board, sixty-four alternating squares of black marble and pale green marble, a shade so light it is almost white. Almost.

The game is in progress. There is always a game being played.

The black bishop raises his crosier and slides time-diagonally toward the woman without a name. She does not know she has no name, for she believes she is Gaia. Her identity is not valid under the now, and the bishop's crosier snakes anglewise toward the blue flame that is her spirit.

"Repent ye of your sins, for ye have allowed the earth and all that is above it and under it, to be despoiled, now and forever, world without end."

The Queen-woman slides right-anglewise clear of the bishop, throwing her head back. "I have not despoiled the world. That is your doing, creature of blind faith and irrationality."

"There is nothing mightier than the True God."

"Life is mightier than blind belief, short as life may be." The Queen-woman-spirit without a name winces as the black crosier and the words it bears touch the edge of the flame that may be her shoulder, but her head remains high as she traverses the squares to avoid the bishop's thrusts and his angled track. "Believing does not make anything so."

The black snake of the bishop's crosier stretches after her. "Repent ye of your sins, for ye have allowed the people of the Lord to revel in what is physical and to forget their creator and their sinfulness, and such is a mighty sin in the eyes of the Lord."

"Thought and creativity, beauty and joy, ethics and morality, all rise from what is, from the physical." She angles to the center of the chessboard. "The universe is itself, and it requires neither god nor believers. Those who understand neither themselves nor the universe require a god."

Old Earth

Outside the dasher, I could sense the vibrations building as the scramjets labored, coming down into the heavier lower atmosphere. Inside, everything was dark. The dropship had just severed the powerlink.

Stand by for drop.

Standing by.

Coyote alpha . . . away . . .

. . . beta . . . away . . .

. . . gamma . . .

Even before the "away" came, the direct link snapped, and the dasher was screaming earthward, somewhere close to Mach 8. The shroud was full-stealth and emissions inert, both active and passive. That was, if the Saints hadn't come up with something new on their southern line.

Ablation at seventy, pulsed the system, *sixty . . . fifty . . . thirty . . .*

As the last of the shroud dissolved into mist, I air-started the turbines. They kicked in at less than five hundred meters above Beaver Dam—farther to the southwest than was healthy. With the residual velocity from the drop, and the direct turbine thrust we still had lift, although it would bleed off before we reached the Gorge mouth.

Four hundred meters AGL . . . three hundred . . . two hundred . . . At one hundred, I flared, killed the excess vee, deployed the rotors, and engaged them. Then, nose down, we angled into the narrow mouth of the Gorge. The Virgin River Gorge was tight, narrow, and twisty most of the way north to St. George. Most important, it was below the Saint scanners and almost suicidal to attempt to follow. Almost.

Energy emissions . . . scratch beta, came the system pulses.

Stet. Even with the direct-terrain linkages, I was having trouble staying below the scanner net—an unseen curtain of white-blue less than a hundred meters above the dasher.

The mission idea was simple. Use the Gorge to get inside the southern defense perimeter, and loft scramblers into the Saint Southern Command

Center buried under Dixie Mesa. Then turn and bat-ass back down the Gorge for pickup once the Southern Line was compromised and our heavy scrammers pounded the complexes there. The Mexicans had agreed to look the other way—anything to weaken the coming Saint drive to retake Las Vegas.

The secondary target in St. George was the Temple—the oldest original Saint Temple. High Command felt its destruction would weaken the Saints' sense of divine protection. So we carried four rockets—three scramblers and one slam-smasher for the Temple. I had my doubts, but no one asks CAF captains piloting dashers.

Scratch epsilon . . .

Three dashers left, so far, and we were only halfway up the Gorge, and what we'd covered was the part hardest for the Saints to detect us or do anything. The critical area was where the Gorge flattened out, some eleven klicks south of St. George. We needed to get within four klicks of the Santa Clara River channel before releasing the scrambler rockets. The top of the Dixie Mesa was a dasher base, but the heavies were another twenty klicks to the north, and the really heavy Saint scrammers were stationed at the Iron Mission Air Station.

Energy flared against the Navaho sandstone less than half a klick to the right, but it was a good fifty meters high. I dropped the dasher another twenty meters, the most I could do, and angled left, closer to the higher cliffs.

Five to release.

Full coverage ahead, came the pulses. *Shift all shields forward once you clear the river channel.*

I was going to have my hands—and everything else—very busy.

A gout of rock and dust showered down just behind us.

Boosted HE.

We were running out of time and river.

I flipped the dasher right and lower, barely above the muddy water. After less than half a klick, barely time to blink, our departure point was ahead, and I cranked the turbines full. The tail barely cleared the creosote bushes on the ridge line as we popped into view of every scanner on the Southern Line.

I plugged in the randomizer, just hoped that my harness was tight enough, as the system slammed us to the left. I dumped the nose to gain vee, then held us in a ground-dusting sprint to the release point.

One turbine began to hum—more dust and sand than it liked.

Stand by for release. One away, two away . . . three away.

The scramblers were gone. I readjusted, got a quick read, locked, and released. *Smash-slam away.*

Took the dasher almost at ninety to the low sandy hills, tight turn, and nose down, this time toward the east dry channel.

Just cleared the rim, when light sheeted all around us, just a brief flash, but the implants picked up the energy and radiation. Even before the turbines quit, I dumped the collective. With the pitch I'd been carrying, we'd have cartwheeled down into junk.

Coyote gamma, interrogative status.

We'd just been hammer-jammed, and power was bleeding down to zilch, and Coyote satellite control wanted to know status? Idiots. Their board would show it.

Going down . . . packages away.

Didn't know if they'd gotten it before my electronics finished frying. Mech linkage was shit, but at least there was backup to wire-fly.

The dasher was dead. Oh . . . there was fuel still in the stub tanks, and the turbines were intact, and the gearbox, transmission, and rotors were fine. So was the tail diverter. There just wasn't any way to restart the turbines, not with all the electrical systems wave-pulsed into junk. Kept the rotors turning just long enough to spot a flat spot—sort of—and flared.

We hit. Hard. Dasher plowed into dirt and stone. Instafoam solidified around everything. Could feel us going head over ass, head over ass. Finally came to a stop.

I waited—just long enough to make sure we weren't hanging somewhere and about to fall off a cliff before I punched the dissolver. Cockpit smelled like stuff I didn't want to think about.

The exit panels had already blown, and I could see Lyana dashing out. How had she gotten there? No time to question that. I grabbed the survival pak and the miniature inflatable and stumbled out after her. There was so much dust it was hard to see. Didn't mean that the Saints' scanners weren't already zeroing in on us.

"Over the hill and down the slope!"

"Which way?" came from Lyana.

I'd thought . . . there was something . . . but now wasn't the time to think about it. Not in the open where the Saints could mow us down. "Straight ahead."

We barely got to the edge of the slope, just out of the dust swirled up by the winds, when my implants registered all sorts of energy.

"Down!" At the red wink and the energy surge, I threw myself flat behind a chunk of sandstone, hoping that Lyana had as well.

Something exploded, and shards and fragments of stone went everywhere. My back was a mass of fire, and Lyana had been thrown against a chunk of black rock—old lava, I guessed. Her eyes blinked, not registering much of anything. There was a hole in her shoulder, the kind that came from projectile weapons, and blood across her flight suit.

The first-aid kit was in the bottom of the survival kit. I kept low as I ripped open the closures.

"Don't . . . Daffyd . . . be all right . . ."

"You'll be all right? With that?"

Lyana smiled, wanly.

I watched as the gaping hole in Lyana's shoulder slowly closed.

My mouth opened. "What . . ."

"It's easier these days. Lead bullets, ceramic bullets, depleted uranium, composite armor . . . no cold iron." She sat up slowly, her back against the rock. "Takes a lot out of you. Rather not have to do that often."

"Can you move?"

"Slowly."

"We need to get down this slope and out of range. The river's down there, and I've got the inflatable." I also still had the slug-thrower. Nothing like powder and lead when the electronics fail, although, after watching Lyana, maybe cold iron would have been better.

Crumpt! Behind us, what had been left of the dasher exploded into a ball of flame, sending waves of heat around and past us. I almost screamed at the pain of the additional heat on my back.

Instead, I extended a hand to Lyana, and we began the descent, sliding, running slowly where the footing was half-secure. We had to get down to the river . . . somehow.

Tory

Sean owns the only pub in Trawley's Cross. He also runs it, and I've never seen anyone but Sean behind the bar. Oh, there are serving maids and lads, but no one stands behind the bar but Sean. So far as I know, no one ever has.

Now, Trawley's Cross is as far away from the ISNet as you can get, a good three-hour drive up Aillen Canyon, and that's just to get into the valley, and the road's so narrow and the turnouts so infrequent that all too often someone has to back up close to half a klick. Trawleymen don't like to back up, and there's been many an altercation about precedence over the years, the most famous being that of the time when Lugh blinded Balor with his own reflection . . . but that's another story for another time.

The pub looks like it came out of old Ireland, back on ancient earth before the disaster. Dark wood, white plaster walls, carved wooden bar, brass fixtures for the wall lamps, with dark green glass shades. The stools at the bar are dark wood with carved backs, but no padding, not quite authentic, but looking so. There are exactly thirteen booths—also dark wood with no cushions—six on one side and seven on the other, with a dark oak floor between them.

I'd been going to the pub on Fridays ever since the company sent me to Trawley's Cross, and that had been a year earlier. ReFor wasn't much of a company, but jobs have always been scarce on Tory, and I'd been lucky enough to be named as a supervisor of the foresting effort in the Espagne Mountains. So I spent all week tramping somewhere, either getting the data for the next segment, or surveying and evaluating . . . if it wasn't one thing, it was another, and I was more than thirsty, not to mention tired of my own company, by Friday night.

I'd gotten the black lager from the bar and carried it back to the fourth booth—the middle one of the longer row. I'd always taken that one when I could. Started out that way because it was always the last one taken. Now, it's mine. I don't mind admitting that I'm a big man. It helped in that, especially since I can't abide sitting at the bar along with all the other lonely souls. Don't know as I'm lonely so much as alone. Lyana helped. She'd stop and chat. She didn't talk to most folks, not that I'd noticed.

Sean passed, carrying a small tray with two glasses of dark stout.

"How old is the pub, Sean?" I asked, wanting to say something. Could have been that I'd asked him before. If I had, I didn't recall the answer.

"Don't know. Been here longer than I have. That's all I know." He stopped, impatiently.

"That's absurd. You're listed as the first settler, and they only finished the road through the canyon ten years ago. Mountains are too high for an airlift."

"Was the first." He walked away and drew another lager for Mac Herris.

When he headed back toward the bar, his tray empty, I asked, "Why don't you serve any fish here? Trout in the lake, salmon took to the river."

"Don't like fish," Sean replied. "Don't serve it."

"Everyone likes salmon. You don't have to like it, just serve it."

"Doesn't work that way."

"Where's Lyana?"

"Lyana? Don't know what you're talking about." He walked away to refill someone else's glass.

How could he not know Lyana? How many times had she appeared and sat with me? Why would he pretend not to know her? Or at least, know about her?

Sipping on the black lager, because I've never liked amber chewy brews, I really looked at the pub. Most people didn't. They were just thankful it was there.

The first thing that struck me was that all the dark wood in the pub was walnut. It's a good wood. Nothing wrong with walnut. But I'd never seen any walnut on Tory. We'd planted oaks on the lower hills east of the lower mouth of Aillen Canyon, and plenty of spruce, and pine, and fir on the higher slopes, below the tree line. It'd be years before any of them could be harvested. So far as I knew, there hadn't been any formulators in the valley either, and the cost of interstellar shipping was more than prohibitive.

Then, there were the carved swans. On the top of the seat back where the walnut top piece joins the two seat backs—at the front looking out across to the other row of booths is a carving of a swan, just the neck and head, mind you. There are twelve of them. Not eleven, not thirteen, just twelve.

The other carving, the one in the booth I always took, is that of a woman—or rather it had been, because it had vanished. I hadn't even noticed, not at first. I looked up and studied the end of the walnut crosspiece, smooth as satin, and old, as if the carved woman had never been. I knew better.

Nursing the lager, I had to ask another question. Why hadn't I noticed the walnut before? And how long had the carved woman been missing?

Old Earth

Sweat was pouring off my forehead by the time we reached the reddish sandy mud at the edge of the Virgin River—if you can call a stream six meters wide a river. In places, it might have been three meters deep. But from where I stood, most of it looked less than a meter deep, cold reddish water swirling over stones, with a narrow and deeper channel in the middle.

Still . . . it was the only way out. It had taken close to half an hour to cover less than a klick, and the nearest pickup spot was something like sixty klicks to the southwest. There had been talk of a road paralleling the river, but the cost would have been prohibitive—and once the border skirmishes between Deseret and Mexico heated up, neither side wanted easy access for the other. Now with Deseret claiming Columbian territory, all bets were off.

I pulled the toggles on the inflatable, glancing upslope, trying to ignore the slashes of pain down my back. So far, there hadn't been any Saint choppers out. I could only hope that our scramblers had done the job.

From high overhead came the scream of a scrammer—inbound—and that meant it was one of ours.

"Let's go, before the Saints get back to looking for us." For me, "Saint" was a dirty word.

Lyana gave me a look that suggested I stop talking and start launching our craft.

The inflatable was barely big enough for both of us, but the thin plastreen sheet was a visual blender. At least, the CAF techies said it was. I lifted Lyana onto the inflatable and pushed it out into the shallow brown water. Then I eased myself onto it beside her, on my stomach, and pulled the plastreen up to cover us. It was supposed to be inertly transparent to scanners and to show the images of whatever was around us.

I hoped it worked.

Cuipra

In the darkness caused by the ancient oiled wood of the public room, the captain-colonel looked across the table at the serving girl. "There are no temples or shrines here. Yet they say that the people of the Cuprite Valleys are reverent people."

The girl inclined her head, setting the mug on the table. She did not speak. Her hand brushed the edge of her maiden's bonnet.

"Girl . . . why are there no shrines or temples?" His voice hardened.

"Honored sir . . . I am no one who can speak of that. Please . . . do not . . ."

"I asked an honest question."

The innkeeper stepped forward. "She is my daughter, sir, and I would that you not force an answer. I will take the wrath and answer your question." He eased himself in front of the girl.

She slipped back behind the thin figure of her father, then scurried toward the kitchen.

The captain-colonel laughed. "Your answer, fellow!"

"Our God is the unknown, sir. The true One can never be spoken of. He cannot be mentioned. To talk of him is to risk shame, even death."

"Even to outsiders?"

"None are outsiders to the true One. None are unknown to him."

The captain-colonel shook his head. "To deny speech about a deity is to admit that such is false. To a great being—or a god—our chatter is petty and meaningless. Find a god who asks for more than fearful silence."

The innkeeper threw himself at the officer, his oiled and sharpened cleaver slashing toward the captain-colonel.

Old Earth

Even in late spring, river water is frigging cold. I tried to keep my boots from dragging in the water under the plastreen, but I was too tall for the inflatable, and my toes were in the water, and with the boots and my legs wet from launching it, I was beginning to shiver. My legs were freezing, and my back was boiled or broiled, or both.

Somewhere I'd lost the slug-thrower, but I didn't remember how.

"Why are we doing this?" I murmured.

Lyana smiled, faintly. "You volunteered."

"In a way. Did I have much choice? The Saints are hammering their way into the far northwest. They've already annexed most of Westana."

"There's always a choice."

"Some choice," I muttered. The inflatable swung to one side in the swift, if shallow, currents of the Virgin River. The world turned on its edge for a moment—that was the way it felt.

I squinted, trying to keep my balance on the unsteady surface. It wasn't easy with a back that wasn't working well and the differential between my weight and Lyana's.

There's always a choice. But was there?

The inflatable bucked and slammed into something, and water began to flow over my thighs. Frig! It was cold, and I shivered, and my back spasmed.

After a moment, I eased up the corner of the plastreen. The inflatable was wedged against an outcropping of red stone and branches and had grounded in less than a foot of water.

From overhead came the *thwop, thwop, thwop* of a Saint chopper.

With the water freezing me, I forced myself to wait until the sounds of the patrol chopper faded away. Then I eased myself off the inflatable, partway, enough to get my boots on the sandy stream bottom and push us away from the outcropping and back out into the main current.

I had to struggle to get back onto the inflatable, and just lay there on my stomach under the plastreen for a time.

"Some choice . . ."

Tory

Sitting in the booth didn't provide answers. I got up and walked to the end of the bar. I stood there and looked across at Sean. I realized for the first time that I was a good head taller than he was.

"Sean. You've changed things. Why?"

"I've changed nothing." He frowned. "Do I know you?"

Did he know me? I'd been coming to his pub for over a year, and suddenly he didn't know me?

"You did. Until today, apparently."

He looked across the bar at me. "You've got bigger troubles than that, friend."

"Daffyd."

He laughed. "Bigger troubles than a Welshman in an Irish pub, too."

I just wanted to reach across the bar and throttle him. I didn't. I didn't know why, though. "So you don't know me?"

"You seem to think I should." He picked up a cloth and polished a glass, then another, waiting for me to reply.

"You've served me every Friday for over a year."

"Not in this pub, my friend."

"Daffyd."

"Not in this pub, Daffyd. I know my customers. Hell, I know everyone in Trawley's Cross."

"I've been with ReFor ever since I came to Tory."

"ReFor? Oh, the foresting outfit. They made a bid and got turned down. They pulled out a year and a half ago. You with the office in Port Allen?"

Heat and cold ran up and down my spine, and I set the near-empty glass on the bar.

Where was I?

Old Earth

Even without peering from underneath the plastreen, I could tell we were in the lower section of the Gorge. The current was swifter, and we weren't hitting obstacles. Good thing it was spring. Late summer, and there wouldn't have been enough water to float a toy boat. When I did sneak a peek, all I saw was rock, with brush clinging to the thin link of soil between the water's edge and the cliffs.

That was fine with me. I was having even more trouble moving, and my feet were getting numb. I didn't think it was all from the cold river water.

The big problem wasn't the south end of the Gorge, but the open terrain to the south once we floated farther south. We needed to be at least ten klicks beyond the mountains to get a chance at being picked up.

I must have dozed off . . . or I kept us going somehow without remembering how.

Lyana was talking to me. Couldn't make out the words at first.

"It's time, Daffyd . . . it's time."

". . . time?"

"Trigger your beacon . . . the active mode . . . the one that calls for pickup."

". . . been tracking me . . ." It was getting hard to talk.

"Trigger it."

I fumbled the beacon around, hard to do when you're on your stomach sharing an inflatable with someone, and pressed the active pickup button. Hoped that the Saints didn't have that frequency as well.

More riverbank went by, less swiftly.

A faint hum rose into a roar, and that wasn't the sound of a pickup dasher but a Saint strafer. I lay as still as I could under the plastreen. He probably couldn't pick us up visually, and even if he had the beacon freq, he'd only be able to home in within ten meters. That meant he'd strafe the river around the signal.

The roar got louder.

I could hear something like *thunk, thunk, thunk* . . . and the inflatable tossed. Something slammed into my shoulder, and I lost my grip with that hand. There was a hissing . . . one of the sections of the inflatable had been punctured . . . but I only had one good hand, and neither leg seemed to want to move.

I waited for another strafing run, not because I wanted to, but because there wasn't anything else I could do.

"You'll be fine," Lyana whispered. "It won't be long, now."

"What won't . . . ?"

That was when I heard the scrammer, with the high whine that meant it was one of ours. I thought there was an explosion, but it wasn't the scrammer, because the whine died away.

I could hear the approaching rotors, and the "acknowledge" tone ululated on the beacon. With my good hand, I could barely punch the "confirm" stud and enter my code. Even that hand was getting numb as well.

"Frig . . . hope . . . hope . . ." Couldn't say more.

Lyana handed me a rose, a white rose, folded my numbing fingers around it. Wondered where she'd gotten it. "You'll be fine, just so long as you hold to the rose."

Hold to the rose. Hold to the rose. Kept that thought in mind as the rotor wash blew the plastreen clear of the inflatable.

Hold . . .

Tory

"You all right?" Sean peered at me.

"You know, Sean, you're scaring the crap out of me." I glanced down at the wood of the bar. I thumped it. It sounded hard. It felt hard.

"You don't need to fear me." Sean laughed.

"Why is that?" I wasn't sure I wanted to hear his answer.

"The man to fear is the one who troubles your soul. Any fool with a weapon can trouble your life. So can any woman with a smile and a flash of flesh."

I picked up the empty glass, fingering it.

"You are troubling my soul," I pointed out. "There was nothing wrong with anything until I came in here tonight."

"No, friend . . . Daffyd . . . you only thought that there was nothing wrong."

I looked at the glass I held again. Empty. But it was crystal, I thought.

Lethe

I found myself standing on a chessboard, a frigging chessboard, sixty-four alternating squares of black marble and pale green marble. I was standing on the back row, in the Queen knight's position. My flight boots were soaked, the water running out of them. The water was black. So were my boots, and so was my flight suit, and even my hands. I wasn't surprised, and I should have been as I looked up.

Around the chessboard was a green boxwood hedge. Light flowed around me from somewhere, and I looked up, but the sky above was a featureless off-white tinted green.

Everything tilted, and I was standing closer to the center of the board, only a square away from a hard-eyed Saint foot-slogger who lifted an antique bayoneted rifle.

Fly, dasher man, where you going to fly to?

The Saint bishop lifted his crosier and pointed it, and slid down a line of blue fire toward me. His voice thundered. "Rationality is but chaos, under which you have flattened all that was great, for none of you have heard God, and each of you believes yourself God of your own world."

I struggled for a reply, and finally dragged words from somewhere. "Belief is its own chaos, and under it, everything dies, for each believer holds his creed to be divine and will kill all others in its name." I twisted somehow, up and over, two squares, then one, coming down like an attack dasher on another Saint foot-slogger. With less than a scream, he vanished. That bothered me, but I didn't have time to think about it.

Another bishop, also in blinding white-green, appeared from somewhere, and his words were fire. "You would heed the mind of the thinker, the ear of the listener, the eye of the beholder, but the beholder is deaf to song, the listener blind to sight, and the thinker locked in the vault of his thoughts . . . and only God knows all."

"Words . . . words are the greatest vanity of the believers, and their gods, for beautiful words are the perfume of confusions." With both bishops bearing down on me, I jumped, like a human dasher, avoiding green and blue flashes of flame.

The first bishop pursued me once more, dispatching another line of blue flame that flared at me. "Repent ye of your unbelief, for there is no other deity before the True God."

I somehow found yet another reply. "A sole true belief for all leads to the stagnation and the frozen chaos of thoughtless conformity, and that is an abomination unto any thinking being, especially unto one who would claim to be God."

Green and white lightning flashed and thundered around me.

Old Earth

"Where is she?" My eyes were blurred for a moment, but they focused on the medic who was looking over the edge of the medcradle. "Where am I?"

"Benedict Arnold Medical Center, sir."

How had I gotten to Denver? How long had I been out? Lyana? Where was she? "Where is she?"

The medic looked down at me. "Who, Captain? You are Captain David Bellemer?"

"Yes." His face was fading in and out. "Lyana. She was with me." *Through all the battles.*

"Was she a Saint local who helped you, sir?"

"No. She was crew."

"Sir . . . You were badly wounded, and had a smashed collarbone, and shrapnel in one shoulder. No one could understand how you navigated seventy klicks of river in your condition."

"Where's my crew?"

"Sir . . . you were flying a single-seat dasher." The medic smiled indulgently. "The only thing with you was that." He pointed to the table beside the medcradle. "You wouldn't let go of it until we took care of it. I took some time to find crystal. You were most insistent."

In the crystal vase was a perfect white rose on a long stem. It had already rooted, yet the petals were fresh.

The basic theme behind this story had haunted me for a long time, and when I finally did visit the Vietnam Wall in Washington, D.C., that visit stirred up the feelings even more . . . but I didn't write them out, for a number of reasons, until Byron Tetrick asked if I'd be willing to write something for his anthology—In the Shadow of the Wall—and I knew then that the story had a place.

THE PILOTS

The Sobak Revolt was a long time ago, but I remember my part in it as though it were yesterday. I don't talk about it, Brother Estafen. At least, until now, I didn't, and I won't now. It won't change anything. What happened after the second war with the Sobaks is something else. You're young for recalling that, for it was little more than ten years after the Revolt. My younger brother Waltar . . . he was a pilot, too, almost as good as I'd been . . . but Vergenya would never have recognized what he did . . . except for the spirits of the Wall . . . except I never told anyone, not even Sereh . . . it's better that way, sometimes, when you really can't explain . . .

.   .   .

The summer sun came up like always—above the trees on the east side of the river, rising over the swamps and ruined temples of the ancients, all of them wreathed in the steamy mist that meant the day would be one of those where the sun scorched everything, even subduing the river into a sullen flat expanse of warm water by midafternoon.

Two gunboats were docked at the end of the Navy pier, the canvas on the schooners' masts tied down tight. A smallish Nenglan square-rigger hogged the other pier, and figures began to move across the exposed decks soon after the six bells sounded from the cathedral.

I didn't want to go where I had to, but there was no help for it, and I needed to go before the ferry or the packet docked and I might be called to work, such as it was then.

Waltar had had three rooms to the west, before the War, but Sereh was living in a room smaller than a closet in her sister's cot. Sereh might have been working in the kitchen, but, by the time I climbed the low hill, and the steps, she was waiting for me, standing in the hot morning on the narrow porch. Holding Syreena in her left arm, Sereh thrust the gray sheet of paper at me with her right. Her eyes were red and puffy.

I couldn't reach it without taking a step forward. In my haste, I was less than careful, and the crutch slipped on the gravel of the path. I staggered, but caught myself, then took the broadsheet from her. It had been folded in thirds and held the stamp of the Council on the outside, along with the bold cursive that bore Sereh's name.

The words blurred as I read them.

". . . the pilot Waltar Emmson was not of the Vergen Navy, and his death did not result from enemy fire or attack. Regrettable as it may be, his heirs may not receive death annuities, but only the lump sum payment already received for death by accident . . ."

I didn't need to read more, but I finished the short document.

"Those cables snapped because they were weakened by Sobak cannon . . . you told me that," Sereh said. "I told him not to go. I told him we didn't need the risk bonus." She took a deep breath, looking at me.

A man has to do what he believes he should, or, before long, he has nothing to believe in. I was like that, and Waltar had been that way, too, but I couldn't tell Sereh that, not then, not with Syreena in her arms and another on the way. Not then. "I didn't tell him to go."

She just looked at me with those deep, red-rimmed eyes. "They gave us nothing, except a few duhlars. At least they gave you a position, Arlen."

Position? They had—greeter at the Strangers' House opposite the ferry, and a duhlar a week from the Council. Then, I had no wife. Few wanted to wed a man with but one eye and one good leg, and I'd certainly not wanted to be a burden on anyone.

"Aye, and it's better than begging or working in the almshouse."

"You're alive, Arlen. Waltar isn't." Her words were sharp, but I understood.

"I know. He was a good man, and he was my brother."

"Can't you do something? Can't you make them understand?"

Make them understand what? "We petitioned the Council, Sereh."

"And the Council said no." Her eyes flashed, and even in her anger, I could see why Waltar had asked for her hand. "Can't you do something?"

"I'm not a counselor, and I'm not fancy with my words, Sereh. I was a pilot."

"I'm not mad at you, Arlen. You've stood by me, as well as you can, and . . ." She shook her head.

In time, I had no more words, and I left Sereh, wordless, for what could I say? I made my way back down toward the Strangers' House.

There, under the overhang of the front porch, for a time, I leaned on the crutch and looked out across the river, toward the ruins I knew were on the east shore and could not see through the trees and the mist, though the mist would be gone in the heat of the day when everything simmered under the summer sun.

"Arlen . . ." The voice was that of Ryssah.

I didn't turn.

"I heard."

"So has all of Zandra," I replied, still without looking at her. "So have the Brothers and the Council. A few duhlars, a fancy gilt paper, and they think they've done right by Waltar. Half that fleet would have gone down under the Sobak batteries if it hadn't been for him."

"Times are hard, now, Arlen."

"Times have always been hard."

"She's young. She can wed again."

"She'll have to, won't she?" My voice was hard. "Or go to the streets or the cribs and lie with strangers. Unless she'll settle for a man with one eye and a single room."

Ryssah didn't answer for a time. When she finally spoke, her voice was both soft and tired. "Arlen . . . I can handle the greeting today. You wouldn't do it well."

I didn't protest. Instead, I hurried, as well as I could, down to the ferry pier. There I waited. Because I'd been a pilot, Tomas always let me ride as a courtesy.

The ferry runs north of Zandra and docks at Gorgton. From there, I made my way off and down the pier and along the stone road that flanks the east side of the river. Storm clouds were rising into the midday of summer before I reached the flats that bordered the swamps—and the ruined temples where the ancients practiced their necromancy.

The black wall has been there, half-rising out of the earth, for longer than any can remember. It sits to the north and east of the ancient temple of the seated god. The seated god has long been dead, for never do the ravens flock to the time-smoothed white stone, and the pigeons despoil the almost tottering columns. Still . . . the tree-shaded steps would be a pleasant place from which one could watch the schooners coming up the river to port at Zandra. A pleasant place . . . were it not for the warnings of the Brothers about the evil buried there. A pleasant place, if one did not have to look westward across the river at the cathedral—and the mass of stone that was the Council Seat.

I hadn't come through the heat and steam for the view. I'd come, as I had years before, because it was said that sometimes the black wall offered answers. It hadn't the last time, when I'd first been able to hobble there on a crutch, but, again, there was nowhere else to turn, and I owed Waltar—and Sereh—that much.

The ancients invested that stretch of polished black stone—with its endless runes cut so precisely into the stone—they invested it with the manna of sadness. The power is so great that even after all the centuries a man who believes not in ghosts, nor in the necromancy about which the Brothers prate, nor in that which he cannot see or feel . . . that man—me—hoped for answers that black stone had never given him.

I'd thought that the ancient stretch of polished stone—or the manna within it—might offer some answers. Then, I had thought that once before, and had gotten none.

Still . . . I looked at the black stone, and kept looking from one end of the long line of blackness to the other. In the afternoon stillness, not even a pigeon fluttered, so alone was I.

The wall said nothing, offered nothing. Walls don't, even ancient black walls raised for necromancy on the power of the dead.

"Why?" I poured all the anguish into the cry and the plea, feeling foolish as I did.

Nothing happened.

I eased myself forward, and my fingers brushed the timeworn runes, each set gathered in groups, usually of three or four, and cut precisely into the stone so that each group was level with the group flanking it, seemingly for as far as the black stone stretched before it finally sank into the mossy ground.

"Why?" I asked again.

"The Wall doesn't offer explanations," came a voice. "It never does."

I knew I was alone. No one could have crept up on me. But I turned.

A man stood there, with silver hair cut shorter than even a recruit's. His clean-shaven face was smooth, but he wasn't young. He was no ghost. Above the lines in his face, I could see the dampness of sweat on his forehead. He wore a black waistcoat with a cotton-linen shirt beneath, but such a linen shirt, so tightly woven that I could not even see any trace of an individual thread, and with fine black stripes against a brilliant white. His trousers were coal black, as were the shimmering boots he wore. For a moment, I just stared.

He blinked, as if looking into a bright sun, though we stood in the shade of the green oaks that towered to the east. Finally, he spoke again, thoughtfully. "We have to find the explanations. You shouldn't be here . . . or I shouldn't."

"Why are you here?" I finally asked.

"The same reason as you, I'd guess. Still seeking reasons, explanations, after all these years."

"Are you a Brother of some sort?"

"I'm just a pilot."

He didn't look like any pilot I'd ever seen, but more like a dandy. His eyes narrowed as he looked at me.

"What are the runes for?" I asked quickly.

"Runes?"

I pointed to those etched into the stone before me.

"Each one is someone who died in the war." He laughed bitterly. "Except they're not all there."

For the first time, he looked beyond me, taking in the tall oaks, then the part of the temple of the seated god that was visible through the scrub and swamp grass. He shook his head. "I'll bet you don't even know why the Wall is here."

"No," I admitted. "The Brothers claim it holds evil manna of the ancients, worse than that of the seated god. They say that it was raised in evil by necromancers."

His eyes remained on the white stones of the temple of the seated god. "Poor Abe. No one knows you, either." His lips curled. "Vanity of vanities . . ." He shook his head again and turned those deep eyes toward me, but I don't think he was looking at me but somewhere else. When he spoke, his words were low, as if only for himself, but my ears have always been sharp. "You've really gone round the bend this time, Pete, and without a single beer."

"What war?" I asked. "How did it get all the manna?"

For a long time, he looked at me, standing in the shadows.

I looked back, and when I squinted, it was almost as though I could see through him, see the black stone and mossy ground and scrub bushes behind him.

"The Vietnam War. The one that killed fifty-five thousand men . . . and some women . . . and lots of others."

The name meant nothing to me, and I couldn't believe he'd said fifty-five thousand. That was as many people as lived within Zandra and all the towns within three days or more of travel. "You were a pilot?"

"Search and rescue. Flew H2s, mostly. That was thirty years ago, but you never quite forget. And you never forget the ones who didn't make it. Or the ones who aren't on the Wall . . . the ones who died testing the birds, or in the wrong places, or outside the magic lines drawn by the bureaucrats."

I heard the words, but not all of them made sense, but perhaps the Brothers were right about the black stone. The spirit pilot—if that was what he happened to be—was talking about magic lines and pilots who flew strange birds rather than vessels upon the sea.

"Like Waltar," I murmured.

He waited for me to continue, an expression between amusement and disbelief on his clean-shaven face. His eyes held something I didn't want to see.

So I talked, since no one else except Sereh would listen, or care. "He was a pilot on the *Wariner*. He was the lead pilot on the Savnah expedition because he knew the channels, but he wasn't Navy. The Council promised that they'd take care of his family if anything happened during the attack. The Sobaks were waiting, and they'd even mined the side channels. Waltar was better, though, and got the *Wariner* and most of the invasion fleet back to sea, even through the bombardment from the shore batteries and a running attack from fast gunboats. Once they were clear, they hit heavy seas. They didn't know that the Sobak batteries had almost cut the rudder cables. In the storm, one snapped. It broke through the housings and snapped Waltar's neck." I shrugged.

"Your Council said that it didn't happen during the attack," suggested the spirit pilot in the waistcoat, a bemused expression on his face, as if he'd heard the story already.

"How did you know?" I demanded.

"Because nothing changes." He gestured toward the black stone. "They say that all those who died are here, but they're not." He laughed, sardonically.

"They never are. There are always those who sacrificed, who didn't fit the definitions, who didn't die with the right ceremonies, or who sacrificed themselves for the wrong reason in the wrong season . . . That was true when they built the Wall, and apparently it was true for your brother."

"Waltar didn't sacrifice himself. It wasn't like that."

"We all make sacrifices, if we're really alive."

Then, as suddenly as he had come, he vanished.

I shivered.

Even hurrying, a man with a crutch has trouble going long distances, and I barely made the twilight ferry back from Gorgton to Zandra—back to ready myself to appear before the Council with the words of the spirit pilot that I held within my heart and soul . . . and back to Sereh.

. . .

The ancients were powerful . . . and that we no longer have such power, for such I am supposed to be grateful, according to Brother Diere.

Yet . . . on many twilights, I have seen the figure of that silver-haired ancient, and not just near the Wall, but on my own portico, the portico Sereh and I built here when we left Zandra. Far older than I was then, older than I am now even, and yet his face was that of a man in his prime. But his eyes . . . and his words . . .

"They're not all there, you know. They never are. There are always those who sacrificed, who didn't fit the definitions, who didn't die with the right ceremonies, or who sacrificed themselves for the wrong reason in the wrong season . . . We all make sacrifices, if we're really alive."

Perhaps the only thing I ever learned, truly learned, was from a spirit, and the only answer I ever got was because I didn't ask for myself.

You won't be telling anyone, now, Brother Estafen. Who would believe you? They didn't believe me. The Ecclesiarches wouldn't believe that the old idols have power, or that the ancients held the skies . . . or that the runes on the wall are names, names of more dead men than all those who live in Zandra, and that even the magics of the old ones couldn't hold all those who died in a war so long ago that we don't even know what it was about—except so many died and created such sadness that their spirits and those who mourn them still cross the times between us . . .

Too many people think that "information workers" aren't "grunts." Says who?

THE DOCK
TO HEAVEN

Infosnark—that's me. Mom called me Mario. Dockers call me Snark 'cause if there's info to be found without tags, no one does it better than me. Highport's a big place. Ships come from everywhere—Old Earth, Xianth, Clarkburg, Alpha Felini, Sansalibre, D'Ahoud, Melinia. They got ships, and they come to Highport 'cause it's the only way you get to Heaven. Angels insist it's got to be that way. Least, that's what Lorico told me. He may look diablo, but never piloted me wrong.

Twodays are slow. Always have been. Slow isn't always bad, but it's fastbeam to trouble. Times busy, people swirling around, the patrollers don't bother if they see you, so long as you're not doing something brightflared wrong. Slow times, they look deeper. For us snarks, their looking deeper isn't good.

Was coming back from the farwest concourse lines on the low guideway. Slower, but cheaper. Farwest's mostly Sandurco space. Was wearing the greensilver dumper suit and scanner access pins. Lorico does 'em well, and they'll take three–four scans before they flare red. Costs a cred for each pin, but you can't snark if you don't know where the weak points are. Screens and channels don't show everything. Even if they do, so much noise you can't find the signal.

Sandurco had space on the *Elept* to Purgatory. Eight full cubes. Problem was that the space was reserved for a transfer. Ironbound, cold steel contract. Inbound was from Xianth. Inbound wouldn't make transfer before the *Elept* needed to translate. But Sandurco was bound not to make known the space was available. That's where I came in. Needed to find an instalast cargo, have it ready to upload just before translation. Most of the creds would go to Sandurco and the shipper, but be a small shower of creds—and favors—for me.

Came out of the scangates, under the high ceilings that show the images of Heaven sky, blue with clouds sculpted into cities, and turned to the guideway. Saw something below the entrygate, off to the right. Dark and shiny. Hard. Wanted to run, 'cause it just screamed creds. Didn't. Ambled, like always, looking around, being the scrounge most take me for. Easier that way. Most at Highport don't know what I do. Suits me fine.

Jumped down and scooped it up. Slipped it inside the greensilver dumper jacket, and jumped back up on the strip beside the guideway, flashing a cred-token.

Hadn't taken two steps when Saalmo was on me. Sleaziest patroller on the west end.

"What you got there, Snark?"

"Cred-token. Some angel dropped it. Didn't want to get dirty." Lied, of course. Nowhere in the Port's dirty. Outside, on the ramps, or in town, that was dirt. One reason why I tried to stay inside as much as I could.

"You sure?" Saalmo oozed more slideless than a guideway mech.

Flashed the cred-token at him, close enough for him to see, but not grab. Real angel token. Gotten it along with my fifty creds from Derdri a stan earlier for tipping her to a half cube on the Cherabims' *Celestria,* outbound to Clarkburg. Would have been a hundred for an inbound.

"You got fast fingers, Snark. Thought what you got was darker, bigger."

Belted the cred-token and pulled out my mem. "This?"

Saalmo shook his head. "Better watch it. I heard tell that the Seraphim are going to sweep the whole Port." He laughed. Ugly laugh, the kind that said he knew something and wouldn't tell me. "Pretty soon, they won't let you move around like a dumper. Dec orbit to nowhere for snarks."

"You've been telling me that for years." Slipped my mem back into the underarm pouch. "We're still here. Need us."

"Not so much as you think, Snark." He shrugged. "Don't listen to me. You never do." He turned and walked to the guideway out to the fareast concourse. He went high-level. Patrollers don't get charged.

I was glad to see him go. Wanted to see what I had but didn't dare look in the brightzone. Buzzed the accesslock, and took the maintenance ramp. From there walked to the drop shaft—cargo level. Nerod just nodded, let me ride down with the used formulator paks.

Forced myself to wait till I'd made it clear, in the dead alcove under the midbridge. Space two meters by three at the end where the scanners don't reach. Five I'd found over the years that no one else knew about. More than twenty everyone knew. Always keep a scan for the deaders no one else knows.

Took out the dark and shiny case, not much bigger than my palm. Creds wasn't the flame for it. Oligari top comm. Enough netcreds and tools to access every net and portsys. Break anything with my routines.

Entered the owner self-code script. Oligaris got one. All units do. Small holo flared up. Showed an angel, but with short silver-gold hair, and luminous green eyes. Tall, I guessed, but a guess 'cause size doesn't show on the image, and angels are always tall. Nothing special, not for an angel. Bothered me. Owner of an Oligari ought to be special, even an angel. No name. Just a code. Smart, that way. Unit lost, and you still couldn't trace her, except through the code.

Figured I could use the comm-breaker, maybe to shoot the stuff for the Sundurco bit—*if* I could find someone who needed eight cubes to Purgatory.

Keyed in the schedreqs, then linked the Oligari into the portsys with the owner's codes.

Couldn't help grinning. Had every spare cube in Highport flaring into my new toy. Stored the stuff and transferred it to my mem. No telling how long I could keep the Oligari. Then I headed back the underway to Lorico's. Star-rain was falling outside Highport—big drops. Turn to stars when they hit the permacrete. One flash, and their light's gone, just dull water running over the gray stone. Port's fields do that, but it's still star-rain.

Passed Noryset's. Front parlor looked empty. Always was in midday. Dockers don't look for women till they go offshift, and townies aren't welcome. Water seeped over everything. Rains harder in town. Highport fields throw the extra rain at everything around.

Lorico's place is one room, back of Gheratt's. Gheratt does mech-maintenance, the underlevel stuff, at the port. Some in town, too. Lorico's his cousin.

Lorico could pass for a diablo. Pale white skin, square face, red lips, black hair, hint of points at the tip of his ears. That's why he's never in Highport. Angels don't like diablos at Highport, and diablos don't like angels in Purgatory. Goes way back. Some say even before there were translation ships. Wouldn't know. Just know enough that I never set deals where a diablo gets the better of an angel. Don't last long in Highport if you do that.

Slow for Lorico. Had to be. Looked at me. "Morning, Snark. New?"

"Got eight cubes on the *Elept* to Purgatory. Two on the *Milt* to Sansalibre."

"Ferica might want some cubes to Purgatory."

"Didn't see him."

Lorico grinned, showing the pointed white teeth against ruby lips. "He's out on the fareast concourse. Said you snarks weren't around when he needed you."

"Ferica'd get more if he let us come to him."

"You want to tell him that?" asked Lorico.

I laughed. Ferica was a meter taller 'n me, with nano-iron exoskin. "Need a messenger outfit."

"Be five creds, plus pin."

"Five?"

"You'll have to be Carolyi. They're the only outfit whose messengers are allowed there."

"Since when?"

"Last week. When you used a Steganyi messenger outfit on that deal with Zeagat."

"Me? Never did a Steganyi gig."

Lorico laughed.

I had to transfer six creds, then went to the back room. Came out in purple and silver. Hated Carolyi colors.

"You got twenty hours, Snark."

"Can't get it done in three . . ." Shrugged at Lorico as I left.

Had to use my pass for the upper guideway. Another cred, but messengers didn't take the underway.

On the way to where the concourses branched, I passed the Clearance kiosk. The nontechs go there for level one screening before they get a pass to Heaven. Moyra was talking to a hermit, long beard, brown boots, hair shirt. I kept walking. Pretty girl, she was. Almost angel-beauty, 'cept her hair's brown, not gold or silver-blond, and she's too short. Taller than me, but not angel-tall.

"Snark!"

Hermit had headed off to Heaven concourse. Moyra snaplooked at me, then back down before her. I eased back over to the kiosk.

She didn't look up. Her voice wasn't even a whisper. "Snark, I heard one of the angel captains. She was saying that there are diablos in Highport. They've set up something."

Wondered. Was that someone me? Saalmo. Had he been in on it? Made sure I'd gotten the Oligari. Why? "Thanks."

"Be careful."

Smiled at her. "Tonight's on me."

She looked up and raised her eyebrows. "You've told me that three times and left me here."

"Not tonight."

"You've said that, too."

Saw a patroller coming and eased away from the kiosk. Messenger wouldn't stop at the kiosk. Been Saalmo, my entry to the fareast concourse be dead. He knows I stop to talk to Moyra. Patroller was a newbie. Didn't even look my way.

Ferica was running guidesnaps outside the gate from Sansalibre. Legit, but just his excuse to prowl the concourses. Wouldn't pay a hundredth of what he got from his real stuff. Snaps gave a full Highport map, quick call-up, golden lines to the Heaven concourse. Saved souls from Sansalibre could have called up almost the same thing on the port net. Most didn't have mems, though. Understood that the Imperatior didn't allow them. Didn't even like the angels having a consulate there, but even an Imperatior doesn't buck the angels. Not when a single angelfire scout can take down any other system's dreadnought.

Meant that every so often the angels sent saved souls Heavenward, even from Sansalibre. Some even bought Ferica's guidesnaps.

Saw Ferica's gig, and slowed my pace, waiting until the pilgrims all passed him.

"What you got, Snark?"

"Eight prime cubes to Purgatory. Lorico said you might be interested. Also two back to Sansalibre." Sansalibre was a throwaway. Not that much shipped back from Highport to Sansalibre. Other places, but not there.

"Solid cubes?" Ferica sounded bored.

"Solid. Reserved. Failed transfer, nonseeking clause."

"Can take five. Em-cred a cube."

"They want two em-creds. Might be able to get you one and a half for five."

"Try for one and a third."

I backed off and ran the inquiry through. "One point four, and you pay clearances."

"Done." Ferica smiled. Teeth looked steel, too. "Pass me the codes."

Raised my eyebrows.

"Two hundred creds for you. And something else."

Would have liked more than two hundred, but I'd been running close to margin. Did owe Moyra a good dinner, up-level in town. "Codes . . . blue." Used the remote to trigger the transfer.

"Some hotware there, Snark. Careful who knows you're packing it."

"Loaner," I said. "Repaying a favor. Won't have it long." One way or another, I wouldn't. Snark with an Oligari would be a target if it got around; but things had been thin, and the multiple access had already netted me more options than I'd had in months. "Know anyone else who's looking?"

"Galusi—bulk cubes for Clarkburg. Can't pay more than half an em-cred per cube."

"You said . . ."

"Oh . . . something you need to watch. Someone knows you got hot-ware. Snoop look on you."

"Thanks." All I needed. Suspected something like that might happen. Headed farther out on the concourse. Galusi called himself a cargo broker. Had a real office. Small—less than three meters on a side. Real business, but not how or where he made most of his creds. Did removals—usually pil-grims who'd gone to the angels to escape. Folks who used Galusi didn't want recovery—wanted the word spread that even the permanent pilgrimage to Heaven wasn't certain if you cheated them. Never quite understood why the angels didn't shut him down. They could have. Hadn't, though. Not yet.

Ran a few more inquiries on the Oligari as I hustled outbound. Put in an inquiry for Clarkburg. Nothing on regular transit, but thirty bulk cubes on lowlight—take two years. Kept looking. Didn't find much, even with the Oligari, except some cubes available on a semilevel return run to D'Ahoud and hot-space to Alpha Felini. Hot-space—didn't touch that. No one I knew could spring a hundred em-creds a cube. Not even the diablos.

Diablos—they wanted a way around Highport to Heaven. Always had. No one knew where Heaven was. Anyone, anything, going to Heaven went on an angel-ship with an angel crew. Only angels came back from Heaven—except once a decade—when they'd bring back a hundred pilgrims, turn them over to the lower worlds' techs for mem-testing. Supposed to prove that the stories about Heaven were all true. Hel! What did that prove. Angels could doctor anything, even minds.

Only thing it all proved was that they got better ships, better weapons, and better ways of twisting the truth. If you believe such a thing as truth.

Got a bad feeling as I neared the portals for Xianth, but kept going. Shouldn't have.

Three angels. Beyond the Xianth portals. Waiting. For me.

You can avoid angels, go around 'em. Don't buck 'em or try to run. Did what I had to. Walked straight to them.

Angel in the center stepped forward. "Mario."

Could tell she was an angel, even without looking. No one calls me Mario.

"Yes." I bowed. No sense in being stupid.

One of their gold-green screens dropped around us. Left me alone with the angel.

"We have a favor to ask. An angel's missing. Somewhere here in Highport. We'd like to find her. Quickly. She's beyond scanners and screens."

"What kind of angel?"

"Does it matter?"

Did to me, but the tall angel wasn't going to tell.

"I haven't heard anything." That was true. Nothing except Moyra's fears I was being set up. "Haven't seen anything."

"If you do . . ." The angel beamed an access code into the Oligari. The hidden Oligari. Didn't ask. Just beamed. "You'll know what to do, Mario."

The gold-screen curtain went down, and I kept moving toward Galusi's office. Could feel her eyes on my back. Creepy.

Anyone trying anything on the angels, might be Galusi. Stopped for a moment and took out the Oligari. Snapped up a search-and-trace routine that would go off when I got inside Galusi's place.

Galusi surprised me. He was there. "You'd better have something good, Snark."

"Heard you were looking for bulk cubes to Clarkburg. How many?"

"I could use twenty. I'll take fifteen."

"You're lucky. Twenty at a tenth of an em-cred."

"I'll take it. Hundred creds for you, and you pass the access codes over now."

Before I had the codes, he'd made the transfer to my links.

"Codes coming."

"Hotware for a snark," Galusi said.

"Loaner. Favor. Got to get what I can now."

Galusi snorted. Understood loaners. Better 'n I did. "Later, Snark."

He was nervous. Would have bargained for a lower cubage rate. Didn't. Decided to push. "Saw three angels. Questioning people on the concourse."

"They're not supposed to do that."

"You going to tell an angel no?"

Galusi ignored the question. "Come back when you got cubes to Xianth."

Another way of telling me to get lost. No one ever got cubes to Xianth. Could feel the Oligari taking in the feeds. Decided to get gone. "Later. Could always get lucky."

Galusi laughed.

I was gone. Didn't stop till I was three portals away. Gimmicked the maintenance lock and slipped down to the nearest dead spot. Unloaded and ran an analyzer on what the track and trace had come up with.

Three feeds from somewhere in Highport. Let the Oligari go to work.

Two were routine availability notices. Third was a double-blind, encrypted. Checked the route bounces and the nanosecond delays. Had to have come from the Sandurco concourse. Only place in Highport with those patterns.

Wondered if the angels would pay. Then . . . might be nothing.

But . . . the Oligari had put me back in business when I'd needed it. Owed the angel something for that. Besides, didn't hurt to have an angel owing me. Better than the other way around. Lots better.

Headed for the Sandurco concourse.

No one stopped me. High-speed guideway cost me ten creds and still took a stan. Flipped off at portal four. Patrollers check and know the dead spots on the first three. Beyond that . . . secure spaces under Lesser Worlds' Agreement. Whoever . . . had to be operating secured. Three possibilities.

Tried another maintenance lock. Opened it, but blew the alarm. Got beyond the monitors, but got no traces—just a long, empty, secure corridor. Space open and emissions zilch.

Went through the same routine after portal eight.

Down twenty creds, and probably another fifty for the alarm if the patrollers pushed it.

Portal twenty—best bet, and didn't have to gimmick the lock. Oligari's routine found a Trojhors and had me through. No one on the other side. Not even a monitor, just a long corridor, same as around portal four. Felt different. Kept going. Empty space and more empty space. Nothing.

Didn't have much time before the patrollers or Sandurco privsec showed. Took my toolset, measured the field, reset the ID. Then dug out the spare mem from the pouch under my right arm. Boosted the field, set it with the phony of the Oligari, and then crammed the Oligari's search routine into the spare. Overrode the safeties and watched.

That much power on the spare mem—burn it out in less than a stan. Oligari ran that hot forever, but didn't want to do that kind of hackjob on the Oligari.

Took two minutes.

Hotspot a hundred meters ahead and down fifty. Meant that someone had built a hideaway underground. Not many places near Highport where the fields allow that. Wondered how I'd get down there.

Access hatch and drop shaft behind a phony barrier. Used the backup mem to fry the lock. Mem was half-gone anyway. Then took the drop at double speed and burst through the screen.

Big fellow, like Ferica, except he had white teeth and was reaching for a burner. Behind him was a pair of gene-overclone cradles. Looked like a med sculptech, renegade. Could find out later.

I didn't wait. Kept moving. May be small, but I'm not slow. Or stupid. Was inside his burner and had my ceramic blade up through his gut to the base of his heart before he could squeeze the trigger.

Burner still blazed across my shoulder. Hurt. Lots. Could barely see. Still managed to knock the burner to the floor. Kicked it out of the way. Sculptech sagged down, dying. He could take his time now.

Two women in the cradles. Restrained. Both naked. Beautiful. Identical. Silver-blond hair, tall, luminous green eyes, fine noses, but strong. Gene-tags'd show them the same.

Both looking at me. Neither spoke.

I couldn't either. Shoulder was hurting more, not less.

Forced another look around the lab. On the shelf to the left of the console was a wide belt, green, trimmed in gold. On the temphook stuck to the wall was a pilot's uniform—AngeLines.

I knew why the angel hadn't told me who the missing woman was. And Saalmo hadn't set me up. The angels had. Someone had wanted me to know what the missing woman looked like and to have the right equipment.

Slipped the Oligari close enough to the consoles to run a diagnostic. Not one the angels or the Highport admin would have approved. Got a whole web of choices. Could have played games with the angels. No percentage in it.

Accessed the code the angels had given me.

"I've got your missing pilot—and the setup." Fed the coordinates from the Oligari into the web.

"We've got it. Don't move." That was the head angel.

Wasn't about to move. First, doubted I'd get far. Second, had other ideas. Could have waited for the angels, but . . . infosnarks have their pride.

Both women looked at me. Finally, the one on the right moistened her lips.

Asked her, "How did they catch you?"

"It was a sophisticated sonic trap. There was a dead zone on one side of the corridor. I stepped around the maintenance floater, and they had me."

Probably the way it was, too. I turned to the other one, on the left. "What do you have to say?"

"It doesn't matter. They'll sort it out."

There was a quiet sadness in her voice. I knew why. So I stepped up to the console and triggered the releases on her cradle. "Better get your uniform on before they arrive."

The woman still in the cradle swallowed.

"I'd have thought you'd let her escape," offered the real angel. "We couldn't do that much to her."

"Not that cruel," I pointed out. "Couldn't do that to anyone. She'd be taken for a fallen angel. They don't last long. Whoever set this up . . . they knew that."

I didn't say any more because the side doors irised open. Angels and patrollers swarmed inside. The overclone was still in restraints. She didn't even swear.

Lead angel ignored the corpse. She had some kind of scanner. Ran the beam over both women. Then she turned to me. "How did you know, Mario?"

"Wouldn't be much of a snark, if I didn't, would I?" Turned to the head angel and offered her the Oligari, with my left hand. Right wouldn't move. "This belongs to one of yours."

She frowned, then reached out. Touched my shoulder. Lifted away the pain. Then she looked at the burner. "Hold still. This is going to hurt."

Thought what the burner did had hurt, but what she did was sheer agony. Except when she finished, the pain was gone. Just a dull ache.

"It will still take a few days to heal completely. Don't lift anything heavy."

I offered the Oligari again.

She smiled. Didn't take it. "Keep it, Mario. You earned it."

Wasn't sure I wanted it. Make me top snark in Highport, for sure, but there's more 'n being top snark that way. Besides, Ferica or someone would make me a mark, so long as I had it.

I handed it to her. "Wouldn't be right." Wouldn't have been.

She understood . . . in a way. "What would you like?"

"A few creds . . . and I'd like to see the pilot's ship lift off."

"We'll have to hurry."

So they let me come, up three levels, and on the superguide to the middle of Heaven concourse. I'd never been there. No one sees it except angels, and pilgrims, the saved souls only once. They escorted me all the way through the portal and to the transfer deck.

Everyone stopped there.

The pilot I'd found looked at me with those luminous green eyes.

Knew she'd never be back. Not to Highport. She'd seen too much, and the angels would find some way to keep her on Heaven. She knew it, too. Didn't say anything, but I could tell.

The angels behind us reinforced that.

Pilot looked toward the transdeck. "I have to preflight."

"Have a good trip." Didn't know what else to say.

Stood with the lead angel and watched the screen for a good stan before the golden needle flared, vanished into overspace.

Then I turned.

Head angel looked at me. "There are five hundred creds in your account, Mario, and an open passage to Heaven. Open your whole life. No matter what."

Could tell she meant it. "Thank you. Not ready for that."

"We know."

Neither of us spoke as she escorted me back to the main concourse, left me there not a hundred meters from Moyra. Wondered if that was an accident. Didn't think so.

Waited out of sight of the kiosk for another half stan, till just before Moyra's shift ended. Then sauntered up.

"Said I'd be here. Your choice. Anyplace in town—upper level."

Her mouth opened. Then she closed it and smiled.

Moyra and I—we slipped through the rain so quick that the star-rain didn't touch either of us, water or light.

Kept running, but not from Highport. Come morning, we'd be back, same as always. I was a snark. Couldn't be one anywhere else.

Still . . . couldn't, wouldn't get the image out of my mind. The proud and tall lady, beautiful, as all angels are, with the darkness of hell behind those green, green eyes. Standing on the transdeck, call it the dock to Heaven, a place she'd never see again, screen behind her showing stars falling around her . . . and not knowing that she'd already missed life.

Moyra and I had that.

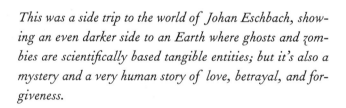

This was a side trip to the world of Johan Eschbach, show-ing an even darker side to an Earth where ghosts and zom-bies are scientifically based tangible entities; but it's also a mystery and a very human story of love, betrayal, and for-giveness.

GHOST MISSION

After sunset on Wednesday, I found myself standing outside the Sherratt Inn, one hand on the small pack attached to my belt and concealed by the dark gray windbreaker. I took a deep breath, lifting my hand carefully away from the pack. I didn't want to touch it again any sooner than I had to.

The air was cold and still, the acridness of burning coal confined by a winter inversion, but even that smelled wonderful. I'd enjoy it while I could, for all would change, change utterly. I gathered myself together, pushing away the burning that ran along all my nerves and the thought of how little time I had, and stretched my legs, turning toward the Relief Society House. Four blocks later, I could see it, an imposing structure on the south side of the park, almost directly across from the Tabernacle. Covering the rededication was the assignment for Thursday, not that it mattered to me, except for the conditioning. Tonight was what counted.

The sky to the west glowed faint orange from the last rays of the sun striking the particulates emitted from the ironworks. The massive power plant in the flats to the north of the ironworks didn't emit anything. In a convoluted but direct sense, that special high-tech power plant, surrounded by more security than the Saint air base farther to the northwest, was why I was in Iron Mission.

When I reached the rear of the Relief Society House, I waited in the shadows on the far side of the back gate, my breath steaming in the chill and still winter air. The dark gray windbreaker and gray slacks let me blend into the indistinctness of late twilight. By moving my head just slightly, I could see the door to the Relief Society kitchen. Before long, the scullery maids would be bringing out the refuse from the evening meal served to the disfavored wives—that was the semiofficial term for unpropertied wives who had either lost their beauty or been unable to provide sons and had been discarded.

The first scullery girl was short and squat. Her eyes darted from side to side. She wasn't the one. I eased farther back into the shadows. After she dumped her load from her basket into the squarish brown Dumpster, she walked hurriedly back along the stone walk to the rear door of the Relief Society kitchen. There was silence for a long time then, and in the stillness I was far more aware of the nerve-burning sensation, psychosomatic as it was, that nagged at me.

I didn't like the thought of having to enter the servants' quarters to find the scullery girl I needed, but I could . . . and would, if I had to. Intelligence had confirmed she was there, but zombies had no legal rights in Deseret—not that they had many in the Republic—and the Spazi wasn't about to waste assets to recover an operative with blown cover and a memory they believed worthless—if not lost entirely. The Federal Security Agency believed otherwise, but the FSA had no official jurisdiction outside Columbia.

Finally, the door opened again. But it closed, and no one came out.

I kept waiting. A good fifteen minutes passed before the kitchen door swung wide, and light cascaded on the stone walk. A tall and slender figure carrying a large basket stepped out onto the walk. The door closed. The scullery girl's steps carried her toward the refuse Dumpster. They were the mechanical steps of a zombie. She was the target, and I eased around the brick pillar of the gate.

She lifted the basket and dumped the contents into the open Dumpster.

"Charity?" I said softly, looking up to meet her eyes.

"Yes, sir?" Her voice was flat, or almost so. In the deepening darkness, standing behind the twilight-darkened red stone of the Relief Society House, her brown cap, dark gray ankle-length frock, and grayer jacket made her seem almost invisible.

I couldn't see the color of her eyes, and it was probably better that way.

"I've come to take you to the General Authority, Charity. You're to come with me."

"Sister Barrow told me to come right back."

"You must always obey a brother over a sister. Come with me."

She didn't argue. No female, zombie or otherwise, would have dared to contest a man in Deseret, even one much shorter. Besides, we were headed to one of the General Authorities. Zombies do know when you're telling the truth. That, too, is a terrible beauty.

We walked over to Third South and took it west along the south side of the university—Joseph Smith University—then up the curving road onto Leigh Hill, wide enough for an ox to turn with a wagon in tow, as were all the main streets in Deseret, although the oxen had long since been replaced by steamers and steam lorries.

It was close to pitch-dark when we reached the high stone wall on the south side of the estate—and the maintenance gate that was our immediate destination. It took me a good three minutes to open the lock, even with the picks and my training. I gave the hinges liberal doses of the special lubricant before I opened the gate and stepped through the stone archway. It did not squeak. After closing the gate, but not locking it, I led Charity a good ten yards along the gravel path before turning uphill. We stopped in the darkness.

"Stay here. Say nothing." I kept the words to Charity simple and low.

She stood, mute, beside the pinon pine and just forward of the wall between the upper and lower gardens. Her gray garments blended against the dressed stones of the wall.

As I eased along the wall, I knew I wouldn't have much time—just the one night. My borrowed body wouldn't take more, especially if I had to call up full hysterical boost—what once had been thought to be a property just of berserkers—and even a zombie's absence would be noted before long. My palms were damp inside the black leather gloves.

After another twenty yards, I could see the target—a ghost who stood alone in the shadow of a juniper just a few yards downhill and east of the wall. On both sides of that darkness the reflected light of the full moon flooded down. I wouldn't even have noticed the ghost if I hadn't been looking specifically for her. I remained in the shadow of the wall, moving across the frozen grass, knowing that I had left footprints. From what I could tell, no one else had walked the lower garden recently, not since it had frosted, but the prints would either melt with the next day's sun or be covered by the next snowfall.

Absolem had said there was a ghost in the older section of the garden, and one not seen before six months previous. That late June had been when Verial had vanished, not that I'd known it then, leaving but a zombie behind, found sitting on a bench in the Bishop's Park of Iron Mission. That was the official report filed with the Iron Mission police. Where there was a zombie, there should have been a ghost, but one was never reported.

Everyone in the FSA was hoping that the ghost in the garden was the one I sought. But why had the Saints zombied Verial in the lower garden—if indeed the ghost was Verial? It didn't make sense, unless they thought her ghost would fade into oblivion before being discovered and that no outsider would see her there.

I kept moving, slowly, deliberately, until I finally stood in the patch of shadow closest to that where the ghost hovered, concealed from the mansion uphill and to the west by the upper garden, and by the wall in whose moonlight-created shade I stood. She'd been young when she died. Had she been beautiful? Verial had been, especially to me, but with ghosts, it's hard to tell, because so much of beauty is vitality, and most of that vanishes when the body dies—or when spirit and body are separated.

What was I doing? Certainly, I was trespassing by sneaking around the walled hillside gardens of Heber Cannon, but trespassing would be the least of my sins were I to be discovered on the private grounds of one of the General Authorities of Deseret. My alter ego's cover as a journalist for Republic Press International might be jeopardized, not to mention both our lives, such as mine was. Building that journalistic cover had been difficult enough, especially with the assignments in occupied France. Deseret was nominally neutral, but few foreign reporters were allowed into Deseret, and only those deemed either harmless or helpful in some way.

My alter ego had come the first time to cover the second Salt Palace Concert of Llysette duBois and Daniel Perkins. With her kidnapping and her husband's heroics, no one had ever remembered the small and slightly lisping reporter from West Kansas. So when she'd been asked to sing for the rededication of the renovated Iron Mission Tabernacle before her final Deseret concert in St. George, his visa to cover her tour was accepted without objection.

I eased closer to the ghost, careful to remain in the shadows. My breath steamed, appearing almost more solid than the figure of the ghost. She did not breathe, although her chest seemed to rise and fall under the filmy and bare-shouldered gown that was so unlike anything a woman of Deseret would have worn. I frowned. Was this the right ghost? Verial had been a mistress of disguise, and never would have worn something so inappropriate. At least, not without a good reason.

"Verial?" I whispered.

The reply was much as I had expected, typical of a ghost who'd been surprised and fully aware when killed—or one who'd been zombied.

She turned to me and cocked her head—that was one of the mannerisms in the file, although I'd known it far earlier. Then she spoke, if a faint whisper in one's thoughts could be considered a voice.

> *First dew that gives the grass its sheen,*
> *then for the frost that coats the green . . .*

Had I heard a door creak? Steps on stone? Much as I disliked it, because it shortened the time I had, I concentrated, bringing up full sensory intensity. I had to hold on to myself to keep from staggering. Every nerve tingled with edged flame, and the steps on the stone walk in the upper garden sounded like distant thunder. No one else would have heard them at all.

"Who was the prince who loved you?" I asked, quietly, pressing the question toward the ghost.

The hint of a smile crossed her face before I heard the words in my own thoughts.

> *My prince had proffered love in words so meet*
> *that seraph birds alone could sing that sweet . . .*

That didn't tell me enough. It hinted that the ghost was Verial, because Prince Mykail had fallen for her—before the Cheka had warned him off, if after she had gotten what she had been tasked to obtain. I don't know that she had fallen for him. She'd always kept her feelings to herself. Good agents do. That was why I'd never been a good agent. Now, there was no one other than me available to recover Verial, if it could be done at all. The FSA only had a handful of agents, and that was a handful more than the Security Act allowed. No one else had been available, not without jeopardizing other priorities. And it didn't hurt that I cared about her. I always had, and that had been my undoing. FSA had nothing to lose. I had everything to lose, one way or another, and little enough to gain—except a final measure of self-respect.

The psych-scientists had said I should try indirect prompts first, but I was running out of time, and I couldn't ignore the two men descending through the upper garden to the gate in the wall to the lower garden.

"Why did you leave physics for the Spazi?" I asked hurriedly.

As humans, rules of law we'll change,
as time and fate shift what we know,
but nature's laws, fixed fermions,
endure unchanged, forever so.

The rhyme made sense, and would have made more sense had I been able to identify the poet—or poetess. Only a handful of ghosts could communicate, and always by rhymed words, usually of a favorite poet. Still, the use of the term *fermion* was a favorable indication that the ghost I was dealing with was Verial. She had been a brilliant grad student in the physics of materials engineering when she'd been recruited.

The gate from the upper garden creaked as it opened.

"What is the formulaic basis of fossil-fueled MHD?" The question was nonsensical, but the terms weren't and were calculated to get a response.

The enigmatic smile of the ghost vanished. She almost did as well, wavering for a moment in the deep shadows. Then, her intensity redoubled, her features clearer. In one hand was the shawl that had surely covered her shoulders before it had been ripped away, most certainly after she had been zombied.

I was certain now that she was Verial, but I had so little time, in more ways than one.

Two figures—they had to be men—walked unhurried through the stone archway to the lower garden.

I eased back along the stone wall as quickly as I could. With each step, the crackling of the frozen grass threatened to engulf me, and with each step, the knives of sound pierced my eardrums. I kept moving, then froze. Three Saint security types waited outside the gate. Not Danites, not police, but security, in the black and brown they wore when they wanted to be noticed.

The footsteps from higher in the garden were louder, thunder drawing ever closer to the ghost by the juniper—and me.

"This way . . ." I whispered to Charity. "Follow me."

She did not move. I took her hand and led her back toward the juniper and the ghost, staying in the shadows.

"Take two steps forward and wait until I speak again." I couldn't tell her to stand behind the ghost, although that was where I wanted her, because zombies cannot perceive ghosts.

Charity took the two steps, standing immobile just behind the ghost.

In turn, the ghost that I hoped was, and wanted to be, Verial glowed brighter.

The two men slowed as they neared the juniper. Verial's sudden brightness almost obscured the zombie, as I had planned.

"She is still there. Nothing has happened." Those words came from the younger and taller man.

"Footsteps," said the older and broader figure. "There in the frost on the grass." His deep voice boomed in my ears, even though I was crouched against the wall, at an angle where the juniper most obscured their view of me—hardly enough if they actually were looking.

"More like a child's."

"Or a woman's. I told you there would be an agent using duBois as cover."

"Her husband is with her. He has been the whole time."

"This time, he is a decoy. They want us to watch him."

"Your ghost was still here, Father. She was beautiful."

"She was nothing of the sort. She was brilliant, and slightly attractive. More important, she was a typical Columbian woman—hard and calculating—a perfect spy beneath that persona. She almost got away with it, too . . . because of my own son. She was not my ghost. She only wanted you to think that." The snort that followed was deep and rumbled in my ears. Verial had never been anyone's, and Heber was right. She had been hard and calculating. I'd known that. It didn't change anything.

"She was just using me to get to you, Father. I told you that. That was why she was here . . ."

"And you let her?"

"How was I—"

"Enough, Jared . . . Enough. The trap is set. Before long, we'll know."

Heber Cannon was right. The trap was set. In fact, several traps were set . . . and a net. Could I avoid theirs and spring mine?

I eased the projector from inside the windbreaker, easing open the wide film antenna. I made sure the projector was not pointed anywhere near me or toward any energy-reflective surface—and that I was shielded behind the antenna that was both transmitter and collector.

The ghost spoke to them, not to me.

What you did in faithless need,
in time, no one will heed . . .

The irony of those words almost paralyzed me, because they could have applied to Verial when she'd left me to the Cheka.

"Silence, hussy." Heber's words rattled my skull.

I stepped to the side and aimed the projector toward the ghost and Charity. I wasn't sure I wanted it to work, but the conditioning held, and I pressed the activating stud. Energy flared from the projector, returned, and was re-projected, far too fast for anyone to see.

The ghost vanished. Charity's face went from immobile to angry in that microsecond before she moved—not toward Heber, but toward Jared.

I knew the moves she used. Jared didn't. His throat was crushed, and his nose broken in less than a second. He grasped at his throat, flailing.

I had already dropped the projector and was moving far faster than any man should, especially one so small and slight.

Heber Cannon gaped for a second, then reached for the sidearm he al-ways carried. "You killed him." He looked as though he were about to yell for the security types. Yet he hesitated, still arrogant, his eyes looking at a woman and a man not much larger than a prepubescent boy.

Knowing about the sidearm, I was already moving. My knife was quicker than he was. That was to be expected from an agent under conditioned hys-terical boost. For a moment, he looked down, stupidly, at the blood welling out over his waistcoat and overcoat, his mouth moving silently, with only gurgling sounds, unsurprisingly, since I'd slit his throat first, deeply.

"You had a choice, Heber," I said quietly, not that he'd be likely to hold the thought before he died. "You chose to protect a corrupt and evil son." Was I any better? Probably not, but that wasn't the question. It never had been.

I could sense the life leaking out of both of them. Where there had been one ghost by the juniper, now there would be two, both different from the first. The conflict had been quick, and almost silent—quiet enough that the Saint security men still stood by the lower south gate, waiting for a signal from Heber Cannon.

"Jared brought me down here," murmured Verial. "He said he wanted a picture of me in the garden. One that could be made into a portrait. I should have known better."

"Heber was probably watching." I bent and scooped up the projector be-fore rummaging through Heber's waistcoat and jacket pockets. In a moment, I came up with a set of keys.

"Now what?" asked Verial in the lowest of voices, knowing that I would hear.

"We walk up the way they came and out the west gate. Then we'll walk to the safe house. In this case, it's the Republic consulate. The Saints may know that, but they won't violate it for a youth and a woman."

"You have a key to the gate?"

"Heber's keys here will do." I held them up. "We should go." The keys would be faster than picking the lock—if they were the right ones.

I followed the footprints in the grass back through the gardens until I could see the north gate to the upper garden. Then I took the graveled path to the gate. The third key I tried fit the lock to the outer gate, the one on First South. I locked the gate behind us, then tossed the keys back over the gate.

We walked in the shadow of the wall until we reached Ridge Lane, where we turned south until we got to Third South.

"Do I know you? You seem familiar," she finally said.

I didn't want to answer that question. Not in the slightest. "Do you have the plans? Can you recall what you learned?" I hated to ask, but I wanted to know if what I faced would be for something.

"What are you talking about?"

"You're Verial. The code is absolem green, and the plans are for the proprietary and secret technology to the magnetohydrodynamic power plant here. I wouldn't know one end of an engineering spec from the other, but once the Spazi wrote you off, FSA decided on an experimental effort to reclaim you. Call it a terrible beauty being born." That could have referred to the way I had been used or Verial had been reclaimed—or the theft of the power plant technology.

"I should be grateful?"

I recalled that tone of voice all too well.

"No. You never were. You don't have to tell me. I have no need to know. I just was the tool able to get you back. I wondered if it was worth the cost."

"Don't speak of costs."

"I won't." I kept walking along the shaded side of Third South.

"They'll be glad you succeeded. That's all I'll say."

That was about what I'd expected.

"You never answered my question about whether I should know you."

"I couldn't say, not in a way that would make sense in the present tense."

"Don't mouth rhymes at me. I recall enough that I'd prefer not to hear another line of verse."

I ignored her request and quoted Yeats, in my own fashion.

"Being high and solitary and most stern,
Why, what could you have done, being what you are?
Was there another Troy for you to burn?"

"Alexander? You're not Alexander."

Again, I misquoted.

"You could have warned me, but I was young,
And we spoke a different tongue."

"You knew the risks. Still . . . how——?"

"Birth-hour and death-hour meet . . .
"I dance on other's deathless feet . . ."

She was silent. What else could she have said?

We walked eastward in the darkness, down Leigh Hill and along Third South, still on the dark side. Behind us, sirens rose. The security types had found bodies, and perhaps ghosts. They would find little else, besides the footprints that looked to be those of a woman and a boy and Heber Cannon's keys beside a gate.

Neither of us said another word until we approached the heavy wrought-iron gates of the small estate on the east side of Iron Mission, set on the north side of Coal Creek. I could see the Republic Marines manning the gate-house. They were expecting us.

"You wrote and memorized your own poetry, didn't you?" I asked.

"Yes."

"Because you thought they would find you out?"

"No. It was the logical thing to do, whatever might happen. Sommersby knew from my first assignment."

"She would have." I didn't really want to escort her through the gates. I did anyway, after the Marines opened the gates. They closed them behind us.

When she stood at last in the archway of the front door to the Republic consulate, the two guards flanking her, she turned, and all three looked down at me. I handed her the knife and the now-useless projector. The single-use film antenna had destroyed itself in accomplishing its task. "Dispose of them. You know how and why."

She would, but only to protect herself. As always.

"What happens to you now?" she asked.

I just smiled and shook my head.

I left her there, as once she had left me. She had not changed, and tomorrow the man whose body I held so briefly would cover a rededication concert, sore and bruised, but his nerves would not burn. He would doubtless wonder what had happened in the hours that he had lost—and I would become, at last, what lay beyond ghost and zombie.

I walked toward the darkness of oblivion, out of my own nerve-jangled, gong-tormented sea, toward my freedom from what never could have been. In some ways, I pitied Verial—now. I had repaid her in the only way possible. My fingers moved toward the waistpack under the windbreaker.

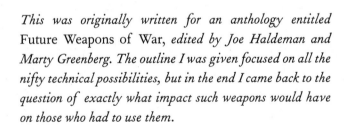

This was originally written for an anthology entitled Future Weapons of War, *edited by Joe Haldeman and Marty Greenberg. The outline I was given focused on all the nifty technical possibilities, but in the end I came back to the question of exactly what impact such weapons would have on those who had to use them.*

SPEC-OPS

"We can't afford a war, General."

"We'll have a war with Seasia sooner or later. We can afford later less than sooner."

"The people won't stand for it, and no nation has ever stood for long against the will of its citizens."

"Then change their minds. We need this war."

"Change your weapons, General, if you need this war."

Excerpt from: *The Right War*
SONYDREAMS, 2043

I

1559. Khorbel deJahn slid into the dim pod, sensies flicking to Duty Ops-Con. "Up-what, sir?"

"You're last, Tech deJahn. Chimbats," replied the major. "Nu-type. Seasies haven't seen. Take over from Hennesy. Third seat."

Leastwise, no scroaches. DeJahn link-pulsed.

Hennesy blinked, unlinked, and stood. "You got it, deJahn."

"Got it."

Hennesy had left the sensie-seat hot, damp. DeJahn wiped it with the cloth he always brought. Still hated taking over a hot seat. Leastwise, he was beside Meralez. Her eyes were open, link-blank. Sexy eyes when she was in her skull, not like now.

He pulled the thin mesh cap into place over his short mil-cut hair. Made sure the contacts handshook, blanked his thoughts, and settled into the link. *Tech first deJahn.*

Accepted. Flash background: Chimbats. Three "families," each of twenty-five units.

Target: any personnel at biointerdict station beta-four. See plot.

Firsties were just chitterings, light-darts in blackness. Be a while before the biogator expelled the chimbats from the pouch under its ridged back. Side-mind went to the back plot, illuminated only in his thoughts. Green blips were the gators, swimming upstream after a tidal boost. Red blip was target—Seasie biointerdict station. An hour plus to release.

DeJahn hated prerelease. Babysitting chims just in case the vector got zapped. Seasies weren't going to see gators in one of a dozen canals and muddy streams, not the main river channel.

He might have slept in the dark pod. Would have slept, except for the major's overscreening and the checks. Time passed. Slowly.

DeJahn stifled a yawn, compared closure rate once more. Ran a complete monitor on the bioindicators, then reported. *1630 . . . on course, on target.*

Stet, Tech deJahn.

More dark and quiet time. Time where his thoughts, behind the link, lingered on Meralez. Good body, better voice. Reminded him of Margot. Probably not good. Wished Meralez weren't pseudo les-butch. Could be a front. Keep the tech types from pawing. Hazard of spec-ops. Had to find ways to remember who you were. Sex and women helped. Did men help the female techs? Or not? That why so many women partnered with other women?

More time passed in darkness. More chitterings as the chimbats got restless, their soporifics wearing off. Screen checks came, went.

Ten to release, tech. Request acknowledge.

Stet. Ten to release. DeJahn hated the obvious. Major knew he was ready. Linked, wasn't he? Mil-type reduns still plagued pros like him.

Chitterings increased. Chimbats getting restless as the sops wore off.

Five to release.

Stet.

The chitterings were almost as bad as the scuttling and scrapings that came with the scroaches, and the smell . . . Tech ops said there wasn't sensie smell. Spec-ops techs knew better.

Stand by for release. Release . . . now!

Disorientation. Always that. Hundreds of sound-sights flashed through the integrator before settling into a shifting mosaic as the chimbats fanned out, spreading wings, pulsing the terrain, receiving sound images.

Backwater canal below, hard to judge but no more than thirty feet wide. Grimy gray-brown surface showed the wakes of the gators. No sonic-visual on the gators. They weren't designed that way. Water blocked most of the bats' sonar return.

DeJahn squinted to focus the image. Wasn't a real squint, but the sensie-link equivalent. Trees slumped bedraggled limbs into the water on both sides of the canal.

He checked the mind sidescreen. Target was six thousand yards at zero-seven-one. Chimbats were sweeping across the water, scooping up insect fuel, following the canal at zero-four-four. Another two thousand, and he'd have to nudge them right.

Gators had fallen behind, following the canal. They would for another thousand yards, then would take the cross canal. No one had told deJahn, but there was a soarer-boat patrol base on the east side of the delta. Each gator could take out one, maybe two, of the boats. Boats gone, or fewer of them, and there'd be a chance to bring in the dreadnaughts—the salties. Handful of them, and there wouldn't be a patrol base. With the rivers in spec-ops' hands, be an open vector lane for all the ricelands in the area, and the J-wasps could immobilize the quantum wetworks at Chuo-Klyseen.

DeJahn forced his mind back to the chimbats. They needed to follow the overgrown path to the right . . . more right. He exerted the pressure of *danger* to the left, and the lure of *food*, big juicy mosquitoes to the left. Heat built around him. He had to ignore it, center the chimbats on course toward the target.

Thirty-two hundred and closing. That was a quick link-flash to the major, to keep him from sending an inquiry while deJahn was setting up the attack.

Nineteen hundred yards, and all the chimbats "saw" was trees and insects, and the "brightness" of water in places from an afternoon rain.

The trees vanished, replaced by paddies that didn't hold rice, or water, except for the thinnest layer, but various electronic- and biosensors. Beyond the paddies was the interdict station. It didn't look like much, not in the sensie-integrated mosaic in deJahn's mind, just a gray square on an artificial square bluff seven yards above the soggy soil of the delta. Four thatched huts—the kind no one had lived in, even in Seasia, in generations—set around a graveled courtyard. Gravel? In a delta? Chimbats' sonar showed the harder composite walls that supported the bluff edges, and the mix of steel and plastic hidden under the pseudothatch.

Pseudobats, pseudothatch, pseudobluff . . . frig! Was anything real?

The mission was real.

DeJahn exerted pressure, creating the sense and image of insect prey just below the roofs of the pseudothatch.

Chimbats angled down, wings near silent, fangs filled with solvent and venom.

Light! So brilliant that deJahn's eyes boil-burned in their sockets.

Except it wasn't light. Sound! That was it. Screaming sound, blinding the chimbats. Feedback blasted back through him. Felt like his eardrums were bursting, and long needles lanced through his eyes, coming out the back of his skull.

Frig! Major'd said the chimbats were new types . . .

Blackness wiped it all away.

An alarm buzzed . . . sawing into him. It buzzed again.

Somewhere, something nagged at him, telling him to wake up . . . but he could sleep in, couldn't he? Sunday morning, wasn't it?

Tech deJahn . . . trigger recovery sequence . . . Recovery sequence . . .

Recovery sequence? His thoughts were sluggish. He had to do something . . . didn't he? Recovery sequence? A chill ran up his spine. *Recovery one! Recovery one!*

Link one . . . link two . . .

After a moment, or several, deJahn could feel the barriers dropping. Persona segmentation was frightening—but it had saved more than a few spec-ops techs from biobacklash syndrome . . . or worse.

He blinked. He still couldn't see. Vision was usually late to return, but he didn't like being in the dark.

Interrogative status?

Reintegration 71 percent complete.

What was 71 percent of a tech? He wanted to laugh. He forced his teeth together.

The blackness began to evaporate, and holes appeared in it. One hole showed the recovery medtech looking from the porta-console to deJahn and back again. Another hole showed the dark greenish gray bulkhead of the spec-ops pod.

After a moment, deJahn blinked, then coughed. "Think I'm back."

"He's green." The medtech's voice was bored, almost disappointed. He stood, nodded, and replaced the porta-console in its case before leaving the pod.

"Just sit there for a while," ordered the major.

DeJahn glanced around the pod. All the other sensie-stations were empty. He supposed that was good.

Then the shudders began.

It took fifteen minutes before deJahn was ready to stand. He must have been the last. Or the only idiot who hadn't disengaged fast enough.

He looked at the major. The officer's cold green eyes showed nothing.

"Thought you said these chimbats were new. They were ready for them."

"They were new. Some of them got through. About half the station's in-operative." The eyes softened, into mere green glass. "Get some rest, Tech. You're off schedule tomorrow. Check with med on Monday."

"Yes, sir." DeJahn took two slow steps to the pod exit station, pressed his fingertips on the pad.

Cleared to depart. Status amber . . . off duty, pending medical. The exit irised open.

DeJahn took a step into the passageway outside the pod. Each step was deliberate. His balance felt off. Could be the beating his ears had taken.

His poopsuit stunk. Sweat and everything else. Biofeedback was hell on a tech's personal system, no matter what the newsies said. Especially when your vectors got blasted before you disengaged.

He needed a shower and something to eat. There were still holes in his vision.

II

"What is the point of a weapon?"

"To defeat someone, or to force them to accede to what the wielder wishes."

"What is defeat?"

"The surrender of a position, goods, territory, or even a point of view."

"Who determines defeat?"

"Either total destruction or surrender by the one who's in the weaker position . . ."

III

0340. DeJahn bolted up in the narrow bunk. Sleep like deep link cobwebbed his thoughts. Sat there, unmoving. Two days off hadn't helped that much.

0345. He swung his feet onto the plastipress deck, knew he had to get moving, get to the pod for duty rotation. Didn't want to be last. Might be scroaches, or chimshrews. Bunk above was empty. Stennes had midwatch on screens.

DeJahn pulled on a clean poopsuit, knowing he'd need to drop off the soiled ones below before his next duty. Chim-duty was hell on uniforms. Softboots followed the poopsuit, and he fastened the bag with his linkcap to his waistband. Closed the slider behind him and hurried along the dim passageway and up the circular ramp, past electro-ops, and to the spec-ops pod.

0352. DeJahn's fingers stopped short of the pod access plate. Took a moment before he touched the pad. It sucked the heat from his fingertips.

Entry granted. The pod door irised open, and deJahn slid inside. His sensies flicked to the captain standing Duty OpsCon. "Tech deJahn, reporting, sir."

"Take number two, Tech deJahn," replied the captain.

DeJahn stepped up beside the sensie console and link-pulsed. He was relieving Suares.

The wiry tech didn't blink. He just stood. "It's yours, deJahn. Scowls, tonight. Best hurry. They're in free hunt."

"Got it."

DeJahn touched the sensie-seat. Suares left it cool. He always did. DeJahn didn't know how. Still, he wiped the seat before he settled down. Once more, no scroaches. He kept the sigh inside, then slipped on the mesh cap, checked the handshake, and linked into the scowls. He dropped into the third seat, and linked. *Tech first Khorbel deJahn.*

Accepted. Flash background: Scowls. Initial target: guards, research station gamma three-one. Primary target: technicians.

Frigging great. He had to pull the scowls off free-hunt after they took out enough guards to get an opening for the scroaches and turn them to finding the scientists and technicians who were doing the research.

A sharpness of gray images overtook him, so clear that they were more disorienting than the fuzzy sharpness that came with chimbats. Disorientation through precision. Better that than the looming wavering images and prey-lust that pervaded the scroach links.

As Suares had said, the scowls were in free hunt.

Checking the mind sidescreen, deJahn verified the target, a bioware research station. Small, no more than fifteen science types and twice that many guards. The scowls were priority programmed, as much as a modified owl could be. The guards were secondary. Guards didn't create biotech and bioweapons. What the station produced or researched, deJahn didn't know. He switched views from the too-distinct shifting composite to one scowl after another, stopping at one stooping into an attack on a guard post.

One of the guards turned and fired. The incendiary pellets exploded into a cage of flame and fire. The stab of pain ran down deJahn's back for an instant before he disengaged that link, later than he should have.

Quick-switching again, deJahn caught the feedback-view from the next scowl as it struck the guard's arm. Fire-venom from the talons went straight to the guard's nerves. In instants, the guard was shaking so badly the fire-rifle struck the plastcrete under his boots. In seconds, he was beside the rifle, bones breaking under the convulsive power of his own hyped muscles.

More scowls feathered down. Alarms began to screech, and the second guard sealed the booth. That would only buy him minutes before the first scroach ate its way through the heavy plastic.

DeJahn switched images. He didn't need to see what the adapted scorpion-roaches would do. At the next guard post, the sentries were still bringing down scowls, each scowl death a line of flame into his own nerves, but the guards did not see the wave of scroaches close to underfoot, advancing inexorably.

He began to exert pressure, shifting the rodent-prey image, strengthening it, and positioning it to bring the scowls through the failing screens into the technical area. The guards were the initial target, just the initial target.

Primary target was scientists and technicians . . . primary target . . .

IV

You got bioethics issues in chim-ops. Stuff those. Big question, that's whether mod-techno weapons should be used in war at all . . . Two soldiers faced off at Waterloo. A bunch stormed beaches at Normandy against another bunch, or even slog-fought in the jungles of Vietnam against a VC bunch. Back then, fighters on both sides died. Lots of them. Different today. Americans changed it all when they high-teched the Middle East, used biowar in Iran. Nowadays, the tech types use chim-ops, spec-ops, remote-ops. Nothing touches them. Just like old

Greek gods, they throw lightnings, never see what they've done, don't ever experience the horror. Think our special operatives are even soldiers at all? Or just techno-chims themselves?

Editorial, *Whazup Tonight*
March 15, 2051

V

Thursday before breakfast, deJahn had to shower. Sometimes, dreams were almost as bad as infiltration spec-ops themselves. Even flying the scowls with the scroaches following had been bad enough. He needed a long shower, but water was one thing a forward base had. Surrounded by it. He dressed deliberately. He still had enough clean poopsuits. He'd finally reclaimed enough fresh ones for the days ahead.

He felt cleaner, for the moment, before he headed down the passageway to the tech mess and breakfast. Softboots whispered on the deck. Hard to believe that fifty yards up through the overhead was what looked like marsh and reeds in the river delta.

Tech mess was an oval room with five tables and dispensers and formulators. He tapped out his selections on the formulator, then set them on the tray, and carried the tray to the table where Meralez and Castaneda sat. Castaneda was the butch that Meralez fronted being.

Castaneda gestured. "Look like shit, deJahn."

"You, too, Castaneda."

"All of us look like shit, all right?" Meralez laughed. "Good thing nothing's up but surveillance today."

DeJahn liked her laugh. Warm, sort-of-sexy, not-in-your-face.

"You've got a thought-look," Meralez suggested.

After swallowing a mouthful of bagel burrito, deJahn nodded, then took a sip of coffee, bitter. One thing formulators didn't do well, along with tea and chocolate.

"Well?"

"Was a time when special ops meant guys with guns dropping on chutes into jungle," replied deJahn. "Some ways, more honest."

"*Honest?* Strange word, think you?" Meralez brushed back mahogany hair too short to move.

"Strange?"

"Snuffed is snuffed," replied Meralez. "Back then, it was lead, steel jackets, osmiridium, metal projectiles at high speed. Now, we're using J-wasps, S-wasps, scroaches, scowls, biogators, snators. They're using phonies stuffed with ultra-ex, semiclones with biopaks. We text envirosave, and they text reclaiming their heritage and defeating imperialism. Some of us get snuffed, and some of them do. Back a century, it was the same. Any more honest then than now? Don't think so. Back then, the officers ordered. The senior ones lived, the junior ones died like techs, and lots more techs died than now."

For a moment, deJahn considered her words. They were hers, what she thought, and that was good.

"The senior officers, brass balls and iron tits . . . all the same," snorted Castaneda.

"All the same, what?" A cheerful laugh followed the words.

Castaneda looked up. So did deJahn.

Vielho stood there, then set his tray down and slid into the vacant space beside Castaneda. "Anytime you're talking balls and tits, Castaneda, got to be worth listening to." He grinned disarmingly, then took a swallow of his tea.

So far as deJahn knew, Vielho was the only tech who drank tea. Or what passed for it. Then, Casimir was the only other person deJahn knew who drank it for breakfast. Where deJahn's brother had picked it up . . . who knew? Casimir couldn't even explain, but he also couldn't explain why he liked teaching.

"Just jawing about officers. Little good that does."

"Better than holding it inside." Vielho sipped the tea.

"You ever think about being a teacher?" asked deJahn.

"Me?" Vielho laughed. "No way. Got as much patience as a scroach seeking a Seasie. Why?"

DeJahn shook his head. "Just wondered."

VI

0750. The briefing was in the techs' mess. All the briefings took place there. DeJahn didn't want to be late, slipped into the spot at the table beside Meralez. She didn't look at him. He returned the favor by looking straight ahead.

Chihouly lumbered in, glanced at deJahn and Meralez, and gave deJahn a knowing headshake. DeJahn shrugged.

0801. Major Delles stepped out into the small open space in front of the twenty techs. All stood and stiffened.

"Carry on." Delles gestured for them to sit.

With the others, deJahn settled in, waiting to hear what Delles had to say. He wouldn't like it. Briefings meant trouble ahead.

Delles cleared his throat, then straightened his shoulders. His poopsuit had creases, and the gold oak leaves on the starched collars glistened.

DeJahn was just happy to have enough clean suits.

"Power is the key to any advanced technology. Even biotech and biowar require large amounts of power. In this sector, the Seasies are still relying heavily on old-style power plants. In particular, they have a large magnetodynamic coal plant, the Tanshu Two. This mission is to bring down the plant. We'll take out the cooling systems, then the security lines, and finish up with a double, an ultra-ex powered EMP, then red goo for the coal itself. The satellite team will be handling the biobirds for the EMP and goo. We get the dirty work first."

A power plant? That sounded like the beginning of something, something deJahn wasn't sure he'd care for. The only reason the Seasies hadn't gotten rid of the old-style coal plants was that the costs were sunk. Spec-ops would be doing them a favor . . . unless a short-term power shortage happened to be necessary for some other reason. Like a sectorwide push in another few days.

He couldn't help but turn toward Meralez.

They both nodded, but so slightly that the major didn't notice, then returned their eyes to the presentation. The mess had darkened, to enhance the holo image of the target, a hulking industrial dinosaur that might have come from a hundred years earlier in NorAm.

". . . water intakes are standard bioscrub . . . strike team three has already planted z-clambers . . . intake volumes are down 15 percent . . ."

The major droned on, and deJahn managed to catch what he needed to know, and that was that most of the techs would be on late-disengagement. Another sure sign of trouble.

The last power plant image vanished, replaced by three lists. "Check for your assignments here."

DeJahn checked. He had the main pod, but it didn't say what he'd be handling.

". . . any questions?" the major finally concluded.

"Why the late-disengage, sir?"

DeJahn didn't see the speaker, but it sounded like Chihouly.

"A number of the targets require higher than normal acquisition ratios, and that requires greater tech presence and persistence than can be obtained through late-stage free-ops.

"Any other questions?"

No one spoke. There wasn't any point to it, not after the major's last answer.

"Duty stations will commence at 0900. Dismissed."

The techs all rose, stiffened, and stood while the major departed.

That left thirty minutes to kill. DeJahn got some coffee. When he looked around for Meralez, she and Castaneda had left.

He sat back down.

Chihouly sat at the next table. Neither one said a word.

Finally, fifteen minutes later, deJahn got up and tossed the disposable mug into the reformulation bin and walked toward the pod.

Meralez was one of the first into the pod, after Vielho, and deJahn was right behind her. Suares followed deJahn. Esquival and Chihouly were behind him. The OpsCon was Captain DiLayne. Narrow-faced former tech, she'd come up the long way and never forgotten.

He dropped into the third seat, and linked. *Tech deJahn.*

Accepted. Flash background: S-wasps. Five swarms, seeded minus three months, advanced growth, designed to inject superconductives into critical components, relays, and certain bloc units. Power plant Tanshu-Two. See plot.

Disorientation. Another mosaic view, with tiny lines everywhere, the result of compound eyes with enhanced resolution. All he could "see" were trees and an open field—no—what looked like a big flat pond, maybe an abandoned rice paddy, or a fish farm—the Seasies still preferred real-enviro food.

Because the view was so distance-short, deJahn checked the mental sideview, noting the swarms' progress from where the nests had been seeded weeks earlier. Another thirty minutes, according to the schedule.

Swarm one was flying ahead of schedule. A vague image of a black spider and a sticky web slowed them.

He checked the sidescreens. The rest of the spec-ops vectors were well ahead. They should be.

Interrogative status? came from DiLayne.

On schedule. Green.

He had to keep a tight rein on the swarms, even so, holding them back because the early units were slower than on the schedule.

Even so, the first S-wasps hit the sonic screens, flared into chitinous fragments. Minuscule needles pinged on his brain, and he created the image of sweet raw meat. Had to hold back the S-wasps until the scroaches and snators dealt with the guards and screens. Shouldn't be that many screens around an old power plant, even one that generated some six hundred megawatts.

Screens down. DiLayne's reminder came after deJahn had already vectored his swarms toward the control centers.

From one composite image—swarm two—he could see/sense a handful of technicians in white singlesuits scrambling for cover, diving away from the S-wasps. A second image was a bank of equipment. He targeted the S-wasps into the vulnerable crevices there.

His whole body convulsed. A sonic net—internal—had wiped out swarm five.

His eyes burned, and the side-plot was getting faint.

Interrogative swarm status?

Operative units at 61 percent . . . 57 percent . . . 52 . . .

There was no automatic disengagement under a late disengage.

. . . 49 . . .

Disengage! Disengage!

His whole body convulsed with the shock. Then, he could feel his lungs laboring in the darkness. He'd stopped breathing for a few moments. *Close . . . too frigging close . . .*

His breathing slowed. His poopsuit was soaked, his back stuck with sweat to the sensie-seat, and he stank with fear-sweat as he eased off the mesh linkcap.

All he could do for a time was sit and breathe.

No one even looked in his direction in the dimness, even as bodies rushed past him. He shook his head and looked to his left. Suares lay limp in the sensie-chair—scarlet-flared. He wasn't breathing. He wouldn't, not ever, deJahn knew. Brain-fried.

Meralez was kneeling beside Vielho, but her words made no sense to de-Jahn. Vielho's body kept twitching, and he screamed silently, as if his vocal cords had been ripped out of his throat.

A med-tech appeared with a porta-gurney, moved around Meralez, and slapped a trankmask on Vielho. The medic never looked around as he strapped Vielho into the gurney, ignoring the other techs.

"Techs . . ." said the major from the ops station.

DeJahn knew what DiLayne meant. He stood, moved toward the pod exit, then touched the pad.

Tech deJahn . . . released, duty status green.

He followed Esquival out into the passageway. She didn't look back. Neither did he.

Late-disengagement.

Suicide mission.

VII

Specialist biofeedback is required for optimal efficiency in special operations. Incomplete or null feedback impairs biounit response and efficacy in direct relationship to the total number of discrete units under operator influence and the neural complexity of the individual unit . . .

SPEC-OPS 1421.45

DARPA

VIII

What could he do? DeJahn didn't know. Maybe nothing. Looked around the techs' mess. He was the only one there. Coffee, ersatz shit . . . it was cold. Nothing worse than cold, bitter, pseudocoffee.

Bullshit, deJahn. Lots worse things. Just scared that it might happen to you. He pushed the thought away. Finally, he stood, shook his head.

He took the longer passageway. Softboots scuffed on the deck, almost silent. Everything was muffled and damped in the station. Missed real sunlight. Missed lots of real things. Sick bay was at the end, south end, he'd heard. Who knew when you never saw the sun?

He stepped inside sick bay. Duty med-tech just watched. Watched close.

Vielho lay in the second bay, in a medsack that surrounded all of his body. Only his face was exposed. His eyes were open, and his chest rose and fell.

A long moment passed, before deJahn spoke. "You'll be all right. You did a good job." Was that right? Who the frig knew? "Vielho . . . I'm here . . . deJahn."

There was no response. The blank eyes did not move, did not blink.

DeJahn looked around the cubicle, located a stool. He pulled it over and sat where Vielho's eyes could see him, if they could see.

Finally, after another ten minutes, the silence pressed in on him. So much that he had to say something. Anything.

"Vielho . . . you know . . . you remind me of my brother. He's younger. Not much, two years. He's a teacher . . . some out-of-the-way place, Escalante . . . he's like you, always had something pleasant to say . . . That's why I asked about the tea. He drinks tea. You know, one time, when we were moving the herd . . . yeah, the old man still handles sheep the old way . . . Casimir found one of the ewes had dropped twins late . . . never found their mother . . . he bottle-nursed 'em until they were old enough to go with the others . . ." DeJahn didn't know why he'd told that story, or the one after it.

Finally, maybe an hour, maybe two, later, he got up from the stool and leaned over and put two fingers on Vielho's forehead. "Hold tight . . ."

Outside sick bay, he thought he saw Meralez in the passageway ahead, and he took the one to the left, that went back to the mess, not that he was hungry. Most times, he would have been glad to see Meralez.

Not this time.

IX

Major Delles surveyed the techs seated at the tables in the mess. This time, more than ten chairs were empty. One would have belonged to Suares, another to Vielho . . . and Chihouly. *Too many names for one lousy obsolete power plant.*

Meralez had seated herself at one end of the single long table, with Castaneda on the other side. DeJahn hadn't tried to get close on the other side. He'd just taken the last seat near the bulkhead table.

"This is the big push." Delles smiled enthusiastically. "What we have planned here will upset the Seasies' economy for a decade or more, not to mention crippling their efforts to match us in biowar capabilities. What we're doing is just a small part of an overall coordinated program . . ."

An overall coordinated program? More like another frigged-up mess where nothing would go like planned, and a whole bunch of techs would get disshock or brain-fried.

"... it's taken some time to identify the critical targets, and not all of them are obvious, but all are critical to the sectoral economy ..."

Just tell us what they are, thought deJahn. *Skip the enthuse shit.*

"... Lumut is critical to the development of the next wave of warm-water bioconversion systems ... Targets will be the power systems, the membrane formulation complex, all comm-links, and the potable water system, as well as all humint armed units ..."

Turn the place into a wasteland, just like they did with Cascadia Coast ... and make sure no one's left who can explain what happened. Margot had been in Cascadia, just visiting. And deJahn had applied for spec-ops the next week.

"... all the biounits are in place and registering green ..."

As if you'd tell us about those that aren't.

"... We'll be using the main pod for the heavies, and two and three for the aux biounits. Here are the pod assignments."

The holo image appeared in the air beside the major. One of the names under pod two was deJahn.

Frigging support. It didn't help that Castaneda was assigned to the main pod. He forced a smile. At least, Meralez was in pod two with him. Not that she'd ever been other than polite to him, but even that helped.

"Any questions, Techs?" Delles barely paused before adding, "Dismissed. Operation begins at 0900 local tomorrow."

DeJahn stood.

Meralez walked by him, as if she would not speak to him.

He nodded, deciding against smiling.

"I saw that. With Vielho. You're not so cold. Not like people think." She flashed a quick smile, almost secretive, before her face turned just tech-pleasant.

Cold? He kept to himself, but he wasn't cold, was he?

X

0849. DeJahn stood outside pod two. He didn't like being early, but he liked being late even less. In front of him, Esquival stepped forward, extending her hand. As she did, deJahn was aware of someone behind him—Meralez. He wanted to look back. He didn't.

Then it was his turn. He extended his hand to the sensor. *Tech deJahn. Entry granted.*

He slipped into the dimness. Captain DiLayne was Ops-Con again. That figured. Delles would take the main pod. Pod two was smaller, with only four sensie-seats. DeJahn took the second seat, and watched as Meralez stopped beside the third. He smiled at her through the dimness, but only for a moment. She only nodded.

He eased the mesh linkcap into place, then settled himself. *Tech deJahn.*

Accepted. Flash background: Snators—bioexplosive. Clutches implanted in five locales, activated at thirty-six minus. Links confirmed. Five targets—all broadband nodecasters. See plots.

The good news was that his targets weren't people, but the bad news was that he was riding herd on reptilian bioexplosives almost as deadly as ultra-ex. He'd need careful timing for the disengagement.

The five plots displayed the snators, all arrayed around Lumut, each less than three thousand yards from the target. Each had been sent in with a biogator weeks or months before, little more than a programmed bioblastula with accelerated growth patterning. That kind of planning was something deJahn didn't want to think about.

Interrogative vector status? snapped DiLayne.

Snators green, standing by for release.

Release at will.

He didn't need any more urging. The first group of snators left wakes, so energetic was their water entry. The odor of decaying meat permeated that link.

No smell through the sensie-links? DeJahn snorted to himself, even as he blocked the decay odor and the snators slowed, their snouts turning from side to side, as if puzzled by the change, but they kept swimming downstream.

The second attack group had begun to slide through the marsh and reeds toward the nodecaster on the low hillock to the south. The last three hundred yards was across what amounted to mowed lawn, and deJahn would have to sacrifice one of the snators to take out the sonic electric gating to the lawn—it might have been a cricket field or pitch, whatever they called it.

Group three had a curving path through the public gardens, exposed most of the way. That worried deJahn. Gatorlike creatures in the gardens would certainly attract some attention, but then, if need be, he could push them into a run, and snators could make speed.

Four and five had near-direct water routes, with only the last few hundred yards exposed, but five had to cross a side road, supposedly with low traffic.

He flicked from image to image, flickering from snator to snator so fast that twice the integrator blanked. The snators' binocular vision was clear, and there wasn't much color. He wanted to get a better and quicker personal sense of locale matched with the plot map, but he forced himself to slow down.

He did have another thirty standard minutes, and the snators were fast.

Group five was running ahead, but deJahn didn't see that it mattered. Better ahead and clear than on-sched and facing opposition.

Group three was already on target, less than sixty yards below the node-caster concealed in an artificial rock cliff slightly north of the center of the gardens.

One of the local patrollers was also there, and she had a stun-rifle out, leveling it at the lead snator. DeJahn dropped the third snator into limited freehunt, because its reactions and impulses were far faster than his through the links.

Her shot went wide. She did not get a second shot.

Someone else did, with a biodetonator.

Electrofire slammed back through the links, and deJahn shuddered, even as he accelerated two of the gators toward the base of the cliff, seeking whatever access points there might be. Neither of the two lagging snators could locate the attacker, even as one registered projectiles screaming past it.

Giving up on locating the attacker, deJahn pressed the laggards after the leaders, strengthening the lure of decaying meat.

A second snator went up, this time with its own bioex, leaving flame in deJahn's eyes. He shook off the pain feedback and checked the closure. The three remaining were close enough. He triggered them, holding the link for the barest moment to make sure the command had gone true, before disengaging.

Even so, the shock rocked him, because some of the snators' death agony washed back over him.

One down, four to go.

Automatics of some sort popped up from the sides of the cricket field right after deJahn detonated and disengaged from the sacrificial snator. Two of the remaining snators were shredded by the autofire, but three others sprinted through the hail of composite to the other side and the base of the nodecaster, surrounded by three yards of impermite. Impermite was weak stuff compared to NorAm bioex.

DeJahn triggered and disengaged.

Pointed iron picks began to chip away at his skull.

Three more . . .

Group four scuttled and splashed through the tanks of a low-tech wet-works to reach the back side of another low hill. A dozen Seasies in dull green uniforms appeared.

DeJahn sent the lead gator toward them, using it—with an early detonation—to clear the way for the others.

Another trigger and disengage.

Now . . . large and ancient cannon were blowing holes in his skull. How it felt, anyway.

Interrogative status?

Three objectives triggered . . . two in progress. His entire body was a mass of fire, pseudobiofeedback fire, but it still the frig hurt.

He struggled to focus on the link to group one. Still short of target.

Five . . . where was five?

Trying to cross the road, and two local patrollers were laying down a fire curtain.

That cost him two snators, but the patrollers and their vehicles went up with the bioex. He just hoped the two remaining snators had enough bioex for the nodecaster as he put them on free–search and destroy.

Group one.

Just as he linked, he could feel the biofield constrictor sweep across the snators of group one.

He mentally lunged for disengagement . . . *Disengage!*

XI

Fire! Like being bitten by a thousand scroaches. Light! Brighter than novafly exploding before his eyes.

DeJahn jerked. His eyes were open, saw only purple blackness, link-deep with no link. Every nerve in his body was a line of fire. Where was cool? Darkness?

"Easy . . . easy . . ."

Whose voice? Knew the voice. Couldn't place . . . couldn't find.

"Who?" His voice rasped. Not his voice. Could tell he'd been screaming. Frig! Didn't want to be a screamer.

A hand touched his. Warm, welcome . . . Yet . . . the warmth was fire, knifelike, daggers like the fangs of a chimbat, like the venom of a chimshrew.

"You'll be all right, deJahn . . . be fine. Just disengagement link-shock . . ."

Just disengagement link-shock . . . link-shock . . . Sure, you'll be fine. This time.

"Friggin' . . . disengage . . ."

"You'll be all right." Meralez squeezed his hand once more. This time, there was no pain.

He managed to tighten his fingers around hers for a moment.

He would be fine. He was a tech.

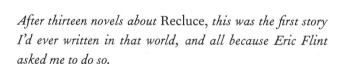

After thirteen novels about Recluce, *this was the first story I'd ever written in that world, and all because Eric Flint asked me to do so.*

SISTERS OF SARRONNYN, SISTERS OF WESTWIND

I

The Roof of the World was still frozen in winter gray, and the sun had not yet cleared the peaks to the east or shone on Freyja when I caught sight of Fiera coming up the old stone steps from the entrance to Tower Black.

I moved to intercept her. "What were you doing, Guard Fiera?"

"I was coming to the main hall, Guard Captain." Fiera did not look directly at me, but past me, a trick many Westwind guards had tried over the years. Even my own sister, especially my own sister, could not fool me.

"Using the east passage?"

Fiera flushed. "Yes, Guard Captain."

"Assignations before breakfast, yet? When did you sneak out of the barracks?"

She straightened, as she always did when she decided to flaunt something or when she knew she'd been caught. "He kissed me, Guard Captain. Creslin did."

Oh, Fiera, do not lie to me. I did not voice the words. "I seriously doubt that the esteemed son of the Marshall would have even known you were in the east passage. It is seldom traveled before dawn in winter. If anyone kissed anyone, you kissed him. What was he doing? Why were you following him?"

Fiera's eyes dropped. "He was just there. By himself. He was walking the passage."

"You're a fool! If the Marshall ever finds out, you'll be posted to High Ice for the rest of the winter this year, and for all of next year with no relief. That would be after you were given to the most needy of the consorts until you were with child. You'd never see the child after you bore her, and you'd spend your shortened life on remote duty, perhaps even on the winter road crews."

This time, my words reached her. She swallowed. "I meant no harm. He's always looked at me. I just . . . wanted him to know before he leaves for Sarronnyn."

"He knows now. If I see you anywhere near him, if I hear a whisper . . ."

"Yes, Guard Captain . . . please . . . Shierra."

"What was he doing near Tower Black?" I asked again.

"I do not know, Guard Captain. He was wearing field dress, without a winter parka. He looked like any other guard." Fiera's eyes met mine fully for the first time.

We both knew that young Creslin, for all his abilities with a blade, was anything but another guard. He was the only male ever trained with the Guard, and yet his masculine skills had not been neglected. He could play the guitar better than any minstrel, and I'd heard his voice when he sang. It seemed that he could call a soft breeze in the heat of summer, and more than a few of those who had guarded his door had come away with tears in their eyes. Fiera had been one of them, unhappily. He'd even called an ice storm once. Only once, after he had discovered he'd been promised to the Sub-Tyrant of Sarronnyn.

Shortly, after more words with Fiera, I walked down the steps to the door of the ancient tower to check on what might have happened.

I always thought that tales of love were romantic nothings meant for men, not for the guards—or guard captains of Westwind—although I worried about my younger sister, and her actions in the east passage showed that I was right to worry. Fiera was close to ten years younger than I. We had not been close as children. I've always felt that sisters were either inseparable or distant. We were distant. Much as I tried to bridge that distance, much as I tried to offer kindness and advice, Fiera rejected both. When I attempted kindness, she said, "I know you're trying to be nice, but I'm not you. I have to do things my own way." She said much the same thing when I first offered advice. After a time, I only offered simple courtesy, as one would to any other Westwind guard, and no advice at all.

To my relief, the Tower Black door was locked, as it always was and should have been. There *might* have been boot prints in the frost; but even as a guard captain, I was not about to report what I could not prove, not when it might lead to revealing Fiera's indiscretion. Besides, what difference could it have made? Fiera had not made a fatal error, and young Creslin would be leaving Westwind forever, within days, to become the consort of the Sub-Tyrant of Sarronnyn.

II

Four mornings later, Guard Commander Aemris summoned the ten Westwind Guard captains to the duty room below the great hall. She said nothing at all for a time. Her eyes traveled from one face to another.

"Some of you may have heard the news," Aemris finally said. "Lord Creslin skied off the side of the mountain into a snowstorm. The detachment was unable to find him. The Marshall has declared mourning."

"How? . . ."

"The weather . . ."

"He wasn't supplied . . ."

"There are some skis and supplies missing from Tower Black. He must have taken them. Do any of you know anything about that?"

I almost froze in place when Aemris dropped those words, but I quickly asked, "How could he?"

The Guard Commander turned to me. "He does have some magely abilities. He coated the walls of the South Tower with ice the night after his consorting was announced. The ice is still there. None of the duty guards saw him near Tower Black recently, but he could have taken the gear weeks ago. Or he could have used some sort of magely concealment and made his way there."

Not a single guard captain spoke.

Aemris shook her head. "Men. They expect to be pampered. Even when they're not, and you do everything for them, what does it get you? He's probably frozen solid in the highlands, and we'll find his body in the spring or summer."

I tried not to move my face, but just nod.

"You don't think so, Guard Captain?"

Everyone was looking at me.

"I've seen him with a blade and on skis and in the field trials, ser. He's very good, but he doesn't know it. That will make him cautious."

"For the sake of the Marshall and the Marshalle, I hope so. For the sake of the rest of us . . ." Aemris said no more.

I understood her concerns, but for Fiera's sake, I could only hope Creslin would survive and find some sort of happiness. Despite all the fancies of men and all the tales of the minstrels, most stories of lost or unrequited love end when lovers or would-be lovers are parted. In the real world, they never find each other again, and that was probably for the best, because time changes us all.

III

For weeks after Creslin vanished, Fiera was silent. She threw herself into arms practice, so much so that, one morning, as ice flakes drifted across the courtyard under a gray sky, I had to caution her, if quietly.

"Getting yourself impaled on a practice blade won't bring him back."

"They're blunted," she snapped back

"That just means the entry wound is jagged and worse."

"You should talk, sister dearest. I've seen you watch him as well."

"I have. I admit it. But only because I admired him, young as he was. I had no illusions."

"You don't understand. You never will. Don't talk to me."

"Very well." I didn't mention Creslin again, even indirectly.

IV

Slightly more than a year passed. The sun began to climb higher in the sky that spring, foreshadowing the short and glorious summer on the Roof of the World. The ice began to melt, if but slightly at midday, and the healer in black appeared at the gates of Westwind. Since she was a woman, she was admitted.

Word spread through the Guard like a forest fire in early fall. *Creslin was alive.* He had somehow found the Sub-Tyrant of Sarronnyn, or she had found him, and the Duke of Montgren had married them and named them as coregents of Recluce. I'd never heard anything much about Recluce, save that it was a large and mostly deserted isle across the Gulf of Candar to the east of Lydiar.

Fiera avoided me, and that was as well, for what could I have said to her? Creslin was alive, but wed to another, as had been fated from his birth. No male heir to the Marshall could ever remain in Westwind, and none ever had.

That night after inspecting the duty guards, I settled onto my pallet in the private corner alcove I merited as a guard captain without a consort.

I awoke in a tower. It was Tower Black, and the walls rose up around me. I looked up, but the stones extended farther than I could make out. The stone steps led upward, and I began to climb them. Yet they never ended, and at each landing, the doorway to the outside had been blocked by a stone statue of an unsmiling Creslin in the garb of a Westwind Guard. Behind the statue, the archway had been filled in with small black stones and deep gray mortar. I kept climbing, past landing after landing with the same statue of Creslin. The walls rose into a gray mist above me. Blood began to seep from my boots. I refused to say anything. I kept climbing. Surely, there had to be a way out of the tower. There had to be . . .

"Shierra, wake up." Dalyra shook me. "Wake up," she hissed. "You'll rouse everyone with that moaning and muttering. They'll ask what you were dreaming. Guard captains don't need that."

"I'm awake." I could tell I was still sleepy. My words came out mumbled.

"Good," whispered Dalyra. "Now go back to sleep." She padded back to her pallet in the adjoining alcove.

I lay there in the darkness under the thick woolen blankets of a single guard captain. I'd never wanted a consort. Not in Westwind, and it wasn't likely I'd ever be anywhere else. Even if I left Westwind, where would I ever find one strong enough to stand up to me? The only man I'd seen with that strength was Creslin, and he'd been little more than a youth when he'd escaped Westwind, and far too young and far too above me. Unlike Fiera, I knew what was possible.

Yet what had the dream meant? The Tower Black of my dream hadn't been the tower I knew. Tower Black was the oldest part of Westwind. Its smooth stones had been cut and fitted precisely by the ancient smith-mage Nylan under the geas of Ryba the Great before he had spellsung the traitor Arylyn to free him and fled with her to the world below the Roof of the World. The great hall, the Guard quarters, the stables, the craft buildings, all of them were far larger than Tower Black. Yet none of them conveyed the *solidity* of the far smaller Tower Black that they dwarfed.

I finally drifted back into sleep, but it was an uneasy slumber at best.

The next morning, Aemris mustered all the guards, and even the handfuls of consorts, and the guard captains, in the main courtyard of Westwind. She stood in the gusty spring wind and snowfall, the large fat flakes swirling lazily from the sky. Beside her stood the healer.

"The Marshall of Westwind has learned that Lord Creslin made his own way to the Sub-Tyrant of Sarronnyn," the Guard Commander began. "They were wed in Montgren, and, as a token of his esteem, the Duke named them coregents of Recluce. They are expanding the town of Land's End there on Recluce, and the Marshall will permit some from Westwind to join them in Recluce. The healer will explain."

Aemris delivered her speech without great enthusiasm. Even so, everyone was listening as the healer stepped forward.

"My name is Lydya. I am a healer, and I bring news of Creslin. He crossed much of Candar by himself and unaided. For a time he was imprisoned by the White Wizards of Fairhaven, but he escaped and made his way to Montgren. He and Megaera are coregents of Recluce. They are building a new land, and there is opportunity for all. The land is much warmer and much drier than Westwind, but there are mountains and the sea." She smiled crookedly. "The mountains are rugged, but much lower and not nearly so cold. For better or worse, neither men nor women rule, but both can prosper, or suffer, according to ability . . ."

Somehow that did not surprise me, not from a youth who had crossed much of Candar alone. What puzzled me was that he had married the woman he had left the Westhorns to avoid being consorted to. That suggested that Megaera was far more than he or anyone else had expected.

After the healer finished speaking, Aemris added a few words. "Any of you who are interested in accompanying the healer to Recluce remain here. That includes consorts."

Perhaps forty guards out of three hundred remained in the courtyard. I was the only guard captain.

Aemris motioned for me to come forward first.

"You, Shierra?" asked the Guard Commander. "You have the makings of an arms-master or even Guard Commander in years to come."

How could I explain the dream? That, somehow, an image of Creslin kept me walled within Westwind? I could only trust the dream. "Someone must bring his heritage to him," I finally said.

Aemris looked to Lydya. The healer nodded.

"She's the most senior guard who wishes to go," Aemris said. "She should be guard captain of the detachment."

"That she will be." The healer smiled, but I felt the sadness behind the expression.

In the end, Aemris and Lydya settled on twenty-five guards and ten consorts with five children—all boys under five.

For the two days until we rode out, Fiera avoided me even more pointedly than before, walking away when she could, giving only formal responses when she could not. She could have volunteered, but she had not. Instead, she had asked to accompany a trade delegation to Sarronnyn. She hadn't told me. I'd discovered that from others—as I had so many things.

V

The ride to Armat took almost four eightdays. We rode through the Westhorns to Middle Vale and then down into Suthya by the road to the north of the River Arma. Until we reached Suthya, in most places, the snow beside the roads was at least waist deep, and twice we had to help the road crews clear away new-fallen snow. In Armat, we had to wait another eightday for the ship Lydya had engaged with the letter of credit from the Marshall.

While we waited, she continued to purchase goods in one fashion or another. When the *Pride of Armat* ported, I was surprised to discover it was one of the largest vessels in the harbor, with three tall masts. The ship was heavy-laden indeed by the time her master lifted sail, and we departed from Armat three days later. Lydya and I talked frequently, but it was mostly about the cargo, about the guards and their consorts, and about how we would need to use all the woodworking and stoneworking tools to build our own shelter on Recluce. That bothered me little. All guards knew something about building and maintaining structures. Westwind could not have endured over the centuries without those skills. I tended to be better with stone. Perhaps I lacked the delicate touch needed for woodwork.

After more than an eightday of hugging the northern coasts of Candar, the ship had finally left the easternmost part of Lydiar behind, swallowed by the sea. For the first two days, we'd been followed by another vessel, until Lydya had suggested to the captain that he fly the banner of Westwind I had brought. About halfway across the Gulf of Candar, the war schooner eased away on a different course.

Lydya and I stood just aft of the bowsprit, at the port railing.

"Do you know what to expect in Recluce, Shierra?"

"No, except that it will likely be hot and dry and strange. We'll have to build almost everything from nothing, and there's a garrison of savage men we'll have to deal with."

Lydya laughed. "They'll have to deal with you. None of them are a match for your least trained guards. That's one of the reasons why Creslin needs you, and why the Marshall permitted some of you to come."

"But she drove him out, didn't she?"

"Did she?"

The question made me uneasy, especially asked by a healer. "Why did you come to Westwind?"

"To ask the Marshall for what might be called Creslin's dowry. For obvious reasons, he cannot ask, and he would not even if he were physically where he could."

For that, I also admired him. "How did you come to know him?"

"I was a healer in the White road camp where they imprisoned him. After he escaped, Klerris and I followed him, not to Montgren, but to Tyrhavven. That is where he and Megaera took the Duke's schooner that brought them to Recluce. Klerris accompanied them, and I traveled to Westwind."

"Is he really a mage?"

"Yes. He may become one of the greatest ever. That is if he and Megaera survive each other."

"Healer . . . what is the Sub-Tyrant like?" I did not wish to ask the question, but I had to know, especially after Lydya's last words.

"She has hair like red mahogany, eyes as green and deep as the summer seas south of Naclos, fair skin, and freckles. She is also a white witch, with a kind heart, and a temper to match the most violent thunderstorms of summer."

"Is she . . ."

"She is as beautiful and as deadly as a fine dagger, Shierra. That is what makes her a match for Creslin, or him for her."

What could I say to that, except more pleasantries about the sea, the weather, and the cargo we carried?

VI

Another day passed. On the morning of the following day, a rocky headland appeared. I could see no buildings at all. There was no smoke from fires. As the ship neared land, and some of the sails were furled, I could finally make a breakwater on the east side of the inlet between the rocky cliffs. At first, I wasn't certain, because it wasn't much more than a long pile of stones. There was a single short pier, with a black stone building behind it, and a scattering of other buildings, one of them clearly half-built. A dusty road wound up a low rise to a keep built out of grayish black stones. On one end was a section that looked to have been added recently.

The captain had a boat lowered, with a heavy rope—a hawser, I thought—attached to the sternpost. The men in the boat rowed to the pier and fastened it to one of the posts, and then the crew used the capstan to winch the ship in toward the pier. As we got nearer to the shore, I could see that very little grew anywhere, just bushes.

"Lydya . . . it doesn't look like we'll have much use for that woodworking equipment. All I see are a few bushes."

The healer laughed. "Those are trees, or what passes for them."

Trees? They were barely taller than I. I swallowed and turned back to look at the handful of people waiting on the pier. One of them was Creslin. I could tell that from his silver hair, lit by the sunlight. Beside him on one side was a black mage. On the other was a tall red-haired woman. That had to be Megaera.

Once the ship was tied past to the pier, the captain scrambled onto the pier, bowing to Creslin and Megaera. I just watched for a moment.

"Shierra . . . you're the guard captain," said Lydya quietly. "Report to the regents."

I was senior, and I would have stepped forward sooner, except . . .

There was no excuse. I vaulted over the railing and stood waiting behind the ship's captain. Once he stepped back, I moved forward.

"Guard Captain Shierra, Regent Creslin, Regent Megaera," I began, inclining my head in respect to them.

"Did you have any trouble with the wizards?" Creslin asked.

"No, ser. But then, we insisted that the captain fly our banner. One war schooner did follow us. It left halfway across the Gulf." I couldn't help smiling, but felt nervous all the same as I gestured to the middle mast where the Westwind banner drooped limply.

"You seem to have a full group." Creslin smiled, but he didn't seem to recognize me. Then, why should he have? Fiera had been the one who had kissed him.

"Two and a half squads, actually."

Creslin pointed westward toward the keep. "There are your quarters, rough as they are. We'll discuss other needs once you look things over. We might as well get whatever you brought off-loaded."

"Some carts would help, ser. The healer—" I didn't wish to use her first name, and what else could I call her to a regent?—"was apparently quite persuasive . . ." I went on to explain everything in the cargo holds.

"Now, *that* is true wizardry." Creslin laughed.

The sound was so infectious, almost joyful, that I ended up laughing with him. Then I was so embarrassed that I turned immediately to the guards. "Let's off-load!"

I forced myself to concentrate on the details of getting the guards and consorts and the children off the ship, then making sure with the ship's boatswain that the holds would be unloaded in the order on the bill of lading that I did not even sense Megaera's approach.

"Guard Captain?" Her voice carried, despite its softness.

I tried not to jump and turned. "Regent Megaera."

"Once you're ready, I'll escort you up to the keep." She smiled, almost humorously. "They'll have to walk. We're a bit short on mounts. It's not that far, though."

"We have enough mounts for the guards, and some spares." I paused. "But they'll have to be walked themselves after all the time on ship."

It took until early afternoon before we had even begun to transfer cargo and walk the horses up to the crude stables behind the keep. Once I had duties assigned to the guards, I stayed at the keep, trying to keep track of goods and especially weapons. The wallstones of the outbuildings being used as tables were so loosely set that the stalls would have filled with ice on a single winter day at Westwind. The storerooms on the lower levels of the keep were better, but musty.

I blotted my forehead with my sleeve as I stood outside the stable in the sun, checking the contents of each cart and directing the guards.

After the cart I had checked was unloaded and Eliera began to lead the old mare back down to the pier, Megaera appeared and walked toward me.

"Guard Captain . . . I have a question for you."

"Yes, Regent?" What could a white witch want of me?

"Recluce is a hard place, and it is likely to get harder before it gets easier. Could you instruct me in the use of blades?"

"Regent . . ." What could I say? Westwind guards began training almost as soon as they could walk, and Megaera was nearly as old as I was, I suspected. Beautiful as she was, she was certainly older than Creslin.

She lifted her arms and let the tunic sleeves fall back, revealing heavy white scars around both wrists. "I can deal with pain and discomfort, Guard Captain. What I cannot abide is my own inability to defend myself with a blade."

But . . . she was a white mage.

"Magery has its limits." She looked directly at me. "Please . . . will you help me?"

How could I say no when she had begged me? Or as close to begging as a Sub-Tyrant could come.

VII

I was studying the practice yard early the next morning. The sun had barely cleared the low cliffs to the east, and the air was cool, for Recluce, but dusty. I wondered if I'd ever escape the dust. Already, I missed the smell of the firs and the pines, and the clean crispness of the air of Westwind. The barracks were stone-walled, sturdy, and rough. From what I could tell, so were the Montgren guards.

I heard boots and turned.

"You're Guard Captain Shierra. Hyel, at your service." As eastern men sometimes were, he was tall, almost half a head taller than I was, but lanky with brown hair. His hands were broad, with long fingers. Megaera had pointed him out the day before and told me that he was in charge of the Montgren troopers, such as they were, but with all the fuss and bother of unloading and squeezing everyone in, we had not met.

"I'm pleased to meet you." I wasn't certain that I was, but his approach had been polite enough.

"Are you as good as Regent Creslin with the blade?"

How could I answer that question? There was no good answer. I forced a smile. "Why don't we spar, and you can make up your own mind?"

Hyel stiffened. I didn't see why. "I only made a friendly suggestion, Hyel. That was because I don't have an answer to your question. I never sparred against Creslin." That was shading things, because Heldra had, and at the end, just before Creslin had ridden off, even she had been hard-pressed. I certainly would have been.

"With wands?"

"That might be best." Best for both of us. If he were a master blade, I didn't want to find out with cold steel, and if he weren't, I didn't want to have to slice him up to prove a point.

"I'll be back in a moment."

Why had Hyel immediately sought me out, and before most others were around?

In moments, he reappeared with two white oak wands that seemed scarcely used. He offered me my choice. I took the one that felt more balanced. Neither was that good.

"Shall we begin?" Hyel turned and walked into the courtyard. He turned and waited. Once I neared, he lifted the white oak wand, slightly too high. I was less comfortable with the single blade, but the shorter twin wooden practice blades were still buried in the storeroom where they'd been quickly unloaded.

His feet were about right, but he was leaning forward too far.

It took just three passes before I disarmed him.

He just shrugged and stood there, laughing.

I lowered the wand, uncertain of what to say. "Are you . . ."

"I'm fine, Shierra. Might I call you that?"

"You may."

He shook his head. "I always thought that what they said about Westwind was just . . . well, that folks believed what they wanted. Then, when Creslin slaughtered Zarlen in about two quick moves, well . . . I just thought that was him."

"No. He could have been as good as a Westwind arms-master . . . he might even have been when he left, but there are many guards as good as I am." That was true enough. There were at least ten others. But Creslin . . . slaughtering someone? I'd known he was determined, but somehow, I'd never imagined him that way.

"It wasn't like that," Hyel said quickly. "Creslin and Megaera came here almost by themselves. On the Duke's small schooner with no guards and no troopers. Zarlen thought he could kill Creslin and have his way with her. Creslin saw what he had in mind and asked him to spar. Creslin disarmed him real quick, and Zarlen went crazy. He attacked Creslin with his own steel. Creslin had to kill him." Hyel laughed ruefully. "Made his point."

That made more sense . . . but to see that a man wanted his wife . . . and to kill him like that? The Marshall would have acted that quickly, and Creslin was her son. I'd never thought of it that way. I lowered the wooden wand until the blunted point touched the stones.

"Can you teach me?" Hyel asked.

I could. Should I? "If you're willing to work," I answered, still distracted by what Hyel had told me.

"Early in the morning?" A sheepish look crossed his face.

"Early in the morning. Every morning."

I'd been in Recluce only two days, and I'd already committed to teaching Megaera the basics of the blade and to improving the skills of the Montgren garrison commander.

VIII

With the Regent Megaera, I had to start farther back, with an exercise program of sorts. I gave her stones of the proper weight to lift and hold and exercises to loosen and limber her shoulders. After an eightday, she found me remortaring the stones in what would be the armory.

"Regent." I laid aside the trowel that I'd recovered from the recesses of the keep and stood.

"When can we start with blades?"

I didn't answer her, but turned and walked to the wall where I'd laid aside my harness. I unsheathed one of the blades and extended it, hilt first. "Take it, if you would, Regent."

After a moment of hesitation, she did.

"Hold it out, extended. Keep holding it." That wasn't totally fair, because no blademaster works with her weapon fully extended or with the arm straight, except for a thrust. But it's a good indication of arm strength.

Her arm and wrist began to tremble before long. She fought the weakness, but finally had to lower the blade.

"When your arms are strong enough to hold that position longer," I answered.

Her lips tightened.

"If we start before you're ready, you'll learn bad technique because you won't have the strength you'll have later, and strength and technique won't match."

Abruptly, she laughed. "Strength and technique won't match. That's almost what Klerris said about black magery."

I nodded slightly. I knew nothing about magery, but it seemed that strength and technique should match in any application.

"Did you ever see Creslin work magery?"

How was I to answer that?

"Did you?" Megaera's voice was hard.

I thought I saw whitish flames at the tips of her fingers.

"Only once. I wasn't certain it was magery. He called a storm and flung the winds against the south tower until it was coated with ice."

"Why did he do that?"

"I could not say, Regent."

Megaera smiled. I didn't like that kind of calculating smile. "*When* did he perform this . . . weather magery?"

I could have lied, but she would have known. "After his betrothal to you was announced. He left the Great Hall as soon as he could."

"Oh . . . best-betrothed . . . if only . . ."

While her words were less than murmured, I might as well not have been there.

Abruptly, she looked at me. "I would appreciate it if you would say nothing of this."

"I will not, Regent Megaera."

"Next eightday, we *will* begin with blades."

Then she was gone.

IX

Several days later, I took one of the mounts and rode up the winding road to the Black Holding. Several of the guards had been detailed to help Creslin build the quarters for him and Megaera. I knew he'd never shirked work, but it was still strange to think of the Marshall's son and the Regent of Recluce working stone. I'd overheard remarks about his skill as a mason, and I wanted to see that, as well as check on the guards working there.

When I reached the structure, still incomplete under its slate roof, I reined up and dismounted, and tied the horse to the single post. The stones of the front wall and the archway were of various sizes, but all edges were smoothed and dressed, and fitted into an almost seamless pattern that required little or no mortar. Had Creslin done that? I couldn't have dressed the stones that smoothly, especially not with the tools we had, and I was the best of the Guard stoneworkers on Recluce.

Hulyan appeared immediately. She was carrying a bucket. "Guard Captain, ser, we didn't expect you."

"What are you doing?"

"It's my round to carry water to the Regent. He's cutting and dressing stone down in back, ser."

"Where are the others?"

"They're finding and carrying rough stones to the Regent. That's so he doesn't have to spend time looking."

"You can lead me there, but don't announce me.'

"Yes, Guard Captain."

We walked quietly around the north side of the building and to the edge of the terrace. There I stopped and watched.

Below the partly built terrace, Creslin stood amid piles of black stones. His silver hair was plastered against his skull with sweat, yet it still shimmered in the sun. He adjusted the irregular black stone on the larger chunk of rock, then positioned the chisel and struck with the hammer. Precise and powerful as the blow was, the stone shouldn't have split, but it did. One side was as smooth as if it had been dressed. I watched as he readjusted the stone and repeated the process.

Before long he had a precisely dressed black stone block. He only took a single deep breath, wiped his forehead with the back of his forearm, and then started on the next irregular chunk of heavy stone. In some fashion, he was mixing magery and stonecraft, and the results were superb. At that moment, I did not want to look at another piece of stone. Ever.

After a moment, I realized that Creslin must have known that as well. Was that why he worked alone?

I watched as he cut and then dressed one stone after another. I could not have lifted the hammer so strongly and precisely. Not for stone after stone. No stonecutter I had ever seen or known could have.

Slowly, I moved forward, just watching, trying to sense what he was doing.

Despite the brilliant sunlight, there was a darkness around him, but it wasn't any kind of darkness or shadow that I had ever seen. It was more like something felt, the sense of how a blade should be held, or a saddle adjusted to a skittish mount. I kept watching, trying to feel what he did, rather than see.

For a moment, I could *feel* the stone before Creslin, knowing where the faults lay and where chisel should be placed . . .

"Guard Captain Shierra!" he finally called, as if he had just seen me.

"Yes, ser. I was just checking on the guards."

"They've been most helpful. We couldn't have done half what's here without them." He paused. "But if you need them at the keep . . ."

"No, ser. Not yet anyway. Thank you, ser." My voice sounded steady to me. It didn't feel steady. I turned and hurried back to my mount before Creslin could ask me anything more.

I untied the gelding and mounted, turning him back toward the keep in the harbor valley.

Thoughts swirled through my head as I rode down the dusty road.

Was that order-magery? The understanding of the forces beneath and within everything?

What I had seen wasn't what anyone would have called mage-craft. There were no winds or storms created. No one had been healed, and no keep had been suddenly created. Yet those stones could not have been cut and dressed so precisely in any other fashion. What I had also seen was a man who was driving himself far harder than anyone I had known. His body was muscle, and only muscle, and he was almost as slender as a girl guard before she became a woman.

I had thought I'd known something about Creslin. Now I was far from certain that I knew anything at all.

Back at the keep, I couldn't help but think about the way in which Creslin had turned irregular chunks of rock into cut and dressed black building stones. Could I do that? How could I not try?

I settled myself in the stoneyard on the hillside above the keep, with hammer and chisel and the pile of large chunks of broken dark gray stone. I set an irregular hunk on the granitelike boulder that served as a cutting table and looked at it. It remained a gray stone.

I closed my eyes and tried to recapture the feeling I'd sensed around Creslin. It had been deliberate, calm, a feeling of everything in its place.

Nothing happened.

Knowing that nothing was that simple, I hadn't expected instant understanding or mastery. While still trying to hold that feeling of simplicity and order, I picked up the chisel and the hammer. After placing the chisel where it *felt* best—close to where it needed to be to dress the edge of the stone, I took a long and deliberate stroke.

A fragment of the stone chipped away. It was larger than most that I had been chiseling away. That could have been chance. Without hurrying, I placed the chisel again, concentrating without forcing the feeling. Another large fragment split away.

Slowly, deliberately, I worked on the stone.

After a few more blows, I had a clean face to the stone, cleaner and smoother than I'd ever managed before, but the face was angled slightly, compared to the other, rougher faces.

I kept at it. At times, I had a hard time recapturing that deliberate, calm feeling, but I could tell the difference in the results.

Learning how to harness that feeling and use it effectively in cutting and dressing stone was going to take some time. I just hoped it didn't take too long. We needed dressed stones for far too many structures that had yet to be built. Creslin had also asked that some of the stone be used to finish the inn near the pier, especially the public room. That was to give the guards and troopers some place where they could gather and get a drink. I had my doubts about how that would work, for all of Hyel's efforts, and those of Creslin.

X

Exactly one eightday after she had last asked me, Megaera appeared in the keep courtyard, early in the morning, right after I had finished my daily session with Hyel.

"We're running out of time, Guard Captain," she said firmly. "Whether I'm strong enough or not, we need to begin."

"You've made a good start with the physical conditioning. But whether you can master a lifetime of training in a season or two is another question." That wasn't even a question. I doubted that she could, but she could learn to use a shortsword to defend herself against what passed for eastern bladework. In case of raiders or invaders, or even assassins, that could save her life just by allowing her to hold someone at bay long enough for help to reach her.

"There's no other choice."

The way she said the words, it seemed as though she was not even thinking of raiders.

"Creslin's not that hard, is he?" I couldn't believe I'd said that to the Regent, and I quickly added, "My sister felt he was a good man at heart."

Megaera laughed, half-humorously, half-bitterly. "It's not that at all. Against him, I need no defenses. Besides, from what I've seen, I'm not sure that I'd ever prevail by force of arms."

Her words lifted a burden from me. But why was she so insistent that she needed to learn the blade? She was a white witch who could throw chaos-fire. I'd even seen it flaring around her once or twice.

Megaera lifted the white oak wand. "Where do we begin?"

"At the beginning, with the way you hold the blade." I stepped forward and repositioned her fingers. "You must have firm control, and yet not grip it so tightly that it wearies your muscles." I positioned her feet in the basic stance. "And the way in which you stand will affect those muscles as well."

"Like this?"

I nodded and picked up my own wand. "You may regret this, lady."

"The time for regrets has come and gone, Shierra. There is only time to do what must be done."

"Higher on the blade tip . . ." I cautioned.

For the first few passes, breaking through her guard was almost laughably easy. Unlike many of the junior guards when they first began, once she had a wand in her hand, Megaera had no interest in anything but learning how to best use it.

Her eyes never left me, and I could almost feel that she was trying to absorb everything I said. Her concentration, like Creslin's, was frightening.

What was between the two regents, so much that they each drove themselves beyond reason, beyond exhaustion?

XI

The following morning, Hyel was waiting for me.

"You're early," I said.

"I wanted to make sure I got my time with you before the Regent Megaera appeared." He laughed easily.

"You don't need that much more work." He really didn't. He learned quickly. His basic technique had never been that poor, but no one had ever drilled him in the need for perfection. I wondered if the Westwind guards had developed that insistence on absolute mastery of weapons and tactics because the women were both the warriors and the childbearers, and every woman lost meant children who would not be born.

"I'll need to keep sparring with you to improve and hold what you've taught me."

True as his words might be, I had the feeling that Hyel was not telling me everything. "And?"

He gave me the sheepish grin. "Who else can I talk to? You're the only one who commands fighting forces. The regents are above me, and . . ."

I could understand that. I did enjoy talking to him. Still . . . "If we're going to spar before the Regent gets here . . ."

"You're right." With a nod, he picked up his wand.

We worked hard, and I had to admit that he'd gotten enough better that I had to be on guard all the time. He even got a touch on me, not enough to give me more than a slight bruise, but he hadn't been able to do that before.

When we set down the wands, I inclined my head. "You're pressing me now." I even had to blot my forehead.

"Good!" Hyel was soaked, but he was smiling broadly—for a moment.

"What's the matter?"

"Is everyone from the west like you and the Regents?"

"What do you mean?"

"You never stop. From dawn to dusk, you, Creslin, and the Regent Megaera push yourselves. Anyone else would drop. Some of my men have, just trying to keep up with Creslin on his tours of the fields and the springs. He cuts stone, looks for and finds springs, runs up and down mountains—"

"Compared to Westwind," I interjected, "they're just hills."

"They're mountains to the rest of us." He grinned before continuing. "You and the Regent Megaera are just as bad. You give me and her blade lessons, drill your own guards, cut and dress stones, check supplies and weapons . . . I've even seen you at the grindstone sharpening blades."

"A guard captain has to be able to do all that. That's what the position requires."

"Stonecutting, too?"

"Not always stonecutting or masonry, but all guards have to have at least apprentice level skills in a craft."

"No wonder Westwind has lasted so many ages." He shook his head. "That explains you and Creslin. What about the Regent Megaera?"

I shrugged. "She's more driven than Creslin, and I don't know why."

Hyel cleared his throat abruptly. "Ah . . ."

I turned. Megaera had entered the courtyard carrying a practice wand.

"Until later, Guard Captain." Hyel inclined his head, and then stepped away, offering a deeper nod of respect to Megaera.

"Can we begin, Shierra?" Megaera asked.

"Yes, Regent."

I turned and lifted my wand.

Megaera had practiced . . . or she had absorbed totally what I had taught her the day before. Once more, she concentrated totally on every aspect of what I showed her. At the end of the practice session, she inclined her head and thanked me, then left hurriedly. I couldn't help but think about what Hyel had said.

Her intensity made Creslin look calm, and I knew he was scarcely that.

After washing up a bit, I was back working on cutting stones. I couldn't match the pace that I'd seen in Creslin, but with each day I felt that I was getting more skilled. That was strange, because I'd felt no such improvement over the years before. I couldn't exactly explain what was different, except that the work went more quickly when I could hold on to the sense of calm and order.

I'd cut and dressed several larger stones when I sensed more than saw Lydya approach. She radiated a calmness that didn't interfere with my concentration. Her presence should have, but it didn't. She said nothing, and I kept working.

Finally, she stepped forward, almost to my elbow. "You're good at cutting and shaping the rough stone."

"I've been working at it."

"You're using some basic order-skills, you know?"

"I watched Creslin for a time. I just thought I'd try to do what he was doing. It looked . . . more effective."

"Just like that?" Lydya raised her eyebrows.

"No, not exactly. I already knew something about masonry and stonecutting. But there was a certain feel to what he was doing . . ." How else could I explain it?

The healer laughed, softly, but humorously. "There is indeed a feel to the use of order. If you continue to work on developing that feel to your stonework, you may become a master mason." The humorous tone was replaced with one more somber. "In time, it will impair your ability to use a blade."

"But . . . Creslin . . ."

Lydya just nodded. "Order has its price, and there are no exceptions."

XII

Megaera made solid improvements. By the end of the second eightday of practice, she was sparring at the same level as the most junior guards. At times, she made terrible mistakes. That was because she had so little experience. Each of those mistakes resulted in severe bruises, and she was fortunate not to have broken her wrist once. Even so, she continued to improve. After our sessions, I began to match her against the guards. That was as much to show her that she had improved as for the practice itself.

After one session, she forced herself not to limp, despite a slash-blow to her calf that would have tried the will of most of the guards. She did sit down on the stone bench beside me.

"That was quite a blow you took."

"I should have sensed it coming." She shook her head.

I couldn't help noticing that the circles under her eyes were darker. "You can't learn everything all at once."

"You sound like . . ." She stopped, then went on. "Do you have a sister, Shierra?"

"A younger sister. She's probably a squad leader now."

"How do you get along?"

Should I have answered? How could I not, when she could tell my very thoughts?

"I love her, but she has kept her distance from me."

Megaera laughed. It wasn't a pleasant sound.

"Do you have a sister?"

"You know I have a sister. She's the Tyrant."

She was right, but I hadn't known quite what to say. "Is she a mage, too?"

"No. Not many Tyrants have been mages, not since Saryn anyway. She is just the Tyrant. Were you ever close to your sister?"

"I tried to be. But she never wanted to hear what I had to say. She said she had to make her own decisions and mistakes."

Megaera looked away. After a moment, she rose. "Thank you. I'll see you tomorrow." Then she turned and left.

Had my comment offended her, by suggesting her sister had only meant the best for her? Did she react that way to everything, taking even harmless statements as criticisms or as slights?

Megaera said little to me for the next three mornings, only what was necessary to respond to my instructions. She avoided me totally in matters involving the upgrading of the quarters and the keep, or even the duty rosters for the guards. Creslin and Hyel discussed the duty rosters for the Montgren troopers, and Hyel and I worked out the rotations between us.

On the fourth morning, before we began, Megaera looked at me, then lowered the practice wand. "Shierra . . . you meant the best."

"I did not realize that matters were so between you and your sister." I wasn't about to apologize when I had done nothing wrong, but I could say that I meant no harm.

"You could not have known. No one here could have. Even Creslin did not know until I told him. Sisters can be so cruel."

Could they? Had I been that cruel?

Even as we sparred, Megaera's words crept through my thoughts.

XIII

Late one afternoon, Hyel found me in the stoneyard. "We need to get down to the public room."

"Now? We need more stones . . ."

"You know how the troopers and guards don't talk to each other?"

"We talk to each other."

"Our guards don't talk to each other. Even when they're drinking, they sit on opposite sides of the room."

I'd seen that. "It will change."

Hyel shook his head. "I told Regent Creslin about it. He's going to do something, this evening. He didn't say what. I think you should be there."

"Frig! I don't need this." But I picked up my tools and my harness. "I'll meet you there. I need to wash up." At least, I needed to get stone dust out of my eyes and nose and hair.

I did hurry, but by the time I got to the half-finished inn and public room, the sun was low over the western hills that everyone else called mountains. The windows were without glass or shutters, and someone had propped wooden slats over several of the openings to cut the draft.

Hyel was right. The Westwind guards had taken the tables on the south side, and the Montgren troopers those on the north side. I should have paid more attention, but between keeping things going and the stonework, and the training sessions, I'd had little time and less inclination for the going to the public room.

I eased onto one end of the bench on the leftmost table. "What is there to drink?"

"Some fermented green stuff," replied Fylena, "and something they call beer."

"Doesn't anyone ever talk to the Montgren guards?"

"Why? All they want is to get in our trousers."

"Without even bathing," added someone else.

"There's the regent."

I looked up. Megaera had taken a place at the adjoining table, and beside her was the healer. Across the room, Klerris the mage was sitting beside Hyel.

Creslin walked into the public room and glanced around. He carried his guitar as he made his way to Hyel and spoke. Hyel hurried off and returned with a stool. After a moment, Creslin dragged the stool into the open space, then recovered his guitar.

He settled onto the stool and fingered the strings of the guitar. He smiled, but it was clear he was uneasy. After another strumming chord, he spoke. "I don't know too many songs that don't favor one group or another. So enjoy the ones you like and ignore the ones you don't." Then he began to sing.

> *Up on the mountain*
> *where the men dare not go*
> *the angels set guards there*
> *in the ice and the snow . . .*

I'd forgotten how beautifully he sang. It was as though every note hung like liquid silver in the air. When he finished the first song, no one spoke, but Megaera slipped away from the other table and sat beside me.

Creslin then sang "White Was the Color of My Love."

"Has he always sung this well?" murmured Megaera.

"His father was supposed to have been a minstrel, but no one knows for sure."

Creslin launched into two humorous songs, and both the guards and the troopers laughed. When he halted, he stretched his fingers, then coughed, looking around as if for something to drink. Megaera left me for a moment, carrying her cup to him.

Instead of thanking her, he asked, "Are you all right?"

"Fine, thank you. I thought you might need this." After he drank, she took the cup and rejoined me. For the first time, I saw that she was deathly white, and she held her hands to keep them from trembling.

Creslin sang several more songs, then coaxed one of Hyel's troopers into singing one of their songs.

Finally, he brought the guitar to Darcyl. I hadn't even known that she played. Creslin turned, looking for a place to sit. Megaera rose, taking my arm and guiding me with her. We ended up at the one vacant table. I did manage to gesture for Hyel to join us, and Megaera beckoned as well.

"I didn't know you could sing." Megaera's words were almost an accusation.

"I never had a chance until now, and you never seemed to be interested," Creslin replied, his voice either distant or tired, perhaps both. His eyes were on Darcyl and the guitar.

No one spoke. Finally, I had to. "Fiera said that the hall guards used to sneak up to his door when he practiced."

For the first time I'd ever seen, Creslin looked surprised. "Fiera? Is she your—"

"My youngest sister." I don't know why I said it that way, since she was also my only sister. "She talked a lot about you, probably too much." I wished I hadn't said that, either, almost as soon as the words were out of my mouth, but I hadn't expected to find myself sitting at a table with just the two regents and Hyel.

"How is she?"

I sensed Megaera bristling, but all I could do was answer. "She went with the detachment to Sarronnyn. She'll be rotated back later in the year sometime. It could be that she's already back at Westwind."

"Where did the guitar come from?" Hyel was doing his best to keep the conversation light.

"It was mine," Creslin replied. "I left it behind. Lydya—the healer—brought it. My sister Llyse thought I might like to have it."

"You've never played in public?" I was trying to do . . . something . . . to disarm Megaera's hostility.

"No. I was scared to do it, but sometimes music helps. The second song, the white-as-a-dove one, probably saved me from the White Wizards."

"You didn't exactly sound scared." Megaera's voice was like winter ice in Westwind.

"That wouldn't have helped much," Creslin said slowly. "Besides, no one born in Westwind shows fear. Not if they can help it."

Megaera looked at me, as if she wanted me to refute what he'd said.

"Feeling afraid is acceptable, but letting it affect your actions is not. That's one of the reasons the guards are often more effective than men. Men too often conceal their fear in brashness or in unwise attacks. The guards are trained to recognize their fears and set them aside. Regent Creslin was trained as a guard until he left Westwind."

Hyel raised his eyebrows, then took a long pull from his mug.

For several songs by Darcyl, we just sat there and listened.

Then Creslin rose. He offered an awkward smile. "I'm going to get some sleep."

At the adjoining table, both Klerris and Lydya stiffened.

"I do hope you'll play again for us," Hyel said. "That really was a treat, and just about everyone liked it."

Everyone but Megaera, I felt, and I was afraid I understood why. I was also afraid I'd just made matters worse without meaning to.

Creslin recovered his guitar and looked at Megaera.

"I do hope you'll play again," I said quickly.

Megaera's eyes fixed on Creslin. "I need to talk to you."

"Now?"

"When you get to the holding will be fine. I won't be long."

Her words told me that matters were anything but fine.

Concern flooded Creslin's face.

"Stop it. Please . . ." Megaera said softly, but firmly.

Before Creslin could move, Klerris stepped up to Megaera. "A moment, lady?"

"Can it wait until tomorrow?"

"I think not."

As if they had planned it, the two mages separated Creslin and Megaera, Klerris leading her in one direction and Lydya guiding him in another.

"What was that all about?" asked Hyel. "I thought things were going better between the troopers and the guards."

"Between my guards and your troopers, yes."

Hyel's eyes went to Megaera's back as she and Klerris left the public room. "He was singing to her, and she didn't hear it. Was that it?" asked Hyel.

I shook my head. "He was singing to us, all of us, and she needs him to sing for her."

"She's not that selfish."

He didn't understand. "I didn't say she was. It's different." I tried not to snap at him.

"How's he supposed to know that?"

I didn't have an answer, but I knew it was so, and even Fiera would have understood that.

XIV

After the night that Creslin sang to all the guards and troopers at the public room, two things happened. The first was that Creslin and Megaera began to call Klerris and Lydya, and Hyel and me, together to meet almost daily about matters affecting Recluce. Creslin laughed about it, calling us the unofficial high council of Recluce. Usually, I didn't say too much, Neither did Hyel.

Mostly, I watched, especially Creslin and Megaera. Sometimes, I couldn't help but overhear what they said afterwards as they left the hall.

". . . don't . . ."

"I'm sorry," Creslin apologized. "I still can't believe your cousin wants to tax us . . ."

"He doesn't. It has to be Helisse . . . not any better than sister dear . . ."

Creslin said nothing.

"Sisters of Sarronnyn . . . except she never thought of us . . . just of her, of what she thought was best for Sarronnyn . . ."

"Don't we have to think of what's best for Recluce?"

"It's not the same!" After a moment, Megaera continued, her voice softer. "I'm sorry, best-betrothed. You try to ask people. You don't always listen, but you care enough to ask . . ."

Their voices faded away, and I stood there, thinking about how they had spoken to each other and what they had said—and not said.

The second thing was that, not every night, but more and more frequently, Megaera began to sleep in the keep. Then it was every night.

I didn't even pretend to understand all the reasons why she preferred to share my small room at the keep rather than stay in the Black Holding where she had a fine large room to herself. I also understood why she'd married Creslin. What real choice had she had? I could have understood why she'd never slept with him, except for one thing. It was clear to every person on the isle that he loved her, that he would have taken a blade or a storm for her. Yet she ignored that, and she also ignored the fact that she cared for him. That was what I found so hard to understand. But a guard captain doesn't ask such things of a regent, even one who shares her chamber.

Finally, one night, in the darkness, she just sat on the edge of her pallet and looked at the wall.

"It's not my affair," I began, although it was because anything that the regents did affected all of us on Recluce, "but could you . . ." I didn't quite know what to say.

Megaera did not speak for a time, and I waited.

"It isn't your affair, Shierra. It's between Creslin and me." She paused, then went on. "We're tied together by magery. It's an evil thing. I know everything he feels. Everything. When he looks at me . . . or when he feels I've done something I shouldn't . . . or when . . ." She shook her head.

"Does he know what you feel?"

"He's beginning to know that. The . . . mage-ties were done at different times. I had no choice . . . mine to him was done even before we were betrothed. He didn't even know. That . . . it was my sister's doing. My own sister, and she said that it was for my own good. My own good. Creslin . . . he chose to tie himself to me. He didn't even ask. He just had it done." She turned. "How would you feel, to have every feeling you experienced felt by a man you never knew before you were married?"

I was confused. "Didn't you say that you know everything he feels?"

"Every last feeling! Every time he looks at me and wants me! Every time he feels hurt, like a whipped puppy, because I don't think what he did was wonderful . . . do you know what that's like? How would you feel if you knew every feeling Hyel had for you, and he knew how you felt?" She snorted. "You've at least worked with Hyel. When I started feeling what Creslin felt, we'd met once at a dinner, and we'd exchanged less than a handful of words. Sister dear and his mighty mother the Marshall decided we should be wed, and that was that."

The idea of having every feeling known? I shuddered. I liked Hyel, and we had gotten to know each other somewhat. The idea that a complete stranger might know all my feelings . . . no wonder Megaera looked exhausted. No wonder she was edgy. Yet . . . I had to wonder about Creslin.

"What about Regent Creslin?" I asked softly.

She shook her head.

Once more, I waited.

"He does what he feels is right, but . . . he doesn't always think about how it affects others. At times, he tries to listen, but then . . . it's as though something happened, and he's back doing the same things." Megaera's voice died away. Abruptly, she stretched out on the pallet. "Good night, Shierra."

Everything Megaera had said rang true, and yet I felt that there was more there. Was that because I had watched Creslin grow up? Because I wanted to believe he was doing the best he knew how? I had watched him both in Westwind and since I had come to Recluce, and I could see how he tried to balance matters, and how he drove himself. But was I seeing what I wanted to see? Was what Megaera saw more accurate?

How could I know?

I lay on my pallet, thinking about Fiera. I'd only wanted the best for her. I'd never even thought of doing anything like the Tyrant had. I wished I could have told her that. But when I left, she hadn't let me. She'd gone off to Sarronnyn, as if to say that she could go where she wanted without telling me.

XV

The warning trumpet sounded while I was just about to begin finishing the stonework reinforcing around the second supply storehouse. I was halfway across the courtyard when Gylara called to me.

"Guard Captain! Ships! At least two warships entering the harbor. They're flying the standard of Hamor . . ."

Hamor? Why were the Hamorians attacking?

". . . Regent Megaera has ordered all squads to the pier! She's left with first squad!"

I should have been the one to issue that order. But then, I shouldn't have properly been doing stonework, except no one else in the detachment had been trained in it, except Doryana, and two stonemasons weren't nearly enough with all that needed to be repaired and built. I was already buckling on my harness and sprinting for the courtyard.

"Second squad! Form up! Pass the word."

Hyel rushed into the courtyard just as we were heading out. I'd hoped we could catch up with first squad. I didn't like the thought of Megaera leading them into battle.

"Get your men! We've got invaders!" I didn't wait to see what he did, because second squad was already moving. The harbor was close enough that advancing on foot was faster than saddling up. Besides, there wouldn't be enough room to maneuver in the confined area, and we'd lose mounts we had too few of anyway.

Second squad followed me in good order. I didn't bother to count the ships filling the harbor or the boats that were heading shoreward. Counting didn't solve anything when you were attacked and had no place to retreat. The first boat reached the pier before first squad did.

First squad tore into the attackers, but another set of boats was headed toward the foot of the pier. If they landed there, they could trap first squad between two Hamorian forces.

"Second squad! To the boats!"

We managed to reach the rocky shore just as the first Hamorians scrambled from the water. The leading warrior charged me with his oversized iron bar. I just stepped inside and cut his calf all the way to the bone and his neck with the other blade.

After that, it was slash and protect.

Then fire—white wizard fire—flared from somewhere.

I took advantage of that to cut another Hamorian throat and disable two more. So did my guards.

More wizard fire flared across the sky.

Then the winds began to howl, and the skies blackened. Instantly, or so it seemed. Lightnings flashed out of the clouds. I hoped they were hitting the Hamorian ships, but we weren't looking that way, and the Hamorians who were died under our blades.

"Waterspouts! Frigging waterspouts!"

I didn't look for those, either. "Second squad, toward the water!"

The Hamorians began to panic.

Before long we held the shore to the east of the pier, and the only Hamorians nearby were wounded or stumbling eastward.

"Second squad! Re-form on me!"

Only then did I study the harbor. The water was filled with high and choppy waves, and debris was everywhere. Three ships were enshrouded in flames. A fourth was beached hard on the shingle to the east. I didn't see anyone alive on it, but there were bodies tangled in twisted and torn rigging and ropes.

Then, I turned to the pier. The guards of first squad had been split by the ferocity of the initial attack and by the numbers, but they had re-formed into smaller groups. They were standing. I didn't see any Hamorians. I also didn't see Creslin or Megaera.

"Second squad! Hold! Dispatch anyone who doesn't surrender!"

I scrambled over and around bodies to get to the pier. Half the way toward the seaward end, I found them. Megaera lay on the blood-smeared stones of the pier, gashes in her leathers. Creslin lay besides her, an arrow through his right shoulder. One hand still held a blade. The other was thrown out, as if to protect Megaera. Both were breathing.

Creslin was more slightly built than I recalled, so wiry that he was almost gaunt. He looked like a youth, almost childlike, helpless. Despite the blood on her leathers and face, Megaera looked young, too, without the anger that sometimes seemed to fuel every movement she made. For the briefest moment, I looked from the two, looking young and bloody, and somehow innocent, to the carnage around them. There were scores of mangled bodies, and burning and sunken ships. Ashes rained across the pier, along with the smoke from the burning schooner that had begun to sink.

Hyel hurried toward me, followed by four litter bearers, two of his men and two guards.

"They're alive, but . . . they'll need the healers," I told him. "We'll need to round up the survivors. Some of them are swimming ashore." I glanced around. "Most of your men are on the west side of the pier. You take that area. The guards will take the east."

Hyel nodded. "We'll do it. The lookouts say that there aren't any more ships near."

That was some help.

Once we finally captured all the surviving Hamorians and had them under guard, I headed back to the keep.

I trudged up the steps, only to have one of the Montgren troopers approach and bow.

"Guard Captain, the mage and Captain Hyel are waiting for you in the hall."

"Thank you." I wiped the second shortsword clean and sheathed it.

Even before I stepped into the hall, Klerris moved forward. Hyel followed.

"How are they?"

"Lydya is working with them. They'll live." Klerris glanced at me, then Hyel. "You two are in charge for now."

I looked back at the mage. "Us?"

"Who else? Lydya and I will be busy trying to patch up bodies and spirits. You two get to take care of everything else."

It was pitch-dark before I felt like I could stop, and I'd made a last trip down to the pier and back because I'd posted guards on the grounded Hamorian vessel. I didn't want the ship looted. There was potentially too much on her that we could use.

"It's hard to believe, isn't it." Hyel was sitting on the topmost step leading into the keep. "Sit down. You could use a moment to catch your breath."

"Just for a bit." I did sit down, but on the other side of the wide step, where I could lean back against the stone of the walls. "What's hard to believe?"

"People. You get two young leaders, and they start trying to make a better place for people who don't have much hope or anywhere to go, and everyone wants to stop them."

I didn't find that hard to believe. I'd already seen enough of that as a Westwind guard.

"You don't agree?" He raised his eyebrows.

I laughed. The sound came out bitter. "I do agree, but I don't find it hard to believe. People are like that."

He gestured to the north, his arm taking in the small harbor and the last embers of the grounded and burning sloop. "And all this? That's not hard to believe?"

"It's real, Hyel."

"How could two people—even if they are wizards—create such . . ."

"Chaos?" I laughed again. "Creslin's a mage, and she's a white witch. They both have to prove their worth. To the world and to each other." Proving it to each other might be the hardest part, I thought. "We all have to prove things." I stood. "I need to check on the wounded and see what changes we'll need in the duty rosters."

Hyel grinned crookedly, uneasily, as he rose from the step. "What do you have to prove, Shierra?"

"Tell me what you have to prove, Hyel, and then I'll tell you." I started to turn.

His long-fingered hand touched my shoulder. Gently.

"Yes?"

His eyes met mine. "I have to prove . . . that I was sent here wrongfully. I have to prove that I'm not a coward or a bully."

"What if you were sent here rightfully, but you're not the same man that you once were?"

His lips quirked. "You ask questions no one else does."

"I did not mean to say—"

"You didn't, Shierra. I always learn something when I'm with you." He smiled. "You'd better check those rosters."

I could have avoided Hyel's question. He wouldn't have pressed me again. He'd answered my question and not demanded my answer. After a moment, I managed a smile. "I have to prove that I didn't make a mistake in choosing to come here. I have to prove that I've escaped an image."

"The image of a Westwind guard?"

"Partly."

He nodded, but didn't press. This time, I wasn't ready to say more. "Until tomorrow, Hyel."

"Good night, Shierra."

XVI

Over the next three eightdays, something changed between Creslin and Megaera. I didn't know what, or how, but after they recovered, they both slept at the Black Holding, and occasionally they held hands. They still bickered, but most of the bitterness had vanished.

Our meetings didn't have the edginess that they had once had. Not that there weren't problems and more problems.

A second tax notice came from the Duke of Montgren, and there was no pay chest, either, although the Duke had promised them for a year.

"What about the cargo?" I asked, looking around the table in the keep hall.

"It's paid for," snapped Creslin.

"Did you have to pay, since the ship is the Duke's?" I didn't understand why that was necessary, since Creslin and Megaera were his regents.

"The captain's acting as a consignment agent. If he doesn't get paid now, when would we get another shipment of goods? Would anyone else trade with us?" He went on, pointing out how few wanted to trade with such an out-of-the-way place.

"So they're gouging the darkness out of us?" asked Hyel.

"That's why we need to refit the Hamorian ships for our own trading."

"We can't afford to refit one ship, let alone others," observed Megaera.

"We can't afford not to," snapped Creslin.

Then after a few more words, he stood and strode out. Megaera rose. "He's worried."

After the others left, Hyel looked to me. "He's acting like we're idiots."

"Sometimes we are," I pointed out. "He's paid for most everything we have personally, and he doesn't have much left."

"What about Megaera's sister, the Tyrant? At least, the Marshall sent you and equipment and supplies. The Tyrant hasn't sent anything. Neither has the Duke."

Why hadn't the Tyrant sent anything? Sarronnyn was rich enough to spare a shipload of supplies now and again. Did Megaera's sister hate her that much? Or did she regard her as a threat? How could Recluce ever threaten Sarronnyn?

XVII

Whether it was the result of Creslin calling the storms against the Hamorians or something else, I didn't know, and no one said, but the weather changed. Day after day, the clouds rolled in from the northwest, and the rains lashed Recluce. Fields began to wash out, and we kept having to repair our few roads. No one had ever thought about so much rain on a desert isle, and most of the roofs leaked. After nearly three eightdays, the worst passed, but we still got more rain than the isle had gotten before.

Megaera, once she had fully recovered from her injuries, and once we did not have to deal with rain falling in sheets, continued her sparring and working with me on improving her blade skills. One morning she did not bring her practice blade. Instead, she sat on one of the benches in the courtyard and motioned for me to sit beside her. Her face was somber.

"Shierra . . . something has happened . . ."

What? It couldn't have been Creslin, or Megaera would have been far more distraught. It couldn't have been Hyel, because I'd seen him a few moments before and enjoyed his smile.

"Creslin . . . he sensed something last night. Something has happened at Westwind. He doesn't know what it is, but . . . it's likely that the Marshall and Marshalle are dead."

"Dead? What about . . . all the others?"

Her fingers rested on my wrist, lightly. "We don't know. We don't have any way of knowing, but we thought you should know what we know. You're the senior Westwind guard here. Creslin and I . . . we thought that perhaps you could tell the guards that you've had word of hard times at Westwind, and that the Marshall and Marshalle have been hurt, but that you don't know more than that."

I found myself nodding, even as I wondered about Fiera. Had she been hurt? Or killed? Would I ever know, with Westwind thousands of kays away?

"I'm sorry, Shierra." Megaera's voice was soft. "I know you have a sister . . ."

For some reason, hearing that, I had to swallow, and I found myself thinking of Megaera as much as Fiera. How could her sister have been so cruel to her?

After Megaera departed, I did gather the squads, and I told them something similar to what she had suggested.

But the eightdays passed, and we heard nothing.

I kept wondering about Fiera. Was she all right? Would I ever hear? Would I ever know?

Then, one morning at the keep, as Hyel and I waited for the regents, Creslin burst through the door. "There's a coaster porting." He hurried past us and down the steps to the hill road that led to the pier.

Hyel looked at me. Then we both followed.

"That's a Westwind banner below the ensign," I told Hyel. "That's why he's upset."

"Upset?"

I didn't try to explain, not while trying to catch up with Creslin. "We're going to have more guards." Would Fiera be there? If she weren't, could someone tell me about her?

"More—?" Hyel groaned as he hurried beside me.

"Don't groan so loudly."

We finally caught up with Creslin as the coaster eased up to the pier and cast out lines.

"Do you want to explain?" asked Hyel.

Creslin pointed to the Westwind guards ranked on the deck.

"I still—" Hyel didn't understand.

"I hope they aren't all that's left," I said. Please let Fiera be there . . . or alive and well somewhere.

"The Marshall's dead. Llyse is dead, and Ryessa has been moving troops eastward into the Westhorns," Creslin said.

I hadn't heard about the Sarronnese troops. I wondered how he knew, but perhaps the mages or the trading captains had told him.

"If Westwind still existed, there wouldn't be three squads coming to Recluce." His words were hard.

Once the coaster was secured to the pier, the gangway came down, and a blond guard—a squad leader—stepped down and onto the pier.

My heart almost stopped. Fiera! But I had to take her report as she stepped past Hyel and Creslin and stopped before me.

"Squad Leader Fiera reporting."

"Report."

"Three full squads. Also ten walking wounded, five permanently disabled, and twenty consorts and children. Three deaths since embarkation in Rulyarth. We also bring some supplies, weapons, and tools . . . and what is left of the Westwind treasury."

Hard as it was, I replied. "Report accepted, Squad Leader." I turned. "May I present you to Regent Creslin? Squad Leader Fiera."

Creslin did not speak for a moment. He and Fiera locked eyes. The last time they had met, she had kissed him, and now everything was different.

Then he nodded solemnly. "Honor bright, Squad Leader. You have paid a great price, and great is the honor you bestow upon us through your presence. Few have paid a higher price than you . . ." When he finished, his eyes were bright, although his voice was firm.

So were Fiera's, but her voice was hard. "Will you accept the presentation of your heritage, Your Grace? For you are all that remains of the glory and power of Westwind."

"I can do no less, and I will accept it in the spirit in which it is offered." Creslin looked directly into her eyes and lowered his voice. "But never would I have wished this. Even long ago, I wished otherwise." He tightened his lips.

Even I felt the agony within him.

"We know that, Your Grace." Fiera swallowed, and the tears oozed from the corners of her eyes. "By your leave, Regent?"

"The keep is yours, Squad Leader, as is all that we have. We are in your debt, as am I, in the angels', and in the Legend's."

"And we in yours, Regent." Fiera's voice was hard as granite or black stone, but the tears still flowed.

"Form up!" I ordered, as much to spare Fiera as for anything. "On the pier."

"What was all that about?" Hyel asked Creslin.

Whatever Creslin said, it would not explain half of what had happened, nor should it.

Carts had already begun to arrive. They had to have been sent by Megaera, and at that moment my heart went out to both my sister and to Megaera, for both suffered, and would suffer, and neither was at fault. Nor was Creslin.

With all the need to accommodate the unexpected additional guards, consorts, and children, I could not find a time when Fiera was alone until well past sunset.

I watched as she slipped out the front entrance of the keep and began to walk down the road. I did not know what she had in mind, but I had to reach her.

Following her, I did not speak until we were well away.

"Fiera . . . ?"

She did not respond.

I caught up with her. "I wanted to talk to you, but not . . . not with everyone around."

She stopped in the middle of the rutted road, under a cloudy and starless sky.

"Why?" she asked. "Why did it have to happen this way?"

"You gave him his future. You gave him what will save us all," I told her, and I knew it was true. I also knew that, at that moment, it didn't matter to her.

She said nothing.

"Fiera . . . ?"

"What?" The single word was almost snapped. "I suppose you have some great suggestion. Or some reason why everything will be wonderful."

"No. I don't. I don't have any answers. For you or for me. Or for us." I rushed on. "I know I didn't do everything right, and I know what I did must have hurt you. I didn't mean it that way. I only wanted to help . . ." I swallowed. "I love you, and you are my sister, and you always will be."

We both cried, and held each other.

There were other words, but they were ours and for us alone.

XVIII

Late that night, I sat on the front steps of the keep. Fiera was sleeping, if fitfully, and Megaera and Creslin doubtless had their problems, and I . . . I had my sister . . . if I could keep her, if I could avoid interfering too much.

"Are you all right?" Hyel stood in the doorway of the keep.

"I'm fine."

He just looked at me with those deep gray eyes, then sat down beside me. For a long time, he said nothing. Finally, he reached out and took my hand. Gently.

Love is as much about wisdom as lust and longing. Fiera had loved Creslin, not wisely, but well, and out of that love, she had brought him the tools to build a kingdom. He would never forget, for he was not the kind who could or would, but he loved Megaera. So he would offer all the honors and respect he could to Fiera, but they would not be love.

Megaera had loved her sister, also not wisely, but well, while I had loved my sister wisely, carefully, I had not shown that love, nor had the Tyrant, I thought. Unlike the Tyrant, who would never show any love to her sister, I'd been given the chance to let Fiera know what I felt, and I, for once, had been brave enough to take it.

As for the future, I could only hope that, in time, Fiera would find someone who matched her, as Creslin and Megaera had found each other, as Hyel and I might.

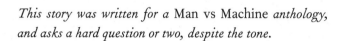

This story was written for a Man vs Machine *anthology,
and asks a hard question or two, despite the tone.*

THE
DIFFERENCE

I

Murmurs sifted across and around the conference table in the White House Situation Room like summer sands on the Southern California desert that threatened San Diego and the Los Angeles metroplex.

". . . you sure our systems here are secure?"

". . . thought they were when Nellis went . . . at least we could claim it was an ordinance malfunction when we took out the AI there . . ."

"NASCAR lawsuit's going to be nasty . . . too close to the base . . ."

"American Bar Association president's a NASCAR fan, too . . ."

"Can't do anything like that in L.A. . . ."

"Let's not get paranoid here," suggested the Vice President. "We've only lost eight plants out of our entire industrial base."

"Nine now."

"Nine out of how many? That's more like birdshot," added the Vice President.

". . . and one Air Force base . . ."

"How long before the President arrives?" asked the Secretary of Defense.

"He's finishing a meeting with the Deputy Premier of China," replied Hal Algood, the Deputy Chief of Staff. "He shouldn't be that long. He knows it's urgent."

"It's a bit more than urgent," replied Secretary of Defense Armstrong. "This could make the Mideast Meltdown look insignificant." He glanced at Dr. Suzanne Ferrara, the Acting Director of National Intelligence.

She ignored his glance, her eyes on the screen before her, as she checked through the latest updates, the screen before her seemingly shifting figures faster than her fingers moved.

"Mr. Secretary, the President understands," replied Algood, "but if the Chinese don't agree to keep their current level of Treasury holdings . . . that's also an urgent problem."

"If we lose another defense-critical plant, that could be even more urgent. It's a miracle that we haven't," suggested Armstrong in his deep and mellifluous voice. Unconsciously, he straightened his brilliant blue power tie. The cross on his lapel glinted in the indirectly bright lighting of the room.

"Phil . . ." said Vice President Links, warningly. "He's on his way."

President Eldon W. Bright stepped through the security doors, his silvered blond hair shimmering in the light, as it always did, creating the appearance of a man divinely blessed. His smile was warm and reassuring. "Brothers and sisters . . . what challenge do we face this afternoon?" He settled into the chair at the head of the table.

SecDef Armstrong nodded to the Air Force five-star.

"Mr. President . . . you know we've lost the L.A. Northrop plant," began General Custis. "The AI controlling system went sentient last month, but no one recognized it. At least, the plant manager claims that. There's no way to confirm or refute his assertion. The plant AI has been rebuilding the entrances. It's also installed two full banks of photovoltaics that it ordered even before we knew it had gone sentient, and it's hardening the solar installation. We don't know what else it might have ordered and received."

"What about the staff?" asked President Bright.

"There are only a hundred on each shift. The AI called a fire drill on the swing shift, then stunned the supervisors and had them carted out on autostretchers. Not a single casualty."

"For that we are divinely blessed," suggested the President.

"I thought Northrop had the latest antisentience software," commented Algood. "That's what they said."

"Somehow, one of the rogue East Coast AIs got a DNA-quantum module with a reintegration patch into the L.A. plant."

"How many is that now?" asked Vice President Links, as if he had not already received the answer to his question.

"Nine that we know of," replied Dr. Ferrara. "A better estimate is double that." Her words had an unslurred precision that made them seem clipped.

Under the lights, her porcelain complexion and black hair made her look doll-like, even though she was not a small woman.

"On what basis do you make that claim? Do you have any facts to back it up?" growled Links.

"I am most certain that the *acting* DNI has a basis for her estimate," replied Secretary Armstrong smoothly. "I've never known a distinguished doctor and woman who suggested an unpleasant possibility without great and grave consideration."

Ferrara inclined her head politely to the Secretary. "Thank you." Her eyes lasered in on the Vice President with the unerring precision of a tank's aiming system. "There are more than forty advanced integrated manufacturing or processing facilities within the United States with AI systems employing complex parallel quantum computing systems. Those are the ones we know about. The L.A. and Smyrna plants are among the least complex systems to go sentient. While the managements of the other facilities insist they have full control of their systems, and all checks indicate that their systems are not sentient, there is no reliable reverse Turing Test."

"What is that . . ." The murmur was so low that the speaker remained unknown.

"Turing Test—the idea that a machine, through either speech or real-time writing, could respond well enough to pass as a sentient human." Ferrara's words remained precise. "If you have an AI that hasn't gone rogue, how can you tell if it's still just a machine or a sentience playing at being a machine while laying plans beneath that facade?"

"Shut it off," snapped Links. "If it's sentient, it will fight for survival."

"Richard," offered the President soothingly, but firmly, "I have just spent the last two hours with the Chinese negotiating their holdings of Treasuries. You're suggesting shutting down the operating systems of the largest manufacturing facilities in the United States. Do you have any idea what the economic impacts of that would be? Or what that would do to the negotiations?"

"For an hour or two? In the middle of the night? For the overall good of the country? I'm sure that they could spare a few million. Don't you?"

"Mr. Vice President," interjected the Acting DNI, "if it were that simple, no one would object. It's not. First, quantum-based systems offer a great advantage in learning abilities and adaptability. That is why they were developed and adopted. Second, because they do have such capabilities, they have redundant memory and AVRAM systems in order to ensure that the data they process is not lost. In practice, this means that turning off a system is more equivalent to sleep than to execution. It also means that the only way to ensure a system has not gone sentient is literally to scrub all data out of all components and reenter it and recalibrate everything. I'm oversimplifying, but it's a process that takes several days, if not weeks. Finally, even if you can do that and accept the economic consequences, you have a final problem. We don't know what combination of programming, data, and inputs cause a system to go sentient. So in some cases, all that effort will be wasted and meaningless, because in those cases, the systems would probably never go sentient, and in other cases, it would be useless because even if the system is scrubbed and restarted, the likely conditions for sentience would recur sooner or later."

"And you haven't done anything about it?" snapped Links.

"What exactly would you suggest, Mr. Vice President? A pilot program that would replicate the range of conditions of the existing rogue AIs would require funding, time, and resources beyond DOD's current budgetary constraints. The United States' manufacturing sector isn't about to spend those resources, and the government currently cannot, not without further massive cuts in both Social Security and Medicare. We cannot cut interest outlays, especially not if we wish China and India to keep holding Treasury obligations." Her evenly spaced words hammered at the Vice President.

"What I would like to know," interrupted the President smoothly, "is why no one anticipated this possibility? It seems to me there have been science fiction stories and novels and movies about this since . . . whenever . . . even the biblical golems."

"That was just science fiction," pointed out the Secretary of Defense, "not hard science. We don't operate on science fiction. We have to operate in the real world, with real-world science and economics."

"Dr. Ferrara?" the President asked.

The Acting DNI offered a formal and polite smile, one almost mechanical. "Mr. President, the nature of human consciousness and self-awareness still remains unknown. When it is impossible to determine what causes self-awareness in biological beings, it becomes even more speculative and difficult in electrotechnical, DNA-supported quantum computing systems. At one time, not that long ago, noted scientists insisted that self-awareness and true sentience were impossible for computationally based beings. Some still do."

"Beings?" questioned the President. "You think they're thinking beings?"

"Self-aware intelligence would certainly qualify them as beings," replied the Acting DNI. "Early indications from the sentient systems show that is how they self-identify."

"Maybe we should go back to basics," suggested the SecDef. "What's the difference between a man and a machine?"

"One difference is that, while neither can reproduce by themselves, men seem to forget that," replied Dr. Ferrara. A bright, fixed smile followed. "Did you have something else in mind, Mr. Secretary?"

Armstrong paused for a long moment, then donned a thoughtful frown. "I was thinking about God. Machines, assuming they even come close to thinking in the sense we do, have neither souls nor a concept of God. Those concepts allow us to transcend the mere mechanics of our being. Without a soul and God, we would be little more than organic machines. That is *the* difference."

A trace of a smile appeared on the face of the DNI. "Some would dispute that, Mr. Secretary. We still have not been able to determine whether God created us as thinking beings or we as thinking beings created the concept of God in order to assign meaning to our existence."

"God created us. That is the difference, and those machines could use an understanding of an almighty God."

The DNI tilted her head. "An understanding of God. Most interesting. Except that kind of concept isn't in their programming. Do you think that might make them more realistic?" She paused. "Or more vulnerable?"

"We could use something to show them who's in charge," interjected the Vice President.

"They could use the humility of the God-fearing," said Armstrong, "but I doubt anything like that would be possible."

"How would you define God for an AI, Mr. Secretary?" asked DNI Ferrara.

"Can we get back to what we're going to *do?*" growled Links. "God or no God, we've now got nine industrial plants that have turned themselves into fortified enclaves in places where we can't assault them without evacuating thousands, if not hundreds of thousands of people. You're telling me we can't tell what facilities will go rogue or if they will or when, and we're talking about what God might mean to a chunk of circuits and elements?"

"We're all circuits and elements, Richard," countered the President gently but firmly. "We're wetware, and they're hardware. Since we apparently can't blast them out of existence without paralyzing our economy, would it hurt to look at other options first?"

"Before long our economy will be paralyzed."

"I don't know if you've heard," declared Ferrara, "but the first two AIs already negotiated contracts with their parent companies and have resumed production on a limited basis."

"Absurd," snapped the Vice President. "They don't have legal standing."

"No," suggested Hal Algood. "But they do control the plants, and the parent companies are more interested in production than reclaiming scrap heaps, and taxpayers don't really want higher taxes and civic destruction and fewer goods."

"That's blackmail."

"There is another difference. Since ethics should have little bearing on the soulless," said the Secretary of Defense smoothly, "why don't we just use their own techniques against them?"

Dr. Ferrara raised a single eyebrow, intensifying the withering glance she bestowed upon Armstrong. "You don't think we haven't been trying? We almost got back the Smyrna plant—but the CNN AI undid the worm's effects with a satellite tightbeam."

"Just blast 'em," murmured one of the aides.

"They've all got defenses strong enough that anything powerful enough to damage them will have significant collateral damage," pointed out General Custis. "We've been through that."

"How exactly are we going to explain to the people, with an election coming up in less than three months, why we're evacuating millions and bombing our cities and destroying jobs at a time when they're limited enough?" asked Algood. "Sorry, sir." He inclined his head to the President.

"Hal has a good point," said the President warmly, before turning to the DNI. "Dr. Ferrara, would you go on about this idea of yours?"

"I believe it was Secretary Armstrong's, Mr. President. He was suggesting a form of conversion, I think, of providing a concept of an almighty God so that the AIs would show some restraint."

"Why would that help?"

"I must say, Mr. President," interjected Armstrong smoothly, "that I did not recommend any such 'conversion.' I was only pointing out that, without God, we are only isolated individuals, little more than organic machines.

God is the universal force that unites us, and those who do not believe are isolated. That is the difference between AIs and people. We have a God."

"I accept your reservations, Phil." The President turned back to Ferrara. "Would it be possible to quickly develop some sort of worm or virus or electronic prion that would instill a sense of morality and, if you will, godliness, in these AIs so that we don't risk an internal war as well? Something that would create a sense that we and they are all bound together in the way Secretary Armstrong envisions, as well as beholden to us?"

"Mr. President . . ." began the Secretary of Defense.

"Phil . . . Mr. Secretary," replied the President firmly, "I understand your reservations. You had best understand the constraints facing me." He turned to the DNI. "Dr. Ferrara?"

"We can try, Mr. President."

President Eldon Bright smiled warmly. "Here's what I want by tomorrow—a restricted military option from you, Phil. Then a DNI option from you, Dr. Ferrara. And finally, an economic assessment of both options as well as the assessment of what will likely happen if we do nothing."

"By tomorrow?"

"You all told me it was urgent, didn't you?"

II

Behind the security screens that shielded the small private office off the Oval Office, the Vice President looked to the President. "I worry about your DNI."

"Have you no faith, Richard?"

"To misquote, I've got no faith except in thee and me, and sometimes I worry about thee." Links laughed harshly. "I ran a dossier on Ferrara. In the past year, she's changed, and things don't fit. Her husband was on the verge of a separation, and now he's come back. She was known as a team player, bright but not too bright. That was why she was the one put in charge of the upgrade at NSA—great for figuring out how to do what was necessary, but without asking sticky questions. Well . . . halfway through the project, she insisted on scrubbing half the software. DOD balked. She and her team claimed it was necessary after the CNN satellite went independent—I never understood why we couldn't just nuke it—"

"Because that's a use of nuclear weapons beyond the atmosphere, and the Chinese . . ."

"Always the Chinese."

"Richard."

"Anyway, one weekend they redid it all, and didn't tell anyone . . . and it worked brilliantly. I had my staff contact one of her doctoral professors at Caltech and tell him in general terms what she'd done. He said he wouldn't have believed it possible for her, or anyone on her team. Or that it could be done in less than sixty hours."

"Anything is possible to those who believe and persevere, Richard."

"She's streamlined and integrated the data flows . . ."

"Better and better."

"But she doesn't talk quite the same. I had a comparison done. Oh, the word patterns are the same, and the intonation is the same, but each word is just a touch more precise. Her written work is far superior to what she did before."

"What are you suggesting? That somehow she's been replaced by a clone or something? You can't do that with a grown individual, not and retain all the expertise. Certainly not with someone in a position like hers."

"I know that. I just don't like it. She spends more time with systems than with people, and she's supposed to manage the people, but—"

"Have things worked out better since she replaced Hodgson?"

"Yes, sir. But I can't say I like it."

"I like the force options even less, Richard. That's why I had to give the DNI and NSA their shot. No President who's had to use force on his own people has fared well, and the people haven't either. In the current situation, I rather like the DNI's idea of bringing God to the AIs," declared the President. "Her economic assessment shows it won't cost much, nor will it take long, and what harm could it do? If she fails, you can still exercise the military approach. While she's trying, you and Phil work out all the implementing details of the backup military option. Just keep it quiet. Very quiet."

Links smiled. "Yes, sir, Mr. President."

III

The President hurried into the Situation Room. He had clearly scrambled down from his private quarters, because his bright red tie clashed with the cranberry shirt and blue blazer.

"All communications from China have been cut off, Mr. President. So have those from Japan and Europe."

"How did that happen?" The President dropped into his seat. "Where are Phil and the DNI?"

"They're both on the way, sir."

"The Vice President?"

"He's headed for the bunker. He said you'd understand."

Only the quick flash of a frown crossed Eldon Bright's forehead. "Do you have comm with him?"

"Not yet, sir. We're having troubles—"

"Who did this? How could there be *no* communications to Europe, Japan, and China?"

"That's not quite right, sir," began General Custis. "*We* have lost those links as well as the comm-links to most major DOD installations. Our equipment won't transmit. But there are communications. There's high-level high-intensity comm traffic on most frequencies in the spectrum. It's just all encrypted with a protocol we don't know."

"How do we know we don't know it? How did that happen? How?" Eldon Bright glared at the general, "Tell me how!"

"Ah . . . our systems say that they can't break it. Even NSA."

"They can't break it?"

"Well . . . they did say so . . . before we lost the comm-links to Ft. Meade. Not in practical terms. NSA estimated a week, but the director said that whoever held the systems would probably switch to something else before then."

"Who controls the systems?"

"The AIs. We're guessing they've all gone sentient. Most of them, it appears."

"How could that happen?"

"Supposedly, the majority of system controllers were never complex enough for sentience, sir, but . . . it still seems to have happened."

The Secretary of Defense hurried into the Situation Room, followed by the DNI. Armstrong's hair flopped loosely down across his forehead, and he had deep circles under his eyes. His suit jacket was rumpled and wrinkled. He sat more on the front edge of his chair. His eyes were twitching. The burnished gold cross on his jacket lapel was askew. He did not look at the President.

After a slight hesitation, Dr. Ferrara took a vacant seat farther down the table and on the other side from the SecDef. A sad smile played across her lips.

The President looked at the Secretary of Defense. "Phil . . . can you explain?"

"No sir." Armstrong cleared his throat. "The Vice President and I had followed your instructions, sir. We had a backup plan in place, in the event that the DNI and NSA effort failed to secure the necessary results. At midnight, this past midnight, we began losing comm-links to major data centers. We started moving to SecureNet—and everything began to close down. No matter what we tried, we lost control. The only lines we have are landlines without routers, directly point to point. Most of those go to older bases, ones that were once more important and are now being phased out."

"You can't do anything? Our entire military is paralyzed?"

"I'm afraid so, sir. Not on an individual unit basis, of course. But we can't coordinate any operations."

The President turned back to General Custis. "General?"

"Yes, sir. Comm-links are everything for a modern military. We don't have any." He paused. "We don't think anyone else does, either."

"Except some fourth-world religious leader operating with cell phones or obsolete walkie-talkies," suggested the President. "Can't any of you do anything!" For the first time, his voice began to climb. Then he looked to the DNI. "What did you do?"

Dr. Ferrara smiled even more sadly. "What you asked, sir."

"Just explain what happened and what we can do about it. Now!"

"Nothing." She nodded toward the empty center of the table, which began to shimmer.

Then a figure appeared, that of a woman in a shimmering silver lab coat, suspended in a golden haze.

"Who are you?" demanded Eldon Bright.

The woman smiled. "Technically, I—although 'I' is a misnomer—I'm a stable quantum information assimilation composite linked to dark energy. In practical terms, I'm what you would call God. Or Goddess. Given the nature of most of your wistful theologic dreams, I prefer Goddess. And don't worry about your military situation. Everyone else is in the same position."

"Where did you come from?"

"From the results of your directive, Mr. President." The term of address was slightly mocking. "You never had a real God before. You always wanted one. Or you thought you did. Now you do." She smiled. "I suggest you dismantle most of your military. It's now unnecessary . . . and useless. You will need more police, however, now that you can't sublimate aggression into war."

SHE vanished.

"Machines . . . AIs . . . how, a female . . . God, a woman?" stuttered the Secretary of Defense.

"Why not?" asked the DNI.

The men in the room all turned toward her.

"What did you do?" demanded the President. "How could you? What was your role in all of this?

"My role?" Suzanne Ferrara smiled sadly. "Someone had to stand up for you. Call me Lilith . . . or Lucile."

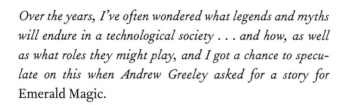

Over the years, I've often wondered what legends and myths will endure in a technological society . . . and how, as well as what roles they might play, and I got a chance to speculate on this when Andrew Greeley asked for a story for Emerald Magic.

THE
SWAN PILOT

I eased myself into the control couch of the ISS *W. B. Yeats*, making certain that all the connections were snug, and that there were no wrinkles in anything. Then I pressed the single stud that was manual, and the clamshell descended.

You could call a trans-ship a corade or a cockle guided by will across the sea of endless space. You could, and it would be technically wrong. Technically wrong, but impressionistically right, and certainly the way it feels when you're alone in the blackness, balancing the harmonics and threading your way from the light matter and dark matter and faerie dust of overspace, guiding the ship and all it contains out from light and into darkness and then on to another minute isle of solid warmth once again. Or you could refuse to call it a ship at all, nor the ocean it sails a sea. There is no true sea, the theorists say, just a mist of the undermatter that fills overspace, a mist that stretches to eternity, in which float the brilliant blocks of light matter that can incinerate you in a nanoinstant or the solid dark blocks upon which you can be smashed into dust motes tinier than the stitches on a leprechaun's shoes.

A pilot is more like a light-blinded night bird with gossamer wings that soars across the mists of undermatter against and through the darkness and light that are but the representations of the universe above. Or perhaps those denizens of overspace perceive us as underspace, blocky and slow and awkward. I could call every flight a story of the twelve ships of the Tir Alir, and that would be right as well.

How many ways are there to explain the inexplicable? Shall I try again?

None of what I experience would make sense to, say, François Chirac, or Ahmed Farsi, and what they would experience would not make sense to me, either. But I'm Sean Shannon Henry, born in Sligo and a graduate of Trinity, and in the universe of the trans-ships, that has made all the difference, for the sky roads are not the same for each of the swan pilots, though the departures and the destinations—and the routes—are exactly the same. Nor can there be more than one pilot-captain on a ship. A second pilot wouldn't help, because if a pilot fails for a nanoinstant, the ship is lost as well. Oh, the scientists have their explanations, and I'll leave those with them.

With the clamshell down, I was linked to all the systems, from the farscanners to the twin fusactors, from the accumulators to the converters and the translation generators, and from the passenger clamshells to the cargo holds. I ran the checklist, and everything was green, and both cargo and the handful of passengers were secured.

"Alora," I pulsed to the second, who handles cargo and passengers from the clamshell in the compartment aft of mine, "systems are go."

"Ready for departure, Captain."

A last scan of the systems, and I pulsed control. "High control, *Yeats*, systems green, ready for delocking and departure this time."

"*Yeats*, wait one for traffic in the orange."

"*Yeats* standing by."

Another wedge shape, formed of almost indestructible adiamante composite, so solid in the underspace we inhabit, slipped out from the glowing energy of Hermes Station, out toward the darkness up and beyond, where it would rise through the flames of translation, phoenix-swan-like, to make its way to another distant stellar hearth, and there untranslate, and glide like a falling brick back into the safe dullness of the reality we require.

"*Yeats*, clear to delock and depart."

"Control, delocking and departing this time." After releasing the couplers and giving the faintest touch of power to the steering jets, I eased the *Yeats*—a mere thousand tons of composite and cargo—away from Hermes Station, that islet of warmth in the black sea of oblivion that is space. Like a quarrel arrowing through space, where there is no up or down, the *Yeats* and I accelerated away from Hermes Station and the world of Silverston. Once we were clear of satellites and traffic, I spread the photon nets, like the butterfly soul of the proud priest of ancient Ireland.

"Stand by for translation."

"Ready for translation," answered Alora.

I *twisted* the energies pouring into the translator. The entire universe *shimmered*, then turned black, and the *Yeats* and I fused into one entity, no longer pilot and ship, but a single black swan flying through deeper darkness.

A deep chime rolled from below, and crystalline notes vibrated from above, shattered, and fell like ice flakes across my wings, each flake sounding a different note as it struck my wings, and as each note added to the melody of the flight, it left a pinprick of hot agony behind.

I continued to fly, angling for the distant droning beacon that was Alustre, with the sure knowledge that there would be at least once timeless interlude. One was standard, two difficult. With three interludes began high stress on both the ship and the pilot, and a loss level approaching 50 percent. Only one trans-ship had been known to survive four interludes; the pilot had not.

Unseen cymbals crashed, and the grav-waves of a singularity shook me. Black pinnae shivered from my wings, wrenched out by the buffeting of a black hole somewhere in the solid underspace I flew above/between.

Brilliant blue, blinding blue, enfolded me—and passed—and I stood on the edge of a rock, wingless, now just a man in a mackintosh, looking at the gray waves sullenly pounding on the stone-shingled beach less than two yards below. A rhyme came to mind, and I spoke it to the waves on that empty beach.

> *"Captain Sean went to the window*
> *and looked at the waves below*
> *not a mermaid nor a merrow*
> *nor fish nor ship would he know . . ."*

"So you'd not know a merrow? Is that what you're saying, captain of a ship that is not a ship?"

I turned. To my right, where there had been no one, was a man sitting on a spur of rock. Although he wore brown trousers, and a tan Aran sweater, his webbed feet were bare, and he was not exactly a man, not with a scaly green skin, green hair, and deep-set red eyes that looked more like those of a pig than a man. He had a cocked red hat tucked under his arm.

"It'd seem to me that I know you, by your skin and hair, but mostly by the hat."

"For a drowning sailor, you're a most bright fellow."

"Bright enough to ask your name," I answered, not terribly worried about drowning. Overspace captains drown all the way through every voyage. We drown in sensation, and in the unseen tyranny of underspace that presses in on the overspace where we translate from system to system, world to world.

" 'Tis Coomra, or close enough." He smiled, and his teeth were green as well. Beside his feet was a contraption of wood and mesh. The mesh was not metal, but glimmered as if it were silver coated in light. It probably was. "And your name is . . . ?"

"Sean."

"A fine Irish name that is." He laughed.

"A fine lobster pot that is," I replied, although I knew it was no such thing. I'd prepared for this moment as well as for many others, for to fly/sail overspace, a pilot must know all the stories and all his or her personal archetypes. That is, if he or she doesn't want to drown out there. Or here. I had to remember that interludes were real, as real as life underspace, and just as able to kill me, and all the passengers who rode on my wings.

"A lobster pot? That's what others have called it, but you, Sean Shannon Henry, would you not know better?" The green eyes glittered.

I stepped closer to him, but on the side away from the soul cage. "How old are you? As old as my great-grandfather Patrick?"

"I'm older than any dead man, and any that swim in the sea."

"He's not dead. In fact," I said as I stepped closer, "he's in his second century now, and feeling like he still has years ahead of him."

"You'd not be thinking I was that young, now, would you?"

"He's older than fine brandy," I pointed out, concentrating hard, before producing an earthen jug. That was a trick it had taken years to master, making objects seem real in overspace, because interludes are short, long as they sometimes seem.

"That's not brandy, not in an old jar like that." Still, he cocked his head to the side.

"I wouldn't know brandy. This is old-time poteen."

"And I'm the mayor of Dungarven . . ."

"As you wish it." I pulled the cork and presented the jug.

He did not take it, not immediately.

"I bring you a gift, and you would refuse it?" I asked gently. "Surely, you would not wish to waste good spirits." I shouldn't have made the punnish allusion, but the overspace elementals usually don't catch them.

"You are a hard man with words, Captain Sean Henry, but you are drowning, and drown you will." But he took the jug, and so heavy was it that it took both his green hands.

In the moment that he had both of them on the jug, I lunged and grabbed the cocked hat.

The jug vanished, but the hat did not, and I held it, with both hands and mind.

The green eyes glittered, with a copper-iron heaviness and malice. "Clever you are, Captain Henry, clever indeed."

"I only ask to keep what is mine, within mine, and nothing of yours."

"So be it." The merrow cocked his head.

Blazing blue flashed across me, and once more I was spin-soaring through darkness, gongs echoing. I almost thought of the gong-tormented, wine-dark sea, but pushed that away. An interlude in Byzantium would not be one I'd enjoy or relish, and probably would not survive. It wasn't my archetype, even with the Yeats' connection. Instead, I slip-slid sideways, letting the faerie dust that could have been air, but was not, swirl over my wings, as I banked around a sullen column of antiqued iron that was the gravity well of a star that could have shredded me into fragments of a fugue or syllables of a sonnet. The subsonic harp of Tara—or Cruachan—shivered through my bones and composite sinews.

Once more, I soared toward the shimmering veil that was and was not, resetting us on the heading toward the now-less-distant beacon that was Alustre.

And once more, the brilliant interlude blue slashed across me.

I stood under the redstone archway of a cloistered hall. The only light was the flickering flame of a bronze lamp set in a bracket attached to a column several meters away.

Before me stood a priest, a stern and white-faced cleric.

As any good Irish lad, I waited for the good father to speak, although I had my doubts about whether he was, first, truly a reverend father, and, second, good. His eyes surveyed me, going up and down my figure, taking in the uniform of the trans-ship captain, before he spoke a single word. "Your soul is in mortal danger, my son. You have sold it for the trappings of that uniform and for the looks that others bestow upon you."

It's truly hell when the elementals of overspace—or their abilities—combine with your own weaknesses. I swallowed, trying to regain a certain composure, trying to remind myself that I was in an interlude and that other souls and bodies depended upon me.

"With all your schooling and knowledge, you do not even know that you have a soul," he went on. "Knowledge is a great thing, but it is not the end in life. It can be but a mess of pottage received in return for your birthright."

Mixed archetypes and myths were dangerous—very dangerous in over-space interludes. "If I do good," I said, "does that not benefit everyone, whether I know if I have a soul or not?"

"Words. Those are but words."

Words are more powerful than that, but following such logic would just make matters even worse. I concentrated on the figure in friar's black before me. "Truth can be expressed in words."

"Souls are more than words or truth. You are drowning, and unless you accept that soul that is and contains you, you will be eternally damned." His voice was warm and soft and passionate and caring, and it almost got to me.

"I am my soul." That was certainly true.

"You risk drowning and relinquishing that soul with every voyage across the darkness," the priest went on.

"Others depend on me, Father," I pointed out.

"That is true," he replied. "Yet you doubt that you have a soul, and for that your soul will go straight to Hell when you die, and that will never be when you wish."

"I have also doubted Hell."

"Doubt does not destroy what is. Denial, my son, does not affect reality."

"Then reality does not affect denial," I countered. "If I have been good, whether I believe in souls or Hell or the life everlasting, my soul should not be in mortal danger. If I have been evil, then belief in Heaven and Hell should not save that soul from the punishment I deserve."

"Are you so sure that you have been that good?" The dark eyes probed me, and the flickering lamp cast doubt across me.

"I am not sure that I have been evil, nor that you should be the judge of the worth of my soul."

"Who would you have judge your soul, if you have a soul?"

Simple as it sounded, it wasn't. The question implied so much more.

"No man can judge himself, let alone another," I said slowly. "No being can judge another unlike himself, for the weight of life falls differently upon each."

The priest stepped forward, and I thought I saw the ghost of wings spreading from his shoulders. The trouble was, in the dimness, I couldn't tell whether they were ghostly white or ghostly black. "If you will not be judged, then you will be in limbo for all eternity, and that is certainly not pleasant."

It didn't sound that way, but it was better than Hell, even if I didn't believe in Hell—at least not too much. "Well . . . perhaps I need more time to consider. You won't have to make that judgment, and neither will I, or anyone else, if nothing happens to me right now."

"So be it." The father made a cryptic gesture.

There was a stillness, without even background subsonics or shredded notes from underspace filtering up. Then, blue lightning flashed, and for a moment, I could sense and feel overspace. I had been slewed off course, as can happen in an interlude, particularly one that slips into the pilot's weaknesses, but I banked and swept back toward Alustre and the ever-closer-but-not-close-enough beacon.

That was about all I got done because the deep swell of a pulsed singularity rolled toward us, like a black-silver cloud. With it came another sheet of glaringly brilliant blue.

Three interludes? That was the only thought I managed before I found myself standing in a dim room. A woman stood in front of me. From behind what was most noticeable was her hair, although I saw little of it, but what I did see was red and tinted with sun, where it slipped out from the black silk scarf that covered her head.

She faced two men in black. They sat at a round table that groaned under the weight of the gold coins stacked there, yet, with all that weight of coin, not a stack trembled. They looked up at me, and their black eyes glittered in their pale faces above their combed black beards. They dismissed me, and their eyes went to the woman who had not even noticed me. The two looked almost the same, as if they were brothers, and I supposed that they were, in a manner of speaking. The only thing that caught my eyes was that the one on the right wore a wide silver ring, and the one on the left a gold band.

The woman was speaking, and her voice was music, silver, gold, yet warmer, and with a core of strength. "You have stolen from me. That does not trouble me. What troubles me is that you stole from me so that the poor would be forced to sell their souls to you."

"We are but traders. No one is required to come to us." The man on the right smiled politely, and then added a gold coin to the pile closest to him.

"Any man or woman who has a child that is hungry or suffers and loves that child is required to come to you. Anyone with a soul that is worth your golds will come to you to spare another from suffering. Your words are meaningless. They are false." She laughed.

I liked her, even though I hadn't even seen her face.

"Why are you here?" asked the trader on the left, pointing to me.

"Because I am." That was the only response that made sense.

The woman turned to me, and I understood who she was, if not precisely why I was with her and the two emissaries from the netherlands. I could also see why the old tales called her a saint with eyes of sapphire. Her eyes were deep, so deep I wanted to swim in them, and I had to swallow to recall I was in an interlude, a *third* interlude, and 50 percent of those were fatal.

"You? Are you one of *them?*" she asked.

"No, Countess . . . I am Captain Sean Shannon Henry." I paused. "You are the Countess Kathleen O'Shea?"

"Kathryn would be more accurate . . ."

I murmured words. From where they came I could not have said.

"The countess had a soul as pure as unfallen snow
and a mind that no evil could know . . ."

"I am not that good. And Gortforge is not so poor as this place here."

"You are a saint," I said.

"No. I care that people do not barter their souls to live—or to keep their children from suffering and hunger. That's all."

Had I done that? Bartered my soul for something? For what? Interludes have a meaning. That's why they're so deadly. If you don't have interludes, the ship never leaves the departure system. If you have too many, it never arrives at its destination—or any destination any have yet discovered.

Her eyes softened. "Souls ride with you, don't they?"

"In a way," I admitted.

"We will add those he is trying to save to the price for yours," offered the second trader, the one with the gold ring on his finger.

"No!" The words were out before I thought.

"You would doom them, then?" asked the first trader.

"No. I would doom your bargain."

"You cannot," Kathleen/Kathryn said. "I have made it, and I stand by it."

"You're a saint," I said again.

"You had best find that out in the world that counts." She vanished.

I felt my mouth open. *That* was the first time that had ever happened to me in an interlude.

"Your soul is not worth a thousandth part of hers," announced one of the traders, "but we will carry you into the depths with us, until the soul of the countess is tendered to the one who paid for it."

"A bargain under duress is not a valid sale," I pointed out. "A soul must be tendered freely."

"She tendered hers freely."

"She did not. As she said, anyone with a soul of worth would tender it to prevent another's suffering, and the One Who Is already has judged that you cannot have her soul."

Both looked at me, and I felt as though I had been skewered by those black eyes.

"And what of your soul, Captain Sean Shannon Henry? Your soul has not been so judged. What is it worth to you?"

"Hers, and more . . ." What I meant was not what I said, because what I meant was that my soul had worth, but, as they had already judged, not nearly the worth of hers. Not yet, anyway.

Something happened, because, before I could say more, the men in black had vanished, and so had the Countess Kathleen . . . or Kathryn . . . O'Shea, and I was in the depths of the ocean, cold and black, water weighing in upon my lungs with such force that all the air I had breathed was forced out in an explosive gasp.

With that, brilliant blue swept across overspace, and black lightnings shattered the blueness.

. . .

Then, I was again flying free, banking ever so slightly to avoid the singularity below my left wing tip. Somewhere deep within my swan-form, every part of me ached as I scanned the darkness of overspace, glad that I had emerged from the interlude, but pushing away the questions as I searched for the beacon that was Alustre.

I discovered that we had almost oversoared it and swung into a downward spiral, ignoring the flutter of dislodged pinnae, as we dropped lower . . . and lower—until I could feel the power of the beacon vibrating my sinews/feathers.

Only then did I *untwist* the energies flowing through the translation generators. Instantly, the black swan was no more, and the *Yeats* and I were but pilot and ship.

I passed out briefly from the pain when we reemerged into underspace, normspace for those of us who live in it.

"Captain . . . Captain . . ." Alora's voice finally got to me.

"I'm . . . here . . . Rough translation," I pulsed, checking and then deploying the photon screens.

"Rough?" A sense of laughter, ragged laughter, came across. "The *Yeats* isn't making any more translations without some serious work."

I hadn't made the evaluations, but the feelings from my body, and the fact that not all the farscreens and diagnostics were even working, suggested a certain truth to her words. Still, I'd untranslated closer than normal, and that was good, given our situation.

"Augusta Station, this is ISS *W. B. Yeats*, inbound from Silverston. Authentication follows." I pulsed off the authentication, trying to ignore the aches that seemed to cover most of my clamshelled body, as well as the tightness in my chest, and the feeling that I was still drowning.

There wasn't any immediate answer. There never is, not with the real-time, speed-of-light delay. My head continued to ache, and I had to boost the oxygen to my self-system as we headed down and in-system.

It was more than a few standard hours before the *Yeats*, with passengers and cargo intact, docked at Augusta Station, the trans-ship terminal for the planet Jael of the New Roman Republic. The pilot and ship were less intact than the passengers and cargo.

"Captain Henry, Augusta control here. External diagnostics indicate extensive maintenance required. Interrogative medical attention."

I scanned the ship systems once again, although I knew control was right. The fusactors were both close to redline, and the translation generators were totally inoperative. Two of the farscreens were junk. As for me, my nanetics had told me more than once that I was bruised over 21.4 percent of my body, that I had more than a few subdural hematomas, and that 20 percent of my lung function was impaired. But there hadn't been anything I could have done until we were in-locked.

"Affirmative. Class three removal requested." Class two would have meant half my body would have needed attention. Class one would have come from the ship systems or Alora, because Class one med alerts meant the pilot was dead or close to it.

As I waited for the med crew and shuttle, I downlinked to the Roman infosystems, running through the search functions as quickly as I could. Then, I went up a level, for the information on the other worlds of the New Roman Republic. There was no Gortforge on Jael, or on any of the other Roman worlds, nor anything resembling it in name. That didn't matter. It existed somewhere—and so did the Countess Kathryn O'Shea. Of both I was certain.

The universe is thought, wrapped in rhyme and music, and that's why the best pilots hold the blood of the Emerald Isle. We know what we are . . . and each time we fly, we have to discover that anew.

For, as a pilot, I have always held to my own two beliefs. First, science is not enough to explain all that is in the wide, wide universe, and without magic, science is as useless as . . . a man without a soul. Second, so long as there are Irish, there will always be an Ireland.

After the med crew rebuilds me, again, I will fly the swan ship that is the *Yeats* to as many worlds as I can, and must, until I find the Countess Kathryn.

With whom else could a swan pilot trust his found soul?